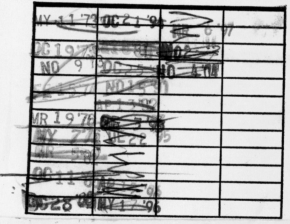

THE

BEST
AMERICAN SHORT STORIES
1972

THE

BEST

AMERICAN SHORT STORIES

1972

&

*the Yearbook of
the American Short Story*

EDITED BY

MARTHA FOLEY

Houghton Mifflin Company

Boston

1972

"Gold" by M. F. Beal. Reprinted by permission of M. F. Beal, c/o International Famous Agency. Copyright © 1971 by M. F Beal. First published in *New American Review* 11, edited by Theodore Solotaroff.

"The World War I Los Angeles Airplane" by Richard Brautigan. First published in *New American Review* 11, edited by Theodore Solotaroff. Copyright © 1971 by Richard Brautigan.

"Covenant" by Kelly Cherry. First published in *Commentary*. Reprinted by permission of *Commentary*. Copyright © 1971 by the American Jewish Committee.

"A Death on the East Side" by Herbert Gold. First published in *Esquire*. Reprinted by permission of Random House, Inc., from the book *The Magic Will* by Herbert Gold. Copyright © 1971 by Herbert Gold.

"The Supremacy of the Hunza" by Joanne Greenberg. First published in *Transatlantic Review*. Reprinted by permission of Holt, Rinehart, & Winston, Inc., from the book *Rites of Passage* by Joanne Greenberg. Copyright © 1971 by Joanne Greenberg.

"The Breadman" by Mary Heath. First published in *The Virginia Quarterly Review* (Summer 1971). Copyright © 1971 by The Virginia Quarterly Review, The University of Virginia.

"Drums Again" by Edward M. Holmes. First published in *The Viginia Quarterly Review* (Summer 1971). Copyright © 1971 by The Virginia Quarterly Review, The University of Virginia.

"The Judge" by Mary Gray Hughes. First published in *Atlantic* (November 1971). Copyright © 1971 by The Atlantic Monthly Company, Boston, Massachusetts 02116.

"In Black and White" by Ann Jones. First published in *The Virginia Quarterly Review* (Summer 1971). Copyright © 1971 by Ann Jones.

"Three Washington Stories" by Ward Just. First published in *Atlantic* (December 1971). Copyright © 1971 by The Atlantic Monthly Company, Boston, Massachusetts 02116.

"His Day Out" by Roberta Kalechofsky. First publishel in *The Western Humanities Review*, Vol. XXV, No. 3 (Summer 1971). Copyright © 1971 by Roberta Kalechofsky.

To
THE MEMORY OF DAVID BURNETT
1931-1971

Acknowledgments

GRATEFUL ACKNOWLEDGMENT for permission to reprint the stories in this volume is made to the following:

The editors of *The Atlantic Monthly, Audience, Commentary, Epoch, Esquire, Event, New American Review, The New Yorker, Occident, Partisan Review, The Transatlantic Review, The Virginia Quarterly Review, The Western Humanities Review, The Yale Review;* and to M. F. Beal, Richard Brautigan, Kelly Cherry, Herbert Gold, Joanne Greenberg, Mary Heath, Edward M. Holmes, Mary Gray Hughes, Ann Jones, Ward Just, Roberta Kalechofsky, Rebecca Kavaler, John L'Heureux, Ralph Maloney, Marvin Mandell, Cynthia Ozick, Joe Ashby Porter, Penelope Street, Robert Penn Warren, Theodore Weesner, Jose Yglesias.

Foreword

DON'T YOU HAVE TROUBLE finding short stories for the book you edit?" a neighbor asked me recently. "Magazines aren't printing them anymore." She is an intelligent woman, fairly well read when it comes to books. She was startled when I told her how many magazines actually are printing short stories and my problem is not in finding them but in choosing from the wealth of stories published each year in America. "But I don't see those magazines anywhere!" she protested. Unfortunately she doesn't unless she has access to one of the better public libraries or to a large bookstore, and today so many communities are without bookstores. How many readers who would enjoy them even know of the existence of such splendid publications as *The South Dakota Review, Sewanee Review, Southern Review, Quarterly Review of Literature, Literary Review,* to mention at random only a few of the more than a hundred magazines publishing good fiction in the United States? To say nothing of *Prism International, Tamarack Review,* and the others in Canada, which is also American. I do wish, however, the word *review* wasn't in so many of their titles. It has a heavy pedantic overtone that scares readers away.

The chief purpose of *The Best American Short Stories* is, and always has been during the fifty-seven years of its existence, to present readers with fine short stories not only from the widely circulated magazines but from smaller circulation magazines whose readers are limited to connoisseurs. Literary gourmets they might be called.

A perennial question asked this editor is what the past year has brought forth. It might be interesting to have first the opinion of an outsider. He is Abraham Rothberg, prize-winning short-story writer, novelist, and book editor who, after the death of my co-editor in November, gave me tremendous help in finishing this collection. His comments show the ambivalence which besets any editor trying to gain a perspective.

"There are a number of themes," he wrote me, "which seem to me most often repeated: violence, madness, rampant and often unconventional sexuality, racial problems and much writing with campus settings. Surprising to see how few war stories there are, how few returning veteran stories there are, how few straight adventure stories. There are more stories about children and old people and the cruelties inflicted on them than I care to read and most of them not very good, but they do indicate that American society is not very kind to its young and its old."

Now comes the other side of the ambivalence. Two days later he wrote: "Just from what I have seen, Martha, the short story is flourishing and you're going to have a fine volume this year." At least Mr. Rothberg was not bored.

As for myself, I find that writers are much more relaxed about sex. There is less writing for the sake of shocking and a more casual acceptance of its physical aspects. There is even a certain frolicsomeness, a healthy sign. There had been so much repression for so long a time — a time when a piano was not supposed to have legs and no one went to bed but instead retired — that there was bound to be overcompensation. No longer, as in the days of my youth, would a dignified judge, when asked by a small grandson who had been reading Fabre's *Life of the Bees* just what the queen bee did, try to explain, fail, and then demand: "Well, you know about men and women, don't you?"

Love stories, good honest love stories, are scarce in American fiction. Why, I have stopped even trying to guess. One of the few I have been able to find and which I reprinted some years ago has since appeared in a number of other collections, evidence of the scarcity. War stories, the better kind, seldom appear close to the time of conflict. It requires Wordsworth's oft-quoted "emotion recollected in tranquility" for them to appear. Why, as Mr. Rothberg points out, there are so few adventure stories I do not know. Nor do I know why, ever since I can remember, stories of children and old people have abounded. Even my own first published story,

printed in a school magazine when I was eleven, was about an old
man. Maybe it is because, as Mr. Rothberg says, American society
is not very kind to them. The kind of person who is a sensitive
writer is bound to be empathetic with the victims of cruelty.

One of the things I like about a book such as this one is that it
tries to hold good writing up for praise. The same neighbor I
quoted at the beginning of this Foreword also told me: "When I
get through reading reviews I am discouraged. Hardly ever is any
writing deemed to be considered worthwhile. Do reviewers want
people to read or don't they? Or do they just hate other writers?"
I told her no. They were trying to be impartial in most cases. I
now think she, as a lay person, was saying something important. In
a page-one review in the *New York Times Book Review* of a book
about Coleridge, the reviewer says ". . . the book cannot be dis-
missed. It is a remarkable exercise of the adversary method when
applied to criticism." It is a hell of a note when critics are supposed to be adversaries of authors. No wonder book sales are so
often low. I do not suggest that critics should overlook serious short-
comings but they are culpable of shortchanging would-be readers
when they emphasize the bad at the expense of the good. I commend to such critics Alexander Pope's wonderful "Essay on Criticism." Especially where he says, "Whoever thinks a faultless piece
to see,/Thinks what ne'er was, nor is, nor e'er shall be."

I am afraid, however, I am becoming an adversary of the United
States post office which plans to increase rates for magazines by 145
per cent. This not only threatens large-circulation magazines but
means absolute death for the nation's literary magazines, such as I
mentioned earlier and which are the lifeblood of the short story.
There is a certain irony in the fact that commercially successful magazines are bending under the threatened blow since they have given
precedence to advertising over reading matter and the post office
is levying only a 24 per cent increase for bulk-mail advertising matter, the kind most recipients disgustedly call "junk mail" and toss
in the wastebasket.

The shock of David Burnett's death is still so close it is difficult
to write about the contribution of his radiant character to my life
and to *The Best American Short Stories* of which he was co-editor
since 1958. He was my son, a fact he tried to conceal because he did
not want to be judged as somebody's relative. He need not have

worried. He introduced me to writing, both American and foreign, with which I was not acquainted, and anyone who discussed literature with him was impressed by his awareness of the true values in it. When I was in the hospital he alone edited *The Best American Short Stories* of 1958. That volume received one of the most enthusiastic receptions the anthology was ever given. Painting was his primary interest. Rockwell Kent praised a large mural David, while still a boy, had painted for his school auditorium. Mr. Kent was not the only admirer of his work. There were many others to follow. Over and over again the numerous letters which expressed grief at his passing emphasized how greatly he will be missed. David died too young.

I am grateful to the editors who have kept this anthology supplied with copies of their magazines, and to their authors for generously granting reprint rights. The editor of any new magazine is urged to send copies to me.

The editors and staff of Houghton Mifflin are entitled to gratitude for their help. Finally, tribute is paid to Edward J. O'Brien, who founded this anthology.

Martha Foley
New Canaan, Connecticut

Contents

THE
BEST
AMERICAN SHORT STORIES
1972

M. F. BEAL

Gold

(FROM NEW AMERICAN REVIEW)

WHERE, WHEN, WHAT:

I've been here almost two months now. I've been staying most of the time, all but the warmest nights, with friends: Evelyn and Peter. Friends, but not old friends; they're far away, some dead, even. Some might not realize I count them that. I'm hoping to see Ruth. I came here in the first place looking for Ruth. It doesn't make me proud to say that; but it's true. I had been looking for her up and down the coast when I heard she was here, too, on the opposite hillside. So I stayed.

Settling down like this has set me to thinking for the first time about why I — we — all left the city. It's almost as if a whole generation has seen itself unable to cope, or as if there has been some sort of pestilence to which certain people are hideously sensitive. That's how it must seem, at any rate, to those deserted. For me it was a simple decision: one night returning from work I realized if I opened the door to my apartment I would be there till I died; so I spent the night with a friend, thinking of how I had, now, to abandon the city and look for Ruth. Or perhaps the search for Ruth was a motive I attached to my decision to justify it.

Her name comes up, of course, fairly often, although generally people on this side of the valley do not visit with and are not overly concerned with the people on the other side of the valley. A curious business. Is it jealousy? It really doesn't seem so. Call it preoccupation with the everyday; life itself is the big preoccupation here — except, of course, for gold. Gold. Continual talk of gold.

But though I am so little interested in that part of this life, everyone is very polite. No one pays too much attention to me; or rather, just enough. The attention, when it comes, is practical, relating to the business of the valley (life) : Evelyn dispenses it mainly, and indirectly, like this: "Did you notice?" she asks, or "Have you ever tried? . . ." Of course it's perfectly reasonable to presume I'm here for salvation — all the rest are.

Ruth and the Mountain:
   I've been trying, today, to remember the hike I took up the mountain the first week here. I have a bad memory. I believe I wanted to orient myself; but I may have been feeling bored, and trapped — isn't that really more likely? It was still May. The nights were cold. I had quite a lot of equipment I'd brought with me in a leather satchel I got in a secondhand store down the street from where I lived the day I decided to start looking for Ruth; a Gladstone bag, the proprietor called it. The evening before my hike up the mountain I went from shack to cabin to shelter and begged a packboard, a hand ax, a canteen; Evelyn gave me rice, my sneakers would do, Peter lent me a sweater to wear under my shirt, so I wouldn't have to lug my jacket along. I also had a bail-handled pot, remnant from a Boy Scout kit; ditto spoon, extra socks, tea, matches, a geologist's pick, several small bags for collecting specimens of rocks and plants, a magnifying glass, a handbook of minerals and one of birds, cigarettes, a blanket roll. What else?
   It was a fine day but I got a late start. The mountain was very impressive, bleak with sunlight. Our two hillsides fingering down from her and the rope of water most think is responsible for the gold stood clearly on her flank like children against their mother. But this mother was no insipid aproned lady; rather a sturdy black woman, basalt heaped from her brow, scoria trailing dark hair streaks in a perfect 45° cape. Only where our creek cut was orange limonite exposed like a tear. A track led to her top.

A Snapshot:
   I could not help but think that in other days there would have been a snapshot of me, standing by the last trees, sunlight splashed on the gray dust. It would have shown me in Levi's, slender, looking not at the camera but into the branches above. The only thing I

cannot see as I develop this snapshot in my mind is the expression my face would wear.

Now the Mountain Herself:

Suddenly the mountain loomed enormous. Where water cut rock the newly exposed basalt was like gashes in her flesh. Viewed afar, from the hillside, she was after one week already familiar; but now as I loomed on her she loomed back. There was a quality in the air like lemon — thin, sharp. It had been only minutes since I decided not to pack the canteen's two pounds of water; but now it had receded in my awareness as if I were some Eocene horse with his three toes who had decided not to wear a man's saddle on his back. I was dislodged, unbraced, overmounted.

A Lava Flow to Negotiate:

I knew man had been here before me by the brightness of the track. But the black lava flow, dodging from the mountain's broken top, left behind a blanket twenty, thirty feet thick, a blanket to bury the sandals of an Indian out away from his camp hunting elk. I sat to smoke and imagine what I would have done in his place.

Some Sort of Rabbit:

As I sat virtually immobile, my cigarette just inches from my face and setting free fine veils of smoke, I saw dots of movement, points, shifts of light in the ropy black rock. At first I thought it was some peculiarity of the rough-surfaced lava flow; but then I realized it was a number of small animals, many of them shifting and moving in their burrows and runs as my presence faded from their memories. Or had they been moving right along, simply counting on me not to notice them in my preoccupation with being myself? The lava face was shimmering with them, finally, going about their business of living in the crisp, decaying rock. There was an occasional tiny piping, and once a landslide of such delicate proportions it could not have consisted of more than three or four grains of cinder. The longer I watched, the more clearly I could see these little animals: their large bright eyes; a habit of squatting briefly on hind legs every few steps; even visits from one to another and small courtesies of the path — nose-touching, touching of feet, squeaking.

Suddenly it became embarrassing, almost frightening, to eavesdrop
and I stood, sending them instantly to ground.

A Banging:
   I was now aware of all sorts of life signs as I continued. The path
wound at the lava flowside for a bit, the dust pocked with footprints
of birds, of the tiny animals; then it climbed steeply in a series of
rough steps, finally coming out on a plateau. From this height I
hoped to have my first sensation of having covered ground.
   The trees, unfortunately, hid the valley below with its hillsides,
and the stream which cut the valley was hidden too. It seemed I
would have to cut back around the flank of the mountain to be
above the valley again. So I was pleased when the track turned not
much farther on and headed to a fair-sized clump of wizened alpine
fir.
   Then, as I reached the firs, I heard a banging. The wind was
fresher the higher I climbed, and sound traveled more distinctly in
the clear air, so as I walked the rustle and clatter of tree limbs far
below drafted to me. But the banging was definitely extraordinary.
   Not much farther I discovered the cabin. It was more of a shed,
really, the tiniest house I had ever seen, and weathered deep-gray
like rock. It stood in a level spot almost in the center of the trail;
on all sides the ground sloped, which made it seem that someone's
hand had flattened the spot. The door was open, banging; it was
such a startling sound I had to go shut it immediately.
   Inside was a bed, almost full-size, *made up with sheets and blan-*
kets. Yet, where the sheets had been turned down were brown sau-
sages of pack-rat droppings. There was a rocker, badly weathered,
the back repaired with strips of rawhide, one rocker resting in a
clutter of old clothing which seemed to have been dropped in flight,
then rained on, then dried again and again to a stiff bas-relief. On
a small oil-drum stove was a coffeepot. A table held a single cup
with tacky rime of coffee residue, and (by far the neatest, most considered item of all) a white handkerchief heaped with nuggets of
a metallic mineral. Now I say "a metallic mineral," but actually it
was clear to me it was a pile of gold nuggets. And yet it couldn't be
a pile of gold, for that defied logic; who would leave gold like that?
So it became immediately in my mind "a metallic mineral," probably iron pyrites: "fool's gold."
   I sat in the chair, before the empty, dirty cup and the neat pile

of nuggets, as if that would make of me somehow the anchorite who had lived in this shack, and tried to imagine why he had left, abandoned his retreat. What had he seen, what thought had driven him from his haven?

A heavy depression came over me. I shut the door firmly, and put my face to the trail.

I Think I Took Water from the Spring Nearby:

Or I may have gotten it as I crossed the stream somewhat farther on. I was preoccupied the whole time thinking of the apartment that first Ruth and then I had abandoned, leaving, I remember, some of my clothes, letters (not Ruth's — those I gave her late one night), books, records; everything whose ideas had been outgrown and, just as important, for which there wasn't room in the back of the car. These thoughts had the effect of deadening me to the passage of time and the weight of the pack and it was not too long before I came to the rock fault.

A Big Smile:

I came suddenly on the crack, first narrow but opening over the next hundred feet surprisingly fast, as if the mountain were a vast chocolate pudding which had dried and split. The gash, with its delicate edges — tiny replicas of the larger split — was deep as well, perhaps twenty feet as it opened out. It lay along the mountainside like a big smile, bisected by the stream which must have teased it forth, and from which came the water the people below thought was the catalyst for the formation of gold . . .

Still, I'm remembering this — I'm sure at the time I didn't think it all. I wanted to get to the top. It had become a passion, and I had an hour's walking to go. I dropped my pack, setting it beside the mountain's smile. Immediately I felt a foot taller and as if my stride were a yard long. Even the ache in my calves diminished. The tuff slid as I dug my toes into it, but still I made good progress; and before I thought it possible, I was within a few feet of the basalt nipple of the mountain peak. Then, like a gift, I found the track again, winding with footholds to the very summit. There, with the heavy blasting wind of early evening on my back, I stood in the fading sun and surveyed what I had done.

Where:

For the first time I could see the valley and the hillsides. The distortion of distance and the shadow which had overtaken them already leached all color from the tiny cabins; there were a few dots I thought might be people, but unlike the conies on the lava flow, concentration didn't bring them into clearer focus. Again I felt the depression of eavesdropping, of seeing aimless patterns in what must be to the people purposeful actions. I forced myself to watch, however, until the notion of patterns separated from the rest of my perceptions as tangerine skin does from the pulp, and the dots that were people came to represent something akin to points of electricity, energy. This perception gave me pleasure, a feeling of inward smiling. I could feel it travel through my organs as a tightening and warming, until my extremities tingled pleasantly. I was not able to refine my perceptions further.

So I turned on my heels and enjoyed the sensation of being clearly higher than anyone or anything for miles and miles. To the east, I saw flat plains and yellow desert; to the west, snow-tendriled peaks, lower than mine, shadowed. The sun, setting into the sheeted ocean, was pure gold.

Below, the gash in the mountainside was a definite smile — deep, black-toothed. The creek which split it moved with white leapings and a foamy urgency from an unprepossessing lens of snow that I realized must be deeper than it seemed. Then farther down, the beard of trees, with a cheek-patch to the side that entirely hid the cabin; and far, far below, the valley, the hillsides where the people, where Ruth was. Overall, a monumental sighing of the wind, blasting at the mountain's bald summit-nipple. I shivered. I started down.

When:

That was in May. I have described it at length, because now it seems to have been responsible for all that has followed — it must be what is responsible. But it is a mystery and you must interpret; I know no more about it than I've just told. When I point to the smiling gash of the fault and ask a friend what he thinks of *that,* he smiles and turns away, as if I am still, unfortunately, too preoccupied with appearances.

This Is Really a Diary:

But even a diary is selective: in the interval between the event and the transcription of it the mind closes itself to much. I could write as if I had rushed from each event to these pages, and then you might *feel* the immediacy; but it would be no more honest than to allow you a sensation of interval. So that is what I have done. Now here is something that happened today: one of the women who has been on the other hillside quite awhile without success, but who has followed the diet, meditated, etc., thought she passed some gold. By the time the story got to our hillside, she was said to have passed a nugget. Evelyn and Peter came up to tell me. I was working on my shelter, having gotten together, somehow, enough tools all at one time to nail up a few boards. But they were so excited (neither has passed any crystals yet) it was really unthinkable to continue pounding, so we talked the afternoon out. Very little gold has been passed on our hillside — why, no one knows. A few theories:

> The average age of the people over here is higher; we are more uptight and can't release body-energy in pure form; some of us take too mechanical an attitude toward the formation of gold. The chemical balance of the herbs, etc., which are considered vital to production of gold, is not the same as on the other hillside.
> The chemical balance of the water is different.
> We get more sunlight than they do.
> Etc., etc.

I was also told to use the correct terminology: the crystals are called *calculi;* they are small regular crystals of gold, sometimes occurring with traces of chemically bonded minerals. I can understand the importance of correct terminology: because of the nature of what is occurring here, it is necessary to have a rational approach to the dissemination of information about it, especially with outsiders.

Late in the afternoon a messenger came over to say it had been a false alarm. The woman had not passed a gold calculus, but rather a common ammonium one.

Thinking of the woman on the other hillside made me wonder about Ruth. Among the things I ask myself often: is she living with someone? (Sometimes this is so painful a thought I can only hold it in my head for a moment at a time. Sometimes it doesn't bother me at all.) Does she think of me? Is she happy? (Also sometimes a painful thought.) As the messenger spoke of the woman's failure to produce a gold calculus I wanted to ask him whether the woman's name was Ruth. But I couldn't. Yet I immediately decided it was Ruth, and I thought of her trying, failing to pass a gold calculus. I was sorry for her pain, but I was happy she had failed; I must admit that. I was happy. That quality about Ruth, her solidness around some center of self-understanding, or, if you will, self-acceptance, was always so painful to me, such a reproach. When I was most miserably unsure, she closed around her center like a clam. It served her right that she had failed, for once.

Gold!

Now here is what happened, what it is like to pass a calculus of gold. On the night described above, tired, sick with loneliness, I decided to fast for a week. Evelyn gathered a bitter weed she calls *pooha* and I ate it; it cleaned my system. The following day I did little but sit in the sun, defecate, try not to think about food. I could feel my body drying, the tissues squeezing from them the excess fluids and poisons of my life. I drank, all day, two cupfuls of water from the creek.

The next day I still thought of food, but it was a vague concern. I felt weak, and when I came out of the sun, chill. My body shook with chill all night; but, strangely, I slept deeply between the waking moments, and had no bad dreams.

Toward evening of the third day, I felt my hunger drop from me like a weight and my head became so clear it was painful. I was able to concentrate fully on parts of my life that have shamed me most: on my time with Ruth, and the things she and I did to each other, on my fear of my mother and father, my fear of becoming a father. I found also that if I turned toward the mountain and looked uphill, I got again the inward smiling sensation I had had that day on her top. As if she was trying — ridiculous as it looks on paper — to tell me something. Some linkage, some congruence of mountain/humans whose meaning would fall open like a Chinese puzzle at the right touch — but I could only look and enjoy the tingling warmth on my limbs, focusing my thoughts occasionally on the colony of conies I had seen and thinking how I related to them as the mountain to us. This clarity lasted almost an hour. Afterward, I fell asleep in the sun and slept for a long time, waking only after sunset with a racking chill. Fortunately Evelyn and Peter came up to check on me, and immediately dressed me in all my clothing. Peter brought up some extra blankets and sat with me until I slept. I remember fragments of what he said: He was depressed about his inability to pass a calculus, even a common one. I tried to reassure him, to tell him how much I admired his relationship with Evelyn, and how solid he seemed to me. This time, in my fever and the clarity given me by the fasting, I was able to admire without also hating; and I told him as final reassurance something which leapt to my head, and which I suddenly realized my father used to say to me: *To him who hath, it shall be given . . . and from him who hath not, it shall be taken away.*

The fourth day I slept.

The fifth day I felt great energy and walked to the stream, where I washed myself with the fine black sand that bedded the shallows and rinsed myself over and over with the icy water. Then I sat shielded by a shadberry bush and let the sun dry me. I found myself remembering the neatly heaped pile of gold (it seemed clearly that, now) I had seen in the cabin on the mountain. Why had I not taken it? Because it belonged to *him*. But then why had he abandoned it?

The morning of the sixth day I woke in pain, cramps in my abdomen so severe I could not stretch out. Evelyn rubbed my back, which helped for a while; but then the pain became so deep and cutting that I couldn't stand to be touched. I tried not to cry out; but the pervasive cramps made me moan and I begged a hand to hold. There were many hands; there were many visitors. Evelyn bathed my face with cloths wrung out of water from the stream. At night a fire was built and the waiting continued. Finally the pain assumed a pulse; bad moments but then better ones during which I caught my breath. During the bad times I cried out freely, and the better times were such a relief that tears came to my eyes. At the end, Peter helped me to stand and we moved to the outer circle of firelight. There the calculus tore my body and passed out.

I slept.

When I woke I had a porridge, a thick gruel of some kind, and slept again.

To be without pain, to be able to sleep, is like divinity.

The Responsibility of Producing a Calculus:

Some of the people who have been here a long time produce calculi once a week, or a series of calculi over a period of hours every month or so. This is why, of course, it is possible for all of us to devote ourselves to the production of calculi; the gold is exchanged for what we need, and while there isn't an abundance there is enough for everyone to be comfortable. Peter also told me I can get money to visit the city, if I want to. He pointed out with considerable pride that while the colony has been in existence for almost fifteen (!) years, no one has had to work out for wages for almost ten. This is not true of other colonies which you may have heard about.

On the other hand, even a regular producer of calculi can undergo a change which stops the process. Everyone seems to believe the deposition begins with a "seed," perhaps a particle of silt. Some claim more calculi are produced in the rainy season, when the stream is slightly cloudy. Some even eat small quantities of silt from the limonite clay bank exposed by the stream. No one knows anything definite about the rest of the process. It may be the water which acts as a catalyst, or something in the *pooha* herb we all eat; it may be the rice, the fasting, the meditation. There are a few who refuse to discuss the process at all, saying it is mystical and not to be plumbed at risk of unbalancing the active forces.

One final point of agreement is that the crystallization process takes a while to get going; all the calculi so far have been regular crystals ranging in size from barely visible to an inch across. This tends to place a value on patience, and in fact the regular producers have all been here many months, if not years. If you lack patience, you move on, for it is an ascetic life; perhaps this, too, has something to do with producing.

So It's Clear I Am an Initiate:

Today people visited me as if I were some kind of display. Many of them — other initiates — take my hand and grasp it lingeringly to tell me something they cannot put into words, looking me in the eyes, almost kissing me. Once or twice this has given me a chill, as if they know something about this business of producing calculi I don't yet know; they are so deeply into this gold thing — more, much more, than I am. It is almost as if they realize we are all only vessels. One of the men (young, though with broad streaks of gray at his temples and fingered into his beard) drew me schemata of the arrangement of atoms within a calculus. It is a crystalline conglomerate, not a pure crystal (in which the pattern of atoms is repeated without variation), nor amorphous (with no regularity of pattern), but something between: small clusters of crystals oriented in different ways. I was taken by his fluency in describing the phenomenon. This was certainly virtually all there was to know in terms of description. But what of all that lay beyond the naming? What of the why or how? When I framed my observations I got a quick, sharp, almost cautionary look back. So I turned to watching his mouth as he talked, the upper teeth hitting his lower lip and at the junction, beads of opaque spittle, almost a foam, springing up, stretching with the next mouth movement, breaking as if he were a fevered dog, a froth of fever working its way into the corner of the mouth before it was licked away.

But most who come to see me wear a face of fatigued gentleness.

Ruth: At Last.

I was sitting on the stoop in front of my half-completed shelter and my eyes were drawn by the form of a woman, heavy-bellied, slow, moving herself and her unborn child up the hill to visit me. Her legs beneath the hem of her dress were slender and she held her arms around her stomach as if trying to carry her load in a more wonted fashion. Her brown hair swept from side to side like the pendulum of a clock. I recognized her immediately: Ruth.

In the instant of recognition I was horrified to think my desire for her might flood back, but lowering myself into consideration of my state of mind, I found instead a clean emptiness. (By the time I knew this she had greeted me.) We sat side by side on the stoop like acquaintances on a park bench; I couldn't see her eyes.

"I'm living on the other hillside with John," she announced. She leaned back against the shelter frame when I said nothing and with the set of her shoulders added: *this thing I am doing now is not conditional.*

Conditional. I understood a great deal suddenly about her and me: and how our being together was never anything but conditional. Then she turned her face to me and her eyes said: *I am no longer an object.*

I said with my arms opening and resting on my thighs: *do you remember the warmth of my body, my presentness?*

"You can see a lot here we can't see on the other hillside," she said. "You can see up the mountain where the stream begins; the hill hides that from us."

"There is a fault up there, where the stream comes out of the ice pack."

"A fault?" But she had already said what she came to say and did not want to learn anything; she turned her head aside.

"What sort of person is John?"

She hesitated a long time — about a month, I guess, or at least a season of the mind, something like passing from spring into summer. "I have passed calculi. I am pregnant. I am happy."

I had to laugh. "You don't sound very happy."

"Well, I am. It's hard to explain, but I think more deeply about these things now. I don't just answer the first thing that enters my head."

This made me very sad. I sat looking up to the gashed smile at the mountaintop, at the black and wrinkled lips of the old lady with her basalt brow.

We talked for a long time, but that is all we said; and when the sun tilted over the old lady's head, Ruth went back to her man.

Pilgrim's Progress:

I awoke desperate to read. There wasn't so much as a book at Peter and Evelyn's, but they said there might be some down in the valley. I went from cabin to cabin: nothing. Finally, hard by the stream I saw a young man — really a child — whose face I knew, and introduced myself; and he took me to his shelter (which in its simplicity and starkness reminded me so much of my own, yet seemed so poor it almost made me cry) and on a shelf, next to his shaving mirror and razor, was *Pilgrim's Progress*.

"I got that because it has such far-out pictures in it, and here, look at this — " He took down a small reproduction of a painting by Gauguin that stood tilted against the wall behind his razor: "Jacob Wrestles with the Angel or Vision after the Sermon." We stood and looked at it. The left side of the canvas held a curve of Breton peasant women, their white headcloths and dark dresses like the uniforms of a religious order, their superstitious faces open in wonder, while on the right Jacob wrestled with the Angel. The Angel's wings were strong, sweeping over Jacob, whose arms, inferior wings, knotted in the effort of fending off God's Angel. There wasn't even a suggestion that Jacob would win.

I took *Pilgrim's Progress* and headed back to my shelter thinking about the boy who had somewhere found this book and the Gauguin print. Just old enough to have been born in the valley, he was one of the few children there. Like them, he couldn't read. I had never been bothered by this: what need, really, was there for reading? But now it distressed me. How would it be possible to understand what happened, knowing less than man did already? As I read, Peter and Evelyn's three dogs came sniffing uphill to see what I was doing and sat down with me. I saw them as distinctly, then, as I would humans: Sam (for Samuel Gompers), Emmett (for Emmett Till), and the puppy, Ché. Sam, oldest of the three, thrust his nose in my hand and moved along under its weight, humping his back and groaning to me to scratch the thick fur of his rump, beating his tail against my leg when I stopped, squinting his eyes shut and panting when I scratched. Ché tumbled whining, clicking his milk teeth together, stump tail furiously beating the stones; Sam snapped, Ché fell back abashed; Emmett set to licking himself noisily, tonguing the bald globes of his testicles, sniffing, inspecting, scratching, yawning. In the city, I had had a dog who smelled sour, strong; these dogs, with their diet of brown rice and *pooha,* smell like a child's stuffed toy. As I saw them in this manner, so vividly, it seemed for a long moment that they were wise in some inscrutable way, that they were teachers. And that was delightful, but frightening, too, because it seemed to tell me about myself. Was I mad? Or had I stumbled on some perfectly reasonable awareness? The word *conditional* leapt to the front of my thoughts; these animals seemed anything but conditional, so firmly were they tied to everything around them. They were dependent and yet independent, accepting the warmth of the sun and my hand as if sun and hand were equal in some equation.

But a Man Is Not a Dog:

I am unable to avoid setting down how Peter died. Quite a while ago he confided to me he was distressed because he had had pain but had not passed a calculus. I should have seen what having been here over a year without producing a calculus was doing to his head. Somehow he decided he could vomit these calculi he believed had formed; so he got hold of some ipecac. Apparently he took the whole bottleful. He began vomiting early yesterday; at sunset when he hadn't stopped, though there was no longer anything to vomit up, Evelyn came and got me. I hadn't even known what he was going to do. He was very weak, but peaceful — so convinced of the rightness of what he was doing that I hesitated to interfere. So Evelyn and I sat with him, helping him when the nausea overcame him, bringing him water to moisten his mouth. The moon had canted down when we first noticed the blood. Less than an hour later he was hemorrhaging, waves of blood that spattered us, the walls, the bed, and he died soon after. Now it seems selfish somehow in the face of his death to have any feelings of my own about it: as if that represented a kind of annexation of his essence to my own. And yet all I could think to do when his body had lost all tone and began to take to itself that freight of dust all dead things — deer, dogs, fish — take up at the end; all I could think to do was to stand in the dark and scream at the valley and its safe fires: *Why doesn't anyone think about these things?*

And then later, the following correlations erected themselves in my head. I do not yet understand their significance, if any:

(A reduction formula)

GOLD = DISCIPLINED ASCETICISM (INWARD SHAPING)

$\updownarrow$

FREE CONTACT WITH COSMIC CHAOS (UNDERSTANDING
ESSENTIAL CREATIVE/CHAOTIC CONFIGURATIONS) = GOLD?

(An expansion formula)

The Mountain Again:

It has been raining. Ruth, fulfilled, is on the opposite hillside, an abyss away. Peter is dead. The summer is gone. I am staying with Evelyn now. We live, we pass calculi of gold, we chink our shelters against the winter winds. The dogs, Sam, Emmett, and Ché, sniff the cooking pot after it has been licked clean, dreaming on the odors which reside in the metal, promising new sustenance. The stream is silted, rich. Ruth will bring her new baby and John to my shelter in the depth of the dozy winter; we will talk. I will be even more alone. I am trapped; trapped to pain and the gold calculi. Everything is very easy. I have been thinking again about the pile of gold in the abandoned cabin. Why did he abandon it? *He,* I

say, coming to know him through his act. Because he understood it
was a beginning, not an end? Do I really believe that? Gold — a
beginning?

Or is it simply that he looked up at that enormous smile gashed
into the mountain, and at the boulder-landslide premonitions which
dribble from her lips moment by moment, now that the autumn
rains are here?

In the book I borrowed from the child of this valley it is written:

FLY FROM THE WRATH TO COME

RICHARD BRAUTIGAN

The World War I Los Angeles Airplane

(FROM NEW AMERICAN REVIEW)

HE WAS FOUND lying dead near the television set on the front room floor of a small rented house in Los Angeles. My wife had gone to the store to get some ice cream. It was an early-in-the-night-just-a-few-blocks-away store. We were in an ice-cream mood. The telephone rang. It was her brother to say that her father had died that afternoon. He was seventy. I waited for her to come home with the ice cream. I tried to think of the best way to tell her that her father was dead with the least amount of pain but you cannot camouflage death with words. Always at the end of the words somebody is dead.

She was very happy when she came back from the store.

"What's wrong?" she said.

"Your brother just called from Los Angeles," I said.

"What happened?" she said.

"Your father died this afternoon."

That was in 1960 and now it's just a few weeks away from 1970. He has been dead for almost ten years and I've done a lot of thinking about what his death means to all of us.

1. He was born from German blood and raised on a farm in South Dakota. His grandfather was a terrible tyrant who completely destroyed his three grown sons by treating them exactly the way he treated them when they were children. They never grew up in his eyes and they never grew up in their own eyes. He made sure of that. They never left the farm. They of course got married but he handled all of their domestic matters except for the siring of his grandchildren. He never allowed them to discipline their own chil-

dren. He took care of that for them. Her father thought of his father as another brother who was always trying to escape the never-relenting wrath of their grandfather.

2. He was smart, so he became a schoolteacher when he was eighteen and he left the farm, which was an act of revolution against his grandfather who from that day forth considered him dead. He didn't want to end up like his father, hiding behind the barn. He taught school for three years in the Midwest and then he worked as an automobile salesman in the pioneer days of car selling.

3. There was an early marriage followed by an early divorce with feelings afterward that left the marriage hanging like a skeleton in her family's closet because he tried to keep it a secret. He probably had been very much in love.

4. There was a horrible automobile accident just before the First World War in which everybody was killed except him. It was one of those automobile accidents that leave deep spiritual scars like historical landmarks on the family and friends of the dead.

5. When America went into the First World War in 1917, he decided that he wanted to be a pilot, though he was in his late twenties. He was told that it would be impossible because he was too old but he projected so much energy into his desire to fly that he was accepted for pilot training and went to Florida and became a pilot.

In 1918 he went to France and flew a De Havilland and bombed a railroad station in France and one day he was flying over the German lines when little clouds began appearing around him and he thought that they were beautiful and flew for a long time before he realized that they were German antiaircraft guns trying to shoot him down.

Another time he was flying over France and a rainbow appeared behind the tail of his plane and every turn that the plane made, the rainbow also made the same turn and it followed after him through the skies of France for part of an afternoon in 1918.

6. When the war was over he got out a captain and he was traveling on a train through Texas when the middle-aged man sitting next to him and with whom he had been talking for about three hundred miles said, "If I was a young man like you and had a little extra cash, I'd go up to Idaho and start a bank. There's a good future in Idaho banking."

7. That's what her father did.

8. He went to Idaho and started a bank which soon led to three more banks and a large ranch. It was by now 1926 and everything was going all right.

9. He married a schoolteacher who was sixteen years his junior and for their honeymoon they took a train to Philadelphia and spent a week there.

10. When the stock market crashed in 1929 he was hit hard by it and had to give up his banks and a grocery store that he had picked up along the way, but he still had the ranch, though he had to put a mortgage on it.

11. He decided to go into sheep raising in 1931 and got a big flock and was very good to his sheepherders. He was so good to them that it was a subject of gossip in his part of Idaho. The sheep got some kind of horrible sheep disease and all died.

12. He got another big flock of sheep in 1933 and added more fuel to the gossip by continuing to be so good to his men. The sheep got some kind of horrible sheep disease and all died in 1934.

13. He gave his men a big bonus and went out of the sheep business.

14. He had just enough money left over after selling the ranch to pay off all his debts and buy a brand-new Chevrolet which he put his family into and he drove off to California to start all over again.

15. He was forty-four, had a twenty-eight-year-old wife and an infant daughter.

16. He didn't know anyone in California and it was the Depression.

17. His wife worked for a while in a prune shed and he parked cars at a lot in Hollywood.

18. He got a job as a bookkeeper for a small construction company.

19. His wife gave birth to a son.

20. In 1940 he went briefly into California real estate, but then decided not to pursue it any further and went back to work for the construction company as a bookkeeper.

21. His wife got a job as a checker in a grocery store where she worked for eight years and then an assistant manager quit and opened his own store and she went to work for him and she still works there.

22. She has worked twenty-three years now as a grocery checker for the same store.

23. She was very pretty until she was forty.

24. The construction company laid him off. They said he was too old to take care of the books. "It's time for you to go out to pasture," they joked. He was fifty-nine.

25. They rented the same house they lived in for twenty-five years, though they could have bought it at one time with no down payment and monthly payments of fifty dollars.

26. When his daughter was going to high school he was working there as the school janitor. She saw him in the halls. His working as a janitor was a subject that was very seldom discussed at home.

27. Her mother would make lunches for both of them.

28. He retired when he was sixty-five and became a very careful sweet-wine alcoholic. He liked to drink whiskey but they couldn't afford to keep him in it. He stayed in the house most of the time and started drinking about ten o'clock, a few hours after his wife had gone off to work at the grocery store.

29. He would get quietly drunk during the course of the day. He always kept his wine bottles hidden in a kitchen cabinet and would secretly drink from them, though he was alone.

He very seldom made any bad scenes and the house was always clean when his wife got home from work. He did though after a while take on that meticulous manner of walking that alcoholics have when they are trying very carefully to act as if they aren't drunk.

30. He used sweet wine in place of life because he didn't have any more life to use.

31. He watched afternoon television.

32. Once he had been followed by a rainbow across the skies of France while flying a World War I airplane carrying bombs and machine guns.

33. "Your father died this afternoon."

KELLY CHERRY

Covenant

(FROM COMMENTARY)

I MET FELIX — that's Seligman, I called him in our conversation — on the twenty-third of December, 1966. I remember the date because it was the date of my wedding. A blizzard had hit Virginia about ten in the morning, so when Felix walked into my parents' gold-papered hallway, he was splattered with snowflakes, lugging a suitcase with one hand and holding a wet gone-out cigar in the other. He's a big man, you know, but the girl he ushered in with him was smaller than I am. Abby wore a black dress. This disturbed me, though later I learned it ought not to have: black is not the color of mourning among Jews.

Felix was our best man. He'd been best friends with my husband since they were both ten years old in Flatbush. In 1966 Felix was one year into the business of getting a divorce from his wife, who, as Ezra explained it to me, had quit sleeping with him six months after they were married, because he'd given up his sales job in order to become a cameraman. He started out nonunion, of course, and earned about fifty dollars a week. Now Felix makes in the neighborhood of fifty thousand a year, but now he screws around with heroin. Anyway, the marriage, his marriage, lasted for five years, and then his wife locked him out one night and he moved in with my husband for a while and then he met Abby. Abby is gone from the scene these days, too; I mean, neither Felix nor I see her, but by her choice. But she was pretty and dark and pretentious, and I liked her. My parents also liked her, and adored Felix on sight, and if they'd insisted beforehand that no unwed couple was going to stay overnight in one room in their lovely house that they'd worked all their lives for, as soon as they set eyes on this good-looking pair of people, they changed their minds, and whispered to me that it was okay. I should have been so attractive — the world would open up, don't kid yourself. Only Felix and his Abigail didn't stay, after all, because they could afford to be appalled at the prospect of being stranded in the suburbs of Richmond, Virginia.

If even I can't mistake the crossness that has crept into my tone of voice, it is because what I am trying to tell you is that so long ago, in that instant when Felix stepped into the house in Richmond, with Ezra grinning from ear to ear, so easily triumphant, with me in a state of panic, I knew I wanted to go to bed with him. *Knew* is maybe not quite the right word. I didn't acknowledge the notion, didn't dwell on it, but it was there, there in my body if not my brain, even as Ezra took him aside and handed him the thin white-gold band that would be urged onto my finger in a few hours. But you won't read this rightly if you don't recognize that both Ezra and I were well-taught children of the Age of Liberalism, prone to psycho-analysis, magnanimously tolerant of fantasy. Why not? Our fantasies were private and could not possibly wreak any effect on a world as incurious or unconcerned as we'd early enough concluded ours was. So the sensitivities of my own rather severe bosom could scarcely disturb my equilibrium, and when Felix flattered me or mocked me with a low drawl, it was only a game. Three years went by before I saw it'd sneaked up on reality. The night was cold, it was late February in New York, and after dinner — chicken breasts in a wine-and-mushroom sauce; how helplessly pleased I was with myself for having learned to cook at last — over coffee, my husband and Felix, each interrupting the other, broached me with the suggestion that I spend a week with Felix at his place in upstate New York. My husband said I needed a vacation. "It will be good for you," he said, "to get away from me for a while." My hands trembled. When I looked at Felix, he reached for the celery sticks: hungry and blithe, he was, seemed oblivious. But Ezra stiffened and I was afraid of the fast smile he challenged me with. He confused me. I didn't know whether to be insulted that I was so sexually harmless, or alarmed at my own ungovernability, or suspicious. My husband was so clever at uncovering guile in others that I assumed he was not incapable of a certain deviousness himself.

Two hours earlier, in the kitchen, as Felix was hanging up his coat, Ezra had caught me by the elbow. Because now that I write this, I remember it was not late February; it was Valentine's Day. That's marvelous. I suppose you had thought to discover in this letter some secret by which to interpret me, content me, but now you see that I am no more than the contemporary female forced by circumstance to deny her inclination toward sentimentality. But you are arrogant and I do not love you. "Happy Valentine's," Ezra said. The present he gave me was a beautiful little Greek vase copy from the Metropolitan Museum; I have kept it still. But the card read, "Will you be mine?" And when you opened it up, it asked, "Or must I take you by force?" I kissed him for the vase. Then I asked him what the card meant: haltingly. He only laughed. "It seemed appropriate," he said. I quickly put them away before Felix returned. It was dinnertime.

We sat in the living room, lamplight reflecting from the snow mounded on the windowsills outside, the aroma of red wine running from the bowl of bones on the table. Felix stretched out in the armchair that had been my husband's before we were married. Was it too ostentatiously that I curled up on the couch next to Ezra and tried to hold his hand? But his face had gone black and he rose to fetch a story I'd done, a story in which the young husband painted his pregnant wife orange. The scene stemmed from Ezra, as so many of my story ideas were his. He showed the story to Felix. I occupied myself with cleaning up, clearing the dishes, while Felix read it, his giggles and snorts exaggerating Ezra's uncharacteristic silence, paining my ears. This story was set in his farmhouse in upstate New York; that had been Ezra's doing too.

"You don't really have the feel of it," Felix said. "You haven't been there often enough."

Three weeks later my husband was still at me, wanting me to go up there, and that was one reason I agreed to the separation when he instead suggested that. There were other reasons that played into it. Ezra, who'd been himself pretty much raised by his analyst, had been sending me to a psychiatrist at the Downstate Medical Center in Brooklyn, a fat and bearded dullard determined to abide by the rulebook to the point where we wasted fifteen minutes each session until I volunteered some stupid matter for discussion. "It's cold out," I said. He said, "Tell me why the cold makes you uncomfortable." But the weather was what we ought to have had in com-

mon. I was lonely, and he merely made me lonelier. So I said to
Ezra, "Enough. If I'm sick, this is no way to get well."

He said nothing at first. He put a cigarette in his mouth, reached
for my lighter; the flame swelled up like a volcano and a tremor ran
up his arm and he dropped the lighter. I jumped for it, smothered
the fire with my boot. "Goddamn you," he cried, "it's our one
chance, don't you see that?" He'd cursed me before, but always we
met in bed. I was crazy for his energy, which fed me, and this night
was no different from the others. But in the morning, a letter came
from my parents, addressed to us both, and he opened it first. It
pointed out that if I worked a few months in Richmond, living
with them, I could give Ezra the extra year he wanted in New York.
"It'll give us time to think in," he said, "and they won't have to
know the real reason behind the separation." Well, it fairly kills my
soul to admit that the first thing I thought of was the midterm coming up in the night school Greek lit class I was taking; I wasn't prepared for it, and this would be a way out. That doesn't mean I
wasn't terrified. "I'll go back to therapy," I said. "Anything." He
called my parents and told them I was coming home that night.
Then he called the airline and made a reservation, and called a
taxi, and packed my things, and took me there, and sent me off. I
swore and said he was an efficient bastard. But when we were picking up the ticket, a black woman with a child stood in line in front
of us. "Thirty-two fifty," the clerk told her. "All I has got is thirty
dollars," she said. She started to weep. Ezra dug the difference out
of his pocket and put it on the counter and smiled at her. I was
heartbroken.

I'd come home from an interview at Midlothian High School,
where the principal queried me on my opinion of *Catcher in the
Rye* and asked how long my husband, doing his doctorate "up
there," wore his hair. My own I'd cut short for the sake of this interview. I knew Ezra wouldn't've approved, but in the Southern sunshine I was living in, all life seemed simpler and earthier, more practical, than he would have it. Now I went into my room, put my
purse down on the ingenious, long desk my father had built so
willingly across one wall, and the telephone rang. It was Ezra. "I've
been thinking," he said. "This is my plan. Come back to New York,
find a job, take an apartment of your own, undergo intensive, long-

term therapy. I'll work part-time and pay our bills. If you can be-come financially and emotionally independent of me, a self-sufficient adult, then it is possible that at some later time we may try living together again." He must have memorized it, and the self-righteous-ness and the vanity of it stung me to the quick. "No! No! No!" I screamed. My voice flew out of me as if it had been caged. "Oh, God, no."

"Then you want a divorce," he said, still matter-of-fact.

"Oh, God, no," I screamed again, but I could hardly believe that it was I whose shrillness filled the room. I cried and pleaded and he hung up. I laid my head down on the desk next to my purse.

My parents are musicians; my mother's hands are rough, the fin-gertips callused, but her bones have a graceful precision, a long, fine line I still would like to have learned. Gently she knocked on the door. "I think," she said, "you'd better tell us what's wrong, now." What Southern delicacy! . . . Insisting I should assume the subordinate position I wanted. What outrage followed, when they learned what was going on. But I would not listen to them. I called Ezra back and told him that I submitted to his plan. "It's too late," he said. "You don't really care about me." Nor did all my tears avail.

Then I wrote to his analyst, a careful, honest letter that he never acknowledged. I called my own analyst, who said, "If that's the way the man feels about you, I can't change his mind." I called Ezra's brother and sister-in-law. They had been my closest friends in New York: "We don't want to mix in," they said. "Our only part in all this is to offer moral support to Ezra." I called Abby. "Men," she said, "they're all nuts." But Abby never called me.

The sole person from that hub of the world who was troubled to get in touch with me was Felix, and he, in his monosyllabic manner, with that hip shrug I could see long-distance, assured me that I was not, indeed, "no 'count" — the mockery was discreet — nor was I so uselessly deluded as Ezra had said or so bothersome as I feared. He wrote me a letter which I saved, since it took off from divorce in general and sailed into a description of his current summertime *ménage à trois* in Woodstock and concluded with a dream sequence wherein he seduced some gaunt lady roundheels from Larchmont, an attorney's wife, mounting all his loathings and his fears on her apoc-alyptically avocado-carpeted floor. I welcomed that letter for its friendliness, and resented it too, because it confined me so closely to the arena of simple friendship. We talked a few times on the telephone. He was in favor of my returning to New York. But that was all. And I accepted the indignity of his disinterest, for if I was guilty of adultery, that sin was not only not palpable, a slight waywardness of the imagination, but had been committed not with him but with the composer in Russia whom I'd once promised to marry. I'd broken that promise in order to marry my husband. Then perhaps the adultery was done with my husband in violence upon the pledge, even upon the very outlandishness of the pledge I'd contracted in a cemetery in Riga to my brilliant and sentimental Russian, who, sick with music and hope, loved me more truly than I felt free at the time to give him credit for, disbelieving his intent because I knew I wasn't worth it. In this way one succeeds in wondering whether Ezra hadn't failed to trust me out of his mistrust of himself, but I can recognize a rationalization when I see one; and surely that kind of melancholic twisting and turning is so far from being true that it was instead the locus of the sickness my husband, probing my psyche even more assiduously than the recesses of my body, stirred in me. In any case, I saw Felix just once right after I returned to New York. Oh, he was hugely altered. His hair was shaggy and unruly, he'd lost thirty pounds, he was dropping acid, he was filming subtle and arch little obscenities for distribution by *Evergreen,* and if he was in bad shape, I was in worse, and we met at the Esquire on Broadway for breakfast and went our separate ways.

Sickness: I am and have always been at the core dogmatic as hell and pitted against the rest of the world but baffled by how ever to make that definition visible, much less viable. You said I am not a woman. You should be able to do better than that. If the accusation is true, it holds for every one of us, including your wife, and if it is true, it is also tired, a ploy, and a threat. "Look here," this man tells me; "you're not a woman until I acknowledge you as one." You can take your sanctions, sweetheart, and shove them. I don't need them. Nor will I allow you to equate my existence with a generality, I am not the womb but only contain one, and my problems are particular and only resemble those of my sisters. Let me tell you something. I went underground quite consciously when I was seven or so; it seemed the only way to preserve one's sanity in a family which was utterly charming, bright, and dedicated to doom. My hus-

band, Ezra Solomon — his father was a small-time judge riddled
with ambition — tried to tutor me into an anger with them that
should have freed me, but, you see, they are *likable*. Just as he
was. And what none of them — he because he believed in "anger"
and they because they believed in "love" — would understand or
even accept was really me, is that I simply did not feel the need for
any radical reconstruction of our mortal souls. I still don't for the
life of me understand why people should not be permitted to feel
hatred and sexual desire and ambition and envy and guilt and
sentimentality and any other thing they care to feel, since what is
conveyed is all that has any effect, or maybe here what I do mean is
affect.

I believe in manners. In appearances. In superficiality, if you
will.

But this passion is off the point and incoherent to boot. What I
started to say, to tell you, if you are in truth listening as closely as
you swear you are, is that I am depressed when I see myself aging,
and whether I look fifteen or not is beside the point because I know
where the wrinkles are and I know where my limbs are losing elastic-
ity and I know how the chances for childbearing daily decrease:
when I see myself aging and yet retaining some undefeatable, some
so help me almost unavoidable, childlike incapacity to translate
what I know into how I reason. How easy it would be if I were only
faced with translating what I think into what I do, but the problem
is deeper, and shows even in a certain translucence of the eye, which
I spotted in my mother ages ago and answer to now in the mirror, a
certain openness which reveals not, haplessly, vacuity, but an incredibly crazy knack for tolerating anomaly after anomaly, if that's
the word I want, for sustaining contradictions without end. And in
fact if I do have any talent at all it is reducible to this, that I can
assume any number of personalities on paper, which has been my
means of survival, and is also the deathtrap in which that core of
dogmatism, me at age seven hearing God in my head telling me to
put aside all argument and go about my work, which was prophecy
(I never told *that* to my bearded friend; it's too simple to analyze
away), has locked itself. Don't you dare choke on this. You asked
for my letter. "I am waiting," you said.

Felix and I talked on the phone occasionally during the year.
After October, it was always I who called: October was when he

informed me that my husband had flown to Mexico, compliments of his brother's money, and obtained a divorce from me. I was divorced for a week before I knew it. Felix tried to placate me, saying, "What good is living with someone who doesn't love you? You're better off out of it. Come on, luv," he said, and giggled, "be a big girl and roll with the punches." But I went on bawling and he said he was sorry. Then after a while, along about March, when Ezra married again, I stopped calling Felix, and it wasn't until almost summer that he rang to say he'd seen my husband who was full of crap and how was my love life. I was surprised. But not entirely. I had, after all, mailed him a poem I'd done about him, which I hoped would set up some echoes in his head. It did, though I knew muse-baiting was an inferior sport. He suggested that we get together sometime. Oh, dear Jesus, was I nonchalant. "Sure," I said, as a year of lukewarm affairs had taught me to hold my tongue in these matters. But that, you see, didn't stop me from glancing at the telephone every time I walked past it.

Then the following week he did phone, and he was in town, and again I met him for breakfast — this was June, and the Esquire had gone out of business and we met at Stark's on 90th — and we went back to my place and turned on with some stuff I had stashed there and then drove to Riverside Park and 96th, where a five-year-old boy black as the Queen of Spades was peeing over the railing. I was too high to concentrate on more than one thing at a time, so whenever I pulled myself back from watching the remnants of cloud that skirted the sun, I found my hemline inching up. Felix climbed a tree. We went somewhere for lunch. I forget where. On the way we passed a young girl selling hotdogs on the street; she was sitting on a stool, and Felix, with the privileges that he was entitled to as a bright and beautiful male making it in Fun City, bent over and patted her knee, but I just smiled at her right alongside him. In the restaurant he said, "Come to the country for a couple of days." He added, "After Bonny leaves." I asked him who Bonny was. "She's been living there," he said, "and she has this kid I'm crazy about. You should have had a kid."

"Are you living with her?" Because one never knew for sure.

"Goddamn! Living? Living with her? I call living with someone when you live with someone for a few years and have a goddamn kid by someone."

He was shaking his head as if he'd like to shatter the air around him, and the motive for his fury escaped me. "What happened between you and Ezra?" I asked.

"Nothing," he said.

But he was deeply hurt because my husband refused to countenance his interest in yoga and the *I Ching*, my husband the arch-rationalist, direct descendant of Elijah Gaon of Vilna who never slept and burned the bad books of the Chassidim, and he felt that my husband was throwing away twenty-some years of friendship. "Christ," Felix said, "friends are for arguing with, aren't they?" Tentatively, I nodded my head, but he wasn't looking at me. "I love him," he said, "and that doesn't seem to mean anything." I would have liked to ask him about Ezra's second wife, but was afraid to. I figured, you see, that he'd just been divorced from my husband and was getting back at him by going to bed with me, but loathed myself for thinking this because it is the kind of deviousness built on self-contempt that I am afraid healthy people don't operate on.

As a matter of fact, when I was seventeen and at New Mexico Tech, a misfit if ever there was one, my closest friend was an older man named Will who said to me that he thought I might someday be the single real woman he knew of if I could rid myself of my deviousness. That is the kind of thing I always took to heart, took to bed, and brooded over. Will later gave up mathematics, it was topology or something, for bear hunting in Alaska. So I tried to lay psychology aside and came on very friendly but calm and Felix was stunned when back at my apartment I seduced him.

It was that, because, like any man, his view of relationships resists expansion, and if I was his surrogate, I was still his ex-best-friend's ex-wife. He knew only what he wanted to do, not what he was willing to do. But for God's sake, accept this much about me: *I* knew that it was too late to wound Ezra by sleeping with Felix. Both Felix and I, in our different ways, had early on transgressed the things that Ezra only toyed with, and we hankered after some conventionality which seemed forever just beyond our reach. Felix sat in my line of sight, across from me, at the desk, licking the edge of a reefer he was rolling, and he has a small wart tucked into the side of his nose that is unaccountably attractive. "What I do like about you," I told him, "is the way you move. It's masculine."

He was as flattered as the most innocent of savages. And why shouldn't he have been? It was sincere enough. He giggled. "I always thought my best qualities were really kind of feminine," he said. "Effeminate."

"Oh, they are."

I sat on the bed. "Why not bring that thing over here," I said, and if I wasn't elegant, at least I wasn't coy. So we sat together on the bed, smoking another cigarette, and the speckles of dust that swam in the sunlight washing over us from my windows grew as enormous as planets. "It's the Milky Way." I laughed, because I was in the one place where the shadow of my mother's smartness couldn't reach me. I was in the one place where no man's wit or coldness could tyrannize me: it's been years since I broke the first taboo, and since then no man can put out my fire. The heat of my body is sufficient to support the cosmos, yes, damn you, to generate stars and suns. I might have spoken aloud, "Try it, Felix, try to pin me down here, try to swing your weight over me and beat me down here, the way you do with your shrugs and your girls and your dope. The way Ezra did with words." He would not even have heard me. He was lost in space already. First I kneaded his thighs, slowly, slowly, and then I sucked the skin of his shoulders, making moons, and touched my tongue to his small teeth, and I revolved around him like earth's solitary moon, slowly, gazing on his blue, glassy eyes until they closed.

He was good, the best I'd ever had, and when we'd done, he kissed my throat, and said, "Well, it was worth waiting for." Such gentleness took me off my guard. I stroked his face. All my energy was spent, and oh lord, oh lord, I knew for how little. I wanted to take it all back, gather it up in my hands, put it to some intelligent, real use. But it was useless, and always was; my energy derives from a stingy source which will not allow a long-term investment. These metaphors were a misery to me, and I turned away from Felix, but not before he caught the cloudiness on my face, so that he held me in his arms for a moment. Then, "I have to be going," he said.

"Right on," I said.

He hugged me.

I had cut a religion class I was supposed to be sitting in on, a doctor appointment, and that was also the first day since I started tutoring her that I begged off on a session with Valerie. She's got cerebral palsy — well, you know — a radiant face, dark brown hair blown

around her face like the emblem of our era, and I was wrong to skip
our session because she has been to me no less than what the child
on the farm was to Felix. When Felix repeated that he wanted me
to come up to the farm, then, still full of his hug, I soared. Even
when he explained that it had to be worked in between when
Bonny, the current girl, was taking off for Mexico, and the following weekend, which was the Fourth of July and he was going to
Woodstock to drop an anniversary tab with the girl of last summer,
or girls, I said, "You bet," and was tickled to death at being listed in
the stable of a hopelessly inarticulate but perfectly fine moviemaker.
He did a film of the subway strike so lyrical, so lovely, it would break
your heart to see it. I showed him out the door and stood in the
doorway and he touched my cheek. His fingers were as swift as rain.

Thursday. A week has gone by since I began this, and I still don't
know what you hope to gain by it. Or I do — you in your unoffen-
sively assertive suit, laced shoes, peeking through this keyhole into
the drug culture, I detest your compartmentalizing, long to do the
same. "Tell me," you said, "why you feel guilty about being unhappy." That was the most splendid excuse I had ever heard: I
wanted to pick it up and raise it like an umbrella over our heads
and with the rain pitching down on all sides I'd let you kiss my
hands and face at least until the sun shone again. Well, as my father
used to say, we'll see. Three minor incidents keep urging themselves onto this paper, and you may as well have them too.

The first is that a few days ago I received a note from Dan Atkin-
son, a writer whom I knew rather formally in Greensboro. He's
thirty-one, married, has two little boys, and from what I gather off
the grapevine, conducts his life with a bit more honor than most of
us who were there at the time. I thought him a good writer; and
he's the only one of the bunch who has had less success than I. To
his note he added a postscript: "I keep on sending stories out, but
each time they sit on them just long enough for my hairline to re-
cede another one sixteenth of an inch, and then they send them back
without any comment."

It's a struggle for power, isn't it? For survival. When we were in
Greensboro, I wrote a story, still unpublished, titled "Portraits."
The hero was Jakob, a Dutch painter of ambiguous aims. I'd always
pictured my Jakob with blond spun-out hair, a pool of hazy sunshine. One night in Brooklyn, my husband, who is as dark and mole-

pocked as any Mediterranean nomad, showed me that nowhere in the story did I indeed specify the color of Jakob's hair. Ezra was smiling when he pointed this out to me, but it was not a malicious smile, or at least I didn't think it was, but it was one which delighted in recognizing something I hadn't, and sometimes still, on the subway or in the store, I think I see his thick lips pulled down like a drapery of flesh over an unspeakably vast and *verboten* abyss. He loved to link things which I would otherwise see as disparate, until it seemed he was weaving a web around my mind, and it was hopeless to argue or struggle against it.

The third thing is not unrelated, though it has to do with Jamaica. Of course I thought about you in Jamaica, in August, but I had an affair there, with the twenty-one-year-old Hindu who managed the hotel in-bond store. His name was Johnny, and except that he had no chin, he was the image of my husband. But the only reading matter in his apartment was a paperback titled *Married Men Make the Best Lovers,* and a stack of comic books, and he knew almost nothing about sex and approached the subject with a scientific mien that was ofttimes unnerving. But he was a nice youth, and he bore me no grudge, and I loved the excellence with which he ran his shop. We stretched out on the sand of the public beach, crossing our legs over each other, listening to the static on his transistor radio. John Crow zeroed in close over our heads, and our heads were buzzing from the ganja. I burrowed my fingers in the sand while he explained to me that the necklace he wore was given to him by his widowed mother in Kingston: it bore the image of a guru and kept the bad spirits away. He carried me back to the hotel on his scooter about one, and when I got into the room I switched on the lamp between Valerie's mother's bed and mine, because I thought I might do some reading. She sensed the light was on and reached up to turn it off, but she was full of sleeping pills, and when she reached up, her pillow slid off, and then she began to slide out from bed after the pillow. She fell asleep again in the middle of all this action, and there she hung, suspended between the bed and the floor, between, I vow, time and space. So I went over and picked her up and swung her back onto the bed. I tucked her in and then started to slip the pillow under her. Suddenly she raised both her arms, her wrists making little clasping motions, and her face was so white and expressionless that *in an instant* my position was transformed, and I was guilty, I was responsible, I was that damned

survivor the corpse clutches at in the hour of silence. What dreams
we have. When I was nine and not yet brainwashed by civilization,
I dreamed of an ancient wooden house. The outside staircase
climbed to the attic. I stood at the foot of the stairs, grasping the
banister, and as I stood there, I saw my family in their various
stations along the staircase shed their skin in flakes like flakes of
snow, until to my huge, crying sorrow their bones showed and shimmered, turning in the pale, courteous light of the stars as if they were
semiprecious stones.

Here is why I tutor Valerie: I make her laugh, my innocence, as
she is pleased to call it, amuses her. Here is why I do not understand the books you patronize me with, Kierkegaard and Saint
Augustine and the rest. All arguments convince only a believer.
To the nonbeliever, the universe is discrete, insane, purposelessly
proliferous, vain and futile. Say that last word with a long *i*. Every
burst of flower, shock of aroma, every high mass sung or thought
conceived or love survived is made irredeemably ugly, is made disgusting, by the death of a child, and every death is the death of a
child. There is no *time* in the world alone. There is no trust, because nothing is trustworthy, nor is there any sharing. Pessimism is
the only intelligent response to fact; and the only fact is the fact
of evil. But what I'm trying to say is that if you ask me to define
God in twenty-five words or less, I'm game, and I say that what God
is, is the possibility of goodness. The possibility. But it is, alas, the
perception of that possibility which without reflection commands
us, binds us in covenant, wrenches us from our natural posture, and
sucks up our energy in an unending effort to bring into being what
can never endure until the End of Days, or, if you will, the Day of
Judgment, and that is what *profound* is, for without personality
there is no morality. Somewhere God and Eros meet. (But it is not
in Dr. Freud's room. I was there and I can vouch for that.) In return for our unholy anguish we receive hope, history, and once in a
blue moon, communication, but this tension, this covenant, is the
bleeding hardest bargain anybody ever drove; selling your soul to
the devil and being sued for gypping him is easy by comparison, and
sometimes I just really wish to hell that somebody would bother to
say this without whitewashing it into terms of conviction or faith or
whatever. What it is, is revelation, and having consented to recognize the revelation, there is no answer open to you but *yes*. Maturity? Maturity is for people who don't have the good goddamn

sense to tremble with terror every blessed moment of their existence, who don't recognize the enormity of the debt of gratitude we owe to God.

So I went upstate, and Felix met me at the bus stop in Hudson, which is not far from Tanglewood.

Too bad for me, he'd got things ordered in his head before I got up there, and as soon as I stepped off the bus he cut me down by asking what I was doing wearing city clothes. We picked up his laundry and when we got to the farmhouse I changed into my jeans and a T-shirt and work shoes. He was wearing wonderfully filthy white pants and the new mustache that made him look down and out in Paris and London. The first thing we did of course was light up and go for a walk in the meadow. "You have to watch out for the gopher holes," he warned me, "you could break a leg."

The sun was bright, the grass was green all over, that gorgeous air sinks in deep. I was glad to see Happy Jack Dog again, and said so. "Son of a bitch killed a gopher last week and brought it in by its neck. Don't want nobody to call him Happy anymore," said Felix. I tripped. "I told you, you got to watch out for four-legged dangerous dogs."

"You don't know what you're saying," I said.

"Sure I do."

"You said you could break a leg in one of these holes. They're mouseholes," I said, "holes in the earth. I'm up on holes because I'm doing *Notes from the Underground* with Valerie."

"I have this feeling, well, I do, that she must be beautiful," he said.

"She's sixteen."

"I read Dostoevsky once. But I wasn't sixteen, I was younger yet. My mother thought she'd improve my mind by checking out books from the Brooklyn Public Library."

"I never realized you had a mother."

"I'm a son of a bitch."

I said, "It's true you're much too tough for me."

We took off our shoes. The pressure of the sun pushed our feet to the earth. Happy Jack Dog nuzzled my feet. "Scram," Felix said, and Happy Jack ran for the woods.

"You're a mean one," I told him, when I tried to kiss him and he pushed me away.

"People drive by, even on this dirt road. You got to watch out for people."

"I know, I know. They're two-legged dangerous dogs."

"If you call him Happy again, I'll strangle you. I used to love him, and that's what you don't understand." He put his big hands on my neck and we walked back to the house. . . . Which is beautiful.

It's fifty bucks a month and he did the insulation himself. A fireplace, a potbellied stove, a darkroom and an upstairs, and the entirety so fragile you feel like you're living on the ground and the whole thing so sturdy you can stay there the year through. Hell, yes, I was there a year. Maybe it was the weed, but I like grass: it is usually fun and it is sensuous and the ritual in its use is peace-making for the mind, even when you are alone. I grant you, I never heard of anybody's getting a good idea on it; but you do sometimes stumble onto interesting notions if you're smoking with someone, because the way conversation works when you're high is that statement A is satisfactorily coherent, statement B is coherent, but B picks up one word or image from A and replies to that, not to the sense of the sentence as a whole. It's like shooting at ducks tangentially.

But Felix and I didn't talk much. Everything we might have said to each other would have rung in a third party, Ezra's ghost. So he loaded his rifle and went out again, this time to take a couple of potshots at rabbits, and the blasts shook me as I rocked in the rocking chair in the living room. There are different kinds of long weekends, and I knew by now that this one was going to be longer than most. My grandmother would have said, "Trouble always comes in threes." My mother says, "When trouble comes, it comes in spades." As soon as I'd entered the house that morning, I saw the book on Cézanne, and knew by the tear on the slipcover that it was my ex-husband's. Felix had left it on the coffee table. He must have known, I think, or ought to have known, that I would recognize it; he knew the slipcover was torn when I hurled the book at Ezra the day he sneered and said my taste in art was "literary." I retorted: "It's not me who's doing a hubristic paper on lithos of Joseph and Potiphar's wife, of all things." Our battles were very intellectual and straight. But I at least knew that for, or in, all his puffed-up rationalism, he saw himself less as King Solomon and more as the handsome and clever Joseph, Mann's lovable unlicked cub, purely oblivious to fleshly lures which would evilly sway him from his righteous administration. *I* knew that when Potiphar's wife, who would be running to a shameful fullness, but harsh with herself, not promiscuous, not oversure, but frightened and bored, said, "Dear young boy, I am sick with the weariness in my womb and desire to teach you the pleasures that are already beginning to graduate from me," Joseph answered without mercy: "What have I to learn from you?" He would not risk Potiphar's sword; neither would he leave Potiphar's house in peace. And with his soft looks and scowl, his curls that whispered when they brushed against her sleeve in the dusk, he drove that woman into madness.

I turned my mind inside out for him, combing all the crumbs of ambivalence from my imagination. When I was clean, he walked away.

The screen door slammed on Felix's entrance. He had with him some stuff from the pot plants he cultivates in between the cucumbers. He'd dried out the tops of some of the plants the day before, and that stuff especially was strong. We smoked it and started to mess around and then he sort of maneuvered me outside into the bushes next to the garage. I didn't altogether comprehend the reason for his grin, since I'd gladly screw in the sunshine any day of the week, but I was afraid to say anything. I could smell his body and it was like the ground. He'd brought the rifle with him and set it down by the inflated plastic mattress we lay on. He knew his way around the country, all right, the route was mapped. We stripped, not touching each other, and the sun sparkled on the hairs of his legs. For the first time, I paid attention to the freckles on his chest; they wiped me out. I wanted to say something nice to him, then, because he was so defenseless against the sky, rooted there like a sapling, bending over me as if compelled to by the wind, but the sun kept shifting, striking first here and then there, so that I was at a loss, I was losing ground. The sun burned up my insides; he stoked away at me as if I were a furnace. His mouth was a glowing coal, I could scarcely catch my breath. The sun beat on the backs of my thighs, and the world kept turning over and over, and then I came, and couldn't stop coming, and for what seemed like forever I had everything I'd ever wanted, because I forgot myself, forgot who I was, forgot him, and was ready to die.

As though it were a rose, he plucked from the nearest bush a straw hat with a short brim and set it on the back of his head. "Oh," I said, "that looks wonderful."

"It belongs to Ezra's wife," he said.

I looked at him in terror. Then I opened his fist and put my mouth to his palm.

"It's too bad, isn't it," he said, "that it doesn't mean anything."

Supper was foul: soup made of radishes, beets, tomatoes, cucumbers, okra, I think, and a salad of unadorned lettuce leaves. I suppose had a girl tried to get me to eat that I'd have laughed at her and fixed myself a hamburger, which means Women's Lib still has some work to do on me, but on the other hand, who needs a hassle. You should have tasted the bread he'd baked, the boy's not going to put Sara Lee out of business. I swallowed what I could, wishing I dared to assert myself, lay claim to the kitchen and bake a blueberry cake. But to my left hung the pegboard Abby had contributed, and the flowers on the table were from the border she'd seeded when Felix first bought the place; or they may have been Bonny's flowers. So I kept myself to myself, and afterward, in the living room, I waited in a corner while he taped himself on a dobro, drums, and the harmonica. He majored in composition at New York University, and he knows rhythm, but somewhere along the line he has lost track of what music was meant to be, or maybe he is shy of it these days, and he pounded on those instruments until the echoes in my head mightily ripped it apart. But that is *not* right, I am being much too crude here. He was hunched over the bongos, the cymbals, the dobro, balling himself into one long roll of sound, and if I felt he'd banished me from the scene, it was my own fault, because he handed me a brass flute, and said, Pan tempting Midas to profane Apollo's godly playing, "Hey, chicken, goof on this with me." I was afraid. I was always afraid. Eventually we went upstairs to sleep.

The silence of the country oppressed me.

In the morning, Felix wanted to find a Sears store, so we got into the car and toked up and started off. We weren't thinking too clearly and soon discovered we were headed toward Albany. It seemed to make sense to continue toward the destination we had evidently begun with.

Somewhere on this side of it, a policeman stopped us, a young cop, skinny and hesitant. We must have looked freaky by that time, all right, anybody who could read the signs could tell we were bombed: I was wearing sunglasses and Felix's fatigue jacket, and there was a tin of about a dozen reefers in the jacket, and Felix's light brown hair curled out uncombed, and the stubble on his face gleamed with sweat. Felix got out of the car. The kid cop said, "May I see your license, please?"

Felix pulled it out of his pocket.

"I see," the kid said. "And where do you live, Felix?"

Felix told him.

Then Felix asked if we'd done anything wrong.

"Oh, no, no. But we're expecting a shipment of two pounds of hash soon, you see, somewhere in the vicinity. Ever use hash, Felix?"

"Well, I'll tell you the truth," Felix said. "Now and then, but only by way of experiment."

"That so?"

"That's so. . . . Now I admit we may have toked up for our journey, just a little grass, but wouldn't you?"

The kid snorted.

Felix said, "God knows it's a long trip to anywhere."

"Just a little pot?"

"That's so, to be sure," Felix said.

I held my breath as the policeman approached me, but he only said, "Excuse me, ma'am," and searched the glove compartment in a perfunctory way. "Well," he spoke again, turning back to Felix, "you know how it is. We don't want any strong stuff coming in here, do we?"

"I should say not, to be sure." I was going to murder him if he said "to be sure" one more time.

The kid smiled, then, and handed the license back to Felix. "Have a good trip, now," he said, and beamed when Felix, cool Felix, gave him the victory sign.

We were approaching Albany. "This reminds me," he said to me, "of a trip I took with Ezra when we were seventeen." I knew the story already, but I didn't forestall him. "Would you believe we drove way the hell up here from Brooklyn, looking for whores to lose our virginity with?" In Ezra's mind, that search had assumed the parodic proportions of a nineteenth-century *Brautshau*. They'd piled into the judge's car on a rainy night, flushed with success be-

fore it was theirs, and when they got to Albany, they'd combed every
back alley the town had to offer. "We didn't find any, of course;
drove home as lily-white as when we left." But Ezra thought that
night was full of laughs, and reminisced about it often, or used to,
because distance allowed him to treasure so rare a lapse into spon-
taneity which was not serious. "It made us blood brothers. My
brother, Ezra," Felix said. "I'll bet he doesn't even remember how
it was. How else could he do this to me?"

"Do what?"

"I told him he was acting the same way his old man acted, ty-
rannical. I thought he'd understand that kind of language. Psycho-
logical."

"So? His second marriage won't last, you know," I said, shaking.

"What do you know about it? Do you know Susan Alexander?
Hell, no, you don't know about her. You're talking through your
hat," he raged. "She's a real fine woman."

"I know he didn't take any time after me to find out anything
about himself." It was a shot in the dark, but I had to defend myself.

"Oh, to be sure," he mumbled. But when some time had passed,
he said, "That mother was always blessed: even with his name;
he could always cut the child in half and still have both halves. May
he rot in hell."

And that floored me. I'd always thought that if there was envy
in their relationship, it must have been Ezra's envy for this laconic,
shuffling, successful man whose hands were so competent and flexi-
ble, who sat beside me, puffing away at a thin stick, the heavy smoke
enshrouding my heavy head. I smirked. "Such an expenditure of
energy, Felix; that's not like you."

He laughed. "No, it's not. But it's pretty funny, isn't it, that after
all these years I should come again to Albany, and with his ex-wife,
at that?"

"Hilarious."

"Well, you wouldn't understand. I've noticed one thing about
you," he said. "You get expectations about things. And when things
don't live up to your expectations, you feel cheated."

He was right on target. There wasn't much I could say, except,
maybe, "No foolin'," milking the South for all it was worth.

"Yeah, luv," he said. "No fooling."

*

We were in Albany, and we bought some peanuts and then asked directions to Sears and I went with him. The garden shop was a broad expanse of concrete wrinkled with potted plants and plastic swimming pools. Everywhere we walked, we passed these pools, brimming with stale water, and pretty soon we started running by them, weaving in and out around the plastic, which was red and blue and yellow, skidding, splashing our hands in the water, sprinkling the concrete with the water, until some clerk stopped us short, but deferentially. Straight people never know, not even you would know, and Felix came on grave as a churchman, and the clerk led him away to the tool department. I found my way back out to the car and let myself in and started to cry. I was crying because I was thinking about how Ezra had divorced me, and I was thinking about the divorce because of Felix, because the book, and the hat, and the blanket that had been a wedding present from my Aunt May, that I'd seen sitting on a shelf in the open closet in Felix's bedroom, told me, no matter whether it was what Felix wanted me to hear or not, that my husband and his real, fine wife, Susan Alexander, had been living in the farmhouse as early as late last summer, all the time I kept hoping, not without encouragement from him, that he'd come to his senses and see what he was throwing away, me, and I was a fool. When Felix came back to the car, he'd charged about two hundred dollars worth of power equipment, everything he'd "always wanted," he said, "since I was a boy in Flatbush." I was still crying, but I had on my sunglasses, and anyway, he was too worked up over his drills and saws to notice. "Hey, Felix," I said, "give me a kiss before we start."

His eyes flashed, blue eyes, and he roared at me the way Ezra used to: "Goddamn!" he cried. "Goddamn! Sometimes . . . some-*times* you really embarrass me," he said, "sometimes you just about put me too uptight to take."

I shivered and clutched at his coat; pulled it closer to my chest. But I was too hurt not to fight back. I said, "It's only a kiss. It doesn't mean anything, and if it doesn't mean anything, why should you mind?" I struck my knee with my fist. "You lie, Felix, you lie. You're as loyal as Happy Jack, and you're bruised all over, or else you wouldn't work so hard at keeping your distance."

"Sometimes," he said, "I think you're crazy. Ezra said you were sick. Oh, dear lord," he moaned, "don't you see, baby, don't you see everyone walks around with his little bag of shit on his back,

and you can't just walk up to them, without any goddamn pream-
ble, walk up to them without even introducing yourself, like you
were God or somebody, and take away what's theirs? My load
is mine."

It was drizzling, a cold, stupid rain. We drove in silence. When
we were beyond the city limits, I tapped him on the shoulder. He
turned toward me and I gave him the victory sign he'd given to our
kid cop. He giggled. "To be sure," he said.

We were still a far cry from home. I sat on my end of the seat.
I was remembering the wedding blanket. Remembering how my
husband and I used to lie under it back-to-back, with him reading
Saul Bellow and me reading Thomas Hardy and each of us interrupting the other to quote nice sentences. We'd have to turn the temperature down — the blanket was electric — when we made love and
then had to turn it up again because he was always as cold as I was.
His black hair, wired in an Afro, spiraled above me like some wild-
flower sprung from hell, an orchid accidental, improbable, violent,
intended for the tropics; when we made love, he held himself apart
from me, the veins of his arms swollen and thick, gorged, and if I
cried out, he never did. But afterward he'd shiver, he was cold, and
he was afraid to go to sleep unless I left the light on for him. Oh,
yes, I knew he suffered, and I will not have you say he didn't, or
that I didn't know it, because if I renounce that knowledge, I am
no better, no more sensitive, than he is, and I must, I *shall*, be better. But I was stoned. I said to Felix, "Am I better than your other
girls?" Which was a silly mistake, the kind of thing I should have
learned not to do long ago. He laughed. "You're all of you different," he said, "so how can I compare?"

"You're such a sweetheart," I said, and was surprised at how truly
tough it sounded.

"Ah, but the loveliest girl of all is Mary Jane."

Dusk had fallen; had dropped over the dirt road we now entered,
the fields, the Berkshires behind us, the garage.

I was depressed. "Felix," I began, "I'm riding a bummer."

"Do you want to talk to me about it?"

He was sitting at the kitchen table, puffing away at a pipe, and at
once the way he switched, from cigar to cigarette to pipe, lacking any
discrimination, bugged me terribly, and I said, "No."

"Then why did you have to tell me about it in the first place?"

That was only too fair, so I went into the living room and put an old Jefferson Airplane on the stereo and smoked some hash. He had a sewing basket on the bookcase; there was grass in it, and hash, and roaches, and pills, which I have never gotten in to, and a couple of hundred caps, and envelopes of the white horse that he said was pleasant to pet and fondle. The only thing he wasn't doing was mainlining, and maybe he was doing that. "You've got quite a stash here," I called. There was no answer from the kitchen. He was reading the *I Ching*, reading with such utter earnestness that I felt sorry for him. I knew the book:

Decay augurs sublime success and the advantage of crossing the great river. What has happened once will surely happen again. . . . When darkness falls, the Superior Man goes within and rests peacefully.

There was a mattress on the floor of the living room, which I sat on, and when the record was over, I played the flip side. Felix came in.

"Want to see some films?" he asked shortly.

"New ones?"

"From last winter."

He set about putting up the projection equipment — he had equipment for this and that, for everything — and I kept to my place on the mattress. And then out of the blue he crossed the room and bent over me and kissed me on my ear, a friendly kiss, a light kiss, an uncomplicated kiss, and looked into my eyes and danced away back to the other end of the room, astonishing us both; and in the hush that ensued, I heard the Jefferson Airplane flying high, out of sight, winging at full volume that insufferable, that brilliant, driving, last stanza to "White Rabbit," which is Alice's song:

> *And the white knight is talking backwards.*
> *And the Red Queen's all in her head. . . .*
> *Remember what the Dormouse said:*
> *"Keep your head!*
> *Keep your head!"*

I forced myself to focus: it was fifteen minutes of filmed water he showed: spring water, sea water, rain water, winter water. Ice floes split and crashed and crumbled; at the shoreline, crystals of

ice reflected each other like a hall of mirrors. The sun on
the screen sugared the snow, and I felt the chill settling on my legs
going numb. In the final shot, snowflakes fell, and I fell with them,
falling, falling past the projector's light that grazed Felix's face,
falling past Felix, spinning, hurtling through space, far past the
sun's edge, far out to the outer reaches of the mind's eye, where I
can see still before me my darkling father at his polished red-gold
violin. When he turns to me, there are tears looped along his lashes,
and the tendons of his hands blacken in pain. He needs me, he is
calling to me, and I *will* hasten to him. I run, I ran, toward him, and
from his mouth there gusted over me a river of lava, and the current of that so brutal heat blasted me back and forth among all the
various worlds, ringed and unringed. How I detested my father
then, hated him, as he gathered the space around him like leaves
of manuscript inadvertently let loose, shutting away his sorrow,
confounding me, and abandoned me to this other, deadly, cold, cold
void. Oh, yes! Oh, yes! I did cry for myself, and cry for myself today, and I *am not* ashamed, beloved, because this I knew in the beginning: that if I fail to do the very thing on my own behalf, there
exists no one else who can.

I left Felix and went upstairs to sleep. I was cold. I went to the
closet and removed the quilt that lay atop the wedding blanket,
thinking, He won't know whether I recognized the blanket and did
not care, or did not recognize it at all; he won't know whether he
succeeded. But I was still cold, so I wound myself in the sheets and
the quilt and went to sleep with my sweaters on. After a while, he
came up too, and I woke up and listened to him shed his clothes.
He peeled the quilt and the sheets from my back, and I heaved upward in spite of myself, loathing my flesh for its willfulness, its ty-
ranny; his flesh slicing into mine was wounding me, and when
mine closed over his, sealing it in like a throbbing sore, I was feverish. I pitched over, and he was moving in and out, beating on me,
inflaming me, the skin of his chest igniting me like a flint, balls of
wool from my sweaters sticking like ash to his chest and armpits. I
ran my fingers down his spine over the small of his back. His waist
was as defined as a girl's, the fullness of his buns angered me. "Oh,
Jesus," he said, "I like to ball." He said, "Anything. Man, woman,
beast." I dug my nails in. He laughed. "That's the spirit," he said.
Sweat dropped from his forehead onto my face and rained on my

clouded eyes and after ages we went together into a cadence of
twitching, groaning, speeding, skidding past each other, shooting.
"Felix, Felix, Felix." I wept. "I hate you!" He buried his head
under my sweaters, his cheek on my breasts, and asked me why. I
wanted to say: because of the loneliness you taunt me with. But
the words filled up my mouth like feathers and refused to fly free.
I pushed him away and reached for the grass sprouting like an oasis
by the side of the bed.

"By the way," his voice followed me, "are you on the pill?"

I began to hit him then, slapped his face forehand and back,
pummeled him with my fists, choked and coughed, and I was crying when he caught my wrists and held me still.

"No," I said.

"Diaphragm?"

"No."

"I see," he said.

"What do you see?" I answered, because I was calmer now.
"I'm not likely to get pregnant. And if I were to become pregnant,
it would not be your business but mine."

"Do you really believe that?"

"No." How would relationships be that rigidly defined, when
Valerie's so softly burnished beauty so plainly showed me that I was
her keeper. Ezra never knew her.

"Did you want him to knock you up?"

"Yes."

"And he wouldn't."

"No."

He lit a candle. He held it up to my face and set it down again.

"I said to Ezra, 'Let's have a kid,' and he looked at me as if I were
crazy, and said, 'If we have a kid, you'll make me wipe its nose,
you'll make me stop in the middle of my work and drive the kid to
his piano lesson.' Would you believe that, Felix? The kid might
have turned out tone-deaf, for all we knew. Whenever Ezra got into
a car, he crashed. Finally I said I didn't care, didn't care so long as
I could have him. He said it was too late."

"He won't be having any kids with Susan. She's forty years old."

"She's Potiphar's wife, Felix. Didn't you know that? He tried
to get me to play Potiphar's wife, but I was too dumb to catch on."

"If you'd known, would you have done it?"

"Who knows?"

"Nobody knows. 'Nobody knows the trouble I've seen,' " he sang. He touched me. "You're a lot like me," he said.

I didn't see how.

"When I got married," he said, "we had a caterer and a photographer. The whole scene. Did Ezra tell you?"

"Is she married again?"

"I tried and tried, but, yes, she's married again. She was such a cold damn . . ."

And the man began to cry. He was out of practice, and his face pinched up and twisted, unaccustomed to that posture, seeming alien and worn in the candle's unforgiving flame. I held his hand and asked him if he were doing any filming and he said no and asked me if I were writing and I said no. "I think I'll go to England," he said, "see what's happening over there."

"Do you want to marry again?" I asked him.

"Yes," he wept, "yes, yes, yes. It terrifies me."

I circled my arms around his neck. "I think I'm going to be able to convert to Judaism at last," I told him; "or at least come to some kind of truce with God. I'm working out an agreement." I was whispering. "Don't you want to know why?"

"It's all the same, sweetheart," he said, but then after a while he said, "Well, I won't knock it. I don't know, nirvana makes more sense to me." He pressed me to him. "Beautiful nirvana." He giggled. "Nirvana's all right, a real good lady. She's got golden hair, magical golden hair, and your Ezra and I spent one night together in Albany, years ago, looking all over town for her. I wonder where she'd gone," he said, and sighed. It struck me that he was a simple man, much simpler than Ezra, and I was grateful to him for that. He moved over to the opposite edge of the bed and asked me to snuff out the candle. I did. I got under the covers and closed my eyes. I thought it was all over, there would be nothing more.

But he pulled me to him, and said, "Put your arms around me, baby, please."

What tenderness was in the way he cradled himself in my arms, I cannot tell you, nor how happy I was and privileged. So the wind moved through the trees beyond our window, music in the air, and I rocked him easily to sleep.

The next morning he drove me in to the bus stop. I had asked if Happy Jack could come along with us, and Felix let him, but he had to stay in the car while we stood unstoned in the clean air. The bus came. "Hey," said Felix, shuffling his feet and nervously punching my arm. He would drive to Woodstock that afternoon. "I'll call you sometime. Well, you know, sometime when the wheel rolls around, and it's time."

How could I hurt this gentle person? But also, how could I let him hurt me. Calling on that convoluted, wrung humor that my family taught me, that Northerners do not commonly grasp, that serves me from time to time, I said to him, "Don't take any wooden nickels," and waited for him to kiss me goodbye.

He didn't. I got on the bus, and our bus driver, may his soul be blessed forever, let me off on the Upper West Side without making me go all the way in to Port Authority. I let myself into my apartment. The bed was unmade, my old stories that I'd been justifying myself with were strewn around the room, my tongue was thick, my eyes kept drooping, and I kept seeing, wherever I looked, old Aunt May's wedding blanket in the closet in Felix's bedroom. I swallowed some Seconal and lay down, until once more I went to sleep.

Aunt May is my mother's eldest sister. She was a librarian, wed late in life, and thereafter has largely devoted her life to covered-dish luncheons sponsored by the Presbyterian church. She's built like the Rock of Gibraltar, and has always looked on our branch of the family with grave mistrust. Her husband, Harold Flagg, made and lost more money in oil and oranges than the rest of us have ever seen, but wound up quite comfortably off; even so, Aunt May with her drawstring mentality was capable of giving my brother, who was then fifteen and very hungry for all the things boys want, a pants hanger for Christmas. Her marriage present to my mother — they despised each other and never forgot their manners — was a meat grinder.

May bore Harold three children. The girl, a kleptomaniac Girl Scout leader, married a Cadwallader from Cocoa; the last I heard from her, she was eager to remove her own daughter to Belgium for a year that she might learn French before the "mimic-center" in her brain closed off at the age of six. The elder boy, Rick, is retarded. May and Harold have set him up with a Seven-Eleven store in Florida; but May, though she is at least seventy by now, has to do all the bookkeeping for him.

Their younger son, Oliver Bob, was my age. The year we lived on a farm outside Richmond, they all came to visit us, and I was humiliated to discover that Oliver Bob played the piano much better than I did. And he had wit even then; I couldn't help liking him, though I tried. We fashioned a tree house in the woods that veered off from the side of the farm; and we bicycled down the hill. He went on to a small college where he majored in Sacred Music, and then, after twenty-one years, he fled the South. Aunt May and Uncle Harold saw no recourse but to employ detectives; but that's usual enough. When they located him, he was renting an apartment in New York City, done all in white with white wall-to-wall carpeting, and he wore a diamond ring on the little finger of his left hand.

They cut off his money and brought him home. He went to work with his brother Rick for a while, stowing groceries in brown bags and taking inventory, and then one day during the dog days he sat down in the armchair in his parents' living room and put a pistol to his temple and blew his brains out. It was Uncle Harold who found him; he picked up the telephone and dialed Aunt May at her church and said, "Mama, I think you might better come on home right now. Babe's in bad trouble." When she asked what was wrong, the old man said, "Babe's in bad trouble, Mama; he won't talk to me. Come on home now, you hear?" She went home.

So sad an excuse for a woman, my Aunt May, torments me, because, for all her paucity of imagination, for all her ill-disguised resentment toward the world, that eternal Mississippi Protestant, like my mother she grew up with, knew enough to know that when your niece marries a Yankee Jew, the only decent thing to do is to send a wedding present; and she had, so help me God, somewhere in her stubborn heart the humanity to choose for that present a wool, electric blanket dyed to a muted mustard, the same hot sweet shade of the strip of sand that used to line the coast from Biloxi to on beyond Pass Christian before the hurricane, I think it was Camille, ripped it all to hell last year. It was one beautiful blanket, believe me, far lovelier than ever my husband dreamed or understood, nor was it ever meant for Susan Alexander to lie under. It was never even meant for Felix. Ah, baby, sweet baby, so in your heart are you covenanted to your wife. Like it or not. Whether I love or have loved you or not.

Whether it's daytime or nighttime.

This fool heater is on the blink again and my fingers are blue. Last week Valerie looked at me, we'd done with tutoring for the night, and said, "I'm leaving, I'm going to a school in Maine." I wanted to tear the smile from her face and shove it down her throat. Then she smiled again and this time I wasn't angry. Or mad. Who can dare that effrontery? Even God, spurned by his own loveliest children, set aside for the sake of a mere image, was moved to repent and restore the two tablets of law that we might live long in the land of our enemies.

HERBERT GOLD

A Death on the East Side

(FROM ESQUIRE)

"WHAT WE LIKE, my friend, is to give away a lot of money so we can catch a little of the overflow for tax savings in line with — oh, well, the federal and state provisions." A boyish forty-nine-year-old man was winking at me. He was also engaged in instruction. "We find that money tends to stick in the nets, a little for everyone, nice like that. Not that you should bother your insides about it. You, sir, are beyond such distractions. You are an artist, head in the clouds, aren't you?"

I would have appreciated his ceasing the flirty winking, and at last, when I looked up from the oysters he was buying me at the Algonquin, he did. He was momentarily busy with his own little-necks — lemon, sauce, salt and wine — or perhaps he was just checking out his next move.

". . . the strength of oysters and the delicacy of clams," he was saying. "For spiritual sorts. The Baroness Blixen lived to nearly eighty on oysters and champagne." He rolled the last clam to its reward. "Isak Dinesen," he said. "We wanted to give her a year to write her final memoirs, but she said she couldn't spare the time. She said she was dying, and she was. Pity."

Philip Grove had served as vice president of various networks, he had been poetically handsome in his youth, he was a delight in middle age (luxuriant gray hair, ironic smiles); he had enjoyed twenty-five years of faithful drinking and seventeen years of psycho-analysis, both of them continuing nicely when we met. Two wives and three marriages confused matters; he had married one of the girls twice, numbers one and three — the oil lady from Tulsa had

leapfrogged the chanteuse from Copenhagen and Cleveland. He
was now redivorced from this first/third wife and paying her double
indemnity, suicide, revenge, menopause, got-the-midnight-horrors
alimony. Her wells had run dry. She was a 3 A.M. telephoner and
even incited their daughter, Carol, to make trouble. "That hurts a
bit," he said. "A lot."

A frequent refuge for Philip in times of stress was to enter public
service. Now he was director of one of America's greatest second-
rate foundations. It couldn't compete with Ford, Rockefeller, or
Guggenheim, and that's how I came in: to help set up a program
for catching the artistic fish and eels that the bigger endowments let
slip through their valves.

Lunches at the Century Club, dinner at the Four Seasons. He
wanted to get a positive result in whatever he did — even instructing me in how to live. I was flattered. We were both recently
divorced, both trying out as gray-flecked Manhattan boys again. He
had read my novels and thoughtfully quoted from me in conversation with me. That man knew how to make joy at small expense.
(The person writing this story is no longer the person telling it.)
I loved breathing the happy air. "Well, sir," he said with the courtly
manner of a slightly older man who is signing all the checks, "I was
probably paid more for reading your books than you were for writing them."

Somehow this made me feel important, though there was surely
an edge to the compliment.

And advice on how to give money to artists? Now, there was a
dreamy, restful deal. So I just let my mind expand, a few folds at a
time. I suggested a program of special vacations for novelists, story
writers, and poets. The idea was to waste and live well for a few
weeks, to refresh the spirit with excess. A large sum of money would
be handed out with the provision that it be squandered in less than
a month. I invoked some traditional models — Dionysius, Bacchus,
and C. Wright Mills (Philip expected nothing less from me). How
would we check against the possibility of practical distortions —
prudent mid-century poets laying on station wagons, laundry equipment, convertible preferreds for the children's education? Well, we
could always go for receipts from Bahamian hotels and chorus girls
freaked out on diet pills. Naturally, I preferred the honor system.
I preferred to go that way.

Philip said he loved the idea, just loved it. As this meant he seemed to like it pretty well, I was sure the foundation would accept it, since he made all the important decisions. It was a brilliant day in the history of philanthropy. I was responsible for a great leap forward from the single flower of Puritanism into the thousand flowers of affluence and ecstasy. "Hmm," said Philip, "a keen article there for Gratefully Yours, the *Journal of Applied Philanthropy*. 'Affluence & Ecstasy: Expanding the Frontiers of Exemption . . .' " I was a mandarin ideologue in my first J. Press suit. Gongs, zithers, wine, silks and dancing girls for the contributors to the *Hudson Review*.

At the next regular meeting of the governing board my idea was rejected.

Ah, so. Another miscalculation. Another case of too much enthusiasm and trust on life's way. Again a deep brainstormer had misplaced his faith in the ability of others to understand innovations in quantum money dispersal. Well, no matter.

Our friendship survived this reverse. I expected a small check labeled "honorarium" for drafting the idea, typing it, too; but evidently the high-level decision was to pay me in lunches, dinners, oral quotation from my work, continuing instruction, and the companionship of Philip Grove. Well, some things are worth more than money, though perhaps a plate of oysters at the Algonquin is not one of them. I put away my mandarin dreams.

Nevertheless, taking a consistent pro-oyster position, one evening I accepted another session of charge-a-plate seafood. Philip wanted to explain. He was tender in his own heart, too. "I know what you think, I'm smart enough," he said, "but the fact is I really want to do something good every time I get into these — oh, complexities. The problem is making it happen. I don't mean gimmicks, I mean the clout, the thrust, the —" He smiled winningly. "The gimmick. I really hate it that you have reason not to respect me, pal. I *know* about respect and self-respect. Those are two of my fields."

It occurred to me, and I should have thought of it sooner, that he really wanted to commit fine acts, read beautiful words, think powerful thoughts, go to bed with sweet ladies.

"Ah-ah." He wagged a warning finger. "I have insights. I stay in touch."

"Sorry," I said. "I really like you, Philip."

"Not really," he said, "but you'll learn. However, I've called this little group together for another purpose." He hinted that he was looking about and planning to leave public service once more. It was not quite — well, take my delicious project, for example. A terrible loss, a personal embarrassment. How the bureaucracy of endowment misunderstands the creative temperament, both administrative and laboring in those lonely rooms which Sherwood Anderson of Elyria, Ohio, described so eloquently in his collected letters.

His large, dark, intense eyes bored into mine to see if I had caught his thought on the wing even before he had filed it along with the request for accrued vacation time.

Yes.

In my turn I hinted that I was nearing the end of the first draft of a new novel. Ah. New phases for both of us. We both sighed. We would digest all this news and return to it in the fullness of time.

We then settled down comfortably to discussing our mistreatment at the hands of women. We did not exactly wallow in our miseries, but we inoculated ourselves against cholesterol and useless fret by not keeping the secret. Although I had entered real life again, chasing limber ladies through the canyons and rushing gorges of Manhattan, I still took pleasure in these restful evenings of commentary and philosophy. Philip, ten years older, claimed to admire my energy, but liked to go at things a little more slowly. Bring them to him by taxi, for example, or by limou when one was available. The permanent truths — friendship, accomplishment, good taste — were what interested him. His daughter, Carol (a "teenie," as he described her), had let him down. "Patience and cunning," he said, "that's what a man needs. But no exile, it's impossible, the whole world is Manhattan now."

"I suppose."

"What good are victories?" he asked me. "What good is the hunt?"

"Are you asking me a question? I feel you're making a statement."

"Well, take Carol for openers. She is bad news for some old man, pal. If not for her dad, for some other chap."

In quest of permanent truth, he left the foundation and went to work for a buccaneer millionaire who had reached the stage in his development where he needed to finance art movies. On the day he told me about his new job I confessed to him that he looked a bit like a leading man. He was tall, slender, handsome, with suave weariness worn like a halo. That's a neat style. In his youth he had

played polo. In his youth, he confessed in turn, he had wanted to
be an actor, but: "I had too much — oh, premature afterthought
you can call it. The lines they gave actors in those days — couldn't
say 'em." His eyes were dark, soft and tender as he explained why
he chose not to be a star of stage and screen. Producer — well,
that's all the difference in the world. Because I had begun to weary
of his dramatic cynicism, I redoubled my efforts to express friendship. After all, he had been good to me. But I began to suspect he
was wearing eye liner to accentuate that dark, soft, and tender gaze.
     Oh, it couldn't be.
     I denied it to myself. He wasn't that sort. I put it out of mind.
I looked for the telltale smear.
     In an agony of difficult friendship we exchanged gifts like shy
romancers. He put me up for his club as if to tell me I should now
consider myself middle-aged. I gave him a copy of *Shakespeare's
Bawdy* as if to tell him he could still have boyish intellectual fun.
He asked to meet girls. I asked to meet interesting people. He was
bored with the girls I introduced him to, and looked wan and
bored. I was bored with the social people he introduced me to,
and once escaped a party on Long Island through the library window. I hitchhiked back to Manhattan, frantic and drunk. We
didn't see each other for a week, but then had a laugh over it and
he wanted to take me to Southampton again so I could repeat my
famous vanishing act. The cream that made me vanish was oil of
small talk. He thought he might sell it along with excursions to
Europe on Icelandic Airlines.
     Ever since the peculiar thought about his wearing eye liner, I tried
to conduct our meetings along with the company of ladies. Four-
somes strolling Greenwich Village, four on weekends to Westport,
that was my new idea. The old male intimacy dimmed a bit in our
new occupations. He was irritated by my increasing implication in
the temptations of Manhattan, as if only he had kept our interludes
of talk pure, free of money and sex and ambition, just two friends
sharing a flight through middle space.
     One night, over the final brandy, he asked, "What's it all about?
We are paper men, air men, we float and .glide over this abstract
town. Who are we? We are what we are — nobodies."
     "I wish you'd speak for yourself, Philip."
     He gazed mournfully into my eyes. Maybe he didn't wear eye
liner, after all. It would be a sin to suspect him wrongly. He had

hard, clear, bluish whites, he had a fixity of gaze. "I suppose I should only speak for myself," he said. "It's part of the disease — abstraction. I want to take everybody my own way, as if a crowd of paper figures could make one man of flesh and soul. I apologize. Nothing personal." He waited for me to reply. "My daughter is breaking my heart."

I had nothing to say. I was tired after the long evening — a divorced Wellesley girl and her best friend — and the abrupt moment of King Lear found me unprepared. We had been amusing the ladies and it left my philosophic skills a bit threadbare. After so much laughter, nudging, and tickling, here came Carol. I must have looked distracted.

"Take the service elevator out," he said. "It's faster after one. Wait, I'll show you."

I found other friends. Philip joined a Unitarian group. We were both in search. He thought up a TV special to promote, something about the revival of irrational religion. He asked me if I liked his working title for it: "The Now! Churches." Rational and irrational, he said; but in quest of some sort of purity. Ninety minutes of stomping and glossolalia, plus Erich Fromm and maybe Norman O. Brown — what did I think?

"Terrific, Philip."

"Sensational," he said, "*and* educational."

Also, as a remedy for that after-five feeling, that void, that anomie, that angst, those mid-century whatchamacallits, he fell in love.

In fact, despite the slow and stately stride of maturity, Philip the Pure was in love with the whole chorus line in the revived version of *West Side Story.* He had a friend whose skinny wife was a featured player and he would stand in her dressing room and look at the girls — High School of Performing Arts, Actors Studio, Merce Cunningham, readers of Buber and Frantz Fanon and *Variety* — through a crack in her half-shut door. They undressed with miraculous calm. Naked but for their eyelashes, long-limbed, cute, oh cute, they primped and jiggled and waited for the Big Chance near massed banks of hot white bare bulbs. Gradually he narrowed his devotion to just one, Sandy Grasset, and gradually she came to understand that he wanted her for his very own.

Okay, one Sunday morning after an ecumenical mass at a Now! church, she gave herself to Philip for his very own. A man deserves a Big Chance, too. But then it wasn't enough. He wanted to marry her, to keep and cherish her. "Will you be my widow?" he demanded, dropping to his knees and mumbling, "George Bernard Shaw, an early play, I have total recall."

"*Wha?*"

"I was quoting. Shouldn't joke at a time like this. Total visual, not oral. Marry me."

She laughed and laughed, though not at the touching whimsy he intended, and he coolly noted that one thin tape of eyelash was coming unstuck. But he only loved her the more for this single blemish on her perfection of greedy little showgirl.

"Naw," she said. "I have my career, and my afternoons I go to the New School." Her evenings, of course, belonged to the Theater. She also studied creative writing, mime (*meem*), and existential psychodrama for a time of crisis.

He stared, hair thick and white, body thumped and worked at the New York Athletic Club. "I need you," he said.

"I like you," she said. "Isn't it obvious, really clear?"

"I would hope it all means something."

"Does, *does*, sweetie. I wouldn't do . . . *that*" — and she made a pretty little moufie, as if to say dirty-dirty. "I wouldn't do that for just anybody. Not even to get a job I wouldn't. I don't have to, besides. I'm well known for not doing it unless — "

"Unless you really like a fellow?"

"Well, you could put it." She got the point a second later. "Okay, then, you be sarcastic and see if it encourages an I-thou relationship between us."

"I'm sorry," he cooed, miserable.

"Aw, come on," she said, wrapping him in her skinny arms.

But she dawdled about marrying him. He worked out a miracle plan: me. I should persuade her, me, with my inspired pleading of his case. *Who?* It was like filling out a recommendation for a foundation grant. It was not like that, but he had his peculiar notion that I could help and he arranged for me to meet her alone at her apartment one afternoon (all of us supposed to be there, Philip delayed, last-minute telephone call, a carefully orchestrated plan). By means of straight talk, full of depth charges there in the shadow of Lincoln Center, I was supposed to win him his third/fourth wife.

I felt a bit wooden and pasted together. I said, "Um, he really cares for you. He wants you badly. I think you would do well."

"Icky," she said. "He's not icky, but he is too old. Hey, how's about I make us some coffee?"

"You said yourself he's not icky," I said, "and with vitamin pills and the new statistics from the insurance companies, he's got many carefree years ahead of him. How long do you think you can dance, Sandy?"

"Three wives. Icky."

"But you're different. And it wasn't really three. And he's a boy at heart."

"Plus he tole me I remind him of his *daughter!* I wanna stay in show business."

"True, he'd like you to be a helpmeet, entertain, spend his money." I hoped she was listening. I'd hate to have to repeat that.

"Hey, he's really loaded?"

"Then you won't?"

She fixed me with her violet eyes in that starved, bony dancer's face. Cheekbones and eyes in the context of violet and good definition always make a fellow think profound. "How much — how much you *bet?*" she asked. First she grinned with elfin humor. Then a hilarious peel of jeering laughter as the implications began to deal with her. Blacch, another natural screamer, I thought. She looks so physical, so much body and dance, but she's like an actress, a nice suburban girl, a nice normal hysteric. Abruptly she stopped laughing. "Maybe I will," she said. "You think the kid, uh — "

"Carol."

" — 'll bug us a lot?"

"No."

" 'Cause I hate kids like that — the selfish age."

"No, the kid is grown up, nearly your age."

That was three fifths of a faux pas, but she didn't seem to mind. She was twitching with thought, tongue working in corner of mouth, Kleenex at eyes, knees jiggling. Perhaps she was just practicing her new role of charming hostess, for she said, "Ooh, ick, the coffee's boiling over. Philip has a Chemex, doesn't he?"

On their honeymoon in Paris he suffered a ruptured blood vessel in one eye and had to go to the American Hospital. Too much drinking or love-making, an expatriate doctor commented, but I never heard that one before. That was one for Neuilly. Personally I thought he got some dirt in it and rubbed. And that's one for Sheridan Square.

They came back and it took a long time before they invited me over to their new apartment (condominium, East Sixties, excellent view of the write-off). Of course, they were busy fixing it up, but other friends got invited two, three times. I was out, it seemed. I had been to close to the premarital examinations, but I still saw Philip occasionally for lunch. He was keeping in touch and I'd be patient. His eye was red for months afterward, as if he had just been crying. Well, let him adjust to conjugal life again. It took some pressure off me, too. Our friendship would find its natural level.

One of the matters we shared was a friend, Baron Clausen, a Danish money pirate with castles in Austria, ranchos in Mexico, and ambitions to keep his tax-exempt fingers in all available tax-free pies. His nineteen-year-old wife (he was sixty) distracted him for a few hours each day, but then there were the sleepless nights and days of Manhattan. He liked Philip for the reasons of Philip's charm and savvy; he liked to discuss himself with me. Philip telephoned me one day at an odd early hour to say, "Clausen — you've been talking to him."

"Of course, sometimes, when he lets me."

"Too much, pal. He's been spreading the gossip about you."

"Clausen? What gossip?"

Philip reminded me of an incident involving — oh, a silly trouble about a party and a wife and her husband. I was irritated with Philip for reminding me of it. I was infuriated with my smiling Danish enemy. As soon as he next proposed one of his damn smørrebrød-and-cigar lunches, I'd give him some honest American lip. Senseless malice: why should he do that to me? I was shaking with the bachelor's dammed-up anger. I fretted, I sulked. I wouldn't deign to reach Clausen.

He never telephoned.

In a few days it dawned on me. Somehow Philip must have made him angry with me, too. What had I said of him? That he was too old for his young bride? That he was hanging about the artists to drink their blood? Well, I might have speculated along those lines — who doesn't speculate?

I should have had an explanation with Clausen, but the whole thing was a nasty bore. Foolish and foolishness. I let it pass. I forgot it. I fell in love. I let them pass, both of them, Clausen and

Philip, and moved into another of the many worlds of Manhattan.

Only gradually, reluctant to admit the loss of friendship, did I guess that Philip was getting rid of me this way. He spread gossip about me among our mutual acquaintances because, well, he needed a bit of a change and he was in the business of opinion and that's how he did things. No matter. Another day, he must have decided from long experience, if I need him, I'll just come with my offer. He'll jump. There's no fun and profit in remembering history, which is mostly a series of grudges. He had once assured me that to his certain knowledge, people operate almost entirely in the light of their present interests. "Not principles or paranoia, friend, but what seems to be in the cards right now. I've found this to be true. It's tough, but it's nice to have confidence in the future, where you get what you want by talking about what's happening this afternoon. Say, listen, it's better that way."

Wine, oysters, talk, and the dangled carrot. Also a continual earnest labor at completing my education. Corrupt and corruption, I thought; no matter. I had other business in life. I felt like Dick Whittington come to conquer the great city. Although Philip had the knack of making his business seem important, more important than anything anyone else wanted to do, I found new routes through skyscraper and across plaza, up subway and into conference room.

Sometimes the crazy orbits of Manhattan intersect or collide. We remained acquaintances, but the old clubby exchanges were finished. We would continue toward new careers, wives, hopes and troubles on divergent paths.

I had a friend, J. Willis, a long-time Village writer, with three stories and a poem to his credit after twenty years and four grants, who turned out to be dating Philip's daughter, Carol. There's a crossed path for you. Willis had presided over self-contempt for so long that it had become a friend to him — a deadly enemy to the ladies he sucked dry. Carol was a pretty thing with long blond bangs that tickled her eyes as if she had no interest in where she was going. Willis took his exercise on such girls and thought he was a man. If I had been Philip with a daughter . . . but I was not Philip with that daughter.

Baron Clausen started a foundation, incidentally, and made Philip the president of it. Philip may have suspected me of wanting to push into the foundation business.

*

Sandy was an odder girl than she appeared — girl making out okay in Manhattan. Dancing seemed to have trained the upturned corners of her mouth, but there were also secret down-turning depths. She had been supported for several years by Rico diRico, the Jukebox King, who had known the joy of seeing his picture in *Life,* not in connection with his Wurlitzer musical activities, but because he was a friend of friends of folks with complex police and FBI records. Rico preserved his friendship with Sandy after her marriage, and also with Philip. It seemed a sporty connection for that elegant veteran of Washington conferences on the arts and network efforts to upgrade popular culture. (*From Shlock to Kitsch,* an autobiography by Philip Grove. That was his idea. Subtitle? "Through Darkest Camera with Grant and Program.") Philip didn't fear for reputation, since most of Rico's arrests had not resulted in convictions.

There is a reason, or a season, or at least a cause for everything, as Ecclesiastes almost says. Philip wanted to produce his first movie, based on a forgotten novel about the Depression. There were many curious elements in the equation. The book was written by a man, now rather elderly and a senior editor of *Reader's Digest,* who at one time had been an iron-willed literary Marxist ("The land is the people! The people is the land!" was the last paragraph and hiccup of the novel). The original story aimed to show (a) the American working and peasant classes oppressed by county banks and agents of Wall Street in jodhpurs, then (b) their gallant uprising at the iron will of the novelist; the movie script aimed to show the warmth and humanity of immigrant racketeers, who managed by means of tenderness and vigor to crash through staid class lines, thereby getting the grateful girl in the end. The suspense for her was terrific. She would have to wait ninety minutes, eighty if cut for drive-ins, to discover she was worth more to the hero than land, people, or his mama's hand-stuffed lasagna. Much more; a symbol of the transcendence of Norman O. Brown's polymorphous perverse eros over economic determinism; a really modern scam, actual, contemporary, today, existential, and within the limits set by the concept of redeeming social importance, dirty.

Sandy played a small part, mostly leaning against a white piano in a speakeasy, looking fearful, as if the chandelier might fall. The financing came from Rico diRico, who may have been crooked but who was not necessarily clever. The film lost money, even with a syndicated sale to TV. The Bonnie & Clyde epoch was not yet upon us. But was it real coin-operated money? Probably the lonely toy money of drugs and gambling that sought warmth and companionship in the real world of tax losses.

Anyway, it made sense for Philip to keep good connections with diRico. Perhaps he could count on cultural impetus in the future, too. I used to run into the three of them, Philip, Sandy, and diRico, at those steamy steak palaces on Third Avenue where you also find popular priests, daytime game-show emcees, and out-of-town buyers working hard at their expense-account cholesterol. Once I sat with them through dessert (I was meeting an option holder from the Coast, who was late). Philip, I noticed, played with his food. He looked pale, and the broken vein in his eye had never quite mended, so that it always seemed as if he were recovering from a recent crying jag or had spent too much time with his accountant. He was hoping to do his second film, maybe this time with Sandy as the star. DiRico was considering it.

Then one morning I got a call from Philip's secretary. Mr. Grove wanted to see me at his office. As soon as possible. Very important. Of course, like all writers, I seek any possible opportunity to avoid work. I was showered, shaved, and in a cab within half an hour. Manhattan traffic jams being what they are, I needed a shower by the time I arrived and wished I had taken a subway, but my shave was still intact.

I carried it through an honor guard of new receptionists and secretaries, Itkin décor, wormwood paneling — the diRico touch. Philip began right off: "What do you do with people, chap?"

"Who people? What people?"

"The public. My daughter."

That pretty girl with the regulation straight blond hair, wan little face, dropout credentials from Sarah Lawrence, and those eye-tickling bangs. She had left J. Willis, my Charles Street pal. She had been moving pretty fast.

"I want to tell somebody," he said, "and then I want to forget it. I'm going to tell you." It sounded like a threat. Before I could say *Oh no you don't,* or *What about your analyst?,* he was on the way and all the way there: she had died of hepatitis in San Francisco.

He looked at me with his peculiar courteous attention. I was frozen with misery and confusion. He waited until he decided I was okay.

"She was taking methedrine sulfate, I think they call it. Speed. Dio-metha-something, I don't know. Affected her mind — memory, reasoning power, she was a skinny thing, not the pretty girl you met. But it wasn't speed that killed her. It was a dirty needle."

"Philip, I'm sorry."

"She was always careless with her things. Her mother used to complain, but what could I do? I wasn't responsible — could I be? That woman really cut me off from her, so how could I?"

"Philip, where is she?"

He looked at me through his one red eye, his two eye-lined eyes. "Ah, she was buried out there yesterday. What's the good?" He shook his head. "I wanted someone to know. Pass it on. Communicate." I realized he was slightly drunk. "I suppose it's better," he said.

"What's better?"

"Hey, fella, let's go to P.J.'s. You can have a hamburger and I can have a freshner."

"No, I can't, Philip."

"Okay, a small salad. I need it. I need to sit with you — someone."

"Okay, Philip."

He smiled, stood up, shrugged his shoulders in that handsome, boyish, stylish way. "What did she have to live for? Her life was a mess. Man, I know about the problems with *my* oedipal hangups. I tried as much as I could, I worried about her, fella. But that rusty needle probably just saved a lot of trouble, agony, and expense."

The secretary came in and he waved her away. "Please. I'm taking an early lunch." He waited until she closed the door. He turned to get his coat and said to me, "Life — what is it? Let's not frighten ourselves with that question, but we got to ask it. China. India. It's time for some perspective. Carol. It's pathetic. But when you've had as much therapy as I have, eighteen years and small fortune, one thing you learn is admit your secret feelings. Expense and worry and what good is it?"

I was out of that office in a few seconds. I noticed I was gone when the elevator door showed me lobby and street. It wasn't grief that made me flee, or not only grief.

*

But it wasn't as if I could shake him so easily. That conversation about Carol had gone past the end for him, too. After I left the office, he waited a few weeks and then summoned me about what he called a "reasonable" project — miscalled. "Let's just discuss," he said, "with no obligations on either side. I always find you have an interesting mind." Which meant: I'm sure you'll want to do what I want you to do. He hired me to work on a film script he was "developing." That means, speculating in. First he told me it was to be based on a story of mine, but it turned out to be based on a story by the network computer which told him what he could (a) get into the nabes and then (b) presell to television. Rico was putting up the front money and Sandy had a slightly smaller part — one scene where we would all presumably share the curve of her dancer's thighs through the magic communion of the cinema art. While I wrote, she became pregnant; no connection. "I'll be an instant grandfather," Philip announced with his shyest smile that invited you to think whatever you liked about his feelings.

However, he didn't look well. His skin had become blue and his body slow and spectral. He should have seen a doctor. He said he was on to what they were selling. His nose bled. He sweated at night and Sandy slept in another room because he felt icky in bed. He refused to go to his doctor. I suppose he knew what he was doing, and buying.

One afternoon we had a meeting about the script. He suddenly closed his eyes as if thinking, as if sleeping. He lay at an odd angle, like a stick in his chair, and I caught him before he fell. He quickly came out of the faint, blinking and smiling, but his secretary called the doctor and we got him to a little private hospital nearby, in the East Sixties. No problem with the heart. Weakness, general weakness. The doctor ran blood tests to confirm what he already suspected.

There was an abnormal increase of white blood cells originating in a disease of the bone marrow. They gave him transfusions to increase his strength for the time being, temporarily. They do that to provide a breathing space. Leukemia.

Philip got the news early. He conned the doctor into telling him everything. Calm and elegant, he heard him out and asked intelligent questions and it seemed the doctor was flattered by the patient's interest. He might live as little as six months. He might last from three to five years. The suppressant drugs have variable results.

When one wears out, or starts to wear out the body — the side effects are often very disagreeable — the doctors shift to another drug.

"And of course," Philip said, "by the time you finish rotating the known drugs, they may have some new ones."

"Or a cure," said Dr. Berman.

"Or even a cure," Philip said, smiling and nodding. "Thank you very much."

I suppose there is no normal routine for handling the friends and relatives. Philip told me, his wife, Rico; he told the poodle and his newborn son; he told the people with whom he did business and cab drivers and stopped just short of writing letters to the editor stating that he had six months left to live. He set up a means for sharing the experience, irony in him, horror in others. He seemed pleased and proud. I wondered if he was taking mood drugs, and perhaps he was, but the euphoria seemed genuine, rooted in the vain and frantic blood. He would call me in the middle of the night to discuss "our" script, and then his illness. He wanted to get the script finished and shot before he "went." He dwelled in an ecstasy of energy and good will, popping into the hospital for transfusions and then flying off to do rapid business with banks and studios and networks. It made story conferences difficult.

"I can't write that girl as man-eater," I would say. "She's sad, but she's not mean."

"Look," he replied gently, "let's cut the crap. I may have only six months left and I see her for what she is: a bitch-whore-destroyer."

The only-six-months argument won his way about character, style, money, whatever the day brought into his office. As some people are name-droppers, he would sit in Sardi's East and death-drop his own death to get one up on me. He was doing it all around, with agents, creditors, secretaries, and even with his wife. Ever since these two events had come to complicate her time — the birth of her child, the announced death of her husband — she had grown quieter and the silliness had disappeared. She had discovered something outside herself. She was interested, frightened, appalled. It was all happening at once. I believe she even stopped seeing Rico, though that may have been his doing, a superstitious fear. She had the eye-liner look which seemed to run in Philip's family — his daughter, too —

but it gave her a bit of staring style. He may have succeeded in instructing her to care for him. For sure Sandy was going through the miseries.

Philip's production staff accommodated his various television and film projects. He used to charm them into working long hours, bending to his will; now he bullied them.

"What are you complaining for?" he would ask a secretary who needed something, such as time off, which he didn't want to give her. "After all, you have your whole life ahead of you."

She blushed.

"So do I, of course."

He got his way. Midtown Manhattan knows how to be nervous and even how to suffer, but this was one boss, handsome Philip, that a secretary couldn't handle.

"What do you mean, you don't like the project. It's changing into, okay, so kitsch. Never mind, listen, now is the time to communicate—gut level. There will come a day," he told me, "when this will be the last project I can close. I won't be able to come to the office." He smiled. "It'll be *me* closing. I'll turn into a vegetable," he said affably, "except it'll hurt a lot, fella."

I was learning to hate him.

"That's for openers and up front," he said.

And yet I couldn't pull out at this stage, could I? Just because he was slurring and jiving and bullying, and using his own death as a marketing and production tool, was that any reason to give him more trouble than usual?

The. job became more complicated than most jobs. Rico and Sandy had me talking to doctors; Sandy because she was brokenhearted, Rico because he couldn't believe the happy-boy partner would really let him down at some point in their business together. Philip was piling ahead, grandiose and furious, with the energy of a pink-cheeked young producer despite his bluish skin and his death's-head eyes.

The doctor said, "Remission. Like a lot of them . . ." He added cautiously, "Mr. Grove — Philip — seemed almost disappointed when I told him his place on the curve may be rather late. It won't be another six-month deal. He might well have five years, and then what? We don't know anymore."

Disappointed?

"You'll see that sometimes — disappointed."

It was a hard campaign to live up to. It was a whirlwind campaign, intended for a six-month promotion; Philip wasn't programmed for a five-year plan. Nobody could put up with his dying for five whole years ahead. Speaking as an associate, it would kill us all. Or at least give migraine headaches, anxious nightmares, Manhattan boredom assaults, creeping paralysis. "They're out to get us," one secretary kept muttering. She meant the leukocytes. We became experts on the disease, as if it were an un-American conspiracy, like Communism or Swedish art films.

He was killing friendship by falsity.

Let me be fair: he was also killing enmity by creating an eerie contempt for his suffering. He made his own suffering unreal by using it as a public relations trick. He was trivializing his own and everyone else's feeling about the primary fact. He was barring his own recognition of death the friend, death the enemy.

Bravado: manipulating his own emotion.

Worse, a public relations bravado: manipulting the emotions of others and calling them his own.

Which?

Both. I wanted to say: China, India, what is life? Your daughter dies. You die. Everybody dies; big deal. Phony trouble. But where then is the real trouble?

I tried to see through the strategy of management to the terror beneath, but felt myself failing beneath my own spite. I began to have nightmares about the emptiness within myself that made me want to destroy this man, or to take relish in his self-destruction; no, not nightmares, black insomnias full of shooting dreams like meteors and murky under-earth movements. Because I found myself hating him and hating myself, I was tied to him by a pity suspiciously like self-pity. What in the past gave him such energy and resolution? How could the mask fit so seamlessly, and leave him so malignant and joyous? He was a mystery to me, and a fearful one.

I visited him whenever I could. I let him work his will upon me. Submissively I awaited new indignities. Confusion. To live with the confusion made the life of New York seem avid, arid, abstract, and horrible. We spent our workday lives in those radiant East Side glass tombs. It was as if I had some wasting disease.

I entered his office one lunch hour — the secretary was out — and found him crooning over a photograph of Carol. He was bowing and rocking and his face was broken. When he saw me, he brightened up immediately. "I didn't hear you come in!" he cried happily.

He had not heard me come in. It was the truth. I had found him alone, entirely alone with his grief and regret.

And it was double the pleasure, double the fun, when he realized that this scene had just come naturally, it was a happy accident, it gave the touch of life and truth to his act, it was sincere. He profited handsomely from his own incontestable sincerity. The incident was proof positive. The secretary had gone to lunch and left him unprotected. I had walked in with no appointment. Who could find a flaw in the deep feeling which I had discovered despite the deep feeler's intent to keep it absolutely mum?

During this same sincere period in his life, Philip was using the opportunity to "speak frankly" — to bad-mouth friends, to encourage confidences and then to betray them, immune to reproach. He stalked like the white death in our midst, swaddled in grave-clothes, clutching at our sleeves and murmuring, "Hey, I'm dying." We wanted to shake him off like those midtown alcoholics who beg for sympathy in the lounges. But he was not dying on time. The months passed. His friends wanted to say to the sleeve-clutcher, "Aw, go away, will you?"

One day I said to him, *"Don't."*

"Don't what?"

He was spreading silly rumors — oh, silliness — such as something, well, on the order of being mean to my former wife. In fact, that was it. Exactly. Mean to stepwife. Now, what a stupid story! Who would ever do a thing like that? But that was what he said — mean (me?) to that dark lady of my miserable twenties.

Of course, I'd have liked to be meaner than I was. As mean as I managed to be, it barely saved my skin. But he tried to tell people I wasn't nice. And you know what? They believed him. People are funny about believing what they are told, especially when the delicious news is coming from someone as credible, as mortally ill as Philip; and especially if there are some really nasty tidbits.

"Don't what?" he repeated with great earnest concern.

"Don't voice your opinions as if you know. Don't tell people you think I'm this and that and wait to have them pick up on it and then tell me what they say and then tell them how I react — just *don't*, Philip. Okay, gossip if you have to, but I'd rather you wouldn't."

"I have no time for small talk, buddy."

"That's not what I'm asking you."

"Wait. You cut the crap at a time like this." He put his hand on my arm and squeezed it gently. He made my gaze meet his. He gave me a long look from dark, sad, beautiful, almost girlish eyes. He squinted them slightly and looked deep into mine. "You fail to appreciate how this changes a man's life," he said, retreating, hurt, leaving me to meditate on his soft turning away of my irritation. He had become a master of the pronoun *this*, a word with a subject and predicate, a dense clause of unspoken explanations and commands.

"Okay, Philip," I said, "I don't suppose I should try to educate you."

"I just try to call the shots how they are," he said. "I've said and done things in the past, things I regret. Carol. Well, you know. Now, with what's left to me, *this*, I'm just trying to be as straight as I know how."

"Okay, Philip, you've explained."

"I want you to understand me, pal, you above all. I've opened up to you. You've seen the worst. I don't even mean I intended it that way, that's just how it worked out. You're someone I really trust and count on."

That's a hard one to answer if it's only the eve of battle, but when it's leukemia time on old Madison Avenue, this country boy from Cleveland, Ohio, found he was losing the argument.

"Thank you, fella," he said, "for understanding where I live."

At first it only seemed like giving him his way on script changes because of *this*, but now it was letting him get away with undoing the little world in which we all moved. Digs, jabs, pryings, and do everything he wanted. Finally one six o'clock after a long session of mixed work and philosophy, I yelled at him, "Goddammit, don't! I don't care! I don't care what's happening to you."

"You don't want to say that," he remarked serenely, coming back into his office to hear me out.

"You have no right!"

He pulled the drapes and stood staring into the swollen orange-gray light of the late-afternoon Manhattan sky. Then he turned back to me, huge and spectral in the altered glow of our glass section of the glass tomb.

"Let's discuss a moment," he said happily. "You've brought this up before. I know I've changed, even as to manner. I feel I have a special emergency built in, a sense of crisis, and it gives me an intensity, a certain clarity and directness — "

I walked out.

I didn't see him for several days. Everyone brings confusion for everyone else. He brought too much of it. He left messages for me, but I took off for Easthampton.

Then Sandy called and got through to me. Her voice gave a correct but incorrect message. "He's in the hospital," she said.

"A relapse? What's up?"

"He may die."

"So soon."

Again the confusion. He had crept close in my life, and lent me moments of power. What right had I to judge him?

"Pills," she said. "They pumped his stomach, but I'm not sure . . ."

He recovered. They gave him blood, they kept him in the hospital for a few days, and then they released him, as good and as bad as ever. He had only taken six or seven Seconals. He apologized to everyone individually, including me. It was just an impulse, he said, a silly one, to spare us all the trouble.

"I'm a little foolish and desperate," he said. "I'm sure I'm being a little, ah, extreme, but who is to say what is proper behavior at a time like this?"

"Philip."

"Please forgive me — please? For the sake of old friendship? You once had a good feeling about me. Will you hold on to it, friend? I know I've done some bad things. We were friends. Try to remember, okay? Please?"

Despite all this busy play, it was finally about to happen. Philip's body began its mortal closing down. The rhythm of trips to the hospital, ameliorations, remissions, transfusions, new techniques, interventions, failures, hopes, desperations, was now a familiar matter. Accelerations did not change the pattern. Hope and despair provided a kind of vividness; then the vividness, like an amphetamine, wore out its host. Sandy became a stilled, sick child with a grin like the beginning of tears and a strangled voice reading the packaging of Philip's old habits: "Hiya, fella." She had learned other things from him, too. "I think he's a little better today. You're going in to see him, aren't you?" She uttered her grief and made his demands for him and slid through the day stricken by the smiling horrors.

Their son was invisible. He had disappeared almost as completely as Carol. Well, this was no time for a baby.

For every man there is a last trip to his office. Philip made that final visit, knowing it was final, and walked out without taking his briefcase. He left his appointment book open, three lunches scheduled for next week. He walked with the stiff gait of a sick man under tight control. He told his secretary he would be back after the weekend; she knew he would not be back. He had drawn into his diminished body. The writer would miss his oysters at the Algonquin; the agent would miss his *scampi* at Fontana di Trevi; the expense account had drawn to its end.

I wonder if many men in business put an exact close to the work by which they think to define themselves. Well, nothing is eternal, not even a great tax gimmick, not even a good East Side address. But Philip made no plans for his uncompleted projects. He left no provisions. He walked out. It was dead to him — the public relations, the TV series, the movie. Someone else could do it; someone else could not do it. He felt nothing for it. Rico might move someone in to try to hatch the eggs, but Philip ceased to fret about it. It was as dead as Carol, and about this retreat from work he was as dry and cold as, it seemed, he hoped to be about his own death. It was no longer what he used to call a plus factor in the daily round.

I came to see him. He was propped in a hospital bed with a lever sticking like a key out of his back. No, there was a thin mattress behind his back, and then the crank. His eyes were burning out of the bluish skin. "They shave me," he said. "I can still shave myself, but this way I have strength left over to waste." He grinned. "I got to figure out what to do with the strength left over from not having to shave myself."

"How are you feeling, Philip?"

"How do you feel when you know the end is near?"

"I don't know," I said.

"You will someday, I trust, fella." As if to soften the malice, he quickly added, "I try to get Sandy to take the towels home from this place. You know what it's costing my estate?"

"I can imagine."

"Oh, boy. Imagine on through."

A nurse was standing in the doorway. "It's time," she said.

"A treat or a treatment?"

"Mr. Grove, it's time now."

He grinned at me and said, "You mind waiting? I'd like to talk to someone when I get back."

"What are they going to do to you?"

"Stick needles. In the veins, that's okay. In the bone to get at the marrow, that hurts. Would you wait? Do you mind waiting?"

The attendants wheeled him out. I waited. He didn't go far. There was an adjacent laboratory. I could hear a distant creaking through the walls, Philip howling with pain, and then abruptly nothing. I was soaked in my clothes when he returned. He looked stunned and goofy. His pajama top was unbuttoned. His chest was covered with unhealed needle marks — deep scars and lesions. He was panting, but quiet. He tried to button one button of his pajamas, but his hand fell away, exhausted. I thought maybe he wanted to sleep.

"No, don't go."

I waited.

He said, "What do you do when you *know?*"

I couldn't answer yet.

"They keep making experiments, I think. Pieces of marrow they drag out. I don't heal anymore, either — the skin — not that it matters. All for sweet research. I'm happy to stop healing."

I had nothing to say.

"Relax and enjoy it, I guess," he said.

The nurse came in with two pills. She held them to his mouth, a glass of water in her other hand. She was a black girl with good country looks, a prim intelligent face, an opulent intelligent body in the rustling uniform. He shook his head to the pills and took them in his hand. "My friend'll give me the water," he said. I took the glass. His hand closely tightly over the pills. "Stay and talk . . ." He meant me. "No, you can go, Nurse. Thank you."

I had nothing to say, but I said it: "That must be painful."

"I'm sorry if it bothers you, pal. I found these tears in a test

tube. The doctor gave me the sample, and I sprinkle them everywhere. It's convenient. Too bad I didn't have them when Carol
died." He closed his eyes. "You're right," he said at last, "relax and
enjoy it."

"I didn't say it. You said it."

"I thought you said it."

"*You* said it."

"Am I getting confused? Now, there's a nasty."

He was stretching and wiggling, and the sweat kept starting on
his upper lip. He wiped it with his sleeve. I stifled my panic.
"Can't they give you something for the pain?"

"Yes, of course, they did."

"Why are you suffering so?"

He opened his fist. The pills were soggy and crumbled. "I didn't
want to get dopey. I want to talk to you first, before I take them."

"Take them!" I said.

He shrugged and put them in his mouth. I held the glass to his
lips. He drank.

Yes, I wanted to turn away. It's not so easy! I wanted to take all
the opportunities he gave me to trim the recognition of decay and
death with disgust at a performance. I assured myself that his re-
fusal to complain of pain, to confess his mortal fear, was just another
matter of style; he knew it would capture me; it was the unspoken
in art, the hidden dream of time in a melody, an esthetic trick like
his other tricks. But no, his discretion was real, I think — the foundation of style and comeliness within all his cunning chic. He
tried not to frighten me with his body so that he could teach me
something with his soul. His selfishness may have been very deep,
as his style was most pervasive. But his intention was also to make
me learn from him. I could complain and strike back. I couldn't
follow my itch to flee. I couldn't be honest and impulsive that way.
I couldn't simply walk out on him. How nice it would be to with-
draw to criticism. He gave me grounds. I had to follow my yearning
in another way.

"Thank you very much," Philip said.

"For what?" I saw the bottle of sedatives by his bed and remembered what the doctor had said: "I give them the pills and let them
make the choice. I warn them: 'Too many and you sleep forever.'
But they just wait, usually until they have no choice. Stubborn —
most men are stubborn."

"For entertaining Sandy, I mean taking her to the movies, talking to her — I mean everything, friend."

"Nonsense."

"Please try to be a little more gracious when I'm being grateful, pal."

My own history with him is not very pretty — a history of falling in with his schemes, taking his money (never as much as I expected), letting the con give me coffee nerves, and then walking out with cold parting shots and angry resolutions. Well, I couldn't just walk out on him anymore. He was in the thick of battle. He — not his words, not even his deeds, but Philip himself, the person hidden beyond all tricks — was telling a part of the truth, like all men, and more of the truth than many. Good-bye to the con. He was suffering. I learned some sour facts about myself from him; that's familiar enough in these days of prideful self-examination and self-laceration; but what was more common, traditional, and yet surprising, I was learning something about him. He struggled for control; he sought to master himself. He no longer thought of killing himself. The rest of life was precious to him, and not merely something he could use. He smiled handsomely, histrionically, and yet he was truly brave in his way.

The disease was marching through his body, consolidating its gains around his organs, receding, sending out marauding scouts, voraciously living off the country, blood, lymph, liver, spleen. First he felt weakness and dizziness, like a rapid elevator to earth, then seasickness and landsickness; remissions, illusions; then pain to breathe, pain around the heart, his body poisoning itself, drowning in its own fluids. This animal suffering he did not include in his public performance. He did not know how to use it; yet he was suffering atrociously. The horror of inexorable, irreversible pain is a great incitement to drama. He refused it. He suffered and left the suffering apart, as if it were the last holy object in his life.

His lungs filled with fluids. The doctors were making taps, inserting drains. They strapped him up like a sick tree and drew interesting substances from the trunk. "Did I tell you I was raised in Vermont?" he asked me. "Maple-syrup time again. Listen, we learned to say very little in Brattleboro, we learned to hide, and when I got garrulous those years in New York — "

"New York'll do that to you."

"I know. That's what I wanted. I never got good enough at it, was what I'm getting at . . ."

He was in torment, and reconciled to the fact that this time he could not pass it on as gossip or conniving. Could there have been some joy in giving up the mission of promoter, of user? No, but relief at defining the area of no copout. Something. Anything. There must have been, I pray there was, some brain flash of discovery and relief. This was not borrowed pain, picked up on the free-lance market. It was his own, his personal creation, he had world rights to it. Once, or sometimes, or steadily through the new and terrible routines of his nights and days, he must have received the message, he must have gotten through to himself. Oh, surely he would have agreed to do without in return for ease, but it was offered anyway — that brain flash, that ebb of sea over the meshed debris of depths, that withdrawal, clarity, and renewed confusion. An accurate, silent, perfect recognition of himself! And still rich in confusions.

He had stopped leaving his room. The transfusions were no longer perking him up; his body said no to the cortisone and mustard and cell suppressants; the organs, the whole system were disoriented.

Now what? How long?

Last week propped lightly in a chair with book and glasses; sometimes shaving himself, sometimes dressed.

Now wearing pajamas and shaved by his wife or a nurse, saving the strength for sitting and talk. It was too much trouble to turn face and lift chin. He should let the gray-mottled beard grow.

"I'm going to sleep," he said. "Wait. Wait a sec." He was working something out, his lips moving, racing the pills in his blood. He smiled as if it were a game. He nodded. He had found what he was looking for. "I'm carrying it by myself for the rest of the way — ah, that's nonsense. Forget it. I'm sorry."

"For what? It's unnecessary."

Behind drugs and coming in after drugs and without drugs at all, in the spaces wrought by disaster, he was finally exploring a territory which was his alone, bordered entirely by Philip, traversed solely by Philip, private beyond any despair or consolation.

"It's soon now," he said.

"Might be."

"First I'll sleep."

"That's fine."

"I'm finished promoting my last asset," he said.

"Shush, Philip."

The panic had left me. I too was calmed, as if for the first time Philip was present in the room with me. The games were done and there was no more advantage.

"There was something I wanted to say before I got confused by one thing or another, but that wasn't it — the romance of my little situation. Not that. Oh, not that, buddy."

"No hurry, Philip."

"Yes, hurry, pal." He winked. "Didn't I do some bad things to you? I seem to remember. I can't remember."

At the last minute, I was thinking, death might come to him as the friend he had always sought, or another enemy, or as an ecstasy of distraction; or merely as a new campaign and project — there was no reason to expect more of death than of life.

"Didn't I?" he asked anxiously. "Bad-mouth you one time? Put you on?"

"Never mind, Philip."

No, none of these. It would slip over him as it slips over animals and men — a diminution, a withdrawal and an acceptance. He would be here like other men and then he would be gone.

"It was someone else then."

"Forget it."

"No, it was you *and* someone else. Plus a lot of others."

"I said forget it."

He shut his eyes. "Next year at this time I'll be a better person," he said. "You wait. This same time next year." There was an almost girlish, peaceful look on his face — eyes closed and mouth in a sensual, smiling pout.

I sat there, watching him, trying for my own sake to try to carry something away with me; and for his sake, too. Despite the drugs and vanity, the money and power and the cleverness, the common paraphernalia of hospitals and the special vaults of Philip's character, his body and soul were falling from him just as other men's do, and I had to meet my own abiding distrust of him in coming to see that he had a soul like other men's, like mine; and he did the best he could for his daughter and his wife, and if it wasn't enough to suit me, it was still all he could do; and finally he held the monster close, as every man one day must.

He seemed to be asleep. I tiptoed out.

"Bye-bye," he said. "Take care, fella."

I looked back, but his eyes were shut and I suppose he was sleeping.

JOANNE GREENBERG

The Supremacy of the Hunza

(FROM THE TRANSATLANTIC REVIEW)

MARGOLIN'S HOUSE WAS four miles down Ridge Road, and part of his keen pleasure in coming home each day was in turning off the highway onto its blacktop. It was a slow road, one of the old wagon trails, lined with trees and made without the raw wounds of blasting. The way wound through hills past meadows and upland pastures. Turning north, a wide vista opened on blue-dark pine mountains, and then the way turned down and Margolin took the dirt road to the right, to home.

It was an old house, square but leaning in its age as the ground did. Marbles put down by Margolin's youngest boy rolled west in some rooms, east in others, always seeming to seek their centers and not the center of the earth. The back of the house looked out over the pine hills and back the way Margolin had come. He and Regina had never owned land or a house before this one. Because of its age, its place and its view, Regina lived with the house's ancient crochets and Margolin became a commuter, submitting to the shocking erosion of his leisure time in travel. It was worth it, they told their incredulous friends. There might not be much time, but there was a sense of time here, and of stillness. Then the power towers came.

The first was neatly placed, whole, while Margolin was at work. It stood ninety feet tall and gleaming silver at the side of Ridge Road. The next day there were two; then five. Then there was a row of towers across the road and down in hundred-foot strides. They climbed hills, walked valleys; they were hung with great muscles of cable. Two-hundred-foot swaths were cut through the

woods to accommodate them until they stood in a cable-hung line
fifteen miles long, crossing all the forest and hill country between
Emmettstown and Hale.

Margolin felt invaded, betrayed. He called the power company
and was told that the land was a long-purchased right of way. He
called his lawyer who looked into it and found that the land had
been deeded in 1913, when there had been no zoning statutes, and
that the owners were held only by what applied at the time of
purchase. Margolin hung up, fuming.

"There's nothing we can do," Regina said. "We'll just have to
learn not to see them, that's all."

"That's the whole point!" he raged. "We came here so we
wouldn't have to un-see everything. They have no right to make
us un-see the damn things! They could have buried the cables and
they know it!" When a neighbor called and told him about the protest meeting, Margolin was eager to go. Regina shrugged, "The law
is on their side — I think it's useless to fight it."

"But if we *all* protest — "

"O.K.," she said, "O.K."

So he sat on the familiar folding chair in the school gym and
waited for the meeting to start. Regina was right — What could
they hope to do? The company was within its rights; its eyesore
towers were on its own land, owned long before the people who
wanted to see these hills and meadows had come and begun to destroy them with houses. A man can spend a lifetime protesting
and petitioning, but there can never be any real protection for the
ephemeral, unnamable joys of life. Across the gym a man stood up
and waved to him. He saw it was Larry Westercamp.

He seldom saw Westercamp except at meetings. There had been
the school battles over sex education and busing and bomb shelters
before that. The Margolins had gone dutifully to be counted, but
Westercamp and his wife seemed to come alive in the atmosphere
of organized complaint. They had been on numberless peace
marches and zoning protests; his was the hand that held the pen for
the petition, and in the meetings Westercamp was always at the core
of the group, passionate and indignant and demanding action. Now
he was coming over. Margolin sighed and began automatically to
formulate an excuse. The meeting wouldn't end before midnight,
and now he had Westercamp, too. Watching the lithe man move

across the gym, Margolin realized that part of his irritation was envy. Westercamp was over forty and there wasn't an ounce of flab on him. His face had a striking, ascetic angularity; it was a face popularly imagined on poets or saints. Margolin was slightly sagging in the middle; he wore glasses and was getting bald, but Westercamp's hair was a magnificent steely gray mass which he ducked and threw in moments of restlessness, like a proud horse or a boy.

"Hi!" and he came over, smiling. He always seemed delighted to see Margolin and sat down beside him with a neatness that made Margolin feel older. "Ave's home with the kids," he whispered. "Measles."

"Oh?" Margolin said.

"She wanted to come, but measles can be serious, you know."

"Yes, I know." Margolin nodded.

"The doctors around here are prejudiced by their union. They're against anyone who wants to keep his health by natural means. Drugs, vaccination — it's all they know. We've had the kids on vitamin C to build them up. The school nurse called us fanatics."

"Oh, well," Margolin said, grateful for something on which he had no opinion.

The meeting began. The problem of the towers was described in agonizing detail. Their height and distance, number of lines and voltage was argued for over an hour. Everyone who said "ninety-foot towers" was reminded by someone else that the towers were 93 feet, 8 inches. Westercamp was often on his feet, explaining, urging. A woman said the towers might be a safety hazard and then the question of their falling or the lines falling was argued for another hour. In the beginning Margolin sat listening in excruciating impatience. Slowly, his restlessness thickened into a kind of leaden boredom which turned down, gentling as it released itself toward sleep. His head moved forward, his arms relaxed. Behind him a chair scraped and he shot up, shocked into wakefulness, not sure where he was. Beside him Westercamp was following each anguished point and question with alertness, rising to explain and embroil himself in each side issue. At last the meeting broke up, having settled nothing but that there would have to be another meeting to decide the main thrust of the protest. It was very late and people left quickly. Margolin was tired and disgusted. He hung back out of boredom, staring at the display of children's artwork on the walls above the gym equipment.

When his eye had worked itself twice around the empty room he knew it was time to go, and he forced himself out through the back door of the gym and into the darkness. The night air shocked him awake. He breathed in deeply and found himself smiling. He stretched and felt the air widening in his lungs. Suddenly he was alert and hungry, his senses keen. The autumn wind had sharpened the edges of everything; a wind-apple scent twisted past him from the orchard farms on the other side of town. There was late cut grass too, and as he turned, a faint, resinous smell — pine trees from the woods miles west of where he stood. He was smiling, relishing the night and his solitude and how ancient a pleasure it was, to sort the scents of the wind. He was sorry he had brought the car. It would have been good to walk the three miles home, warming himself from the work of it. He looked out toward the parking lot. Beyond it stood the line of towers, now with red lights on top of them to warn away aircraft. The pyramid, he thought and sighed; the most stable structure there is. They were in for good and a million meetings wouldn't move them.

"Civilization!"

He jumped. The voice was Westercamp's, behind him. Damn! Margolin felt caught at something. He turned and there was Westercamp pointing to the towers.

"Why do we let ourselves be used by these . . . gadgets! America's gone soft."

"I don't like the towers either," Margolin said uneasily. He didn't want to hear about Soft America. Searching for something else, he remembered a half-heard fragment of table conversation. "Hey, the kids say they saw you on TV. How does it feel to be in Show Biz?"

He saw he had said the wrong thing. Westercamp tossed his head nervously and dug his hands into his pockets. "It's just another part of what I've been trying to fight; the mechanization, the reduction of everything. The news media made a big joke of it."

Margolin wished he had remembered more of what had been said. "Uh . . . I didn't see it. What happened?"

"Our section in Fish and Game has been working on a new strain of brook trout. We needed a species with a high tolerance for the common pollutants. Last week the governor invited the four other governors here for those Regional Conservation talks of his. We were supposed to give a demonstration of the trout, but we didn't know it was rigged as a stunt. They announced that the five governors were going to do a little fishing, that away from all the pressures and publicity they might be able to work out the issues. Then Fish and Game got the word that the governors had better catch something, and what better than the new trout? I had to take almost all of our new fish upstream of their 'secluded spot' and release them to be dragged out three-hundred feet away."

"That's kind of standard, isn't it?" Margolin said. "Honor of the state and all that?"

"There were newsmen in that 'secluded spot' taking pictures of me throwing the fish *in* and others taking pictures of the governors pulling them *out*. On the six o'clock news they mentioned the specially developed trout, and they mentioned conservation talks, but nobody paid attention. It was all a big comedy. They had spliced my section and the governors' sections together and speeded up the film. They even set it to music. Me throwing and them catching. It looked like a sort of dance, fixed in rhythm, in, out, my face, the governors' faces, and then the fish, so we were all doing a kind of dance . . ."

Margolin had begun to laugh. He couldn't help it. He imagined the look on the faces of the men and on the faces of the fish. The governors were clad in skins, grunting as they pulled out fish in a steadily quickening rhythm, Westercamp working faster and faster, the wide-eyed fish more and more confused — He tried to stop and tell Westercamp that he wasn't laughing at him or his job. The man just stood there looking wounded until Margolin forced himself to stop and offer a ride home. The answer was stiff, but Margolin hadn't wanted to be cruel and Westercamp knew it.

"I'm sorry, really," Margolin said. "I suppose feeling strongly about a thing puts it out of the joking category."

They got into the car. Westercamp, still earnest, persisted. "It's just that you, of all people, must know how important it is — not only conservation, but human — dignity. The average man doesn't see, but you're an anthropologist, you study uncorrupted people, people who live as nature intended."

For a minute Margolin didn't understand. "What?"

"I mean you can see how far we've gone from the true pattern, the way people were meant to live."

He had turned out on the road and then glanced at Westercamp. "Larry, all man imposes a pattern on nature. The lives of the people I study are often more artificially determined than ours. I just study the pattern, I'm not looking for Utopia."

"But there are people whose lives aren't complicated by . . . by . . ." and he gestured out the window to the few lights in a deserted shopping center.

"I don't know that it's better to have a life complicated by dead ancestors whose clan taboos must be remembered and followed — "

"I'm not saying that others don't go wrong — tribes full of superstition and fear, but there are others, certain groups — "

They pulled up to the house. Margolin wondered if he should shut off the motor. It was late and he was tired, but he didn't want to seem impatient or draw attention to his waiting. Westercamp was still working. "Doesn't it disturb you that we, the richest nation on earth, are plagued with mental illness, moral decay, pollution of our air, our water, our values — ?" He was aware that he had lost a connecting point in his idea. "Well, you *understand*," as though Margolin had only been teasing him. He looked up at the dark house. "Ave's probably gone to bed." He opened the door, got out and then turned back to Margolin. "Look, we've got to fight those towers. We can't give up. Come to the meetings — we need you. People get excited at first, but after a while they drop away and without organization, we're lost. You have to be vigilant — so vigilant, all the time." In the dashboard light, Margolin saw his tight little smile, a condemned saint, encouraging at the fire. Then he turned and went to his house. Margolin could see by his walk that Westercamp was tired.

The youthfulness seemed to have fallen from him like a disguise, with only the physical props still there, the hunting boots, the soft old shirt with half-rolled sleeves; young Westercamp forever just returning from the woods strong and uncompromised. Except that suddenly the forty-three-year-old man was in disguise and admitting to his age. Margolin wondered why he should be so comforted by that admission.

He headed home, keeping the window down and trying to relive some of the enjoyment he had had in the beauty of the night. Now it was only cold and late and going to be hard to get up tomorrow. "Primitive man!" he muttered. Then he thought about Westercamp again, beautifully choreographed, feeding fish to the governors' mountain stream, and by the time he got home he had orchestrated in order, a minuet, a tango, a wild "primitive" native dance.

In following weeks the Margolins began to get phone calls and mail from some of Westercamp's conservation groups. Regina laughed at Margolin's "new hobby" but he found himself inordinately angry at Westercamp's violation of his privacy. The letters and calls were so importunate, so desperate and convinced: Did he know that Strontium 90 was building up in our bodies? Did he know that the water table was dropping, the world was burning its resources, wastes were poisoning its soil, war eroding its morals? *Act Now!* He put the pamphlets in the bottom of the filing cabinet when Regina wasn't looking. The second meeting about the towers was held on an evening when he had to be at the university and he was relieved not to have to go. The next day Westercamp called.

"Ted, I didn't see you last night. I hope you haven't been sick or something."

"No, I had to stay over at school."

"I hope you can make it next time. We're getting up a petition. Frank Armbruster is going to see if we have good grounds for a lawsuit and he'll let us know."

"Uh . . . Larry, I've been caulking the windows, and I left things where the kids . . ." But Westercamp wasn't listening.

"It's going to pick up this time. This time we'll make them see. Oh, and I was talking to someone there and we got into a discussion about the Chontals. That's the way you pronounce it, isn't it, Chontals?"

"Who?"

"Chontals, those Indians on the southern Isthmus of Mexico — "

"Oh?" Margolin tried to sound professional and interested, but he was fighting an annoyance out of all proportion to the cause. Spontaneous Discussion of the Chontal. He sighed.

"I was reading," Westercamp went on, "about this man who went there. He never saw an adult strike a child. Crime and insanity don't exist there. He never saw violence. The people live on their land simply and in peace. He saw women of seventy and eighty carrying water in huge jugs for miles without tiring. I admire people who can live like that — simply. Don't you think that's wonderful?"

Margolin wanted to say, yes, wonderful, and go upstairs and caulk

windows and curse, but he couldn't conquer his irritation. "I've
never visited that group," he said, "but I know the area. I'll lay
you odds that the 'women of seventy' were thirty and *looked* seventy.
Employment means staying alive till tomorrow; the absence of
crime is the absence of an idea of private ownership. The harmony
is chronic malnutrition, the tranquillity is cocoa leaf."

"Ulcers and heart trouble are unknown," Westercamp argued
doggedly, "diabetes and mental illness . . ."

But Margolin couldn't stop either. "They have rickets, pellagra,
TB, smallpox . . . the infant mortality rate culls out everyone
but natural survivors. Mental illness 'exists' only where people accept the possibility of changing human behavior."

"But diseases like rickets are cured by decent diet, medical knowledge that we — "

"Larry, if the Good Life depends on decent diet and medicine,
then the Good Life isn't Chontal, is it?"

"Well what about Tristan, then, Tristan da Cunha?" The big
proof, the cap.

"What about it?" Margolin said, remembering the magazine
stories. "The islanders were warned and later evacuated to Liverpool because an earthquake had been predicted."

"Yes," shouted Westercamp in triumph, "but they found themselves getting cavities in their teeth, they saw their old people getting respiratory diseases and their children picking up the values of
the gutter; so they packed up and they got out, all of them, back
to a decent life, a life away from 'civilization'!"

"After seeing six months in a Liverpool slum as 'civilization,' "
Margolin said acidly. The magazines had played it Westercamp's
way, he remembered, the *Good Life* vs. *Sin & the City*. "The men
with the rotten teeth and bad morals were the ones whose machines had predicted the trouble and saved the islanders in the first
place. Too bad about cavities, but the people of Tristan were un-
skilled and illiterate in a world that demands both skill and liter-
acy. The population in paradise is dwindling anyway, aging and
dwindling, because in spite of clean air, good morals and no cavities,
the general health is poor. With a single occupation possible and
almost no choice of mates, there is very little dimension to life on
Tristan, because Tristan as Utopia just doesn't work, O.K.?"

The phone voice sounded wounded. "Well, you know more

about them than I do, I guess," and he said good-bye, leaving the victory of the dead line to Margolin.

"Be as a little Chontal," Margolin muttered, and hung up. His mind passed over other words to where his envy was: what right did they have to make heroes? That ugliness scared him so badly that he had to promise himself to be decent next time, and generous, and leave Westercamp's illusions alone.

In time the mailbox glut slowed a little, and it became peacefully automatic to put the tracts away in the filing cabinet. They had a place. Outside the power towers showed no sign of departing the landscape, and he tried his best to ignore them, look through them, adjust them to his eye in some automatic way, but none of the tricks worked. He missed the third meeting and the fourth, and after that he wasn't called again.

The autumn moved from abundance to its lean old age. The trees shriveled and darkened, the frosts fell dry. Winds screamed in the towers. Margolin began to have daydreams about those towers blowing over; they were juvenile, self-indulgent dreams and they made him ashamed. Then it snowed and the towers stood out like skeleton sentries overwhelming the hills where they stalked, watching. They had been up for five months. He knew they would never come down; he knew that defacing the land with them was wrong, in Westercamp's words, unnatural, and that there was nothing he could do.

It frightened Regina to see him sitting in the chair by the window, looking out dully as an invalid at trees, sky and the graffiti of birds and small animals in the snow. The sun picked out the towers in a blue-white blaze. He knew she was able to strike their ugliness from her mind. If she had been asked to draw the meadow in front of their house and the hills stretching beyond, her painstaking sketch would have shown no towers. They had spoken about her gift for ignoring ugliness once or twice, and when he thought about it, it frightened him. Now it was one of her sources of strength. He thought she might try to coax him away from the betrayal by keeping him busy. His special project was coming in December. He would be home until then.

He was correct. She began to invite people over for dinner, for cards, for nothing. Soon the guests reciprocated until every evening was filled, until he complained that he didn't have enough time for his reading or his work. What was the matter with her? Why was she so restless?

It was at one of these automatically reciprocating forced marches that he saw Westercamp again. Remembering his stubbornness, he thought that Westercamp might turn away, but whatever losses Westercamp had suffered, he seemed to have forgotten them and he hurried over smiling to greet Margolin.

"Ted, hi!"

"Hi, Larry," he said. "How's it going?"

"Fine, fine," and Westercamp grinned again. They went over to get drinks and Margolin dug around for something to talk about. "Say, how is the group coming on the towers?" Westercamp gave the dip of his head that showed he was embarrassed.

"Well, it's just about disbanded." Margolin realized the embarrassment was for him — one of the Righteous who hadn't been there.

"We had too few coming to make a real fight of it," Westercamp said. "We did make some calls, we sent the petition and Armbruster is still looking into the legal angle, but" — and his taut, ascetic's face gave a quick twitch of a smile — "people aren't willing to back up their beliefs."

"Oh, come on, Larry," Margolin said, "a well-led group could have gotten it done in fifteen minutes, and instead of group therapy we could have had our petition going right away. I went to the meeting to register a protest, not start a career. There was no firm leadership and we got bogged down in side issues. The thing didn't die of apathy, but incompetence." Westercamp stared at him with the shock of having heard something obscene. Margolin muttered an excuse and slipped away.

They left early. It was a thick, ugly night. As they came toward home he looked around for the towers, but they were hidden in fog; even the mean-eyed red lights. "Damn things. I hurt him again, Reg, but he's so naive!"

"Then why are you so hard on him — why can't you leave him alone?"

"I don't know. He's using me, and — I don't know."

He escaped into work gratefully. It was almost time for Christmas vacation and he had been asked by a therapist at the state hospital to spend some time with three Sioux who were patients there. "They dream," the therapist had said, "and I'm out of my depth with the symbols they're using." Margolin had been looking forward to going. It would be a relief to be called from the twilight window where he could see the towers closing upon his house. Perhaps he might be able to help in some way although he was no expert on the Sioux. Some insight here might freshen his classes, anyway. When the day came he packed delightedly and told Regina that he would come back rested and stimulated and looking forward to writing *acculturation* on the blackboard again. He left earlier than he needed with a feeling of excitement, as though he were going to set off cross-country to a place unmapped but where all towers were his to deal with. He called her from a hotel near the hospital and a few times after that to find out if everything was all right, and he called her when he was getting ready to leave. His voice on the phone hadn't prepared her for the way he looked when he walked into the house again when the project was over. He stood without moving, gray and sick and deeply tired, so changed that she was stunned and couldn't think of anything to say. For a while they simply stared at one another.

"Ted?"

"Hi."

"Darling, what happened? You look exhausted."

"Tomorrow," he said, "not now."

"Let me take your coat — come on in the kitchen and have some coffee. It's all ready — "

The whole house had been readied for his homecoming; Regina in her diaphanous blue thing, the kids in bed, the rooms orderly. He sat in the quiet room with his coffee and realized that as exhausted as he was, he wouldn't sleep. He was afraid even to try.

After a while she asked, "Did you have a nice room at the hotel?"

"It was fine." Then he laughed, shaking his head at the lie he was beginning; he would have to tell her something, and if it wasn't what had happened, it would have to be some kind of lie. "It wasn't fine," he said. "I can't even remember what it was like. What I remember is a series of gray-smelling interview rooms, two senile old Sioux and Benton Song . . ." He spoke slowly, seeing himself again in those rooms, listening as he had, cold and alone, to tapes of Benton breaking asunder with astonishing dreams. In the nightmare landscape's vastness, the symbols of The People had become cheapened parodies, like the Made In Japan trinkets Benton sold summers from a plastic wigwam off the highway.

"Start at the beginning," she said.

"In the first place, Benton isn't Sioux at all. He comes from Arizona; his mother was Navaho, his father one of the Tewa living in Taos Pueblo. At the staff meetings they talked about The Indians, not Navaho or Tewa. Benton is the product of a marriage like that of a Japanese geisha and a Sicilian grape-grower. I tried to help him, Reg, and I couldn't. I didn't patronize him or play the scholar, but I couldn't help either. In the middle of our first meeting he got up and yelled, 'Your mother is full of cowboy pictures!' and left."

"What happened? Did he come back again?"

"No, I went to see him on the ward. We talked there at first. He needed all kinds of proofs of my honesty and competence — you can't give that in two weeks and he knew I had that time limit, that neat vacation. 'Two weeks with The Savages,' he said. There've been too many fake-authentic Indian things and too many bad books. Even the simple facts of Benton's life give him pain. Sometimes he was — well, never mind. His mother was a professional Indian, going around the country to march in parades and 'do' conventions while his father waited back in Taos and wondered why his wife couldn't be the way women are supposed to be. Later she took Benton on tour with her."

"But that's no Indian background — it's . . . nothing."

"It was this Indian's background," and he smiled sourly. "At one time I did try to pin him to a category." (With which people were you most at home?) "He only shouted at me." (With the warriors of the Silver Screen! Apaches in feathers, bathing trunks under their breechclouts, Sioux in sneakers. Tonto, him my brother!) "I tried to make him see that even his mixed symbols had meanings that Anglos might not know." (The hawks you see in Dr. Ferrier's tests and the ones you dream about — he's trying to find a way to help you . . . "I don't know! They threw me out before the movie ended!")

"You can't be expected to do psychoanalysis in two weeks," Regina said, defending.

"I was supposed to know the context of those dreams — to show Ferrier where the symbols carried cultural weight." He began to repeat one of the dreams that Benton, tongue-tied with tranquilizers, had given to the tape recorder to haunt Margolin's evenings.

"The sky is clear — it's someplace near Window Rock. It's noon and the sun is riding the world. Something is going to happen, but I don't know what, and I'm afraid it's a sign I won't see or recognize — that I'll miss it. I'm sitting on a mesa, a small mesa, all piled with rocks, alone. I'm watching everything, and I'm watching me. I'm born from the sun — I look down and see the me that's down there, far, far down. I'm a hawk. I despise that crawling thing so far down there. I begin to dive toward it, to kill it, and I feel a heat and a chill in me, a kind of crying, like crying for air when you can't breathe. I open my big wings and my shadow darkens the man and the rock. What the wanting is — it's to join that shadow — to be all one. I scream, dive head-on toward myself, man and shadow, and hawk, all one, and when I hit, it's dying, the end — a terrible pain, and I wake up."

"It has a beauty to it," Regina said.

He sighed. "I suppose it does," and looked around at the kitchen, shining and clean for his homecoming. "There are tribal realities in it, and universal ones, and a self-wounding satire of the White Man's Red Man, and I can't really tell where one leaves off and another begins. We soon stopped having 'interviews' and just talked, that is, when we could. He would fight in the ward at night sometimes. Then he would come in the next day black and blue and groggy with drugs. I liked him, so it hurt — that business. Before I left this morning, I stopped in to say good-bye and we shook hands. I hadn't thought he would commit himself like that. I wanted something, anything, that could make it better for him. He's intelligent and he knows it in spite of all the 'injun-talk.' I told him to help Ferrier and the group therapy people by telling them about the differences between Navaho and Tewa, not letting them get away with phony symbols and a phony reality. He shook his head, and said, 'Maybe it's better to be a character in a white man's movie. When the Eagle speaks for my life what language will he use? A language I don't know? A language nobody knows anymore?' I told him to keep trying to hear the words. He looked at me and shrugged and said that at least I have been a change from sitting around on the ward, and we laughed. Then very quietly he said, 'You tried.' I — uh — gave him our address and told him to come and see us when he got out. Don't worry, he won't. He folded the paper up very carefully and put it away, but we both knew he wouldn't come."

"Oh, Ted, you don't know it wasn't more than that. Maybe he

will. Maybe you did do more than he said, even more than he knows himself, and then too, you helped the doctors — "

"Sure. I took the notes I'd made and brought them to a big hospital staff conference. Everybody listened politely and when it was all over they thanked me and complimented me and kidded in a very gentle way about the scholarly monographs to be derived from this source anguish."

"They tried to make you see that you had helped."

"Oh, Reg! They were pitying an amateur who couldn't fight away the awful hopelessness wound up in those damn tape spools. They'll forget Benton isn't Sioux, they'll forget I told them I hadn't helped. They'll take the notes and make them law and do more studies on The Mental Patient, and I'll do one or two on acculturation when I need something published, and Benton's pain is so awful and so frightening and nobody knows how to help!" Then he stood up and shook his head and went to bed, leaving Regina alone in her sexy blue, staring at his half-finished cup of coffee.

The next day was Saturday and he resolved that if he didn't want to be ministered to, he'd better stop acting like an object of pity. He dressed quickly and with a great show of heartiness, fixed the loose steps on the back porch, and took the kids out for hamburgers and a monster movie. Although there was nothing real in his good spirits, he was comforted by the deception. He was standing in well for the real owner of this life. The movie struck him as being subtly obscene. Its symbols, which he understood more clearly than Benton Song's, were homosexual and fetishistic, and, worried for his children, he questioned them afterward about what they had seen. They answered from untroubled, open faces and spent the ride home delightedly reliving the crucial scenes with themselves the monster and the world gone small and helpless. Regina looked at the greasy-fingered, bleary-eyed spectacle they made and her face relaxed. "Honey, I forgot to tell you last night — I put all the mail in the top drawer of the desk so it wouldn't get misplaced. There were some calls. I took the messages and they're in there too."

"I'll look at it all later," he said, and, still working, went upstairs to see Mark's science project.

When he did get to it, he understood why Regina had let it wait. It was madman mail; Westercamp again, and oh, the air, the water, the food, outer space! The benthos off the continental shelf! And the phone calls. They had heard he was interested; did he wish to become a member? Did he know there was a group to — ? a council for — ?

"*Regina!*"

"I had to save them for you . . . Now that you've seen them you can throw them out."

The phone rang. It was for him. Did he know about the protest against mass shooting of elk in Wyoming? He hissed his answer into the phone and hung up. Regina was standing in the middle of the room, watching him, her hands raised slightly, defensively, and the gesture infuriated him.

"This is ridiculous!" he said. "I won't have that damn fool involving me in every hysterical cause he's hooked on!" He went for the phone book to get Westercamp.

"Ted . . . Just a minute. I think you should know — something's happened to Larry. Avis told me while you were away. He's sick, Ted; he's been home all week and it has to do with his job, somehow."

"What's the matter with him?"

"Avis never talks about their troubles. She must have thought it was important that you know, because she told me to tell you. You're a very special person to Larry."

"I know, I know," he said.

"Maybe you should call, but not about the protests."

"I'll tell her to put him on vitamin C," Margolin said, and felt ugly for having said it and so had to defend the ugliness. "No wonder he's sick, with all the fuss they make over health and vitamins. Reg, how am *I* supposed to help him? I just got back from *not* helping someone I *liked,* someone I'm 'trained' to help." Her eyebrow rose slightly. "Okay," Margolin went on, "he's naive and I'm jealous of it, but I resent being used as a talent scout for his damn tribes!"

"You don't own primitive man any more than he does," and, getting his look, she shrugged. "Well, I've told you about him; you can do what you like." She left him and went upstairs to oversee the baths.

"Do what I like!" he muttered, and dialed Westercamp's number. He had concocted a vague, neighborly beginning, but when he heard the hope in Avis Westercamp's voice, he knew he wouldn't be able to use it. What did they expect of him? Westercamp got on and Margolin was unprepared for the lowered, pinched quality

of the voice; its youthfulness had been conquered, the naive enthusiasm was gone, narrowed to the effort necessary to lift the phone.
He was even puffing from the walk. They traded greetings and
Margolin found his neck and arms aching with the strain of holding the phone to his ear. He began to throw words into it, needing
the sound to listen to. He told Westercamp a wildly doctored
story about his visit to three Sioux Indians, and how one had
turned out not to be Sioux at all. He tried to make a little joke
about the mailing lists. He pushed away heedlessly and the
thoughts fled before him into hiding. When he stopped he was
winded. Westercamp began to speak slowly.

"I suppose your wife told you what happened."

"Not really," he said.

"Trout . . ." Westercamp whispered. Margolin held his breath.
"We were developing . . . uh . . . resistant to certain . . . uh
. . . contaminants in the water. I told you."

"I remember," Margolin said.

"We put some in Ede Lake about two months ago. By last
week they had died . . . all of them. And in Swanscombe Creek,
too. The fish could live in foul water . . ." — his newly old voice
cracked — "but not in sewers . . . The river . . . is a sewer. The
lake . . . is a sewer."

"I know they took time to develop — "

"Not the *time*," Westercamp interrupted querulously. "It's us.
We had everything, everything, and we burned it, poisoned it.
Why didn't we stop before it was too late? Why can't we stop de-
stroying? Why can't we live *simply*, like the Hunza?"

Margolin caught his breath. The Hunza. New entries in The
Noble Savage Sweepstakes.

A student had asked him something before vacation — he should
have seen this coming. His old notebook had given:

The Hunza: small group of Moslem, subsistence herders, slopes
of Himalayas. Close, precarious adaptation to high altitude, short
growing season, rugged terrain. (P.8, C.50, IC. 6)

The codes indicated the typical Tibetan pattern, but the Utopia
hunters must have been there and come back with the eternal,
impossible tales — no anguish, no crime, no locks, men living in
vigor to great age. The old dream was blowing into bloom, like a

wild poppy. It would be cut back on the edge of fact and lie dormant for a winter only to come bright again somewhere else. Margolin sighed and thought, Your mother is full of cowboy pictures.

He said gravely into the phone, "Yes, the Hunza." He could hear Westercamp breathing in his ear, sick now, and wary of more pain. Suddenly Margolin wanted to beg his forgiveness; for polluting his air and fouling his water and for permitting the hideous towers to stand.

Westercamp breathed into the phone again. "People who have seen them say there are no words for greed or envy."

"There probably aren't," Margolin said gently.

"They live simply, pure food, good water."

"They are a small, closely knit people," Margolin added quietly.

"And they reverence wisdom. The elders live to a hundred and twenty." Westercamp's voice had lightened.

"Moslems," Margolin said, "tend to venerate age." He was glad when Westercamp missed the point of this.

"Yes, and wisdom. They don't worship fads, material things — they're happy, I think, because their lives are natural. It's good for men to work hard . . ." The voice had some of its suppleness again. Margolin was moved. His own torment could never have found relief in some unknown tribe's good fortune. He knew that if Utopia existed, he would have envied it, and not, with Westercamp's singular goodness, wished it well. "You see," Westercamp went on, "they're not compromised and humiliated all the time. They live as they should. They don't have to try to convince everybody of the simplest truths . . . the most obvious truths . . ."

"A Hunza can understand another Hunza's work," Margolin said, "and I think that is a beautiful thing."

"I'm glad you agree. If only we were like them!"

". . . And their language is interesting too," Margolin said, "an old and complex tongue."

When he hung up he found he had a headache. At three in the morning it was still pounding. The red lights on top of the power towers were winking on and off, on and off, outside the window.

Margolin sometimes used a handmade spear thrower to shock his freshman classes on their first day. He would send the spear into the wall at the back of the class and then, in the sibilant wash of amazement, wade dramatically to his beginning: Primitive Man. At six in the morning Regina traced the strange sound to the basement and found him practicing with the spear thrower, sending the makeshift spear across the laundry room with terrible savagery. When she asked him what on earth he was throwing it for, he said, breathing hard, "Ninety-three feet, eight inches."

MARY HEATH

The Breadman

(FROM THE VIRGINIA QUARTERLY REVIEW)

MRS. SPROUT'S WEDDING day dawned clear as a bell. Up with the birds, she was elbow deep in dough by seven. Her daughter Eileen came down to the kitchen in one of the negligees that had been part of her own trousseau a year ago this month: peach with spidery white lace around the neck and wrists, ill-fated, for the marriage had barely lasted out the honeymoon.

"Sweetheart, I haven't even made coffee yet," said Mrs. Sprout. "That was a good buy, you know. Half price, but it washed up like new. You have a real eye for a bargain." It was the negligee she spoke of.

Eileen held out the wide hem and dipped it back and forth. Mother and daughter studied its peachy mothy glamour. "Shame I never really got my money's worth out of it," said Eileen, and they both laughed gaily.

"Well, follow my suit, sweetheart," said Mrs. Sprout. "If at first. Now look at me, and I could of done it before only it never seemed worth the trouble. Just take your time, Eileen. You're honey to bees, you don't have to settle for just anything."

Eileen was making the coffee and lighting a cigarette and getting out the oranges to squeeze for juice. She was humming. Every now and then her eyes met her mother's and they smiled at each other. "Six dozen," said Mrs. Sprout. She rolled out the dough, sprinkled it with cinnamon and brown sugar, then rolled it back up and cut, every inch along the long roll, and crowded the little swirls, cheek by jowl, into baking pans, and set them in a row, ready for the oven. "Chicken salad and aspic ready," she said to herself. "Cinnamon buns ready. No oysters. Pity you can't have oysters in May."

The coffee and juice were laid out on the little round table, and the two women sat down to it. "There'll be three at table next week," Eileen said suddenly, and both fell to weeping; and then to hugging each other.

"Sweetheart, you'll always come first."

"I know that, Mother. For all we've been through."

"That's right, you and me. But you have to marry sometime, right? And you'll be next. Oh, yes you will. You're not going to give up that easy. Reverend Highrider said himself just after your tragedy, what a fine spirit you have. Now just take a leaf from your poor old mother's book."

"Frankly, I just haven't seen anything I'd want, for a start. Or a finish."

"I never did like that Ronald, if I was to be perfectly honest," said Mrs. Sprout. "It was something about the look of him, Eileen. Now I'm not saying I told you so, because I didn't, and maybe that was my mistake. But I think it was those pale blue eyes. Now your father had blue eyes, but they were dark and could just look right through you sometimes. I wish you remembered him better. It would of given you some standards. I think," she mused, "that's why I never really felt any urge to marry again. I mean I never really saw a man would of given you those standards. Edwin's all right for a husband or I wouldn't be marrying him, would I, but I wouldn't want you to get the idea that he was some kind of ideal."

"Don't worry about that," said Eileen cheerfully. "Ronnie's trouble was he was just a kid. He didn't know a thing. Funny how a fellow could know just nothing about anything, isn't it?"

"It was the mother," Mrs. Sprout said promptly. "I took one look at her at your wedding and said this will never work. Well, who were they, anyway? Just someone you met on a bus, just ships that pass in the night."

Eileen said: "You know, I can't even remember what he looked like. Don't you think that's funny? It's like I never was married, even for a week. He could be dead, think of that."

"Oh, Eileen, don't get morbid."

"Well, boats are torpedoed every day. All hands lost. And then I'd be a widow. It just makes you sad, if you stop and think. A girl getting married now may not be doing anything but making herself a widow."

"You can't count on anything," her mother agreed. "But some people come through thick and thin. My, it's getting warm though. But I'm going to wear my fur piece anyway. They do at weddings, even in July. Next Christmas, Eileen, you're going to have a genuine mouton coat, I promise. I've already said to Edwin how you never had a fur coat and nearly thirty. It's your turn next, sweetheart."

The meal was finished. Neither of them really ate breakfast; mid-morning was the first meal of the day, and Mrs. Sprout's romance with Edwin Doty had begun at that point. Delivering bread and pastry at just the right moment, he had found a market. Doughnuts were Mrs. Sprout's weakness; Edwin had said that the second week, delivering his fourth dozen, and she'd agreed, adding: "From now on, you bring the doughnuts and I'll make the coffee." So Edwin Doty gave up his mid-morning coffee at Gus Whipple's store on Tuesdays and Fridays, and for two years had it at Mrs. Sprout's on Broad Street, winters in the kitchen, summers on the back porch.

After the first year Mrs. Doty said he could have his breakfast, lunch, and dinner there, too, and packed up his clothes and personal effects — a stamp collection from his boyhood, an album of their wedding trip through New England, a chess set she'd given him one Christmas, which he'd never learned to play but liked to have set out to look at — and left them on the front porch. He'd showed up at Mrs. Sprout's door, just at suppertime that night.

"Why, I don't take roomers, Edwin," she'd said. "Why, what would people say?"

"My wife says they say I live here anyway," said Edwin.

"Now don't be funny," said Mrs. Sprout. "You and I know perfectly well you don't live here." And added touchily, "What's wrong with coffee and doughnuts?"

But it had not always ended there and while Mrs. Sprout herself overlooked these bursts of passion — passion was not a word she used; that was pure Edwin — Edwin could or would not. "I love you," he said, and continued to say during the second year, until at last, not as a roomer, but as a husband, he was moving suitcase and duffle bag from Mrs. Knipe's boarding house to what he would ever after call home.

Love, resolving itself into marriage, had not been simple. Mrs. Doty divorced Mr. Doty, and agreed, in exchange for the house and a monthly allowance, to charge Mr. Doty with nothing worse than mental cruelty. But the living Mrs. Doty was not the only obstacle. There was, strictly speaking, the possibility of a living Mr. Sprout.

Almost twenty years before, Mr. Sprout had locked up his hardware store one night and, with only the clothes on his back and the day's receipts from the cash register in his pocket, walked to the train station and bought a ticket to Philadelphia. It did not come as a surprise to anyone but his wife that the business turned out to be in a bad way, and that a thin yellow-haired girl named Junie Frontz never showed up again behind the notions counter at Hall's store. Mrs. Sprout weathered the shock. She showed up at the store, after two weeks, ready for business. She said herself she had no head for business, but she managed to make enough out of it to feed herself and Eileen, pay off the mortgage on the house on Broad Street, and send Eileen to a secretarial school. When Eileen finished her course and got herself a good job as private secretary to the president of the bank, Mrs. Sprout retired to private life.

But as the moment of changing into Mrs. Doty drew near, she became, as she confessed to Eileen and Reverend Highrider, confused. Was she, after all, a widow? They advised her to see a lawyer.

"Bigamy," he said easily. "Not really, of course, though you ought to have Thomas Sprout declared officially dead."

Mrs. Sprout cried for three days. When Edwin or Eileen remonstrated, she said, "Officially. Oh, dead is all right. I've lived that way for years. But now he can't ever come back."

Edwin took Eileen aside and said, "She still loves your father. She loves another man."

Eileen got out the Christmas whiskey and poured drinks for all three and said, "Of course she does, Edwin, a woman always loves the father of her child. But you aren't going to complain about what's natural. You have to see what my mother's been through. And people saying he and that girl had gone off together. Why, whatever he did, he did for us. He might just have thought that creditors would be much nicer to a widow and orphan, you know, and they were. They certainly weren't going to let *us* starve."

"I don't see anything so wonderful about that," said Edwin. "He just went off and left you, and took money that wasn't rightfully his."

"Now I won't sit here," cried Mrs. Sprout, "and hear you say things like that. Are you calling him an embezzler? And that lawyer insinuating I'm a bigamist. Why are you all hounding us down like common criminals? My husband, wherever he may be," she said slowly, "is suffering from amnesia. He doesn't know who he is, let alone that he has me and Eileen. Now that is no crime. And I," she added, "have been a widow for nearly twenty years, and that is no bigamist. And that is that."

And so Thomas Sprout, wherever he might be, whomever he might believe himself to be, was declared dead, and Mildred Sprout his widow. A fox-fur neckpiece and a diamond ring were presented in the presence of a few select friends. Plans for the wedding were drawn up.

Eileen carried the cups to the sink and rinsed them out. "You go up and have your bath, Mother, and I'll tidy up here," she said. "Edwin'll bring the cake when he comes. I'll just tie the ribbons on the knife while I think of it."

"It just makes me think of your wedding day," said Mrs. Sprout. "It should be you. I wish it were."

"Not marrying Edwin, thanks," said Eileen.

"I know you don't really love him," Mrs. Sprout said, her eyes filling up. "Would you rather I'd just lived down the scandal and gone on alone?"

"No, of course not, I only mean I don't love him and I'm not marrying him. And he'll make a good husband."

"A good husband! Oh, Eileen, what do you know about good husbands?" And Mrs. Sprout, in full tears, fled the room.

"You're past all that," said Eileen in a reasoning voice, bent over the sink and not noticing that her mother had gone. When she looked up, she went on talking anyway. "I mean, not first love. You can love him and all, but not like the first time. Now I've never told a soul this, but I just never got over Dan Ritter, and Ronnie wasn't a man to help you get over things, was the trouble. And I'd settle for a good husband, though I might hope for something better. And I'm glad I had a proper wedding in a white dress while I was young enough to enjoy it, to have something to remember, even if it wasn't worth having to live with Ronnie forever. Have my cake and eat it," and she began to laugh, thinking about the cake Edwin's bakery was giving him as a wedding present; three tiers, bride and groom on top, frosting roses garlanding the edge. Her own cake had been topped by a bride and a naval officer, and she had wanted to cut it with a sword, but of course Ronnie hadn't been an officer, and maybe sailors didn't have swords anyway, much good it would do them unless they were attacked by pirates. "You can't have everything," she said to herself, and nodded in agreement.

Four blocks away, on Main Street, Mrs. Tennyson said, at her own breakfast table, "Mildred has a perfect day for it," and, to her daughter: "Don't eat too much before you sing, Mary Ella."

Mary Ella put down the piece of toast she had just bitten into and pushed back from the table. "Can I be excused?"

Her mother said yes, but to stay around the house. From behind his paper, her father said, "When is this thing to be?" and her mother said, "Noon on the dot. But I have to get Mary Ella there by half-past eleven."

The paper was folded and put down on the table. "Second weddings," said Mr. Tennyson, "should not be performed to music."

Her mother said bitterly, "Or in the company of your family and friends. Or at a decent hour of the day."

Her father took out his watch, and stood up. He bent over to kiss his wife who, pulling away, received the kiss on her left temple, and nodded to his daughter. He had stopped kissing her good-bye in the morning, unless she insisted on it. Now she stood up and put her face up to his so that he brushed her cheek, then awkwardly patted her shoulder. He left the room and crossed the hall, and the little temple bells that hung inside the screen door rang out as he closed the door behind him.

"It's too bad Mrs. Sprout isn't a little thinner," said Mary Ella guiltily; she wished so much to be walking with her father to his office. "I mean, then she could wear Eileen's dress. It seems a pity to wear a dress just once."

"Wedding dresses are meant to be worn just once," said her mother. "That is, unless you have a daughter coming along to wear it later. That's my real regret, you know. Married as I was, no dress left behind for you. Married at six o'clock in the morning! By a minister I'd never laid eyes on before, Mary Ella, and haven't again to this day. No mother, no sister there, no friend. All in secret, as though it was something to be ashamed of. He was a divorced man," the old story continued, "but I wasn't ashamed for that, and why should he be? I'd done nothing wrong. I hope," she added, taking Mary Ella's hand, "I hope you are never, never ashamed. Never ashamed of feeling, of true feeling. Love. Now there's just nothing shameful in it. You aren't ashamed of anything, are you?"

Mary Ella said quickly, "No." Then: "But I think I might like to elope. I think that might be interesting. I like the way weddings look, but I think it might be exciting to just elope." In her mind there was a ladder against a wall, herself carried off, through the night, to a minister she had never seen, escape with a man she had never seen. Her father, of course, had not used a ladder; once, asking her mother about the famous elopement, her mother had laughed and laughed, and later, embarrassing Mary Ella, said to her father: "Do you know, Jason, Mary Ella imagines you carried me down a ladder?"

"You are not going to elope," said her mother, and began gathering up the breakfast things. She rang the little bell for Ida to come and clear away. "Now I'm going to give myself a facial and you stay around. When I finish, I'll call you and we'll do something about that hair."

"Can I just run over and speak to Rhoda?"

"Well, stay out on the porch so you can hear me when I call."

For a year, since they'd turned fourteen, Mary Ella and Rhoda Highrider had been singing at weddings. It had begun with the marriage of Janice Scott. That had been a quick wedding because the groom, a paratrooper, was being shipped overseas. The church soloist had suddenly developed laryngitis and there had been no time to find another choir member. Mary Ella's mother, who often got the two girls to accompany her while she played the piano, had volunteered their services. They had sung "Oh Promise Me" and the marriage hymn "Oh Perfect Love." Neither, when the moment came, had wished to sing. But after that first time some of the nervousness wore off, and they had become popular singers for weddings. There was something in their style that spoke right to the hearts of the women: they stood surrogates for the nervous bride, the image of innocence and sacrifice. Their repertoire increased, as did their wardrobes and the carrying power of their

voices. Mrs. Tennyson began to talk about their beginning regular
voice lessons. She said that the sweet uncertainty of their voices
must be replaced, not by untutored self-confidence (in argument
with Mr. Tennyson: "You don't want them to sound like Fern Miller, do you?" Fern Miller, roaring and booming through anthems,
crashing in and out of all hymns, overtaking and subduing both the
bass and the baritone, triumphantly overcoming all melody, demo-
cratically proclaiming all voices, tunes, words equal and indistinguishable), but by poised and educated interpretation. "You must
think about what you are singing," she would cry to them. "Think
of the words — oh — per-*fect* — then pause, then, softly, tenderly
— love. L-O-V-E."

They practiced and practiced, and achieved success through par-
ody. Love. Love. The dying fall, the swoon. They could not do
it without laughing, except in public where nervousness still re-
pressed spirit.

They collected trophies. Each had a compact, for that day when
she would use powder. Each had a silver-plated charm bracelet,
and charms on it to date their performances: Janice and William,
Eileen and Ronald (they had asked Eileen should they remove
that one, she had said it would spoil the looks of the bracelets);
Miss Rogers, their Sunday school teacher, and R. C. H., Jean and
Donald, and now Mildred and Edwin. The bracelets jingled, they
could not wear them to school or church. They had a large collection of lace hankies — each time they promised that they would
carry this particular hankie on their own wedding days — and a
variety of bath salts and sachets. They had become, finally, cynical,
betting with each other whether this time it would be another
hankie or Apple Blossom cologne.

Rhoda was on the porch, sitting on the swing, her hair up in curl-
ers. Neither said hello, but took up with the conversation left
over from the night before: "I still think it must be sex."

"Not at that age."

"Love?"

"Could it be?"

"Oh, Mary E, it just couldn't. Not *real* love."

"My father was forty-eight."

"Yes, but your mother wasn't much past twenty-five, which isn't
all that old. Besides, your father's different. I mean even now he

looks younger than my father even if he is twenty years older. He doesn't count."

"My mother says it was a great love."

"Mrs. Sprout and the breadman?"

"Don't be silly."

Then Rhoda said, frowning, "I really think that when it comes to it, I could understand sex better than love. I mean, love may just not happen. But I think sex probably always does. It's just biological, I mean, part of your system whether you like it or not. It's sort of superficial, really, like the way people look. I think that probably explains a lot."

"But then — Mrs. Sprout — and sex?"

They stared at each other a moment and then began to laugh. "It can't be that," said Mary Ella, turning serious again. "It must be — well, companionship. Like someone to keep you company."

They began to swing, back and forth, eyes closed, humming. Then Rhoda started, in her strong alto, and Mary Ella picked up the melody: "Oh promise me that someday you and I/Will take our love together to some sky" — and a deeper voice, but disguised as falsetto, joined in, rose above their harmony, scattered it.

Eugene Darby, sponge in hand, came through the border of shrubbery, vaulted over the porch railing, and threw the sponge at Mary Ella. "You need some variety in your act," he said. "Take me along. I know all those ditties by heart from listening to you practice all the time."

"You're supposed to be washing the car," said Rhoda. "I heard your grandmother shouting at you about it this morning."

"It's done," he said. "I made that old Buick do eighty-five on the cemetery road last night. What do you think of that?"

They knew, and he knew they knew, he was lying. Two years their senior, he had a driver's license, but was never allowed to take the car out without either his grandmother or her companion sitting in the back seat. On Sundays he drove them to church, on Tuesdays and Saturdays to the store. "When are you going to take us for a ride?" said Rhoda.

"Any time you say."

"I bet. Your grandmother wouldn't let you. Maybe Toby could go along as your chaperone, though."

Toby, outlaw dog, loved Eugene, next best Mary Ella, tolerated

the immediate family and Rhoda, viciously attacked postmen, sales-
men, all dogs; had killed, two years earlier, a toy terrier. The dog
died, not from wounds, but a heart attack, and the owner had sued.
The grandmother had proved Toby belonged to her son, Eugene's
father, a wanderer, never long in one place. The suit still hung
fire.

"Toby's all right," Eugene said stiffly. "He's high-strung is
what."

"I know," said Rhoda. "His grandfather was lead dog for Ad-
miral Byrd. He has a lot to live up to."

"I'm giving him to Mary Ella when I join up."

"Her daddy won't let her keep him," said Rhoda. "Besides, this
war will be over before the air corps will take you."

"You can join up at seventeen."

"Your grandmother won't let you quit school. Who wants to be
in the air corps anyway? I think the navy uniforms are nicer. My
father says if he had to go again that's what he'd pick. Cleaner,
he says."

"He was just an ordinary soldier."

"He was gassed, remember. They don't gas people like that anymore. He said once the rats in the trenches were the worst part.
Ugh — I couldn't take that."

Mary Ella was scratching Toby's ears. "Sometimes people talk
as though the last war was somehow better, though, than this one.
It was was supposed to be the war to end all wars."

"Oh, there'll always be a war," said Rhoda. "The Bible says so,"
and she began to hum "Oh Promise Me" again.

Eugene broke in. "Today's the day," he sang, "they give bread-
men away, with half a pound of butter."

"Soybean butter," Rhoda corrected, laughing, and all three began to improvise a scene of mass poisoning. Edwin Doty, facing up
squarely to the butter shortage, seeing that bread demands butter,
had sold to every housewife on his route a pound of soybean butter,
assuring them that even the most discriminating taste would be
fooled. It hadn't. The following week he had carried away the remains of a hundred pounds of the stuff. It was a minor trouble;
but jokes keep their flavor longer than scandal, soybean butter out-
lived mental cruelty.

A voice called: "Eugene. *Eu*-gene. Eu-*gene*."

"Sorry to break this up," he said cheerfully, and swung back down over the railing and disappeared through the hedge. Mary Ella still held the sponge.

"Do you like him?" Rhoda demanded. "I mean, *like* him. You know, as a boy."

"No," said Mary Ella. "I wouldn't want to live with his grandmother though. My father says she ruined her own son and now she'll do the same to Eugene. My father thinks it might be a good idea if he joined the air corps. Only I don't think he wants to leave Toby."

"Or you."

"Or you, either, then."

"He likes you best."

"No, he doesn't."

"Does."

"Doesn't."

Silence. Then, "Mary Ella, Mary Ella, Mary Ella," trippingly, lightly. Mary Ella got up and took the sponge with her.

"Will we ever fall in love," said Rhoda.

"Oh perfect love," said Mary Ella. "Oh — Per-fect — L-O-V-E."

When Mary Ella and her mother came down the front steps at half-past eleven, Rhoda and her father, Reverend Highrider, were just turning out of their own front walk. Mrs. Tennyson and Mary Ella waited for them. Reverend Highrider shook Mrs. Tennyson's hand, bowing slightly over it, and said, "You two look just like sisters," and then, as Rhoda and Mary Ella moved off ahead, "They look like sisters. You've been like a mother to Rhoda," which he said at every opportunity, to which Mrs. Tennyson always replied with a sad smile, "Well, she's as dear as a daughter to me."

Rhoda and Mary Ella gave each other sidelong looks, then quickly away. Once they had longed to be sisters, had cruelly widowed Mrs. Tennyson, married her off to Reverend Highrider. The memory filled them with horror, and Mary Ella with anguish. She could not bear to remember their appalling ignorance, to contemplate the possible consequences of it. Behind their backs Mrs. Tennyson was explaining that Mr. Tennyson would be coming directly from his office.

In a low voice, Mary Ella said, "What do you suppose they'll give us."

"Wish it would be money," said Rhoda. "My father says the

church soloist always gets ten dollars at least for doing this. But she gives half of it back to the church, can you imagine?"

"I'd buy a pair of green sandals. I saw them at Asher's last week. And you don't need coupons because there's no leather, just rope soles. Mother says they look like something gypsies would wear."

Mrs. Sprout's house was two blocks off Main Street. As they turned the corner they could see Edwin's bread truck pulled up in front of it. "Will they take their honeymoon in that?" asked Mary Ella, and Reverend Highrider, smiling, said, "I believe Eileen's lent them her car for the occasion. Destination unknown, of course."

"Why of course?" asked his daughter. "I'd tell people where I was off to. What's so secret?"

"I rather agree with Rhoda," said Mrs. Tennyson. "Weddings are public occasions. Joy should be shared."

"Oh, yes indeed," Reverend Highrider agreed. "Quite, yes indeed. When Mrs. Sprout spoke to me about performing the service I said why of course I would. Though Mrs. Doty remains a member of my congregation, too, but it is my duty, you know, to serve all my flock. If the shoe were on the other foot, I said. If it were Mrs. Doty who was marrying."

"Divorce," said Mrs. Tennyson sadly, "should not cast a shadow over marriage."

"I still don't see why we can't know where people are going on their honeymoons," Rhoda insisted.

"Well," said Mrs. Tennyson, "I'm afraid I can cast some light on that, Rhoda. When I was just a girl, not much older than you two, a friend of my sister's got married. And she and her new husband were to spend the first night in Sunbury before going on to Atlantic City. And we knew about it, and, I'm sorry to say, took advantage. We left the wedding party and went on to the hotel ahead. I pretended to be the bride and Billy Turner was the groom, and we went up to the desk and got the key, registered and everything. Now that's really awful, you know. And we went up to their room and made a pie bed. And unpacked their cases, and — oh, the pajamas, I shouldn't laugh, but I've never seen anything like them. All striped, every shade of the rainbow."

"Joseph's coat," said Reverend Highrider.

"And then rushed out. And this friend, Helen Fague now, but don't you breathe a word of this — well, she said to me, years and years later, that I'd just spoiled her honeymoon. I don't know what made her think of it after all that time. She just came up to me at a party once. And I was so sorry I could have wept," Mrs. Tennyson insisted. "I said to her, I never meant any harm, Helen, and I don't think you should let it eat away at you like this."

"But that's the heart of it, isn't it," said Reverend Highrider. "We can forgive but we can't forget. Now if she could just see it as childish. Thoughtless, but without malice; insensitive but certainly not intentionally cruel."

"Well, not cruel really," said Mrs. Tennyson. "She's just an awfully serious person. Needed a bit of fun, don't you think?"

They had arrived at the door.

"You can't see the bride," Eileen cried out from the kitchen, and stuck her head around the door. "I thought it was Edwin," she explained when she saw them. "Hello, Lou, come on out. Mother won't trust me to do anything. Go in and sit down, Reverend Highrider. Help yourself to some punch. The bowl on the left isn't spiked."

The girls followed Mrs. Tennyson into the kitchen. "Mildred Sprout, you aren't even dressed," Mrs. Tennyson cried, and Mrs. Sprout said, "Oh, Lou, I'm too nervous, got to keep busy. Oh, don't they look sweet!" catching sight of Mary Ella and Rhoda. "Oh, you little sweethearts! It'll soon be your turn, just a few more years."

"A bit longer than that," said Mrs. Tennyson.

"That's right, take your time. Oh, I hope they're spared what my girl went through," and Mrs. Sprout began to wipe her eyes.

Mrs. Tennyson said, "Why don't you girls go out on the porch where it's cooler," and gently pushed them toward the kitchen door. "You're just in the way out here."

On the porch they sat close together on the railing, not talking. The living room had looked so small, the chairs crowded up against each other. The thing about a church was that the singers were far enough away from the audience so there was an obliterating space between them: no face was distinct.

After a while Rhoda said, "I think sometimes maybe I won't do this anymore. I think we're getting too old for it. I really don't like singing this stuff, do you?"

"No," said Mary Ella. "I don't like weddings so much anymore. I mean, everything is supposed to be so secret and you aren't supposed to know things, but then they act so silly sometimes. Everyone knows why people get married."

"Sex," said Rhoda. "You can have love without marriage."

"We couldn't just come out and say that, though, could we? We won't sing because —"

"It's too sexy," said Rhoda, and their nerves gave way, laughing they clung to each other, helpless.

From the doorway Eileen called, "Well, let me in on the joke," and came out onto the porch.

Fifteen years older than they, she still liked to play at being one of them. She had let them try on her wedding dress, even before she herself had worn it as a bride, even before there had been the clear prospect of a wedding. Hearing that no more wedding gowns would be made for the duration of the war, she had immediately purchased one. A year later she had found the groom, but in the meantime the dress had hung in its cellophane wrapper on the back of her closet door. Once she had invited them up to her room, and closed the door, and said solemnly, "I am going to let you try it on." First Mary Ella, then Rhoda, had been carefully buttoned into satin, been veiled, and led to the full-length mirror in the upstairs hall. Afterward they had confessed to each other their feelings: it had been like seeing a ghost, featureless and remote.

But if this apparition had not forearmed them, Eileen's varied experiences and advice might. They tried her lipstick and eyeshadow, followed her advice on skin care and how to talk to boys; listened, fascinated, to her accounts of dates, proposals, close-calls; took quick looks into the marriage manual she allowed to lie forthrightly on her night table. She said they could read it straight through when they were sixteen. She said, right to Mary Ella's mother, that in this day and age every girl ought to know what's what and that was better protection than a lot of do's and don'ts.

Wishing to distract Eileen, and to compose herself, Mary Ella asked politely, "What's your mother wearing?"

"Dusty pink," Eileen answered promptly. "Fox neckpiece, long white gloves, small hat with veil. Corsage of gardenias, double strand of pearls, beige pumps. Because of her weight she can't wear bright colors or large prints. No big hats because she's so short. And no dresses with well-defined waists." Eileen had a book called *Dressing for Your Type,* and was also an authority on disguising figure problems.

Now Mrs. Tennyson appeared in the doorway. "Girls," she said, "Mrs. Sprout wants to see you upstairs. She has a little token for you." The moment was upon them. They had no time to exchange looks, but went along.

Mrs. Sprout was standing in her slip, rubbing the rouge carefully along the curve of her cheek. When they entered she threw her arms around them, gave each a kiss, stood back and looked at them, kissed them again. "So young," she cried. "Enjoy it, enjoy it. And I want to give you something to help you enjoy it. I thought and thought — Eileen had all sorts of ideas — but finally — " she went over to her dressing table and picked up two envelopes. Money. They were going to get money. They took the envelopes, but did not dare open them until Mrs. Sprout laughed and said, "Go ahead, go ahead." Inside each envelope there was a little card with love from Mildred and Edwin; and a ten-dollar bill. Gasps, speechlessness, then stammered thanks. "This is far too much," Rhoda said bluntly. "Nonsense, you darlings, oh, you're like having my own little girl back. I just want you to promise — promise me, now, a sacred promise — that when you fall in love and plan this big step you'll let me know. Promise I'll be at your weddings. Now, promise. Oh, it's the biggest thing in life, let me tell you."

They were saved from promises by a knock on the door, then Mrs. Tennyson, all smiles, coming into the room. "My, you two look happy," she said, and looked around for the boxes. "What's made you feel so good?" Mary Ella held out the bill. Mrs. Tennyson went on smiling, but looked rather sternly at Mrs. Sprout and said, "You shouldn't have done this, Mildred. They just sing for the fun of it. Just a little something to remember the occasion by."

"Now today I do as I please," said Mrs. Sprout gaily, and took the dusty-pink lace dress off its hanger. "Who's going to snap up the bride? Oh, where's my garter? Do you know what? This morning Eileen said to me, she said, 'Mother, will you do something for me, will you wear the garter I wore on my wedding day?' Wasn't that something? Where is it?" Rummaging, she found it, forced it up her leg. "Tight," she said. "Well it won't cut off the circulation too much if I just wear it an hour."

"You two go down now," said Mrs. Tennyson. To Mary Ella: "Your father's come."

Below them they heard voices. Terror returned. They descended single file, slowly, holding back. Mary Ella saw her father, but he did not glance at her. She and Rhoda took their places beside the piano, and watched for Mrs. Tennyson to descend. She came down the stairs quickly, smiling this way and that, nodding to her husband; then she sat down at the piano, looked at the girls, struck the first chord. She was to play softly through one verse first, then they were to come in. Too late to avoid the mistake, they began to sing, one note behind her. She paused a moment, gave them an encouraging smile, took up where they were. They sang so softly they believed they were not singing, half leaning against each other. In the small room their voices slipped in behind cushions and curtains and under rugs, absorbed by the furniture; gone the great open space before them of the church. "Louder," Mrs. Tennyson breathed, still smiling. Mr. Tennyson coughed, the half dozen ladies smiled and smiled. They finished "Oh Promise Me," took up "I Love You Truly." Their breathing eased, Mrs. Tennyson's shoulders relaxed, the voices found their harmony. Mary Ella thought, I shall never sing again.

They came to the hymn. Mrs. Tennyson's eyes always filled at this point, but it didn't matter; she knew this one by heart. Hearts cold as stone, they sang through it. Then, their part done, they went and sat on two straight chairs in the hall. The bridal march began, Mrs. Sprout appeared at the top of the stairs on the arm of her daughter. They had to part to go down, Eileen first, winking at Mary Ella, at Rhoda, at Mr. Tennyson. He winked back; Mary Ella stared, shocked. Mrs. Sprout reached out and patted the girls as she passed.

And so they were all there: Reverend Highrider, prayer book open, smiling, composed; Eileen, gay, head high; Mrs. Sprout, gently nodding at everyone in the room. Not quite all there: the groom with his best man was missing. They were to have appeared through the kitchen door. But there was no sound from the kitchen. Mrs. Tennyson kept on playing. Organists are employed as much to cover lapses as to make music. Desperately she played; then flung a look over her shoulder, caught by Mr. Tennyson, who got up gravely, went through to the kitchen, returned in a moment with the groom and his best man. "The cinnamon buns," Edwin said. A pause, and matters drove to their practiced conclusion: Mrs. Sprout became Mrs. Doty, the ring was placed, the kiss exchanged, the music began again, then stopped abruptly as there was no place for bride and groom to go. They remained where they were and received their congratulations.

Mr. Tennyson went up to his daughter and Rhoda and asked

them to eat lunch with him. "That's how it's done," he said. "The gentleman sizes things up, picks out his choice or choices, and feeds them up. Go out on the porch and save me a place."

He brought them plates of food and some of the cranberry punch. Sitting between them on the swing, he said, "It's time you gave this up. I can't attend many more weddings." They showed him the ten-dollar bills. He looked thoughtful, then said, "I may reconsider." Mrs. Tennyson appeared and said, "Oh, here you are." She saw the money. "I knew your father wouldn't like that. Do you think they ought to give it back? Or give some to the church?" Mr. Tennyson said, "No. Sit down and let me get you some food." She said there was still too much to do, and went back into the house. In a few minutes he got up and followed her. "I'll just see that your mother gets something to eat."

When they could eat no more, they went to inspect the gifts. They were, for the most part, documentary: the choir had given a silver plate, all members' names inscribed; the Rotary Club a silver beer mug, more names; from the Bridge Club, a pair of bon-bon dishes, initialed, dated; from the church, where Mrs. Sprout-Doty had always been a member of the Altar Guild, a plate with a colored engraving of the church front. There were a few housewifely items: a pair of linen sheets from Mrs. Tennyson, saved from her own trousseau, no longer available in stores now, thanks to the war; a damask tablecloth and napkins; a martini pitcher with little glasses, which would do nicely for orange juice. The girls were able to take it in with a glance. Nothing remarkable, nothing to learn from any of it. They went out through the kitchen, thinking to sit on the back porch until the cake was cut, and work out the spending of their fortunes.

In the small kitchen all was confusion. The scorched cinnamon buns remained stuck to their pans, and dirty dishes were piled around the sink. They went on through to the porch, screened in, hidden under honeysuckle and morning glory.

"We probably ought to save some of it," said Rhoda. "Buy savings stamps."

Tired from their morning, they sat silent, waiting. After the cake cutting there would be the cake eating; then the bride would go up to change and Eileen would pass out the rice or confetti. After that, a wait; then, running after the couple and shouting and throwing the rice; then collecting the little boxes of cake to sleep on, and that was the end. There was nothing to look forward to. Long ago they had given up hoping to dream while their heads rested on wedding cake. "At least nobody cried," Mary Ella said, after a bit.

But she spoke too soon. Through the kitchen window, high over their heads, at that instant they heard a sob; not a stifled one, but loud as a hiccough. It was a sob too loud and deep for a woman. Rhoda got up on her chair and peered through the curtained window. "It's Edwin," she hissed. "He's bawling."

They were too surprised to move. The sobs increased, unselfconscious as a child's. Neither of them had cried that way for years and years. "What shall we do?" Mary Ella whispered, and wondered where her father was. They began to giggle, then, confused, stopped. "It's really awful," said Rhoda. "He doesn't know we're here." The sobs went on until they heard Eileen's voice saying, "For goodness sake, Edwin, what's got into you? Mother wants to cut the cake." Now the sobs became a kind of gulping, but did not altogether stop. "Now look here," said Eileen firmly, "you're not going to ruin this. Now just pull yourself together. Why, you act like getting married wasn't your idea all along. Now what are you afraid of, I'd like to know."

"I — just — I don't know — know how it happened," Edwin managed to get out. "I'm not sure — sure it's right."

"Well this is no time to think of that. You just come right out here and cut this cake. After all my mother's been through. And you, too, for that matter."

"I do love her," Edwin cried. "But I'm not sure I can do right by her. Or you. I just don't know."

"That's all right," Eileen said in a kinder voice. "You just got worked up. But I want you to know that this is your home now as far as we're concerned, and I expect you to treat it as such. And make Mother happy. Now come on, wash your face. The cake has to be cut, and that's all there is to it. You'll feel better once that's over."

Someone ran water in the sink, there was splashing around. Then Edwin's voice: "I'm not used to strong drink."

Eileen laughed at that and said, "Why there wasn't more than one single bottle of wine in that whole punch bowl, Edwin Doty. You've just got bride jitters," and she hooted.

In a minute the kitchen was quiet. Rhoda got back up on the chair to make sure they were gone. Then, without a word to each other, the two girls went into the house, through the kitchen, to where, with much laughter, the cake was being cut.

They never spoke of it. After supper Rhoda did not go over to sit with Mary Ella, Mary Ella did not go to Rhoda. She went instead into the back yard and sat on the swing that had been slung from the elm tree to celebrate her third birthday. It was much too low to the ground, her knees were nearly up under her chin. Pretty soon Eugene came around the side of the house with Toby, and sat down on the grass a little distance from her. "You want to go to the lake tomorrow?" he said, after a while. She answered, "Rhoda can't go swimming on Sundays."

"Well, I'm asking you. Grandma says I can have the car from after lunch till five."

She twisted herself around on the swing, then let it spin out. Once that had made her dizzy, almost sick. "My mother wouldn't let me go alone," she said.

Eugene threw a stick for Toby, but he refused to fetch it. "How was the wedding?" he asked. And then he lay back on the grass, and began to sing. He sang, his voice firm and clear, surer, warmer as the song progressed:

> "Oh, promise me that someday you and I
> Will take our love together to some sky;
> Where we can be alone and faith renew,
> And find the hollows where those flowers grew."

He sang right through to the end. She had not known he could sing; only to make fun had he ever sung before in front of her. This, she thought, is how it ought to sound; not the way she and Rhoda must. That never brought tears to her eyes. But they rose now, into her throat, her nose, her eyes. He finished and sat up and grinned at her. She gave herself a violent push, and swung up toward the lowest branch. Above her head the grandmother's voice called once, sharply: "Eugene!" He answered, "Coming, Grandma," stood behind her, waited for her to sail back, gave her a tremendous push that sent her up high enough so that her toes brushed the leaves. When she came down to earth, he and Toby were disappearing around the house.

Her father came out on the back porch. He came across the lawn, stopping to look at the peony bushes; then on toward her.

He came up behind her and began, gently, to push her. She could just remember: now we go to Chicago, and now to California, and now — China! And then, very nearly, she would sail right up over the tree limb. He pushed her now, carefully; the tree branch creaked, and he said, "You're too big for this," but went on pushing for a while, back and forth, back and forth.

EDWARD M. HOLMES

Drums Again

(FROM THE VIRGINIA QUARTERLY REVIEW)

ALL THE TIME I was on the phone trying to talk with Karl Anderson, up to Ellsworth, saying "Who?" and "What?" and Karl trying to
tell me, Marie had this thundering and then quiet thing on her record player, full of horns, drums, pauses, and no tune, and sometimes just the deep, gentle *th-r-umb* of one of them big drums that
make a man shiver. Through the window I could see the mast-
high spruces sway and bend in the gale, and hear the snarl of
wind beating against shingles and clapboards, and behind the
music I kept seeing the winter seas hurling themselves to death on
the boulders at Schoodic Point, like they was trying to destroy the
trees, the soil, and the little earth, and then that tense frightening
quiet between waves when the last one has rolled back and the next
hasn't struck yet.

"I'm only third selectman," I told him. "Why don't you call
Mace Gifford?"

"Out of town," he said.

"Well, then, Phil Ackerman."

"Gone to visit his daughter up to Portland," Karl said. "You
know, Easter weekend."

"Yeah, maybe I should have gone somewhere myself."

"Come on. What are you going to do about him?" Karl asked.

"The State will kick in a hundred dollars," I said. "You know
that."

"And the rest? There's laws about this sort of thing."

"Well, if it's got to cost more than a hundred dollars — "

"You can't do nothing decent at that price," Karl told me.

The horns came in again, soaring high and sharp like a gull wing-

ing above the surf; then there was one of them pauses — louder
than the music itself somehow — and then one deep, hollow boom
from a drum as big as half the earth, not loud, but threatening, like
it was announcing fate, and then again, the same boom, lonely and
solemn. And I shivered, and instead of the telephone and the window, I was seeing the rocks out to the end of Petit Manan when the
storms hurl themselves in off the Atlantic, towering up, up, black
and white, monstrous, like they would destroy trees, buildings, and
all life, soon as they could reach, and then toppling, thrashing at
the jagged rocks on the shore.

"It's plain you didn't know him," I said. "Suppose I'd said 'No':
would you have delivered him on my doorstep in a basket or something?"

That made Karl mad and he hung up. I stared out the window
a minute, watching the spruce branches bend in the northeast wind.
Then I stood in the doorway to the setting room where Marie was,
and her record player, Marie listening to that what-I-would-not-
call-music-at-all-really (no tune to it; only once in a while I remember a piece of it, can't help it), them sounds tearing into my blood
and flesh and raising pictures I am not used to, or anyway usually
push back out of sight. And Marie said, "What was that about?"

"Ralph Leighton. Dead," I said. "What is that thing you've got
on the player?"

Marie answered.

"I won't have you cussing at your age, at least not in the house,"
I told her.

"It means 'Twilight of the Gods,' " Marie said.

"What language is that?"

"German."

"I thought you was studying French," I said.

"So I am."

"Well?"

"We get this in music appreciation," she said.

Christ Almighty! High school is not what it was. And I thought
of Christine, like I often do, and what life was like for her, what
there was of it, until Marie's birth, and what mine was like. Well?
And Ralph Leighton's . . . ?

Back there in October on one of them bright, chill days, I had
stopped in at the town office to pretend to ask Mace Gifford what

there was I could do, or ought to do, in the way of town business, but really just to remind him that he wasn't running the outfit all by himself. I could hear Mace talking even before I reached the door, and see Phil Ackerman balanced on the edge of the office desk.

"So I went to his sister Amy over to East Point," Mace was saying. "You know: the one with the crinkly black hair looks like a feather bed with a belt around it — and I says: 'He's your brother, ain't he?' And she says: 'That's right.' 'Then are you going to care for him?' 'I'll care for him cheaper than anyone else,' she says. 'I'll go halfway on expense and I don't know but more. But before I do it, you'll have to find me a rent with running water.' 'Is that so?' I says. 'Yes,' she tells me. And I ain't found no rent that's plumbed, and I ain't going to find none that's plumbed neither, because they ain't any."

"Who is all this about?" I asked.

"Ralph Leighton. The damned fool had a stroke."

"You can't very well blame Amy for wanting running water, not to care for an old fellow," Phil said.

"Maybe not," Mace said. Mace has always expected the world to do exactly nothing for him, no matter what, and to be fair about it, he returns the compliment. "So there he is up in that camp of his to the West Side," Mace said. "I got Crow Carter's boy going in twice a day to build up the fire and get him water, but damned if I know whether he eats. Come to think of it, I don't even know if he lives. You fellows are younger than I am: one of you better go up there and find out."

His camp squatted in a dark hollow down away from the road. It was not very different from a hundred other shelters on back roads that I know about: the roof sagged; the walls bulged; the shingles were rotting on the vine — if that's where shingles rot — and the rusted metal stovepipe — an insurance underwriter's nightmare if I ever saw one — stuck out drunkenly from the roof. The door was partly open, for the frame was too warped to let it shut. I knocked, then pushed the door open and went in. There was Ralph, laying on what used to be called a sofa. His eyes was open; his mouth hung slack; his whiskers was growing.

"Ralph!" I said. "Ralph, how are you making out?" But he didn't speak. He didn't even move so I could tell whether he was alive or not. "You getting enough to eat?" I said. "The boy keeping the fire burning?" There was a fire in the stove. I could see it through the wide cracks, feel it. Ralph never budged. I watched him to see was he breathing or not, and he was; he was alive all right. Finally I left.

I recalled what Father used to say about Ralph, that there wasn't another man to match him on the East Coast, a man who would turn handsprings a quarter-mile from his house all the way down to the shorefront, pull a skiff two, three hundred feet over winter ice on the low-tide flats, row to his boat, and go out to haul a hundred or hundred and fifty traps in a day when that was about the physical limit. And for him, every day was a fishing day, no matter what. I had heard how he built fish weirs, two, three to a time ("Don't build just one weir, boys. You can't lose money fast enough! You got to do more than that.") How he quarreled with Cliff Evarts over shore privilege until either one of them was ready to fillet the other with a fish knife, and then one February he comes in from outside in a blinding northeast blizzard, and there is Cliff's boat broke down, with a burned-out bearing, and Cliff, who has been hearing the boats go in right and left of him, unseeing, unseen, for the last three, four hours, about ready to give up. Cliff begged Ralph to take him aboard and let go the boat — or so Cliff told it later — but Ralph says, "Not by a damned sight, by Jesus! You need that boat to make a living with, same as the rest of us." And Ralph passes him a line and they made a long, hard tow of it, the line parting three, four times when the seas yanked them apart, and each time it took them twenty minutes of cold, wet, numbing labor to get the line spliced and rerigged. It was near morning before they got into sheltered waters, and the next day Ralph was down to Cliff's house, offering half the use of his own boat, until Cliff's was out of the shop.

And Father told too how Ralph had gone off to Vermont or some such and come back with a young woman, but Father couldn't remember how many children came — whether it was eleven or thirteen — and how Ralph, or his wife, or both, brought them up hell-raising and working and learning, all three to once — the boys carpenters or mechanics or seamen or woodsmen, and the girls cooks or seamstresses or nurses or teachers — and give each of them a shove off the edge of the nest as you might call it, with some dollars in their pockets, whatever they could scrape together at the time, and how once launched, the kids apparently stayed afloat although never near home port because neither Ralph nor his wife had ever asked or even encouraged them to do that. So we stopped seeing them and kind of forgot they had ever existed, I guess.

So after a minute I went back to the phone, called Karl Anderson, and told him we would pay the extra hundred, or hundred and fifty even, if that was what was needed to buy a decent burial, whatever that meant, the day after tomorrow; and we would have a preacher there, and get somebody to dig the grave, and not only that, we would have another one to fill it up. Which more or less satisfied Karl, who almost pretended I hadn't been insulting.

And I figured that until tomorrow at least I could put it out of my mind, but that was a mistake, because three or four hours later, right bang in the middle of supper, the phone rings again, and this time it is Walter Farnum to tell me that two of them Leighton boys from North Torrance, Emmet and Dick, are taking stuff out of Ralph's camp and going off with it.

"Well, you're the constable," I said. "Go up there and tell them to stop."

"I will," he says. "But I want to have someone with me when I do it."

"What for?" I asked.

He was silent.

I coughed. "Well, all right," I said. "Stop here for me on your way up."

"I'll do that."

"What now?" Marie asked.

I told her about Emmet and Dick and what they were up to.

"And Walter's too chicken to go up there and stop them without you."

"He just wants a witness," I told her.

"Well, that's a nice way to put it," she said. She turned away and stared out the window. "Emmet and Dick — and their brother's body ain't hardly cold yet, is it?"

"I dare say not."

"And then they talk about teen-age guys," she said.

"Jim and Charlie?"

"Sure, Jim Adams and Charlie Blake."

Jim wore a helmet and flew low over the highways on his BSA, and Charlie, who brought Marie home from time to time or called to take her to a ball game or something important like Coke and

hamburgers, drove a battered stock car with roll-over defenses and a
flower decal on the stern: MAKE LOVE, NOT WAR.

"Who was it," Marie asked, "pulled that kid out of the harbor
the night he fell through the ice? And wasn't it high-school guys
that saved the firehouse?"

"I never said it wasn't."

"Well, there," she said.

About then we heard Walter Farnum's car out front, and I went
out to go with him up to Leighton's camp.

Emmet and Dick was at it all right, looking as crummy, as dis-
organized, and as pitiful as ever. Emmet was dragging a chair up
over the bank and getting ready to set it on top of a load of cultch
he had in the wheelbarrow; and Dick was filling a croker sack with
nut coal. Walter put his flashlight on them and told them they was
to put that stuff back where they got it, and put it quick.

"What for?" Emmet said.

"Because it's Ralph's," Walter said.

"Ralph's dead," says Dick.

"Don't think I don't know that," says Walter. "But it don't make
no difference."

Emmet put the chair down and sat on it. "We his brothers."

"I didn't see you doing nothing for him when he lived." Walter
took the badge out of his pocket and stuck it on his jacket, letting
the flashlight glint over it once or twice. "Anyway, it don't make
no difference: the town's got a lien on this camp, and the state
too."

I set out to tap Walter on the arm and tell him it would be worth
it to let them take the stuff if only they would stay over to North
Torrance one more year and be permanently off our relief roll, but
I didn't dare say it for fear they might hear me and move back into
town just for spite.

As slow as they dared, they unloaded and dragged everything
back, inch by inch. Walter latched the door to the camp, put a pad-
lock on it, and the key in his pocket, and after Dick and Emmet had
gone down the road wheeling their wheelbarrow and pulling a little
cart the three miles to North Torrance, Walter and I got back in his
car. I said something about giving Dick and Emmet a lift, but Walter said, "Where am I going to put the barrow and cart? And anyway, I won't have that much stink in the back seat."

Back at the house, Marie had finished the dishes and was doing her homework. She asked me what had gone on, and I told her about it. "Unh-hunh," she said.

"The funeral's day after tomorrow, and I want you to go with me," I said.

"Why?"

I stared past her and out the night-blackened window; there was nothing to look at. But I remembered Christine, and Christine cooking at the stove, and doing the dishes at the sink — that same sink — and then setting in the chair Marie was in now, writing a letter to her folks, or filling out her diary, or such a matter, and I said: "I'll be damned if I know why exactly, but I want you to do it."

"And you'll write my excuse to take to school?"

"I sure will," I said.

Next day the storm had moderated, and the glass, which had fallen like the bottom was dropping out of it during the storm, begun to climb at the same rate. Those of us that knew anything at all knew what to expect — a skin-flailing northwestern — and the day of the funeral it struck, bending the trees back toward the ocean, and enough to make a man stagger against it when he walked.

I had got Sarah Williams to read the service. She is a preacher who used to have a church out on one of the outer islands until her husband grew tired of isolation and moved in here to the mainland. I figured even if she did not know Ralph Leighton, she must have known men more or less like him out there in the offshore fishing villages, and I figured perhaps she was human as well as pious.

Karl Anderson's hired help and hearse was all tied up at other burials morning and noontime, so it was quite late when they got down to Oak Harbor with the body, and Marie had been in school all day and not missed anything.

Sarah Williams had tried to get the church up to the head of the harbor for the funeral, but there was more things against it than I could count: the place was locked, and no matter where you went, somebody else had the key; then it wasn't heated, and the light wasn't turned on, and I don't know what else. I set out once or twice to offer the deacons twenty-five dollars to see if that would unlock it, but I was afraid to risk the money; I thought sure they'd grab it. The result was Sarah said she would read the whole service out to the burying ground.

Mace Gifford gathered up Amy Standish, Ralph's sister, over to
East Point, stopped to pick up Marie and me, drove over to Sarah
Williams's, and once she was aboard, waited outside the Town Office. That was all there was, just the five of us, and I was not certain
Mace did not plan to put in his time on the town account. But
where none of the town had turned up, perhaps it would not be un-
just at that.

When the hearse arrived, Mace walked over to give the driver
directions, and we followed them, slowly, over the humped and
gullied road out to the cemetery on Fishhawk Point. Mace and I
helped Karl Anderson's boys and Tony Mason, our gravedigger,
who had been setting there waiting for us, to lift the coffin and
lower it. Then Marie and I and the others, except Sarah, stood to
one side, and Sarah, at the head of the grave, opened her leather-
bound black book and begun to read.

The wind blasted across the point; it whipped our coats and
jackets; it burned our cheeks, our ears, our eyes with the cold.
Marie stood beside me and I grasped her hand. Sarah Williams was
reading, but I did not hear the words. The sun was getting low,
those hundreds of thousands of miles away across the bay and beyond; and the wind was whipping the bay feather white and jagged
black. Suddenly what I heard was not just the wind, not just the
waves, not just Sarah — what I heard again was that music Marie
had played in the house two days ago, the horns soaring, like announcing a judgment, and then a pause, the deep drums again,
thr-u-u-mb, and a hollow silence.

"Know ye not that a little leaven leaveneth the whole lump?"
Sarah read.

Spray flew up over the rocks into the browned grass, and the
horns again, high and sharp, like a gull winging above the surf . . .

"For I am a stranger with thee, and a sojourner."

The soft, quiet pound, the *thrumb* of doom . . .

*"O spare me a little, that I may recover my strength before I go
hence, and be no more seen."*

The deep tones picked it up. They soared with the winds above
the spruces. I trembled and shook, but it was not with the cold.
Across the tortured bay, the sun, like blood, was crimsoning the sky.

*"One generation passeth away, and another generation cometh:
but the earth abideth for ever."*

All to once I see the *Simoon,* the herring smack from the canning factory, fighting her way west across that chop, into the sunset, driving west after a load of fish; and I remembered Charlie Blake was now deckhand aboard the *Simoon*. Whoever was at the wheel was giving her hell all right; she shot her prow up over the black, jagged seas just like a shark. Ralph Leighton . . . pine box . . . horns again, mightily sighing, and then the drum, like the last stroke . . .

"The sun also ariseth, and the sun goeth down . . . The wind goeth toward the south . . . it whirleth about continually . . . according to his circuits. All the rivers run into the sea . . ."

"Daddy, Daddy!" Marie was whispering to me. "You *hurt*." And then I knew I had been clutching her hand too tight, pressing it between fingers and palm. It was not what I had meant, and I let it go and put my arm around her shoulders.

"Ashes to ashes . . . dust . . ." A bit of frozen earth dropped from Sarah's hand. The wind careened, whistled, and across our faces snapped like a whip.

> *"Lord, have mercy upon us.*
> *Christ, have mercy upon us.*
> *Lord, have mercy upon us."*

Then a gull screamed, wings spread, high over us, like a wandering soul, and I knew the tears were rolling across my face, but I was damned if I knew exactly why. I picked up the shovel myself and put in the first scoop of crusted earth.

Back away from the grave, Mace waited, holding the car door open for us, but I told him we'd walk.

"You're sure?"

"We're sure," I said. And we walked along, after the car and the empty hearse, and for quite a ways we were both silent. Then the cars were gone; we were alone; and on the crest of the hill, a quarter-mile ahead, we could see our house, its southwest windows bright in the sunset, and I thought ahead to the warmth inside, the familiar chairs, and tables, and beds.

"What do you want for supper?" Marie asked.

"What've you got?"

"I'll pour you a glass of wine."

"Good."

"There's leftover biscuits."

"You call that a meal?"

"Boiled potato, pork scraps, corned hake . . ."

"Now you're talking. Come on. Let's run," I said.

We ran, and Marie of course ran ahead. Watching her, lithe, strong, blown by the wind, running still in the last rays of sunset, I thought suddenly and joyfully of Charlie Blake. The horns rose again through the gale and the swaying spruces, and I clenched my teeth.

Hit those drums; hit them again, solemn and deep and noble. Hit them, dammit . . . .

MARY GRAY HUGHES

The Judge

(FROM THE ATLANTIC MONTHLY)

THE MEXICAN'S NAME was Baille. "Pronounced 'Buy-ye,'" the Judge liked to explain with amusement, and for the past three months now, at least once every week, the Judge had driven out through the flat countryside to where the Mexican lived to try and make him sign some papers. So far the Mexican would not do it.

"You'd think I was trying to sell him snake oil," the Judge said. "The old charlatan. I can't help liking him. Last time he came out with the statement that he didn't even have any rights in the claim at all. Just after I had shown him, with genealogical charts, how I had traced him. He says he's Basque, but that's nonsense. The name is pure Spanish. You find it all over this part of the state and in northern Mexico, going back, with a few orthographic variations, for two hundred years. There were never any Basques around here."

The Judge would know. He knew about languages and races and the origins of people and their names. He had made a study of such things. He could speak five languages and read two more. He knew Baille personally, too, though it was only in the last year that he had come to know the Mexican well. "It's not that he's an important claimant," the Judge said. "His portion is one of the smaller ones. But when it is a question of the heirs in a petition against the States, then it looks better to have all the heirs file. He's the only one who won't sign. One hundred and twenty-seven depositions I've got, two of them from as far away as the state of Oaxaca, and a brief that is easily the most complicated ever submitted in this jurisdiction, and I'm held up by a country school janitor. It's good I can appreciate the humor of it. Nonetheless, time is getting short.

I must try to move him along this Sunday. I'll tell you one thing, if I have to drive out to that place of his many more times, I'm going to get the county to do something about that road."

Not the highway. The Judge did not mean that. The highway was fine; laid flat and dead straight on the ground, it fell before him across the countryside like a clap of thunder, splitting the gray brush in two. On Sunday afternoons it was usually empty, and the Judge's solitary car hummed along at the fifty miles an hour advised by the instruction book as best for breaking in a new car. They had offered to let him keep a state car when he resigned. "No, no," the Judge had said, "you know me better than that."

The first turn off the highway to Baille's came just beyond the railroad crossing. From there the Judge's car followed a gravel road past the country school where the Mexican was janitor. Beyond that there was a bend crowded by willow trees and then a sharp right turn onto a narrow dirt road. Dust spilled out under the wheels and rose up beside the car like a giant gray dog and ran around the curves with it, brushing against the bushes in the narrow places. When the Judge stopped at last before the Mexican's house, dust poured up and over and through the car and on ahead down the road before collapsing back down into the ground again.

The Judge spat out the window to clear his mouth and honked the horn once, then again. Nothing happened. He knew Baille would not come out. He honked again, longer.

"Baille," the Judge yelled out the car window. "Hey, Baille."

"You know, I took a Sears catalogue out there to him once. And a big black pencil in case he didn't have one. I told him to put a check by all the things in the catalogue he wanted, just go ahead and mark everything he would like to have, anything and everything, and to keep on marking, and I would tell him to stop when he had used up the money I could make for him in one single year. He wouldn't do it. He wouldn't even look at the catalogue. Wouldn't even open it."

The Judge sat in the car staring at the shack and rubbing his nose, which he did in a very distinctive way. He held his hand still and moved his head gently up and down, sliding his nose between his thumb and forefinger. It was occurring to the Judge that it would all be a great deal easier if the Mexican had more of the world's goods, for then there would be more places where pressure could be applied.

The Judge honked again, and called, "Baille," louder, but without really expecting any result. He got out of the car and started over to the gate. A short man, with most of his height from the waist up, the Judge walked with his back rigid and his big powerful stomach firmly leading so that he looked in profile like a chair being pushed steadily forward.

Around his feet two bulbs of dust spouted onto his shoelaces and his trouser legs and then settled back down on the tops and sides of his shoes when he stopped before the fence. It was a fence made of barbed wire and mesquite. The wire was a dull color, with rust exploding around the base of each barb, and the untrimmed mesquite posts were knobbed and twisted and so dried up that the old shallow, hand-dug post holes gaped open around them.

The Judge established himself by the main gate post to wait. He lifted a foot to rest it comfortably on one of the lower strands, but the wire twanged loose onto the ground, throwing the Judge forward.

"Damn," the Judge swore. And yelled, "Baille!"

"It's true that it is not precisely flattering to be kept cooling my heels outside his fence until it suits him to come out. I need my old bailiff to hail him for me. Still, they have a sense of dignity and pride, these Mexicans. It denies our tempo of doing things. They insist on time, they respect it. And let me make one other point: he has some strange, absolutely perfect sense of just when it is the right time to come out."

The Judge pressed his stomach against the gate, moving it back on the tripled loops of wire that served as hinges. His hand eased along toward the latch. From around a corner of the shack the Mexican appeared, walking quickly with little low steps that moved him over the bare ground with no up-and-down movement at all but simply a fast unbroken propulsion forward as steadily efficient as the towing along of rakes or harrows after tractors, or the dragging of dead things behind the low rear bumpers of cars.

He was a man in his fifties, and so short he was forced to tip his head back to look up at the Judge. When he did, the Mexican showed his face with all the flattest angles exposed, showed his quick blinking eyes and soft squashed nose.

"How can you stand the heat out here?" the Judge said in a friendly tone.

The Mexican stared at him with the wild surprise the Judge's lisping Castilian always brought to him, for how was it this man could go on sounding like a drunken bird every time he spoke?

"Doesn't it bother you?" the Judge said again.

"You don't like the heat?" the Mexican said finally, hopefully.

"I can take the heat. It's the dust I really don't like. I swear, if you don't start acting sensibly, Baille, I'm going to get this road blacktopped."

The Mexican peered in amazement at the thin dirt road running along his fence and beneath the Judge's car, for the Judge had just announced that he intended to take an oath to do away with the road in darkness with a coating of perpetual obscurity.

"You don't like the dust then?" the Mexican said, trying again. "There is certainly much dust here. Much dust. You should stay in town. You stay in town, and I will come to visit you there."

"There is an innocence, or rather an obviousness that reminds one of innocence, in some of his ploys. At times it is terribly poignant. A touch . . . not of childishness, they are not childish, these people, he's a grown and very tough man, but a touch of the basic, unconcealed, open human being that can be very moving. Would any of you believe that I feel I have actually learned from him?"

"I think not," the Judge said to the Mexican. "I think not. You might forget to come. But I never forget, do I? And the Judge began to fan himself slowly, swinging his hat in wide arcs. His clothing was sweated through. "Listen," the Judge said, "why won't you trust me? All I want is to make some money for you. Why won't you do what I tell you?"

"Don't think the irony of it has escaped me. Mrs. Easterbury reminded me only the other night that I was the one who got him his job. Otherwise he might not even be around here. Well, I don't regret it. He came to me for help about two years ago. I'd hardly spoken to him before, but he knew who I was, so of course I had to help him. His wife had just left him, and he had some scheme in mind, some absurd plan for getting her back. I got him the job as janitor. I told the school board he would never steal. I took the responsibility for that and gave them my assurance, and he never has stolen a thing."

"No papers," the Mexican said, shaking his head. "No papers for signing. Absolutely no."

"You can sign your name," the Judge said. "I've seen it written down at the courthouse."

The Mexican neither moved nor spoke, but the Judge became instantly alert, for he knew, just as he would have in a courtroom, that the Mexican was running inside, running and running while he was standing still. The Judge was sure of it.

"What's the matter with your name on the records?" the Judge said. "Hm? What's wrong with it?"

"Nothing, nothing," the Mexican said. "It's my mother's name for me, why not? So if you don't like it, what will you do? Shoot me?" And he burst into a fit of giggles snuffled out against the back of his hand. For the phrase in Spanish was *Fuegame*, and it could mean either "fire me," as from a job, or "shoot me," as with a gun. Months ago when the Mexican had first said it, the Judge had been so delighted he had laughed out loud, and after a few seconds of uncertainty, Baille had joined in, laughing harder and harder.

"Their humor. Even when used as the most pathetically obvious smoke screen, still it is always appealing. Superb, poised, and proud. It's dour and simple, yet with sophistication, too, and with that special cast of appreciating language. That's what I relish most of all, the gift of language that they have. You see it right from the earliest days of the nation's history and down through all the major shifts in the language itself. They have a racial genius for language. Do you realize that even the poorest, most uneducated Mexican uses the subjunctive tense?"

"*Fuegame,*" the Mexican said again, giggling behind his hand.

"Maybe, maybe," the Judge said. "Or better than that, if you don't act sensibly, I might have a look at those records in the courthouse. The ones with your name." He said it pleasantly, and aware that the expression on his face was one of brightness and humor, with his eyes twinkling, yet he wanted a threat in his words, and there was. The Mexican was running again inside.

"How old are you?" the Judge asked suddenly, trusting it was the right question.

Intelligence flicked and vanished in the Mexican's face the way a lizard's tail slips away between sun-baked rocks, and the Judge was left gazing at the place where understanding had been. And slowly, with exquisite precision, the Judge's mind eased open and gave up to him his secrets in the order in which he needed them: the Mexican's age did not match his name. This Mexican's age was decades short of what was needed to match those yellowing, smudged courthouse records. He had "bought his name," as the Mexicans put it, and his papers were forged.

The Judge was home free.

"I was reminded of the last will and testament of one of the first Spanish conquistadores. 'Before us,' he had written, 'there was no evil, now there is no good.' A moving sentiment, but is it history? The Aztecs could not have been conquered if the majority of the Indians in the Valley of Mexico had not joined Cortez' crew precisely because the Aztec rule had been so cruel; so evil, indeed, that they were willing to follow anyone else in order to overthrow that rule. Our Spanish testator erred in the way we all do — what we do not understand, we always simplify."

"Has the Sheriff ever looked at those records of yours in the courthouse?"

There was no more running now inside the Mexican, just the quick blinking of his eyes, the rabbit caught, and waiting.

"You look to me, Baille," the Judge said, "like a man who may have himself some trouble."

The Mexican waited.

"Listen," the Judge said, "I could go on away from here right now without any signature of yours on any papers. I don't need it. I can prove from the records in the courthouse that I don't need it. But I'm not going to do that. I've made up my mind to help you. I know all about you, and you'll have to do what I say. Do you understand?"

"It would be all right if you went away from here now," the Mexican said. "You can do that."

"Don't think it is just altruism on my part," the Judge said. "If I don't get your signature on the papers, it will not look right, because there are people who know your name should be in this case. So if you do not sign, I will have to explain why you did not, and I will have to tell about your records. Do you see? I will have to tell, and then the Sheriff will know about you, and then he would come for you. Understand?"

The Judge set himself to sound absolutely commanding, and it was easy because he had come to that key moment when he knew he was winning and was enjoying his skill at closing a case.

"Now, you go on in there and change your clothes," the Judge said firmly. He knew better than to give the Mexican any time. "I am going to take you with me into town to sign those papers." The

Mexican's fast-blinking eyes kept wavering away, glancing off toward the road and the brush around. "Oh, yes," the Judge said, "yes, right now. You go put on something else, something cleaner that you can wear to the courthouse. Go on. Now. And while you're changing, I'll go take a look at your lake."

"Mud pond — that's what I usually call these unimproved water holes when I'm not trying to be nice to the people living near them. Little indentations in the ground they are, no deeper than the hollow in a beggar's palm and filled with thick brownish water evaporating away from the muddy banks. Often one end will go deeper, keeping a permanent water supply, and willows grow up all around it. Any of you noticed these little ponds? Ah, you should. These sites are going to be worth good money one of these days."

The Judge crossed the road and walked alongside it, and the soles of his shoes snapped down the brittle grass that grew and burned and grew again out in the sun beside the road. Once into the shade of the willow trees the grass thickened and made a soft cushion under the Judge's feet. He went straight to the deep part of the pond. As he went he kicked in the reeds and fallen tree limbs for frogs or turtles or any signs of the small animals that exist in the banks near water. Just at the end of the pond, there was a little rise of ground. It was not more than three feet high, but in the midst of the violent flatness of the countryside around it seemed higher, and the Judge, coming out from the fringe of willows and putting aside their frail branch tips with the side of his hand, pulled himself up onto it with his short legs and felt he could see a long way, felt he could see for miles. He looked across the pool to the low brush beyond and the dense trees of pale green and gray on the other side. He would have been embarrassed to say how stirred he was by the countryside, or how much beauty he saw in the tangle of mesquite trees growing in a solid cloud on their thin, crooked trunks. He would not have wanted to tell of a game he played, when he was out in the country, of letting his eyes rise only slowly, slowly along the low line of brush and small mesquite, and inch by half-inch go along the solid mass, then slowly lift to the first few broken spaces in between, and moving faster, a little faster and rising again, up and farther along, and going with joy now, joy, up and faster and off over mesquite and willow to the horizon and the dumb unbelievable idiot palm trees grinning like God, he told himself, over the long flat landscape running beneath them all the way to the sea.

"It wasn't easy. I tried just about everything on him. I made three trips out to the school to see the principal, and I made sure each time that Baille saw us together. That preyed on him. He would hang around in the hall pretending to sweep out but watching us. That fool principal spent all the time carrying tales to me against Baille. He told me the Mexican sneaks the lock shut on the boys' washroom once a week or so, and then hangs around in the hall to watch the fun. I was supposed to be shocked at this. Especially shocked because Baille thinks it's funny. The principal is naive. He doesn't understand their humor. More than that, I think it bothers him that I like Baille. He can't understand why I want to help him. At heart, the principal has no feeling for them."

The Judge's attention was caught, by a sound? a smell? and he turned his head and the Mexican was there beside him. The Judge opened his mouth to speak, thinking to ask why the other was in the same clothes and had not changed, when all at once the whole of the Mexican — body, head, shoulders, arms, legs — came leaping into the Judge and jolted him so hard that he hurt all through his body. The two of them fell, not backward and so down the slope of the little hill and into the shallow water as the Judge thought they would and the Mexican intended, but straight onto the muddy lip at the deep edge of the water, just below where the Judge had been standing. For the Judge had been felled absolutely, had had his short legs collapse right under him and had fallen with the Mexican on top of him. They rolled from side to side on the muddy ground, and the willows shaded them some of the time, and the position of sky and lake and trees kept shifting in their line of vision.

All the time the Judge kept grunting and trying to get his breath to say something like: but this is an accident and I accept your apology for stupidly and clumsily and accidentally knocking into me; I understand; while the Mexican pulled at the Judge's head and shoulders trying to haul and shove him further forward into the water, deep enough to cover his head and face entirely. Reeds at the water's edge snapped beneath the Judge's head, and a rock under his shoulder made him arch his back up in pain as he tried to roll free from the Mexican's hands which fled from his head and face back to his arms and tugged and pushed at him again, moving him forward once more, further into the water.

This time the Judge realized what was happening, and focused his eyes finally on the Mexican's face close above his own. The Judge's body jerked rigid and then turned frantic with terror. He grabbed at the Mexican's wrists, uselessly, then tried to get a hold anywhere on the skin that was thin and taut over muscle and bone, and not able to do that, clutched at the worn overalls, but he could not grasp hold of the Mexican in any way. "Knee him in the groin, knee him in the groin," yipped some part of the Judge's mind, delighting him with his own tough knowledge. But his legs thrashed foolishly and uselessly up and down, miles, it seemed, away from the Mexican straddling his chest. The Judge could not even kick the man in the back. The Judge pulled again, and again with no effect, at the Mexican's small hard wrists. With a hiss the Mexican shoved and slid him another few inches into the water and once more tried to submerge the heavy, golden head. There was not enough water, simply not enough water, and in a rage of despair the Mexican grabbed the Judge's head and pressed it deep into the mud. The shallow sludge filled the Judge's left ear and shut one eye, and the nostril on that side was plugged as solidly as by a finger. But the Judge's entire head would not go under. His free eye saw a reed inches in front of his face. It seemed gigantic, the strands that formed it long and beautifully green, and the edges of it the most incredible sharp yellow. The Judge strained toward it, moving with great effort, his head rising out of the mud and water. The Mexican hissed by his ear and got a different grip under the Judge's shoulders and hauled him forward again, deeper into the water. The Judge could feel mud under his shoulders now and dampness down to his waist, and water washed against his neck and up to his ears. With a deep grunt of satisfaction the Mexican pushed the Judge's head down again, hard, and this time the whole head and white face went beneath the water.

It was shocking. The Judge's eyes shut at first, but his ears heard all the sounds water takes in from the air but does not give back to it. He could hear hands thrashing in the water, and the sound of the Mexican's voice cursing. He opened his eyes, and he could see the Mexican, could see everything; it was there, but changed because of the layer of water over his face. The Judge went limp and the Mexican, too ignorant, too eager (*"Poor son of a gun. They're so often like that, defeating themselves by lack of experience or lack of self-control"*), pushed forward too fast, thinking it was over, thinking to finish it, rushing, and so rising up on the Judge's neck too high and getting himself off balance for just that instant (*"Timing has always been one of my greatest courtroom assets, you know"*), so the Judge gave a heave of his powerful stomach and short legs and rolled up and over his own shoulder, tossing the two of them backward, half-somersaulting, and crashing through the reeds and over the muddied lip of the pool and down into the clearer, deeper water. Wet now to hip, to chest, and at any minute over the head possibly, but the Judge was not to know, for the Mexican had turned and flung himself at the shore, crying out for it, lunging back to the bank with the Judge hanging on around his hips while the Mexican grasped and tugged on the reeds, pulling great, sucking chunks of them out of the mud and lunging back again at them and seizing thick sheaves of them in his hands. And all the time the Mexican kept making hoarse, gasping noises, steadily louder, until with a burst of strength he tugged the two of them out of the lake and plunged onto the muddy bank where they fell crushing the reeds down into the mud.

The Judge propped himself on his knees but kept hard hold of the Mexican as they panted side by side. Streaks of mud curled down the sides of the Judge's face. "Listen," the Judge gasped. "Listen." But he could not get enough air for the words. He was bursting, bursting with joy. He had had a fight. He, the Judge, at his age, had had a fight, like any man, and with a Mexican.

"Listen," the Judge said, holding on to the Mexican's arm just under the shoulder, holding tight, lovingly. "Don't be frightened," the Judge said. "I understand. I am a man, too. I won't bring any charges against you for that. I know how you feel. I won't call the Sheriff. Understand? I know you had to fight."

"Have you ever seen a Mexican cry? A Mexican man, I mean? A grown man? Not the way we do, but with a little 'hee hee hee' noise. Sitting back on his heels with his head pressed against his knees and crying 'hee hee hee,' like that. Just like that."

"See here. Now, see here," the Judge said. "It's going to be all right. It's going to be fine. You can trust me."

The Mexican would not move or lift his head from his knees.

"I'll come out here tomorrow," the Judge said. "At ten. Ten in the morning. And I'll take you to town. And I'll call the principal personally and explain to him that you won't be at work so you won't have any trouble there. You be ready at ten sharp. Understand? Then you can sign those papers. Look, it will be fine. Fine. Don't be scared. Don't . . . don't make noises. Please. Don't. Why listen, listen, you may have . . ." and he stopped. "Saved my life," the Judge wanted to say, but inexcusably he could not remember the verb "to save" in that sense is Spanish. "You may have kept me from drowning," he said. "Saved my life," he remembered, "that's it. You may have saved my life."

The Mexican at least stopped making the noise. The Judge shook his arm in comradely fashion.

"That's right. That's right," the Judge said. "See?"

"No, of course we didn't shake hands. They don't make agreements in that fashion. But by an old, mutually understood joke I became his attorney. Yes, that's it, that's the truth, I was made his counselor by humor, and to be honest, I don't have a better contract, I can swear to that. It was an extraordinary experience; he's an unusual man. All the same, I think I may take up judo on the side if my practice continues in this way."

"Of course you understand now," the Judge said. "Certainly. You probably saved my life, and so I want to help you, too. I'll come out here for you tomorrow at ten. Ten in the morning. You be ready. Hear? You be ready, or I'll have to go get the Sheriff to shoot you. Our joke. Right? Ha ha. Our joke."

In the morning the Judge changed his mind. It seemed to him the best and most courteous thing would be to save the Mexican the trip into town and to the courthouse. Instead, the Judge decided to take his secretary, who could act as notary, and the necessary papers, and go out into the country and let the Mexican sign the papers there. The Judge liked the idea of the gesture. He would meet the Mexican more than halfway. And in any case, the Judge did not know how he and the Mexican, with the closeness that they had between them now, would manage in town, for the town was not ready for that yet.

The Judge went first thing, as he always did, to get his morning newspaper. The newsstand attendant was waiting for him. An obese man, he was squeezed into the narrow doorway of the shop with the Judge's paper held folded and ready.

"You heard?" the attendant asked eagerly. The Judge, as was his custom, dropped a quarter into the brass bowl although the paper cost only ten cents. The attendant kept hold of the paper until he could finish his story. "Haven't you heard? Really? They's a Messgun drowned in the river. Sheriff says it's one you know. Says you know him for sure. I was the second one down to the bridge to see him. I could see him plain as I see you. He was washed up nearest the American side, and he still had a bundle with his things in it tied around his wrist. He was curled up and lying real funny, sort of right on his head and knees, like a little brown snail, and down back of him there was a trail going all the way he'd come out of the river. Everyone wondered where his hat was, but I told him any idiot would know a hat would be the first thing to float on off. Isn't that the truth, Judge? Any idiot ought to know that. But you know something I don't get, how come Messguns don' learn to swim since they keep crossing back and forth in that river all the time? You'd think they'd learn to swim, I say. Now, you take my sister's boy, he's learned to swim good and he's only fourteen. If they'd have learned to swim, them Messguns, none of them would have never drowned."

The Judge stood on the sidewalk with his feet planted square and carefully apart. He had a wide staring look on his face as if an arrow had shot straight through him from back to front going at a great speed and he was looking way off in the distance after it for some vital part of him that was being taken away faster and faster and faster away over the long, flat Texas landscape. Then the Judge gave a sudden, violent jerk, as happens sometimes when falling asleep, or waking.

"So what I say," the attendant said, "is someone ought to teach them to swim. That's what I say."

The Judge turned and began walking away, stamping off with hard steps pounding on the sidewalk.

"Want your paper?" the attendant called after him. "Judge?"

The Judge did not answer. He was getting into his car. He turned it around in the middle of the street and started straight out into the country to the Mexican's home.

He drove the distance in the same way that he always did, at the same carefully restrained rate of speed. There were not even many other cars on the highway, and he got there in the same time that it took him on the quiet Sundays.

There was no sign of life from the shack or from the treeless area of dirt around it. The gate hung open, slanting crookedly onto the ground. The Judge turned off the engine of his car.

"Baille!" he yelled at the shack. "Baille!"

The Judge got out and slammed the door hard and began to walk through the sparse grass and the dust which heat and wind had worn to a powder. He walked cautiously, as if at any minute he expected to be struck lame by a stiffening in both knees, an affliction he had felt creeping up on him from a long time past and which he dreaded because he knew that like old rusted locks, it was something no oil or ointment or paid-for expert he might hire was ever going to loosen for him again.

"Baille!" the Judge yelled.

There was no point in standing still before the open gate. The Judge went through it into the yard where he had never been before. He walked toward the corner of the shack around which he was used to seeing the Mexican come. He supposed there must be some sort of door on the other side. When he turned the corner he saw a square black opening in the wall before him. "Baille?" he called again, when he had reached the door, "Baille?" and there being no reply, he lowered his head and plunged into the darkness inside.

There was no one there. The Mexican was gone. And the second shock was the size of the room. For somehow the Judge had always imagined rooms and rooms expanding within the small frame of the shack. In his mind the Judge had thought of the Mexican waiting for him while sitting in a living room or small reading room, with a kitchen off to his left somewhere and at his back a bedroom. The Judge had placed the Mexican there, sitting comfortably, reading perhaps, or walking around at his ease while he waited for the Judge to come so he could match wits with him again. But there was instead a square of space marked off by gray wooden boards and covered with a tin roof and with the bare ground underfoot. There were not even windows cut in the walls. Threads of light spun themselves down through gaps in the roof, and a block of light fell through the doorway like a hunk of wall collapsed onto the floor.

The Judge's eyes adjusted to the dimness, and he could see every part of the room. Quite obviously the Mexican was gone, gone and had meant to go. He had left a coat the Judge had given him, and a pair of pants the Judge had given him, and two black shoes the Judge had given him. But all the rest was gone except the heavy things he could not carry, a table made of railroad ties and next to it a three-legged stool; an old kerosene stove that was thick with rust; a brass bedstead with no mattress.

A cup, still half filled with coffee, was on the table, and the Judge put his palm against its side. It was cold.

"Damn him," the Judge said. He struck the cup a flat blow, lifting it up through the air to smash into the wall. "Damn, damn, damn him," and the Judge kicked the small three-legged stool. It rolled under the table. The Judge kicked one of the table legs, but the table stood firm on thick square legs. The Judge bent over and caught the edge of the table to upend it, but it would not move. He could not budge it. He tugged again, heaving on it, and when it still stood motionless he bent lower, his head just above its surface, and pulled harder, his mouth strained open with the effort and his face glazing with sweat as he pulled and pulled — and he was seeing through the bright sunlight his car just beyond the gate, and realized he had been seeing it for several seconds before he understood that it was possible, that he had been seeing it with that special clarity of vision given by a peephole, a tiny tear-shaped opening between two warped boards.

And he understood that the Mexican had seen him this way. The Mexican had sat there in the dark at this table and had seen him, the Judge; had watched and waited, all the time looking out through the little hole, and seen the car arrive and the Judge get out of it, and watched it all in a flood of garlic-smelling sweat and terror while his heart leaped and raced all over the place inside his frozen, terrified fraud's pose of stillness.

"Your simple Mexican has a grace of bearing and manner that is hard to believe if you have not seen it. Or experienced it, perhaps, is a better way of putting it. Let me give you an example. I drive up to his house, you see, and of course he hears the car, but first I have to sit and wait. There is to be no rushing. Finally, I get out and walk to the gate, and sometimes I call out to him. Nothing happens. Some ethnic formality of time has to be satisfied first, some proper amount of respect allowed for. Then he emerges and comes forward to meet me at the gate. But it is always just as I become restless and impatient, yet most receptive, that he appears. He comes when I am most alert, most open to meeting with him.

He knows this somehow. Then he comes forward, and every time it is done with pride."

"Damn him." The Judge slammed his palms down on the table so hard his cheeks quivered with the blow. "Damn him for a rotten fraud. Damn him." He leaned forward over the table with his arms braced stiffly straight on it. "Damn him to hell, I swear if I could I'd kill him . . ."

He stared straight ahead at the empty air, and slowly his body sagged down onto the thick black table. His hands slid across the rough surface to the opposite side so that he was half lying on it, almost embracing the wood, with his heavy stomach pressed against the edge.

"I wonder when he started packing?" the Judge said. "I wonder what he used to make the bundle — a second-hand gunny sack and some old begged-for, handed-down rotten piece of twine?"

The Judge's cheek rested flush against the table. Suddenly he stretched out his tongue and licked across a section of the surface, violently hoping it was thick with germs.

He raised his head, and drawn irresistibly, put his eye to the peephole and looked out again through the bright sunlight that was another dimension of his country, and saw his new blue empty chrome-iced car winking and flashing back at him.

"St. John of the Cross," the Judge said, "as we know perfectly well from the writings of Alonso de la Madre de Dios and the dissertation of the brilliant medievalist Jean Baruzi, made a point of choosing for himself the smallest, meanest, darkest cell in the monastery because he knew that from there, when he looked through the tiny window out over the fields of Spain, he would see visions. Visions."

ANN JONES

In Black and White

(FROM THE VIRGINIA QUARTERLY REVIEW)

PATRICIA WALKED through the empty house, finding herself alone in all of its comfort. She was the owner now, but loss surrounded her, footsteps echoed in her mind, eyes filled with patterns that were now a few ashes scattered over a mountain. Ben was gone, but the house didn't seem to know this. Objects waited for his touch. Clothes waited for his body. Cold white gin waited for his thirst. It was merciful that things could not talk. Although the real miracle, she decided, was that anything at all remained, as the day outside the house seemed to remain, warm and soft, edges shaped by morning shadow.

Another morning, other shadows had held the swift cutting of the catamaran through gray ocean water, just beyond the breakers, parallel to where she was walking on the beach near the school she was attending. The fog was coming in, touching everything with light fingers, and there the boy was, seen through the mist, brown skin in bright yellow trunks, lying stretched out on his side beneath the small sail, waving to her as though he knew her and had expected, maybe even hoped, to see her walking on this strip of sand between the water and the pressing rows of city houses. She had waved back, feeling something catch in her throat, surprised almost to the point of tears. And then he was gone, knifing through the gray water. It was right somehow, that none of these actions had made any more sound than the fog touching the sand. She remembered hoping that he would turn around and come back, but he hadn't.

Instead, it had been her father who had come jogging back toward her, the heaviness of his body concealed by the gray sweat shirt he wore over his black swimming trunks. Only his legs remained uncovered, huge and hairy, marked by blue veins that stood out on the bulging calves. He must have run three times as far as she had walked, never leaving her out of his sight, back and forth as a dog would run, up and down, up and down. He had certainly seen the boy on the catamaran.

He stopped running. "Friend of yours?"

"Oh, Ben."

He wiped his sweating forehead with the back of his sleeve. Goose pimples sprayed over his thighs. He began to run in place looking down at her. "You think I'm a bastard now, but you just wait, Patty. It won't always be like this. Your old man will take care of you and someday you will see that he was right. I promise." He slid his finger gently across her cheek and then he was gone, running slightly ahead of her.

Strange that she should think of this now, although some days she had the feeling that the truth of everything was locked into this type of fragment-memory, that all she had to do was relax and everything would be revealed. She thought that way today. She could walk anywhere through this day. She could do anything, without the imploring silences, the recrimination, the reproachful watching, and this in itself was a kind of revelation.

Barefoot, she stepped out the sliding glass door onto the stones of the terrace. She thought she saw Black Cat, her father's cat, watching her from the brush partway up the hill, but if it was him he didn't come when she called. Water slipped from tall rocks into the small pool beside her where reeds of horsetail rattled when the wind blew. Up above, on drier rocks, in more remoteness, lizards clicked their tongues in and out catching insects, or slid blue bellies down the rough-edged granite.

In her new freedom she left the house behind, walking down the game trail to the river, seeing the stark fire damage above her as she went. Tree skeletons stood out on the skyline, and rocks, like bones, showed through the blackened skin of the earth. It was quiet, almost peaceful. Even the song of the few birds that had returned seemed subdued. It was as though everything that was going to happen in her lifetime had already happened, leaving her alone in her survival to walk along the river if that was what she wanted to do. It was all she wanted to do. She walked and walked, her bare feet clinging to the rocks, snake-watching, mind-consuming, whatever she thought she might have become, escaping into the morning air as smoke had escaped above the ridge fire.

All day they had stood and wondered as the wind shifted and the fire came dangerously close to the isolated house. The professional fire fighters were lined in strategic places, their hard hats reflecting the strange light flickering through the smoke, barely touching the earth. She watched their faces change from pink to orange to pink again. It was a beautiful visual experience, seeing the look of Jason, for instance, so familiar and yet so strange, moving through this light as though a spell had been cast upon him. But who could cast a spell upon Jason? Nobody on this earth. He was beyond influence, and that was why years ago her father had chosen him for his one true friend. "Don't let the bastards screw you when I'm gone, Jason," she had heard him say not long ago. "You know how my negatives should be printed and that's the *only* way I want them printed. By God, I'd destroy them right now if I thought there was a chance some fool would pretty them up! They are all I have to leave Patty."

"You have the house and the stocks — "

"God damn it, man, you know what I mean!"

"Look, Ben. Granted, now that you put it that way, I do know what you mean, this time. But I don't always know. And I don't want to guess at something this important."

"Oh, for Christ's sake, Jason."

From where Patty had been standing, she could not see her father's face, but she had known the helpless bewilderment that would be showing in his eyes as he turned to his friend. It was showing more and more often lately, as though in dying, he was finally meeting something he could not understand. She could not bear the thought of him this way and had begun to cry. Both of them had come to her. She remembered looking between them through the windows to the floating tops of the newly leafed buckeye and oak shivering in the small wind of early spring, and she had let herself be comforted.

Fool, she thought looking back, *you* should have done the comforting. She looked down at her own skin and saw it was touched with the same pink light that was touching everyone, and somehow this pleased her, as though in spite of all her mistakes, she had been accepted. Jason looked up just then and shouted to her, waving. She laughed and waved back. He looked as excited as she felt.

In contrast to her father's almost rigid neatness, he had always had a wonderfully fluid appearance. He seemed to have the aura of a magician, in control of vast stores of arcane knowledge. No one, she least of all, could ever expect to know what he was thinking because everything about him was changeable, his expression, his moods, the sometimes clear, sometimes murky gray-blue of his eyes. Even the prominent bones of his nose added to this illusion. He was long-limbed and long-bodied. His skin had the rough, real, imperfect look of the outdoor man. Nothing of the plastic look for him, the smooth shave, the measure of cologne carefully placed. He was different. Although sometimes, and she hated these times, his skin would smell of the darkroom chemicals he had been working with and she would draw away from him in childish anger as though she had been betrayed.

The truth was she wanted him always the way he was in the fall, when the only thing he smelled of was the ripe yellow apples in his orchard. She remembered him in his blue overalls, leaning down, arms outstretched as the child she had been came running up the dirt road toward him, afraid but altogether willing to be swung high over his head in an indescribably exciting arc just beneath the yellow leaves of the apple trees. It was because of him that she and her father had finally settled in this canyon.

She watched while Jason and two other men moved through dreams toward the house aiming hoses limp with falling water pressure. Other men were running with shovels and heavy rakes breaking a path for the fire to die against if it should reach this far. Bulldozers roared further up canyon where high on the hill, burning debris would roll down through the rocks and trees, starting new spot fires as it went. The call echoed down to her: "Hot one!" and she moved around to the front of the house to see better. Just then, borate bombers roared in over the ridge dropping their smothering load, and the smoke shifted, rolling like a baited animal, now this way, now that. Huge oak trees, exploding in the heat as though set off by dynamite, shattered the air with a burning as beautiful as anything she could ever remember.

Her father had stood in the curved driveway, red-veined and expressionless, his stomach round and soft beneath his folded arms. He was looking uphill toward the fire and she thought he had not seen her coming up behind him, but he spoke without turning around, cutting into the excitement of the day. "Get the bar going, Patty."

People wandered into the house and she served coffee or made martinis for them, or gave them beer. She cut the fresh rye bread she had just baked and made corned beef sandwiches. She set out crackers and sharp cheese. The little glasses glinted in a party way on the counter between the kitchen and the dining room, and the house itself seemed warm and friendly, something to be cherished and loved at all cost. It was more important than ever, and they would have to save it.

Even a few local people, glasses in hand, drifting over the flagstone entry hall and down into the big living room, seemed to be looking at things with more than mere curiosity about the way they lived. Maybe they felt it, too, that the house was more than a house, although she knew it was still strange to them after three years, the way it floated out in a round curve over the edge of the hill, the way the glass walls made shining contours that reflected down into the furthest part of the empty canyon. Her father had always held open house on New Year's Day and they were careful to buy everything they could from the local stores, but a certain amount of sometimes contemptuous curiosity remained. She saw one of the men in the living room now nudge another man with his elbow and smile as they looked up at the intricacies of the polished wood ceiling.

She shivered, feeling as though someone had sneaked up behind her and put cold hands on her neck. Impulsively, she sipped a half-drunk, too-warm martini that had just been set down. Part of her was saying, "Kill it, fire! Kill the house!" and it was this realization that had chilled her. It was as though she had spontaneously seen the fire as an agent of release, a Prince Valiant of the spirit, and now she would never be able to deny it.

"Do you need any help, Patty?"

She jumped guiltily. Jason came around the counter and took the drink from her and poured it down the sink. When she picked up a knife to cut some corned beef he took that from her, too, his hand just for a second covering hers with the familiar comfort of his callused skin. She remembered all the walks the three of them had taken, her child-hands held firmly by theirs as they swung her along between them, lifting her over the rocks and puddles. She pulled her hand away.

"Don't drink slop, Patty. If you are going to drink, fix yourself a fresh one."

"How long have you been watching me?"

"Not long."

"Well, I don't like it, Jason!" she said angrily. "Sometimes I think he pays you to watch me."

"Now, don't be silly. A little paranoia is all right — but too much, and away you go." He did a little soft-shoe dance, the reflection of the mad-colored world shining in the window behind him.

She had to smile. "All right. All right, what do you want to say? You're wearing your lecture face."

"Just a small one today, Patty. Don't drink for the wrong reasons. It's a waste of good liquor. Do you know what I mean?"

"I know, I know."

"What I really came to tell you was that your father wants you in his studio. So get along, girl."

She found him alone in the finely lighted, white-walled room, his photographs on every wall. "I need your help, Patty. I think we should move these over to Jason's ranch just in case. The negatives are already there."

"Then why worry," she said before she could stop herself. "These are only prints and you can always make more of them. Anyway, I don't think the fire is going to reach us at all." Even to herself her last words sounded sad, as though she had been deprived of something.

"Well, little Miss Know-It-All," he said bitterly, shaking his head. "It just so happens that I don't want *any* of my things burned. So if you will leave the conjecturing to the professionals and bring me that box over in the corner, we will start right here."

She packed and repacked, as meticulously careful of every detail as her father required. The voices of tired men passing on the road above the house drifted down to them. Before Ben was satisfied, two hours had passed, with only the roar of the helicopter to punctuate the strange silence that had fallen between them.

That night, looking out the window of her bedroom, she could see the spots of fire on the hill as though a city of lighted houses and streets had suddenly been terraced into the night. And then a buck-eye or an oak would leap into flame, or a sycamore in the canyon begin to burn wildly, and it would become the enemy again or, she thought wonderingly, the friend.

She sat now on a rock, her bony feet slipping into the water. The river ran quietly. The air was soft around her. She leaned back, the arch of her spine sweating along the hot slanting rock. Sun burned into the lids of her closed eyes bringing kaleidoscopic designs of crashing, changing color. She loved color, although all of her father's work had been done in black and white.

"Why not color?" she had asked once. "Jason sometimes works in color. And even you say he's a good photographer."

He turned to her, looking up from his camera in exasperation. "He is not only good, Patty, as I have told you many times, he is a *fine* photographer, truly unique."

"I'm sorry, Ben," she said, speaking to the expression on his face. "I didn't mean — "

"Well," he interrupted, "it's just that God alone knows how many times I have told this to you. Maybe now you are ready to listen. I am not Jason. Color disintegrates images for me. I don't see things in color. It scatters. It widens — that is not to say broadens, or deepens. Black and white has a sense of limit, a kind of endless range of depth and tone, but always within limits. I can find infinity in your bones, Patty, if I look long enough."

"And I live long enough." She laughed nervously.

For just a second, anger lit his eyes and then he laughed with her. "Come on now. Shape up. We are in this together, aren't we? Have I ever made you feel you weren't a basic part of this team?" He left his camera and went over to the lights, adjusting them so they cast a knife-edge of shadow behind her leg. She felt it creating a reality far more important than the reality of herself, whatever that was. She was lost in it.

"Why me?" she asked suddenly. "Why do you so seldom photograph anyone or anything else but me?"

He was very patient. Again he stopped what he was doing and made sure they were looking directly into each other's eyes before he started talking. "The same limiting factor is at work here, too, Patty. Selection is everything when you work within such limits. Besides, my camera saw you born. It saw you before your mother did. Why should I want to photograph anyone else? Use your head. Limits. Limits. Now be quiet, breathe slowly. Turn your head a little so the hair falls forward — just a little more. Lean to the right — now hold it. Wait. Your leg is improperly placed." He began again.

Sound stirred around her like soft animals. Her father's face diminished in her mind, drifting away like the face of the magician in an Oz book she had read as a child, disembodied, hanging in the air, threatening, but definitely drifting away. The grass was already coming in green over the charred black. One heavy rain and the ash would settle forever, the plants spring back to life, the trees grow.

She felt a rumble of hunger in her stomach and started back toward the house. A house should be full of food after a funeral. She knew how it should be. There was something unnatural about one that wasn't, but the local people at the memorial service had been mostly tradesmen, and they had turned away uneasily when she approached. They hadn't liked the cremation of the body. She could feel this. They were people who still buried each other whole in the crowded earth, and the thought of ashes floating down on the surrounding mountains disgusted them. Also, the people from her father's world had seemed alien to them. Not that there were that many of them at the funeral, but she could sense the mistrust between the two groups. She knew what the local people were thinking all right: If he was such a famous man, why had so few people shown up for the memorial service. There was no answer.

But she had done what she could. With Jason's help she had managed to feed everyone who had come back to the house after the service and later, when she was alone, Black Cat had come and eaten off the table with her, his jade eyes glinting. The dishwasher had sighed to a stop. Humming in the distance, the pump at the well had also ceased, but the house itself had gone right on talking. It cracked in the heat of day and cooled in the evening. It sent messages of maintenance she could not understand. Tomorrow she would need help.

Today, she left the river and walked back to the house where she made herself a salami sandwich on sourdough bread with thick slices of onion. It was not bad having only oneself to consider, she thought, remembering the noon meal she should be cooking. There is nothing wrong in being alone. She was amazed that this small good feeling was not obliterated immediately by guilt.

For dinner tonight, she thought, I will have broiled mushrooms stuffed with cheese, and a martini before dinner, and wine. Yes, definitely wine. This made her think of her father's wine supply which was kept in a pantry especially designed by him. Light, dry red wine, sweet, fruity white wine. She had had it for dinner for years but now it would be different. A certain excitement rose in her and she moved uneasily beneath its weight, remembering when it had first begun. She stopped eating.

It was true. She had first felt this excitement the moment she had found him lying on the floor of his bedroom, one hand clutching at the bedding, pulling it off the bed in a twisted mass that almost covered him. Light from the morning sun had flooded his balcony, cutting softly through the glass doors to drop on his face, blurring the distorted features. Oh, God, she remembered thinking, I have killed him.

Now, it was as though she were finding him dead again, as though all of that moment were happening simultaneously with the croaking of a frog in the terrace pool at noon today. She went to the doorway, the small sound making the day seem larger. When would she stop double-seeing, as though today was a transparency placed over a yesterday that showed through in every way?

Part of her problem was that she had never spent one day completely alone until now. At least Black Cat would have been with her, or the television would be on. Her father had never understood how much the television meant to her, and yet now, her impulse was to leave it off, to disturb him no longer. It was strange how the habits of another life clung to her. She had the urge to clean and to sweep, to strip the house and polish it into an inhuman brightness, replacing each object confidently and lovingly or boldly discarding it.

And yet she dreaded the end table where her father's pipes and tobacco were waiting for him. She truly feared the closet with all of his waiting clothes. And the papers and old photographs . . . surely to God, he could have burned more of them the night she had come down from her bedroom and found him at two in the morning sorting papers and negatives and prints and burning, burning in the large stone fireplace. She had the feeling that all of these things, even the burned ones, were waiting for her behind every cupboard door, inside every closet and chest.

She hurried down the two stone stairs into the white-carpeted living room and standing before her father's record collection, put on the first record she touched. At such a time the wildly military music of the band made her jump, but not with surprise. He had hundreds of such records. She was startled only because she had thought the familiar music would be different, too, as the day was different, as food was different. But it was exactly the same. Her first impulse was to turn it off, to stop its mad flowing through the speakers into every room in the house, but she didn't touch it. It was better not to cry and yet she wanted most terribly to cry.

She thought mercifully of no return, but went ahead, with the music around her, into his room where the bed looked up meaningfully and the closed windows called to be opened. She went forward, opening the glass doors onto the deck that spread out into the tops of the oaks and sycamores. The hummingbird feeders were almost empty of the red-colored sugar water, and small birds were darting in and out fighting with the yellowjackets to be fed. The iridescent blues and greens of the little birds flashed familiarly among the dull leaves of the oak trees. Up canyon, the blue mountains rose above the hills creating a jumbled skyline whose ever-receding peaks seemed to go on and on and on, threatening her with an interminable kind of eternity. Ashes would float forever over those peaks, a drift of dust never to settle on the earth again. She could visualize it seeking, probing, finding.

Behind her, like a presence, the unmade bed challenged her. Gathering the soiled linens she put on fresh, repeating the image of life that lingered in every corner. Black Cat suddenly appeared in the doorway behind her, but he wouldn't come in. He sat there with his tail wrapped around him, watching her move through the familiar ritual, his eyes flashing amber in this light. He had slept almost every night of his life in here with her father.

Patricia picked up Ben's clothes and went to his closet, but she couldn't put them away. She pressed her face to them and felt his long arms around her, his hand finally going to her chin, forcing her to look up into his tired face. "Jason is a very special person, Patty. He is going to go on with my work as well as his own, making prints, selling them, seeing they are shown in the right places. Museums will want them. Collectors. You have no idea how valuable my portfolios alone will become and Jason is trained to carry on in my place. You can trust him completely to do what is right for you."

She could feel the distraction behind his words, as though he was not really saying what he wanted to say.

"It's the terrible finality of it, Patty, the ending of a work you feel has only begun." He pulled away from her and slammed a tight fist into the palm of his hand. "Right now. By God, right this minute I think if I could begin again as though I had never photographed anything in my life, I could do it — I really could."

"But you have already done so much! Oh, Ben, is there really that much to do?"

He turned to her and smiled, although his eyes remained sad. "You are her daughter. Even the words are the same."

She couldn't stand the loneliness. She pushed herself back into his arms and said what she thought he wanted to hear. "Don't worry about me, Ben. I can find work, you know. There are lots of things I can do."

"And leave this house?" She felt the shock run through his body. He looked over her head, into the curved contours of the floating room and she realized that he had never thought of her leaving, but when he spoke again it was to say, "Well, and maybe you should. Maybe that is exactly what you should do. One thing though, in the light of what you have just told me. Listen to what Jason has to say, but don't be too influenced by him. Jesus, how can I tell you to listen and not be influenced after what I've done to you. Oh, it's all so wrong. It's all so goddamned wrong."

She stood now in front of his mirror and carefully put his shirt over her shoulders. She held both of his shoes in her arms as though they were twin children. And then she lay on his bed and stared at the ceiling. Ivy, trailing over the railing of the deck, seemed to be encroaching upon her quietness. Soon enough it would be lacing itself across the windows, sliding tendril by tendril across the floor. How could death mean so much to one person and so little to another? She folded her arms and relaxed.

When the music ended and the first second of quiet fell on her, she sprang to her feet, pierced and broken by the huge sound of silence, as though what she wore was a pottery shroud that had suddenly cracked and opened, leaving her exposed to the world. She suddenly realized what her father had been trying to tell her and ran down the hall toward the studio.

Here, there was no escaping the deadly symmetry of line and limb and light. It surrounded her. Each photograph, beautifully matted, expertly lighted, showed her father's mind in as many facets as had ever existed. He was here, watching her. She withdrew into the shell of her skin and bones, deeper, into the hollows of the spirit known only to herself. She could not stand the sight of the photographs, and the certainty she had felt moments before deserted her.

She went to one of his few landscapes for comfort, but it was herself again. Her contours in the hills, her bones in the rocks, her fear in the trees. How did he know me like that? How could he have seen what I would be like today? Because it was herself today, this second, that she was seeing, even in the photographs of infancy. Had she never changed then? Would she ever?

The afternoon sun disappeared beneath the saddle of the hills, flashing orange on the underside of white clouds. She watched it through the one long narrow window the room contained. For a moment something of its afterglow filtered into the room and then it, too, was gone. She was surrounded by photographs disappearing into the background. She began to relax as abstractions of her imperfect body faded into the walls, blurring into a formless continuity that had nothing to do with her.

And then silently the lights went on, again revealing herself to herself, each ingenious spotlight adding its own tones to the grays and whites and the blackest of blacks. She stood in the center of the room, hiding her face in her hands, her short blond hair swinging forward. The quiet of the room finally became too much. She looked up into Jason's eyes.

"I didn't expect to find you here," he said, glancing around the room. "I can imagine how you must feel about all of this now that it is over. I mean, I think if I was you, I would be frightened — I would actually be running."

"Where would you go?"

"Honey, there is everywhere to go."

"Alone?"

"Don't look like that, Patty. Nobody's going to push you. I'll always be here, but you should get away and gain some perspective of your situation."

She looked at him sadly as his eyes passed from hers to the photographs. The distance of the reversed vision neatly severed from life separated the two of them as she watched him looking from photograph to photograph and finally back to her.

"I never get used to them," he said. "I simply don't know which is more astonishing, them — or you."

She wanted to shout at him, but she didn't speak. His hair, wild and dark, hung around his neck and curled over his collar. He looked down at her and his eyes seemed to be asking forgiveness in an archaic manner. She remembered the smell of ripe apples in the fall.

When people die, she thought, they tip the edges of the world, and you fall off whenever you think of them. She could clearly see this happening to Jason now, and she pitied him. It was happening to her, too. It was not good for survivors to be together like this, so soon. Visions could flash from eye to eye. Curtains could swing open. Nothing might become something.

She thought of him as he must have looked coming down the driveway in his tennis shoes. He never drove his car if he had time to walk where he was going, and one of his small cameras, loaded with color film, always hung around his neck like a talisman. "I'm a slow thinker," he had told her once. "Walking gives me time to reflect on what I want to say when I get where I am going. I don't like to do anything fast."

If she had been looking out the front window just now she would have seen, when he was directly below her, the thinning spot in the wild hair, and the sight would have reassured her. She would have watched him coming up the flagstone steps, the neglected rosemary plants trailing around his feet, their pale blossoms full of wild bees. He seemed more real to her when she imagined him than he ever did in person.

"What are you thinking about, Patty?"

"Nothing." Dreams of color overcame her. Pink against violet. Orange against red. Green on yellow.

"Leave this house, Patty." He stood uncertainly. She knew he was waiting for her to speak. "I saw you all the way. From the very beginning. I saw you every way your father did, and I am telling you to get out of here. Leave."

The mirrorlike house echoed around them. They stood there abstracted from all that was going on. She walked finally over the polished and waxed floor into the living room, and he followed her. It was a relief for her to be free of the photographs that had surrounded her, but it was an emptiness, too. She reached for his hand in something like fear.

The woodwork gleamed. The wind struck the wind-bells attached to the eaves, making a fluid sound of water running over rocks. A memory of movement seemed to fill the corners and slide over the white carpeting. An oak branch rattled on the terrace making a last-winter sound of embers falling into themselves in the fireplace, a last-summer sound of laughter on the beach drifting up through the alders. Black Cat cried harshly. They looked down, astonished to find anyone but themselves alive in this house.

He pulled himself free. "Stop it, Patty! Do you know how this makes me feel?" Turning his back to her, he took his camera from around his neck and laid it on the coffee table.

Defensively, she walked over and turned on the television. Before her, in the blue light, a comedian patted his huge stomach and strutted to the accompaniment of timpani. The way people die, she thought, feeling herself sliding off into death, the interminable way they find to go on dying over and over and over. She understood him, of course.

He walked across the room and sat down while a commercial began and ended, the play world sliding back onto the screen as though the interruption had been imagined.

"If you will turn that goddamned thing off, maybe we can talk sensibly."

But she didn't turn it off and with no other lights in the room, the screen glowed menacingly. For a moment she thought she saw the future in it, as though she were looking into a crystal ball, and a great sadness related panic to her bones. And then the sycamores, with the early rising moon behind, papered the walls with their flowing shadows, summer stars and constellations, murmur of a universe. She turned to him, seeing because he saw, her leg stretched out on the couch. It was an abstract shape in the uncertain light, and nothing more. She saw through his eyes, her arm, her neck, her breasts, her jawline, her soft hair falling forward and she looked away quickly, keeping her eyes hidden.

They came together. Weeks had hollow sounds, months had nothing more. Years stood against today like death and nothing mattered. They walked down the curving hall and pondered movement, swept along by the swaying tree shadows. Behind them the television's blue light obtruded into the soft darkness, the deception of white mountains floated in the moonlight, her father's ashes drifted on and on and on.

She closed her eyes and when she opened them again, there was only the night pressing against the glass, dissolving into shapes of emerald and sapphire and topaz.

WARD JUST

Three Washington Stories

(FROM THE ATLANTIC MONTHLY)

1. Noone

THE EMOTIONS OF IT were fairly straightforward, and I don't want to make too much of them in any case, either way. She was crying on the bed, or it sounded like crying, and I was in my rage at the doorway. I had said the words so many times in my head that when I said them out loud, they sounded false. I told her we were finished, and I was leaving. She told me to get out then, and I did. After I slammed the door, I couldn't hear her anymore. I stood for a moment in the street, then began to walk down Dent Place to Wisconsin Avenue. I was walking very quickly, head down, looking for a taxi. The regular Yellow would arrive at eight, but I didn't feel like waiting for half an hour. My knees were shaky and I kept to the inside of the sidewalk. Then I collected myself and slowed up. My briefcase swung in rhythm, my footsteps even on the sidewalk. *Click click click click.*

I arrived at my office in thirty minutes; only a few people were in. The receptionist, one or two others. My secretary followed me through the small offices to the large one, bearing a cup of coffee. She remarked on the weather, hot, and the day, heavy, and handed me the appointments list and waited.

"Is Noone in yet?" I asked.

"Noone's downtown this morning. Back at eleven."

I nodded, irritated.

"At eleven, then."

"Shall I telephone?"

"No need," I said.

My secretary made a small note on her stenographer's pad.

"And hold all calls."

There were two meetings that morning. We were having trouble with a transcript. I wanted State to agree to release an uncensored version of an ambassador's testimony, and State had refused. Can't conduct diplomacy in a fishbowl, the Secretary said; not so much a fishbowl, more a muddy river, I replied. He smiled. I smiled. *No*, he said then, very politely, knowing he had the strength. The White House would back him, so the thing was hopeless. That was where Noone was now, at the State Department talking to their legislative man. Making everything as difficult as possible for them. Like everything else, it has its positives and negatives. I was getting solid publicity, and the cause was a good one, which it isn't always. But the dispute had gone on for a month, and people were tiring of it; some of my colleagues on the committee were tiring of it. Noone and I agreed that there should be one last press release, then forget it. An issue that became a bore was worse than no issue at all. But others had come in behind us, and the two meetings this morning were to let them down gently. To tell them we weren't marching anymore, at least at the head of the parade. This will sound fatuous, but it is true: I have always tried never to let people down without warning them.

I have two offices, a public office and a private office. The public office is very large, with a huge mahogany desk in the center of an oval rug. The Capitol building is in the background, visible over my left shoulder through the windows. *What a wonderful view,* the visitors say, and I smile, *isn't it?* The desk belonged to my uncle, when he was in the Navy; it is a beautiful object. He bought it in Honduras and gave it to me when I first came here. The walls of this office are crowded with pictures of me and my family, me and politicians, me and military men, me and important constituents, and plaques with my name on them. They are commemorative, of this and that — Rotary, AUSA, AFL-CIO, the United Jewish Appeal. That sort of plaque. The other, smaller, office is personal and difficult to find in the maze of rooms in the Capitol. I have a small bar in the corner and an old Underwood typewriter and a bookshelf full of mystery novels. I have all of John D. McDonald's

sixty-odd books, plus Ian Fleming and Ross MacDonald and the
others. No photographs, no plaques. A comfortable couch along
one wall, leather chairs around the room, stand-up ashtrays, a gov-
ernment-issue desk. There is a seascape, a self-conscious impression
of a slice of American coastline, Maine or California, Castine or
Big Sur. I am in the smaller office now, waiting for Noone.

Gloria Noone is thirty-five, dark, compact, austere. She is divorced from a lawyer, and she pronounces her name "new-nee."
Before she came to work for me she handled public relations for a
television network, and although she is ten years younger than I
am, I trust her judgment and her instincts. I trust her absolutely
when it comes to dealing with the press. We did not get on well at
first, owing mainly to her unfortunate habit of correcting the smallest mistakes. In the first interview we fell to talking, for some reason, about Iowa. I was making a point about redistricting.

"In the eight congressional districts of Iowa . . ." I began, but
she interrupted.

"There are seven congressional districts in Iowa," she said, and
named the congressmen.

It vexed me, and she saw that, and smiled. Of course then I had
to hire her.

She knocks, is in the room.

"How did it go?"

"Fine," I say. She is talking about Nancy, but I am talking about
the meetings this morning. "They took it very well. They seemed
pleased that we had gone along as far as we did. Kudos. We get
kudos."

"I'll get the last press release out right away." She looks at me,
bland as warm milk. "As long as it went so well, we might think
about a press conference."

I smile. Score one for Noone.

"I'll concentrate on the Secretary personally."

"You do that."

"Pompous bureaucrat. Another Wall Street fool."

I laugh.

She puts up a hand; she's steady, resolute. "Senator, we will
get the last *ounce* . . ."

Gloria Noone is talking, and I am looking over her head. The room is small, so comfortable. Sometimes I think she is a touch paranoid: she had it swept for bugs. Of course there were none. But the knowledge gives me a strange satisfaction. We are absolutely private in this room. We have a code word for it. The Vatican. I have only had the office for two years; they gave it to me after my tenth year in the Senate. But now I never talk about confidential matters in the large office; it is as if that office were ceremonial. Noone and I and sometimes Walter Mach go to the Vatican in the evenings. We do our business there, over a drink. They are for me the best hours in the day, sitting and planning; scheming, Noone says. The day they gave me the key to the office, Noone insisted that I go inside and talk in a normal voice, and she stayed outside with the door closed, listening. She wanted to be certain that nothing could be overheard in the corridor. And it can't be, even when you shout. The soundproofing is gorgeous. When I call her paranoid, Noone smiles and says she is cautious.

She is silent now, waiting for me.

"Well, we are quits."

"Sorry about that," she says. She manages to make it sound both sympathetic and ironic. So I can go either way, and she can follow.

We are both quiet for a moment, and I see her pick up a pencil and begin drawing boxes. One box is fastened to another, a series of boxes slanting down the white paper. She shifts on her chair, sighs, and rubs the flat of her hand along her cheeks. She pushes her hair back behind her ears, then she looks at me, a long moment.

"Nancy *is* staying."

I nod.

"And you're moving out."

I nod again.

"Well," she says. "Well." Noone is carefully inking in the boxes she has drawn, turning the paper as she does it. Now she is using a felt pen, and the ink is staining her fingers. She is unconscious of that. "I think," she says, "a short, blunt statement."

"The shorter the better."

"Two sentences," she says. She has stopped doodling altogether and is staring at the pad. Then she says, "Due to irreconcilable family differences, Senator and Mrs. Hayn . . ."

"Christ, no," I say. "Jesus Christ, no."

Noone shrugs; I am angry. But the anger does not concern her. She is silent for a moment, then tries another approach.

I am a fatalist, and that has served me well in politics. When I am in a tight spot I try to remember that life is capricious. Life is unfair, Jack Kennedy said. He could afford to say it, although he didn't believe it, really, and I do. He was more romantic than fatalist. Noone and I talked about fatalism once, just once. She said fatalism was for losers, and I laughed at her and called her Horatio Alger's mother. She looked at me as if I were insane.

There is a funny aspect to this. A month ago we looked for precedents, and could find none. It isn't the sort of problem you can refer to the Legislative Reference Service, so Noone went personally to the morgue of the *Times*. I wanted her to find out how these problems had been handled in the past, specifically what was said, how it was explained. She drew a blank; perhaps the *Times* did not consider a politician's personal life news fit to print. So we are operating on our own instinct because it would have been awkward to ask questions, even of close friends. The place is like a sieve, Noone says.

She has tried two or three approaches now, and they are improving.

"Senator and Mrs. Tom Hayn have decided to seek a legal separation . . . well, no." She pauses, thinks, begins again. She is writing the statement as she recites it out loud. "Senator Thomas Hayn's office announced today that the Senator and Mrs. Hayn . . . no." She begins again. ". . . the Senator *and his wife* have decided to seek a legal separation. Mrs. Hayn will continue to live in their Georgetown . . ."

"Huh-uh," I say.

"Oh, right. Dumb of me," she mutters. ". . . *their house in Washington, D.C.* The Senator has moved . . ." She looks at me, her eyebrows up, inquiring.

"A downtown hotel," I say.

She smiles. "Right again. You should have my job."

I am thinking that after all I was right, and we should have prepared a statement in advance. But she argued against it, worried about a leak or the possibility of a misplaced piece of paper. We can work it up in two hours, she'd said. That would be a bad piece

of paper to have lying around. I agreed finally. But now I don't
see the need for all the detail, and I tell her that. I want a simple
statement of fact. A one-line statement of fact.

"Tom, you have got to say something," she says. "You have got
to give them more than the fact that you and Nancy are quits. So
it has got to be in two sentences, and maybe three. This is not major news, but it is news. You have got to give them more than the
blunt fact. If you don't, they'll know you're hiding something.
They'll speculate."

"They'll speculate anyway."

"Of course. But if you give them something to chew on, the
speculation will be built around that. I mean, it doesn't matter an
awful lot what it is. What the extra fact is. I think that the place
of residence is the most neutral, and it fits; the impression is that
you've nothing to hide. This is a family tragedy, politics be
damned. That's the point we want to make."

Noone is at the bar. She fixes a martini for me and a Dubonnet
for herself. She is lost in thought, worried now. The dining room
has sent up sandwiches. There is no telephone, so we are quite
alone. I smile when I think of that. It is the only office in Washington without a phone. If there is no telephone, Noone said, there
will be no spur-of-the-moment, ill-considered calls. She prefers to
conduct business face-to-face.

"How difficult is Nancy going to be?" She looks at me before she
asks the next question, which I ignore. "How difficult was she this
morning? Or was it last night?"

"I don't know," I say, which is the truth. We have been married
for twenty years, and have been in trouble the last ten. We are disconnected now, I don't know her feelings. I am preoccupied with
the immediate problem, which is the statement; I have lived with
the other long enough to know it is insoluble. "I honestly don't
know," I say. "Depends in part on that son of a bitch." I mention
the name of Nancy's priest, and Noone smiles.

"Rasputin lives," she says.

"The hell with that, Gloria," I say.

She is back to business again.

"You are going to have to take gas."

"Unavoidable."

Noone is thinking, very quiet now. She is circling the subject, closing off the routes of access. She is very thorough. "Think about this," she says, leaning across the desk, concentrating on her drawing. She is very slowly inking in all the boxes. "It might be advantageous to leak it. It might be better to get the word out informally, to prepare the state for it. Then, in two or three days, make the official announcement." She looks up. "I don't think I would recommend this course, but it's one possibility and we ought at least to consider it."

So we talk, and finally I shake my head. "It's going to come as a hell of a surprise. Best to come from me, this office, officially. Better that than rumors for a week, followed by an announcement. They'll have me in bed with every woman in Washington anyway."

Noone nods gravely.

"Have the kids been told?"

"Nancy will do that," I say.

"But Tom Junior's in Europe."

"She'll find a way."

"It'll be a surprise," she says.

"No, it won't."

"I mean in the state, and that's the bad part. The surprise."

"The Knights of Columbus," I say, grinning.

"The Holy Name Societies," she says.

"Monsignor Shaw," I say.

"The Cardinal!" she cries.

And we both laugh.

Noone has prepared three statements, and I am reading them now. She gave them to me on one sheet of paper. They represent three different "spins," she said. This is how they look on the paper.

1. Senator and Mrs. Thomas Hayn have decided to seek a legal separation. Mrs. Hayn and their three children will continue to live at the family home in Washington, D.C. The Senator has moved to a downtown hotel.

2. Senator Thomas Hayn's office announced with deep regret today that the Senator and his wife have decided to seek a legal separation. Mrs. Hayn and their children will continue to live in the family home in Washington, D.C. The Senator has moved to a downtown hotel.

3. Senator Thomas Hayn's office announced today that the Senator and his wife, Nancy, have decided to seek a legal separation.
Senator and Mrs. Hayn emphasized that their decision came
most reluctantly and was made, finally, in the best interests of
the family. Mrs. Hayn and their three children will remain in
the family home in Washington. The Senator has moved to a
downtown hotel.

I chose the third, naturally.

I am thinking of adding a single sentence: "There is no question
of a divorce," but Noone is against it.
   "The word looks terrible on paper and raises questions," she says.
   "But it will be the first question they ask."
   "Of course. And I will answer it: 'There is no question of a divorce.' It will give them a second story, which they will have to
have. There will be other questions about the children and their
ages and Nancy and her age and so forth." She stops, smiles.
"Thank God, there's no need to clear the statement with her."
   I look up, startled. I hadn't thought of that.
   "Not to worry," Noone says. "If she objects to a decision made
'in the best interests of the family,' then she's on the hook and
you're off it. There's one thing in our favor. These stories are
really awkward for them to pursue. The locals will be reluctant
anyway, and you're not so famous that the nationals can really bird-
dog it. If they do, it looks like a vendetta. Unless, of course, they
smell real scandal." She smiles. "Then anything can happen."
   "Thanks for all the good news," I say.

Noone is pleased; the statement has just the right tone, melancholy but dignified, she says. "When I talk to them privately tonight, I will stress the family tragedy aspects. I will not talk politics
with them at all. I will tell them that you have gone away for a
week. Tom, I am not going to close any doors." I return her stare.
"It isn't unheard of. You will take gas, but attitudes have changed
now. Even back home. I could foresee circumstances . . ." She
does not finish the sentence. She types a clean copy of the statement
on the old Underwood, and leaves to return to the big office. Perhaps she is right; she is a smart woman. Times change. But I am
feeling a little melancholy myself. If I'd been a Protestant, there'd

be no trouble, or anyway less trouble. I think about that for a moment, then turn it around. If I'd been a Protestant, I would not be a senator.

The statement is typed and Xeroxed; it will be given the press at eight or nine tonight. I leave the small office and walk across the street to the large one. Everyone is gone now, except for Noone. I look in on her and motion for her to follow me. She does, eagerly. We march into my office, and she places the call.

I talk to His Eminence.

His Eminence talks to me.

Because the question is lying there, palpable, a shadow on the mind, I try to reassure him. "John, I want to tell you personally that there is no question of any divorce or remarriage. Nor any third parties either. That is definite."

The old man grunts, and says that he is glad to hear it.

But he doesn't believe it.

"You have let me down," he says. "You have let me down badly."

While I am talking, trying to explain the situation, I am watching Noone. She is taut, excited; she seems to me like an athlete before a game. I cannot tell what she is thinking; her mouth is set in a hard thin line.

She'd insisted that Walter Mach not be brought into this, and I reluctantly agreed. I used to think that she and Walter were close, but now I am not so sure. She didn't want anyone brought into it; otherwise it would look like a council of war. "Bad atmospherics," she explained; "too political." She catches me looking at her, and smiles slightly, distracted; she is perched on the edge of the big desk, her hand under one elbow, concentrating on the conversation. Her hair falls wonderfully over her face; she turns now, and her mouth and eyes are obscured. Her left leg swings free, describing a circle. The Cardinal is silent, and there is nothing to do but say good-bye and hang up the telephone. I have known this Cardinal since he was a bishop. I am in politics largely through the early patronage of this Cardinal. We were friends.

Noone listens for two clicks, then puts down the extension phone.

"Pretty frosty," she says.

"Balls like ice cubes," I say absent-mindedly.

"That bastard," she says. "With *his* record."

"Well, he is an old man."
"But he won't help."
"Why should he?" I ask.
We make six other calls after that.

I am walking down the Capitol steps. Very theatrical: it is raining softly, and wisps of steam rise from the still-hot pavement. The
late-working secretaries are going home now, and I watch their
bodies move. I am walking with another senator, and he nudges
me, nodding at a miniskirt ahead of him. He shakes his head, grinning. *Quiffquiffquiff*, he murmurs. I laugh.

2. Slayton

All marriages have private jokes; mine has just one. The joke is
Sylvia. When my wife and I have stayed late over the chessboard,
or become hypnotized by "The Late Show" on the television, we
will leave the debris of the evening and go to bed with the words,
"Sylvia can clean up in the morning." On the rare occasions when
we have guests, we insist that they not worry about the dinner
dishes. "Sylvia will take care of it." Of course there is no Sylvia.
There never was.

I have breakfasted on coffee, two coddled eggs, and the newspaper, and now I am waiting on the corner for my ride. I look at my
watch; Jack Fowler is late. Today I am the fourth man, and Jack
drives a Volkswagen. I will be in the rear seat with my legs
cramped, squeezed like an orange next to Bill Day. Jack will be
talking football with Gershen. A thirty-minute ride to Langley,
stop-start, stop-start. I close my eyes, I doze; it is Monday and I
think of my vacation, two weeks away. Presently, Bill nudges me
and I awaken and see the guard through the window. My ID is
in my hand, and I press it against the glass. The guard looks at it
and nods. The car moves through the gate, up the road, and into
the underground parking lot.

Noone is still in the big office. She said she would make selected
calls to selected members of the press. Different men, different
spins, she said. Not to worry. I leave her at her desk, her hair
freshly combed, new make-up on her cheeks, two packages of cigarettes next to the telephone. Coins lay atop the cigarettes. She is

excited, anxious for me to be gone so she can begin her telephoning. Straight-faced I say that I think I'll wait and listen to the first call, see how it goes. She shakes her head quickly, *No.* She would be inhibited with me on the extension phone. It is better if she does it alone. This is her job, she says. The reason she is paid $28,000 a year.

"Twenty-eight, five," I say, and her humor returns.

"It's cheaper than a trip to Rome," she says.

I know her friends, so I know where to look tomorrow. I mean which newspapers, and which network. They will be very interested in this story because I am on all the short lists for Vice President. They will say this will take me out of the running, and they are right, although Noone will not believe it. I tell her she is crazy, she had better set her sights elsewhere. A Catholic separated from his wife, three children.

"I can live without the vice presidency," I tell her.

"There are seven congressional districts in Iowa," she says, and begins dialing.

It is a routine day, until three in the afternoon. My secretary brings me a cable, covered by the familiar black-bordered folder.

TOP SECRET
(this is a cover sheet)
Basic Security Requirements
Are Contained in AR 380-5
THE UNAUTHORIZED DISCLOSURE OF THE INFORMATION CONTAINED IN THE ATTACHED DOCUMENT(S) COULD BE PREJUDICIAL TO THE DEFENSE INTERESTS OF THE UNITED STATES.

The U.S. government is careful, thorough. There is a parenthesis at the bottom of the sheet: "(This cover sheet is unclassified when separated from classified documents.)"

I have read the cable, and now I am thinking about it. It is one of the things that fascinates me about my work. I have not been in the field for fifteen years, and all I know is what I read. I see nothing firsthand; my objectivity is complete. And as my superiors have reason to know, my judgments are accurate. I have learned to distinguish good cables from bad, and the writer of this cable is quite nimble, a man with a sure grasp of government form. The paragraphs descend down the page, numbered 1 to 23. But it is a puzzling cable, and I read it three times. Now I am drinking a cup of tea, waiting for the telephone to ring. I have already told my secretary to call Jack Fowler to tell him not to wait, and my wife to tell her I will not be home for dinner.

There are six of us in the conference room; the deputy director, one of his assistants, an area chief and one of his assistants (that is me), and two spear carriers, strangers. We are very anxious to keep this inside the agency. The deputy director: "This is our affair. It has nothing to do with Defense or State or anyone else. We will handle it in-house on a closed basis. This meeting is being held at the request of the director." He does not say what is obvious, that it is a confidential meeting, no written record. Then we talk about Slayton.

I am wrong about the other two. They are not spear carriers at all, but two of Slayton's close friends. I have read their cables for years but am meeting them face to face for the first time. We have generally worked different countries. It is typical of the agency that they should bring these two into this meeting, although they are both outside the chain of command in this matter; strictly speaking, they should not be involved at all. They are part of the old agency, very — what was the word we used to use? — la-di-da. Good schools, rich wives. History majors from Yale, bored lawyers from Wall Street. It's changed now, and we favor mathematicians from UCLA or the University of Chicago. In the general conversation before we get under way, I notice that the blue-eyed one has a Southern accent; Virginia, I think. I remember one of his cables that I read years ago. It was from Warsaw, Prague, someplace like that, some Cradle of Western Civilization Enduring the Long Night of Soviet Communism. It read like an honors thesis, and the last line made me laugh. "Such, anyway, is the melancholy prospect from . . ." The old-boy net at the agency was great for melancholy prospects.

We have all read the same Top Secret cable, from Slayton's Number Two in N——. His nerves show a little in the language, and it takes him a hundred words to get to the point: he thinks that Slayton is having a nervous breakdown. He recommends an immediate replacement. You have to be inside a large bureaucracy to understand the delicacy of this undertaking. The Number Two is running considerable risk, unless he can make his case stick and stick fast. I am reserving my voice, for the moment.

There are several unspokens, for this after all is Slayton. Wonderful Slayton, battered Slayton, Slayton-the-widower, Slayton-the-linguist, protean Slayton. Slayton and his private income. But Slayton has been under very heavy pressure for two years. He has been on station for three, longer than is either usual or desirable. He had — has — excellent contacts, and speaks the language. Oh, fluently. And has the credentials.

The embassy has been bombed twice, and Slayton is on all the blacklists. Blacklisted Slayton. Eighteen months ago he was infected with hepatitis, which laid him up for ten weeks. The deputy director wanted to remove him then, but Slayton pleaded to be kept on. It was an elegant cable. Removing him from N——, Slayton told the deputy director, would be *coitus interruptus*. Worse, it would jeopardize the operation. The two were old friends, and the remark gained a certain celebrity around the shop — I mean among those who had access to the cable. It was very highly classified. The DD bent the rules, and Slayton stayed. Now, according to his Number Two, he was bats.

It requires felicity to talk about a man's personal life in a cable. There is no satisfactory way to put it in government language. *Subject was observed drinking twenty-two Scotch-and-sodas in the Palace Hotel bar, then was seen to pitch and fall into a lamppost on Ledra Street, where a native seized and made off with his briefcase containing the ciphers* . . . No, no. So there are code words, and I do not mean of the five-numeral variety. These are the words: eccentric behavior, slurred speech, abnormal working hours, and the most damning of all: "A frequent loss of control." The phrase "erratic personal life" meant a sexual irregularity of some kind.

This meeting is a strange one. It is odd that it was called at all. The normal procedure, in matters of this kind, is for the Number Two (or whomever) to call the DD on a secure line and tell him the facts face to face, or voice to voice, and get a third party on the scene to make an evaluation. Naturally, if it is a chief of station faulting his deputy or anyone under his command, his word alone is sufficient. The man is removed. But a deputy breaking dishes on his boss is something else. Normally, an independent evaluation is ordered. A station chief does not live in a vacuum: his behavior is known to the ambassador, among others; the chief of the military mission, if any; and there are a number of discreet ways, even in a very large organization, to monitor a man's performance. These devices are built-in. But in N—— the U.S. government has no ambassador, and since the bombing, no embassy. The military mission is small and the colonel in charge of it incompetent. There is a consulate, staffed by three frightened Foreign Service officers. None of these is suitable, and only *in extremis* would we call on an outside agency in a matter of this kind; I cannot recall a time when it was ever done. At any event, in N—— there is only Slayton and his Two and six others scattered around the country. Still, it would have been simple for the Two to telephone. But a cable is more efficient. In a cable, words have weight.

I am not expected to say anything. I am at the meeting because I am the officer assigned to country N—— in Washington. My immediate superior is the area director. He will wait for a signal from the DD before he speaks, and then he will be cautious. Not that it matters at all; I knew what I would do the moment I read the cable. *Get him out,* I said to myself. Right away.

The area director is asked to assess Slayton's performance from this end. He says: "Objectively excellent, although as we all know, he has a tendency to operate on his own overmuch. He is the only officer at that rank in the agency who speaks the language, and writes it. His contacts in N—— are wide and varied. He has shown unusual discretion. In two matters" — he looks at the DD, and at the two strangers — "of great delicacy Slayton performed superbly. One of them went haywire, but that had nothing to do with him." The DD nods, and the area director continues. "A quality man. If it were not for this cable" — he picks up the paper, holds it a second, and lets it fall — "there would be no question in my mind about Slayton's suitability. Of course, he would have been withdrawn next month anyway. I would not keep a man in a station

like that for more than three years in any case. Not for any reason." I smile. It is the first time I've heard that.

The deputy director has turned now to the "friends." He lifts
his eyebrows: "Charley?" This is the blue-eyed one, the older of
the two. He lights a cigarette, and looks at his colleague. Now they
will close ranks. I can't believe it," he says, speaking directly to
the DD. "I saw Slayton two months ago in Rome, and he was fine.
He said he'd recovered from the hepatitis, and was enjoying his
tour in N——. As much as you *can* enjoy N——, which is not a
garden spot, as we all know. He was with one of his daughters in
Rome. I think she lives with his brother. I ran into him by accident at the . . . circus." Blue-eyes smiles, looking at the DD; the
DD returns it. Some private joke. "We had a drink later; he
laughed about drinking Vichy and soda. He looked very fit, although he'd lost some weight. With his record . . ." Blue-eyes
trails off for a moment, as if looking for words. "We know his C.V.
France during the war, then Eastern Europe, Hungary, Japan,
Cairo, back to Eastern Europe" — he smiles at the euphemism, and
slides on — "the tour at Bragg, and now out there. A volunteered
second tour. *Coitus interruptus.*" The DD smiles; the area director
smiles; the two friends smile. "This is not a man to let an operation go out of control. We know that from the past. What the hell,
this agency is Slayton's life. In view of what I gather is a certain
urgency . . ." The words come out *gyathuh's a suht'n uhj'ncy.*
"Well, the record . . ." Blue-eyes's voice is soft, persuasive. "I'd
trust him with anything," he says.

We are silent, waiting for the DD. "Is it possible the whole
thing is an act?"
"It's possible," I said. I did not add that it was not likely. In
twenty years in this work I have never heard of a man faking a nervous breakdown. For obvious reasons.
"How well known is he in N——?" This, from the area director.
"Well known," I said. Stupid question. Any man who is station
chief for three years in a country like that becomes known. He is
probably better known than the foreign minister. It is impossible to
be unknown. Also unwise. If they know who you are, they know
where to go with their information. I mean the friendlies.
"If this is an act, would he tell his Two?"

"Be very foolish if he didn't," I said.

"Be very foolish if he did," Blue-eyes cut in. "No reason to. He couldn't've suspected that his Two would try to break dishes on him." He nodded at the DD: yes, certainly that was it. That was the explanation. "It's a setup," Blue-eyes said.

I looked at him. "Why?"

"You would know that better than I," he drawled. This was not a man to go beyond what he knew, or was supposed to know.

"On the other hand, Slayton's been out there too damned long," the DD said. "The operation is too important to be entrusted to a man who is possibly . . ." The DD shook his head. "I don't understand why the Two waited until the last bloody minute to send his cable. I assume there was a good reason. Also a reason why he did not call. But a thing like this doesn't come out of the blue, not usually."

"Well, he's been accused," Blue-eyes said. "There's no proof."

"The Number Two is an excellent man," the area director said mildly. I waited for the qualification. "Though of course a younger man."

"He's under forty," I said dryly.

"There is no plausible reason for the Two to undercut Slayton. If what he says is false, that will become obvious straightaway. I find it bewildering. Of course, now there is no way to get a third man into the country. There is no way to *know*, and I have been unable to raise the Two on the radiophone." He looked at his watch. "As of just now communications will go *kaput*. Except, of course, our own X-communications. Which are not of much use if no one is there manning the radio." The DD pursed his lips.

"I'd stick," Blue-eyes said, and his friend nodded.

"The only alternative is to put the Two in charge. I wouldn't like to do that, in a situation of this delicacy. Slayton's kept his plans very close." The DD glanced over at the area director, who was staring bleakly at the table. Blue-eyes and his friend were smiling ever so slightly.

Blue-eyes had mentioned "a certain urgency." What that was about was this: Slayton was managing a coup, all by himself. It was known in the cables as Rampart Street; that was the operational code word. Doubtless it had some special meaning for Slayton and his cronies. In this particular coup there was meant to be no American participation at all. Zero. Entirely indigenous, as we say. Three years ago, a half-dozen young Army officers approached Slayton, and the plans proceeded from there. Of course, there was no way for my bureau to know all the details, because Slayton did not let us in on his plans; I mean the area director and myself. Slayton made his reports verbally — I suppose there are pieces of paper somewhere — to the director and his deputy. He did not go through channels; he was too old-boy net for that. So those of us here who had the responsibility did not have all the facts. Slayton ignored my messages demanding more information. He fobbed them off on his Two, and had enough personal clout with the DD to get away with it. The agency was very excited because Slayton had seemingly squared all the circles. All the negotiations and planning he did himself, personally. Not that there was much of either; all the rebels apparently wanted was Slayton's neutrality.

At any event, he did manage to import Swedish weapons: I heard the DD refer to that in an admiring way one day; yet it was my bureau that found the weapons, that paid for them and arranged for delivery in S——. There were one or two other items of that kind. But officially, the agency was not involved in Rampart Street, and if it succeeded, we were way ahead; if it failed, we'd lost nothing. That is, Slayton lost nothing. Those of us here would lose a great deal. For we would be asked to pay the price for an operation in which we had no more than nominal control. That is a fact of life: when there is a failure, someone must pay up. The thing would leak; it always did, sooner or later. So that is what Slayton had been doing in N—— for three years, and it was the consensus within the agency that no one could put it together except Slayton. Slayton had the finesse. That was the "certain urgency" about the meeting now, because the coup was supposed to get under way today. Or would if Slayton were sane.

The DD has gone through all of Slayton's personal files, and finds nothing to suggest imbalance. *Au contraire,* the printout indicates unusual stability. A photo accompanies the file. I see a middle-aged, red-headed man, scowling. A bit fleshy, standing in a slouch, a cigarette holder in his left hand. I look at the picture upside down: Slayton is quite mad, no doubt about it. Blue-eyes and his friend have long since been excused, and it is just the four of us now. The DD goes around the table, requesting recommenda-

tions. The truth of the matter is that he has no options, at this
late date; he had them this morning, but he does not have them
now. He must go with Slayton or abandon the game altogether.

I am in my office now, drinking a cup of tea and waiting for the
first cables. I have asked my secretary to stay, and she is in the outer
office, waiting as I am. We have heard nothing from the Two since
his cable this morning. I have a bad feeling about this operation,
a feeling that it will fail. The psychology has gone wrong, as it
sometimes does in the middle of a chess game; the atmosphere darkens, and you know you are going to lose, although you do not see
how or why. I am ashamed to admit that I almost hope it does. It
will teach them a lesson: field men cannot be entrusted with operational control. They are too close, they lose their perspective; it is
a question of limited parameter. That is a fact of life. If you surrender control, you surrender responsibility. What is the value of
an area director or a bureau chief if he is not permitted to control
operations in his zone of responsibility? It is pointless not to use
the resources of the agency. What is the point of the apparatus here
if it is not used? It is not entirely my problem, because I have been
here for twenty years and I will be here for twenty more, and the
situation *is* improving. It is better than it was, thanks largely to the
computers. They have simplified some of the problems. There are
only a few Slaytons left. There are fewer of them every year.

The cable from the Two finally arrived, brief, too brief. It turned
out more or less as I expected. Slayton did have a breakdown, and
the coup did fail, although there is some difference of opinion here
as to what "fail" means in this case. Slayton is now in a private hospital in S——, and the Two is on leave. We were lucky to get them
out of the country at all, particularly Slayton, who was completely
haywire. It was done this way: with a show of compassionate concern, the White House ordered Army medical teams to N—— to
care for the wounded and the homeless. This was done very neatly;
the Army was in and out, no permanent presence of any kind;
Slayton and the Two left on the first flight. There were a few rude
remarks in the local press, but these will be forgotten in time.
N—— is back to normal. I had one small satisfaction, which I
shared with my wife the night we put together the rescue plan.
Since the operation was an agency matter from the beginning, I in-

sisted that we be given overall control; that is, one of our people in the field supervising the Army units under orders from me. This is a departure from the normal procedure, and it took me twelve hours to fight it out with the Pentagon; but we prevailed, and I directed the operation from my desk in Washington. I was in personal charge, so it fell to me to choose a code name. I chose the name Sylvia.

3. The Brigadier General and the Columnist's Wife

The columnist had been active in his trade for thirty years. He was one of those who had made his reputation in World War II — *war two,* he called it now — marching across France with the Ninth Infantry Division. It was in France with the division that he met Hemingway, who took a fancy to him. The two shared foxholes and danger and, according to at least one contemporary account, a woman. When acquaintances asked the columnist about Hemingway, he would shrug his shoulders and say very little. War two was a wonderful experience, and the columnist wanted to keep it to himself.

After the war the columnist's reputation grew. He spent the late 1940s in Greece and China, and in 1950 he was evacuated from Korea with a bullet hole in his left shoulder. The authorities set him up in a private room in an Army hospital in Japan, so he could continue to write his column. He read the dispatches in the morning and composed his column in the afternoon, writing it with his good hand on a portable typewriter. The wound became infected, and the columnist had spent six weeks in the Army hospital.

One day in September the chief surgeon brought a movie star in to see him; she was making a tour of the hospital with a USO troupe. She stayed for drinks and dinner and then she stayed for the night and in a month they were married, quite privately, in Kyoto. Acquaintances were stunned; the columnist was then forty; the movie star was thirty, and at the top of her trade. The acquaintances gave the marriage six months, but they were wrong. It lasted two years, and supplied the columnist with a fund of stories on which to dine. In the property settlement, the movie star was awarded the mansion they had occupied in Holmby Hills. The columnist said good riddance; he had called the place *Berchtesgaden.*

The columnist and the movie star had divided their time between New York, Washington, and Los Angeles. Now the columnist returned full time to Washington, and resumed his military writing with vengeance. But the 1950s was a bleak period, for the wars were small and of little account. Nig-nog wars, the columnist called them; gratuitous insurgencies in the Middle East and the Orient, squalid little generals' coups in Latin America. The columnist returned from his trips depressed: he said he was too old to backpack with the infantry; now he could concentrate on grand strategy. His editors were disappointed, for the columnist had no equal in the description of violent combat.

So he turned to strategy and took six months to refresh his memory on that subject. He went through the commentaries of Caesar and Marcus Aurelius and the memoirs of Foch, the contemporary accounts of Liddell Hart, and much more that was less well known. It was in the midst of his book on grand strategy that he met Caroline, a quiet Washington young woman with no military background at all. The columnist was instantly enchanted and courted her with the single-mindedness that had been his trademark in the war: he took her with him on lectures, and once to France, where they spent a week with one of his old Resistance friends, now a distinguished publisher. With the publisher in tow, the columnist returned to the Normandy Beachhead, where he embarked on an eight-hour exegesis of the assault and the fortifications, the manner in which the battle proceeded, and the blunders. So many blunders. At one point the Frenchman and Caroline were in tears together, listening to the columnist describe a repeated assault against an entrenched enemy gun position. The publisher devoted a page or two of his memoirs to the incident, describing it as "extraordinary, an afternoon of inspiration."

The columnist treated Caroline as a singular object of art, a serene and delicate event. Then forty-five, he married her in a small ceremony in his house in Georgetown. The ceremony was large, the reception small; fifty guests, most of them journalists and military men, a few movie people, Washington lawyers. Caroline was dazzled, perhaps in part because of her age. She was nineteen.

The columnist's acquaintances were amazed at the change in their friend. He lost weight, and returned to his column with a new zeal; his intelligence, always formidable, broadened and deepened. His book on strategy was wonderfully reviewed, and it was a rare week when one of his observations was not quoted in the na-

tional press, or on television. He and his adoring wife were fixtures at the White House during that period, "both of them handsome as box tops," a gossipist wrote, chic together in a way that a
very successful man and a beautiful young woman are chic. His
interests widened: always bored with domestic politics, he covered
the 1956 election campaign as if it were the breaching of the Rhine.
On a tip from a family friend, he wrote a series of articles on conflict of interest within the Eisenhower Administration that won
him a Pulitzer Prize. And canceled all further White House invita-
tions. He was more pleased with that than with the other. The
columnist disdained honors, believing them beneath him. But the
Pulitzer came at the right time, and caused numerous magazine
"profiles." Suddenly the columnist found himself a celebrity. He
had always been "known," his name recognized by anyone who
carefully read newspapers. But now he was likely to be interviewed
at airports, and in the spring sought for honorary degrees. A television network offered him a large fee to do a five-minute commentary three times a week. Pressed for cash, the columnist accepted,
and the commentary became one of the ornaments of television in
the late 1950s.

While his interests did widen to include politics and economics,
his preoccupation remained the Army. Strategy, tactics, ways of
war, military personalities. When a young major he had known in
Korea was promoted to brigadier general, the columnist wrote him
a long letter of congratulations; then he asked him around to dinner, not once but half a dozen times. The columnist "talked
him up" (as he said) and wrote two glowing accounts of the officer's
heroics in Korea almost a decade before: in fact, it had been the
major who was responsible for the columnist's war wound; he had
encouraged him to accompany a dangerous patrol. Far from ending the friendship, the incident strengthened it. A brigadier general
three months, the officer found himself named secretary to the joint
staff.

The columnist was pleased with his coup for his protégé, although he did not speak of it to anyone save Caroline. Gradually,
in the late 1950s and early 1960s, he discarded the other interests
and came back to the military. He refreshed his memory on weap-
onry and orders of battle, and commenced to cultivate those new
officers who had made their reputations in his absence. His anal-

ysis of the British Army, written in 1958, stands as a model of its kind; his inquiry into the temperament of military leaders, *Eminent Warriors,* is now a standard text at the command and general staff school at Fort Leavenworth. He hastened to Cyprus and Kenya and Malaya and Indochina and all the other places where there was fighting. These were brave moves on the part of the columnist, because the public then, as now, was bored with military affairs. In the early 1960s, there were no wars of consequence.

In Washington there are people who remember, and can cite, the column that signaled the decline. Except that it is always a different column. Acquaintance A is entirely convinced that it began with the vendetta against the Secretary of State. There were twenty-one straight columns, seven weeks of columns, each one attacking the intelligence and integrity of the Secretary, a harmless New York lawyer, long active in the Council on Foreign Relations. Acquaintance B is equally certain that it began six months later, with the column on farm price-supports. What was odd about this column was that it had been ten years since anyone cared about farm price-supports, and the article itself was incomprehensible. At the time, it caused more laughter than dismay; readers assumed that lines had been dropped somewhere in the transmission, and the copy had become garbled. Acquaintance C, with considerably more authority, is certain that it came later still, the column that everyone now calls "the war column." It was quite simply a celebration of war, of blood and of killing, of "the cleansing nature of armed combat." In it, the columnist announced his theory of war and human progress; that is, the one was impossible (he used the incredible word *indispensable*) without the other. It was a circular theory, working both ways. Appalled, his acquaintances sought out the columnist's wife: what had happened to him? Tight-lipped, she shook her head, refusing to explain. The columnist's wife, clearly upset, would blandly change the subject, and go on to other things.

The war column appeared on a Monday, and that night the columnist and his wife had eighteen in to dinner. There was the usual array, journalists, a senator, two lawyers, a visiting academic, an intelligence official, and the brigadier general, the columnist's old friend. The senator knew the columnist best and over drinks put the question to him. Immediately the party fell silent, listening.

The senator dispensed with all preliminaries and asked straight off: "What the hell was that column about this morning?"

The columnist smiled.

"Damndest bilge I've ever read."

The columnist selected a canapé from a tray.

"I think it goes beyond all bounds."

"De mortuis nil nisi bonum," the columnist replied, which explained nothing and satisfied no one.

There were other columns after that, and in Washington these had the effect of heightening interest in his work. He was the most closely watched writer in town. Between explosions there would be a series of reasonable, even deft, sometimes brilliant columns about missiles or new tanks or aircraft, with occasional skillful excursions into the national economy. But the television network, fearful of slander or worse, canceled his contract. For his acquaintances, picking up the newspaper in the morning was like picking up a hand grenade. On the morning of the sixth of June, 1962, appeared the most alarming column of all. It was a movie review. The film was an adaptation of a celebrated novel of the period, a novel written around the Korean War. The co-star was the columnist's ex-wife, and the last line of the column read: "Anyone venturing an interest into the noblest endeavors of our time must witness this film. Miss Harrison's performance is as luminous as a star, and as moving as death itself."

The columnist and his wife did not have friends the way other people had friends. They had companions, acquaintances, chums. Their house was a salon, and people felt free to stop by. The caterers arrived every Saturday and left again on Wednesday morning, after four nights of parties. In the beginning, Caroline found this exciting. The columnist knew everyone in town, and introductions to anyone he did not know were easily arranged. His brief connection with the movie industry had given him a wide acquaintance in the theater, so the weekend parties were interesting and vivid. The columnist presided over these affairs with style and consideration. He arranged the seating (always placing his wife next to the most interesting, rather than the most prominent, guest), and if conversation fell, he pumped it up again, with an anecdote or outrageous war story. It was in this way that Caroline fell to talking a good deal with the brigadier general; both of them knew the anecdotes and the war stories by heart.

New acquaintances were conducted on a tour through the study, a room which Caroline called "the armory." It was filled with military artifacts and photographs of the columnist in Army fatigues: with Bradley in Europe, with de Castries in Indochina, with the movie star by his hospital bed in Japan. His favorite photograph was of himself in a trench. In the photo he is intense and scowling, squatting in the dirt with his typewriter on his knees. The trench is filled with dead.

The columnist's weekend parties became unpopular not long after the appearance of the movie review, owing to his habit of conducting strange monologues in the early hours of the morning. He would address the two or three stragglers, pulling his chair up close to the edge of the rug in front of the fire. And reprise the wars. He did it quietly, in blackest humor, precise minute-by-minute reconstructions of forgotten engagements, so many dead in the first five minutes, so many wounded in the first ten. Their names and ages and ranks. He would describe the setting of the battle in the larger context of the war, whichever war it was. He once saw a man shot in the heart, and took to describing that with such care and loving attention to detail that once a guest walked out of his house physically ill. He would speak of the camaraderie during wars, the closeness of men and women; the community of it. But he would not expand on that. He thought of the century as a gigantic hecatomb. But exhilarating, he'd say. And war two the best war of all, the most violent, the most profound. Late at night he would talk about the major, now a brigadier general, in the same breath as Guderian or Patton. Occasionally, he would seem to be confused over the nature of his wounds. Just a kid then, he'd say, just a kid. The major, he'd add, "my priest."

Every year the parties ended on October 1, and resumed again late in December. This was the period when the columnist took his trip, to view for himself the various wars then in progress. There were always one or two, somewhere around the world. His reputation was such that he could secure interviews with anyone, and each trip included an example of his old style. It was a visit to a field hospital or a guerrilla command in the bush or something of that sort, and it was then that his prose took flight, there that he was most comfortable and in command. He'd be gone a month or six weeks, then would meet Caroline in Athens or Cairo or Madrid. He would write a month's columns in advance, and they would take a trip: the Pyramids, the bullfights, a tour of Berlin, and once a magical two weeks on the Trans-Siberian Railway. In the beginning, he was a wonderful guide, because he had been everywhere once and could reminisce about the old days. About Segovia in 1938 or Kasserine in 1942 or the time he went on the bombing mission from the north of Scotland in 1944. Tourane in 1952.

"Is there any place where you haven't been in a war?" Caroline asked him on one of the early trips.

He thought a moment, then shook his head.

"No place at all?"

"New Zealand," he said finally.

"Let's go there."

"Dull country," he said. "What's the point?"

"I'd like it so much."

"Oh, sure," he said, but they never went.

It was during one of these absences, in the period before she was to join him in a capital somewhere, that the columnist's wife had the affair with the brigadier general. The affair was reminiscent of another, and in the columnist's younger days he would have laughed about it, perhaps with Hemingway or Capa. The brigadier general came by the Georgetown house one afternoon with a manila envelope full of documents. He stayed for drinks and dinner and then for the night.

No one knows what animated the affair, nor what kept it going. Caroline had seemed happy, if distracted; there was always an exquisite poignance about her, as if her life were lived on the edge of something. Often at parties she'd stare at her husband across the table, desperately protective of him — his vitality, his easy dominance, his pride, and of course, his prejudice. On the evenings he talked about the war she would retire to another corner, but there is no evidence that she ever abandoned him in any traditional way. There is a single written record from the period, and for obvious reasons it must be read with skepticism. It is a novel, a *roman à clef,* written by the columnist's former secretary. The novel was published in 1963, enjoyed a brief success of scandal in Wash-

ington, then died. Two picturesque chapters purport to describe
the love affair between Caroline and the brigadier general. One
passage suggests the entire dreadful book.

*They lay in each other's arms, apprehensive, as if watched by
the photographs on the walls. The general's uniform lay crumpled
beside the couch, the single star on his epaulet lit by the soft light
of the room. It was as if he were there with them. His presence dominated the room.*

"Do it again," she said.

And he did, as if on command.

"Doesn't he do it at all?"

"Oh, yes." She seemed quite appalled by the inference.

"Well . . ."

"It isn't that. He's fifty-three now, he's done . . ."

"I see."

*The brigadier general was a plain-spoken man, and he did not
understand why he was there, on the couch with her. He was enjoying it, but he didn't understand it. But then, he didn't understand the columnist either.*

"Why me then?"

"Well, you were there in Korea. His friend."

"I still don't get it."

*She smiled, and pointed at the pictures, all of them. The
pictures from all the wars. She was pointing at the pictures and
laughing. Her laughter grew in volume, louder and louder until
she was hysterical and finally collapsed in his arms, sobbing and
crying for him to do it again.*

The author of the *roman à clef* didn't understand what it was
about, because the chapter ends one paragraph later. Further on
in the book there is an account of what happened when
the columnist found out about the affair, but that account has no
value because the secretary by then had quit, and was in New York
selling an outline of her book.

The affair with the brigadier general began in late 1962 and
lasted through most of 1963. The columnist returned from his trip
in November, a month ahead of schedule, ill with fever contracted
in Central Africa. The trip had not been a success anyway, and he

took leave from his column and of course never resumed it. The column just trailed away, as he did.

Friends found him one afternoon in his study, the armory, staring blackly at a thick loose-leaf folder. The folder contained hundreds, perhaps a thousand, names. They were carefully written, three names to a page, in the columnist's thin script. He refused to speak, and for a time no one could decipher what the names meant; they were names in numerous languages. It should have been obvious, but it was not, until Caroline explained. They were the names of dead, she said. Companions, acquaintances, chums. Soldiers, war correspondents, various political people. The columnist was seated at his desk, staring at the list, defiance on his face. He gripped the loose-leaf folder with such strength that it was impossible to pry it from his hands. It stayed with him, part of him.

That is close to the end of the story. The brigadier general was transferred from the Pentagon to Fort Carson, his career in ruins. Caroline followed him there, stayed six months, then returned to the house in Georgetown. The general went on to the Far East, and when last heard of he was still there. No one has heard anything of Caroline except a rumor that she was in the Far East, too. Though not, of course, with him.

ROBERTA KALECHOFSKY

His Day Out

(FROM THE WESTERN HUMANITIES REVIEW)

LIONEL ENZINO HAD BEEN in Craigmore Institute for the emotionally disturbed for almost two years. For the past three months he had had a day a week, usually Sunday, to go home, visit relatives, friends, stroll on a beach, wander through a park, or just plain "have a ball," as Dr. Benson had said. Lionel dreaded his day out. He wished he could give it as a gift to someone who would appreciate it. He did not. If he were taking Sunday out, panic began to build by Friday night. Saturday was destroyed, he could hardly read a book or play a game of bridge. By Sunday morning he prayed war would break out and all "inmates" be ordered to stay put. His day out was a misery. He had to think each move in advance and felt as if he were swimming in the Sargasso Sea. What to wear, what to do, what to say, how to put his tokens in the slot, what train to take, not to panic if he got lost, what restaurant to eat in, what movie to see, if any, what museum to visit, whether to go home, whether to see a friend, whether to date a girl. He never just went out, he never just was. From the moment he knew he was taking a day out he scheduled each move. He could not stand surprises. He took the same trains, he ate in the same restaurant, he walked the same streets; he always went home. He could not stand not having a roof over his head.

Dr. Benson usually came to his room and asked him how his day had gone. Lionel only knew that, thank God! it had gone. He felt ludicrous that what he had managed to live through was ordinary stuff. He knew that people lived through it every day. They took trains, visited relatives, went to museums, caught buses, pushed up umbrellas in the rain. He watched them, envious at their non-chalance.

Craigmore was outside of New York, past Nyack, on the Hudson. When Lionel had first seen the old Craigmore Mansion, imitation medieval castle, modern convert into asylum, sunning itself in a dip between two hills on the Hudson River, he felt his esthetic bone bruise.

"What corn," he said to himself. It took him eight or nine months to get up enough nerve to tell Dr. Benson that the Institute, this miracle of rehabilitation, was 30 per cent corn, 30 per cent mechanical gaiety, 20 per cent inefficiency, waste, boredom, languor, 10 per cent sadistic attendants who watched you through slitty eyes to see how funny you could get, 5 per cent indifferent attendants and 5 per cent Dr. Benson, who held the whole thing together with inexhaustible patience.

Dr. Benson brushed his nose with his index finger, a gesture he made so frequently that Lionel imagined he had softened the cartilage at the end of his nose. "Eighteen ninety was a pretty corny period in a lot of ways," he said. "Men who made money then went as European as they could get. You wouldn't believe that this place was something of a bunny club in its day."

Lionel sensed that Dr. Benson was offering a masculine turn to the therapy and he felt calm enough by then to rise to it. "What happened to it?" he said lightheadedly.

"Jasper Craigmore — he made his money on some silly invention that had to do with amplifying sound — got tired of bunnies and went in for hunting lions. He got lost on an expedition in Africa and was never heard from. His wife, who was Roman Catholic, had the house converted into a museum for medieval art. Concentrated on the thirteenth century. No one knows why. Basement still full of jars of kneebones and fingers, bits and scraps of wood and veils. Was frugal. Lived by herself in a cottage up the hill."

"The sculpture school," Lionel said. He tried not to snicker, but he hated dabbling in the arts for the sake of therapy, esthetic snob that he was.

"She died at the age of eighty-three. Always wore black. Left one son, Hellman. He never liked the house. Was a Baptist like his father and went through the halls smashing the jars and tearing up the mummies as soon as his mother was buried. Hellman's wife aspired to the jet set and they're somewhere out there now, two daughters, two poodles and a Siamese cat. Hellman's uncle, Jasper's brother, had become psychotic (Lionel felt his heart jump. He hated such definitive terms. He knew he was sick and it terrified him to think that anyone might define his sickness like that) in his middle years (Lionel felt sweat on his back at the thought of the future). Hellman had always loved this uncle. Only friend he had ever had. Came to his wedding when his father didn't. Soon as his mother was buried, he cleared out the medieval and devoted the house to the Harkley Institute for the Mentally Ill. That's us."

Lionel looked down at his thumbnails and scratched them. His stomach fluttered. "That's us."

"More or less," Dr. Benson said.

Lionel's eyes shot up. "You mean I'm less than more."

"What about this Sunday?"

Lionel's mouth dried. "I'll go if you want me to," he said. He felt silly to flatly decline an offer to go out.

"Why don't you want to, yourself?"

"Because the whole thing's a bore." Lionel wasn't sure whether he was lying. He knew he was bored because he was paralyzed. Living in a mental strait jacket wasn't the liveliest way to stay alive. The fountain of youth is love of life, he had said to himself. One loves life when one finds it interesting. One finds life interesting when one is not frightened of it. He was paralyzed because he was terrified. A ride on a train was a stupefying collision course between those thoughts which he must not think because they put him in a state of panic and those other thoughts which made him nauseated. He veered and careened from station to station between nausea and panic until he got to Queens, where his mother eyed him with distraught and guilty love for every sign of improvement and hushed his father all afternoon in fear that he might say a wrong word, threw a ball to his younger brother, listened to his sister's records if she was home, and gnawed his soul all afternoon in worry over the trip back.

Once his brother, sixteen, had asked him what was wrong with him. "You look all right," he said.

"I get this thing on trains," Lionel said.

"What thing?" Lionel felt Franklin eying him.

Lionel drew in his breath. They were lying on Franklin's bed, looking at his stamp collection. Lionel did not know whether to tell him or not, or how much to say. Now, after two years, he had a great sense of security in talking to Dr. Benson about it, but talking to Franklin about it was like plunging off a cliff. He shrugged his shoulders. "This thing."

Franklin turned the gum in his mouth. "What thing?"

Lionel's mouth dried. "All sorts of things. First, when I get on the platform. People standing so close to the edge. It gives you the creeps. One push and it's all over." He shuffled some loose stamps into an envelope. His hands were wet. "I bet you don't think such things."

Franklin rocked on his heels. "All the time. I don't stand near the edge."

Lionel looked up at him. He was intrigued by Franklin's insouciance. It was a revelation. "How come such thoughts don't bother you?"

Franklin shrugged his shoulders. "Don't know. I think them and then I don't stand near the edge. Is that why you went up to Craigmore?"

It was plain Franklin didn't think that much of a reason to be in a nationally renowned Institute for the Mentally Ill, draining the family of its money. Lionel felt confused, even piqued. "There are plenty of other thoughts. When I see the doors close I want to scream."

"You did scream, remember?" Franklin said. "When we were in that elevator. You mean you still feel that way?" Clearly, Franklin thought the family money was being wasted.

"I don't scream anymore," Lionel said.

"Yeah, but you still want to. Why don't you scream now and get it over with. I mean do it in advance to see how it feels. A train's only a train, no different from anything else."

"Exactly," Lionel said. He got off the bed feeling undermined and boyish discussing his problems with Franklin. "It's not just trains. It's buses, elevators, escalators, airplanes, tunnels, bridges, tiny rooms and wide open spaces. It's too many things, too many things."

"Don't be upset," Franklin said, fearful he had stepped over a mysteriously "healthy" boundary. "I'm just trying to understand. You seemed to be having a ball at college."

Lionel picked up a hairbrush. He put it down and turned to Franklin. "No," he said in an even voice, "I was not having a ball in college. I was locking myself in my room every night after supper. I hated the food, I hated the classes, I hated being away from home, and then I hated the idea of graduating. Sorry about that, Franklin."

"And you couldn't even take the train home," Franklin said with sudden insight.

"No, there was nothing to do. So I broke up." Lionel felt extraordinary relief saying it like that. It had seemed bitterly dramatic to have his mother and father come to Ohio to take him home, three months before graduation, the first child in their family to go to college, second generation Italian immigrants. His mother sat weeping in the dean's office. "Why my son? Why my son? He was such a good boy." The dean tried to tell her, without resorting to modern linguistics, that this was not a matter of good and evil. But his mother, whose psyche had been nourished on other ideas of justice, was sure that mental illness amounted to an indignity that was a cruel punishment and she was confounded by her son's innocence.

She sat in Dr. Benson's office, having found by instinct "the best doctor in the whole country," and cried, "Why my son?"

Dr. Benson rubbed the cartilage at the end of his nose. "Why not your son?" he said.

"Did you mean that?" Lionel had asked him after his mother had gone.

"Of course. Who's immune, and what's immunity?"

Dr. Benson was part of Lionel's problem. He liked him so much he never wanted to be away from him. He had not wanted to leave home, he had not wanted to graduate and he didn't want to leave Craigmore. It was a big mistake to send him out once a week. It was almost as bad for him when Dr. Benson took a holiday, for Lionel worried fearfully for him.

"You're not flying?" he said anxiously.

"Sure am. It's the only intelligent way to go."

Lionel would pin a note on the wall in his room giving him complete information about Dr. Benson's movements, what plane he was taking there and back, time of arrival, hotel he was staying at, approximate traveling time from airport to hotel. His estimate of this part of the trip could never be better than approximate, which put Lionel into deep depression. As soon as he knew Dr. Benson's plane had arrived safely — he always checked — he went into deepest panic because there was no way to contact Dr. Benson in the complicated mess of trains, subways, taxis and traffic. Lionel could not tolerate a situation in which Dr. Benson would not be available to give immediate response to his panic. He rarely asked for this response, but he liked to know it was there. That's why he hated trains more than bridges or small rooms. Because if he began to have his eerie thoughts on a train he knew there was no way he could call Dr. Benson from the depths of the subway. He was locked in with his own mind and there was no getting away from it, he and a few hundred other people. He had only to think to himself — as he always did — as soon as the doors closed, that now he was in for it, there was no way out. Counting helped minimally. It was three hundred and forty seconds of agony from the 14th Street station to 42nd Street on the express. He told himself that only a worthless person couldn't put up with three hundred and forty seconds of agony, but he knew that it would have been better had he taken the local, for he watched the local stops sail past, helpless that he could not step out on one of them.

It did not give him a feeling of achievement that he had been making these disastrous rides every week for several months. As soon as he was back at Craigmore he felt relief that it was over and foreboding that he would have to do it again next week. After all, the fact that you have walked through a ring of hell doesn't mean that you can face the same ring of hell next week with cheer. Hell, Lionel discovered, was an absolute and always felt like hell. That's what gave it its terrific quality. You couldn't extract courage or hope from it. Lionel never had the satisfaction of saying to himself, "By golly, I did it and I can do it again." He said to himself, "Thank God, that's over and I'd give anything never to have to do it again." When he had gotten back to his room and gone through these thoughts, he often ended with the worst thought of all: Dr. Benson didn't know what he was doing; Dr. Benson was a poor doctor and he, Lionel, was never going to get well. The pain of that thought was intolerable. Lionel would lie down on his bed, flaming with agony and all night float in a miasma of pain.

Once Dr. Benson asked him, as they were walking down the corridor together, "I'd be interested in knowing what you think of me, Lionel." He opened the door to his office and invited him in. Lionel felt unchecked admiration and affection for Dr. Benson. Those were his daytime thoughts. He knew he wasn't going to make it without him and he told him so.

"No doubts?" Dr. Benson said.

Lionel reddened.

Dr. Benson gazed at his mail and without looking at Lionel said, "You can't be sure."

Lionel felt pursued and vexed. Dr. Benson was being tricky. "How sure can anything be?" he said smartly.

"Exactly." Dr. Benson leaned back in his swivel chair and put his hands behind his head. "You have to learn to live in the margin of gamble." He threw that out in a more comradely fashion than the doctor-to-patient relationship augured, and then changed his tone. He brought his chair forward, placed his hands on the desk. "That's where you have to go, Lionel. How did things go yesterday?"

Lionel felt immediately depressed. "Same as usual."

"Same train, same stations, same restaurant, same streets?"

"Yes, yes, yes, yes."

"How was your mother?"

"Same as usual."

"Franklin?"

"He wasn't home. He went to a baseball game."

"Why didn't you go with him?"

The thought of the crowds at the stadium made Lionel shudder. "I'm not particularly interested in baseball."

Dr. Benson put his hands behind his head again. "You play a good game here."

"That's different."

"How so?" Dr. Benson said.

"All right." Lionel snapped. "I like baseball. I hate crowds."

Dr. Benson came forward again and put his hands on the desk. Lionel knew he was waiting for him to continue. All of a sudden the son of a bitch had slid into the good old classical session. Say it, Lionel, Dr. Benson's eyes said. Say what's on your mind. Your frame is too small to stand all that howling inside. Let it out. I'll never say it, Lionel laughed behind his closed lips. I'll never say it because if I do you'll know for sure I'm nuts. Dr. Benson stared at Lionel as if for two people to look at each other in silent and fierce antagonism for fifteen minutes was ordinary behavior.

"Because you never know for sure," Lionel cried. "God, you never know for sure when one of them's got a gun or a knife and will get you in the back. There are hundreds, thousands, pushing all around you and you never know which one of them's a freak.

And one of them's bound to be a freak. That's the law of averages.
And it only takes one freak to kill a dozen people."

"That's true," Dr. Benson said. "Crowds increase the chance of
danger. Always did, and human nature can get freaky at times. Always was. But what's that got to do with Lionel Enzino?"

Lionel felt crushed by his admission. "How the hell can I escape?"

"Why not? Some do."

"But it's all a matter of luck," Lionel said bitterly.

Dr. Benson looked at him down the slope of his nose. "What
bothers you about that?" Lionel felt nauseated. "It's not good
enough," he whispered. His hands were wet. Suddenly he had a
vision of Franklin, rocking on his heels, telling his friends, "Man,
you shoulda seen that car go outa control. Smashed into the super-
market and all. People scattered like mad. Just an old lady and
her grandkid got it. I'm tellin' you what luck." Lionel drew in his
breath. He would be crying if he were alone, but he never cried in
front of Dr. Benson. That much he kept for himself.

"Besides," Dr. Benson said. "Lionel?" he called, because Lionel's
mind was still listening to Franklin.

"What?" Lionel said, detached.

"Sometimes it is, and sometimes it isn't," Dr. Benson said. "Don't
overestimate luck. Don't underestimate it either." He laughed.

"What can you do about a guy sitting behind you who pushes a
knife into your ribs?" Lionel asked hotly.

"Not much." Dr. Benson smiled. "How many people have been
killed at ball games lately?"

Lionel's eyes narrowed. "You want me to go to a ball game
next week, right? A trial run at being normal."

Dr. Benson rubbed his nose. "Sure, Lionel, if you'd like to."

Bull! Lionel said to himself. If I'd like to! Why don't you ask
me if I would like to jump into a vat of boiling oil. "Dr. Benson,"
he said, "I don't even want to go home next week."

"Then don't. Take the day out and do something else. It's
spring. Take a walk down a country road."

"Doctor Benson," Lionel said.

"Come in around Wednesday," Dr. Benson said. He got up and
put his arm on Lionel's shoulder. "We'll talk about it then."

"Doctor Benson," Lionel said, finding himself at the door.

"And try not to make out too many lists and itineraries of how
you're going to spend the day. You have a good memory, Lionel.

You'll remember from this Sunday to next Sunday how to spend the day," and Lionel found himself outside the office, facing his next day out, another Sunday, another train ride, another mealy tuna fish sandwich in Katz' Kozy Korner. Maybe he would go to a ball game and show Dr. Benson. No, he wouldn't. He didn't care to show Dr. Benson anything. Maybe he wouldn't go home. This once he might try the Whitney Museum, which wasn't too big or too small. He'd take the train to the 58th Street station, walk one block east and two blocks down. But the Whitney was on 54th. Are you sure? he said to himself. Better check it out thoroughly before next week. Maybe he would be lucky and die before next week.

But he wasn't. Worse, Sunday dawned clear as a bell, not a cloud in the sky, birds singing, April beauty. Wearily, Lionel put on his clothes. He changed his tie three or four times, brushed his hair forward to look modern, then brushed it back to feel safer. Took a close shave and then was sorry he had done that. Dead giveaway, looking so spic and span, careful like the guy on the dance floor counting his steps. But I am, Lionel said grimly. He took a deep breath and went out for his day.

I am counting, he said breathlessly. Three blocks to the bus stop. Street deserted, feel conspicuous like an invader. Eight minutes on the bus. Just him and the bus driver. Sunday loneliness setting in. A six-minute wait at the station. He stood with his hands in his pockets, well away from the edge. He could smell his pomade, Listerine, Mann deodorant and Savage aftershave lotion. The small Tudor houses, still-life peace, surrounded the station. All was quiet with Sunday shades pulled down. Never was fond of Sunday, he thought. It always shut him out. Surprised that Dr. Benson didn't steer him in the direction of Thursday or Saturday. Two girls came on to the station platform, chic to their eyeteeth. Lionel felt his insecurities pop like blisters. He smelled pomade and Listerine all about him. His face reddened, his hands got sweaty. Dr. Benson, he said to himself, you're making a big mistake.

The train pulled in, he got on, clutching his soul. The girls eyed this seat, then that one, and finally drifted into the next car. Lionel felt better and settled down to count something, anything, birds, trees, telephone poles. He thought of his mother counting beads. Don't see much of that anymore. Certainly not in the streets the way she used to do it. Always there by her side whenever she needed them. Comfort in mechanical repetition. It might not be too bad to be a machine, Lionel thought, but even as he thought that to himself, cleverly, panic fell upon him. The thought scared him out of his wits. He felt sweat in his scalp. What the hell *am* I scared of, he said, trying to get hold of himself. Does anyone know? Or care how scared I am? He looked around at the train. Sunday never brought many passengers, mainly dissidents, old beggars. Families travel by car on Sunday. There was only one group at the other end with a guy in the middle playing a guitar. They were dressed tough, motorcycle club, leather jackets, studded belts, spurs. Lionel felt shaken to his toes. When the train pulled into the 125th Street station, he bolted out the door to the strains of "Ya Gotta Tell It Like It Is to Your Mammy That Is 'Cause Your Mammy Is All You Got, Son."

Actually, he thought, fleeing to catch his next train, it probably is safer in a crowd. He had never seen it that way, and the thought was cheering, like the sunniest of revelations. He thought of putting a dime in the phone slot, calling Franklin and telling him to meet him at Shea Stadium. But he didn't.

By the time he got to 58th Street, it was almost twelve, as he knew it would be, and he decided to stop for lunch. He might, he thought, he might make up his mind about Shea Stadium after his sandwich. Study the situation. Consider all possibilities. What a strike for freedom if he went. Dr. Benson would never believe him.

Katz' Kozy Korner was closed due to a death in the family, and Lionel went flat. He stared at the closed door with disbelief and terror. Not possible, he thought. Oh God, yes! Never mind lunch, he said to himself quickly. That was just an excuse to act normal. Get back on the train quickly and get on home.

I cannot go back on the train quickly, he said to himself. I have not gotten on a train quickly in three years.

Call Franklin and tell him to come get you.

Franklin will think I'm mad.

That's all right. At least he'll know the family's not wasting its money.

I will not call Franklin, who is sixteen, to rescue his brother, who is twenty-four, and help him find another restaurant to eat in.

I thought you didn't care about dignity.

True. Mine's gone, but there's still Franklin's.

Bet he'd enjoy it more than a ball game.

Don't be cynical, Lionel said to himself, he'd never forget it. Pick up your leaden feet and find another restaurant.

Where? If I wander from this block I might get lost.

How?

That's what I don't know.

Try it. Get going. Lionel stuck his hands in his pockets, wheeled on his heels, sucked in his cheeks and started up the street. His eyes burned. The harder he practiced nonchalance the more unrelaxed he felt. He wanted to scream. That would relax him. He walked three blocks, leaden-footed, his stomach swollen with all sorts of juices. There was another restaurant, another Kozy Korner. Same kind of lunch counter, island in the center, booths along the sides, telephones in the back, magazine rack near cash register. He felt a dry-mouthed gratitude for familiarity and haunched himself on to a stool.

"What'llya have?" the counterman said.

"Same as usual," Lionel said. Then he sat up erect. "Sorry about that," he mumbled. "Tuna fish sandwich and coffee."

"Toast?"

"Toast?"

"Yeah, toast?"

"Toast — Wait a minute. Change that to egg salad on white."

Lionel ran his tongue over his gums and around his teeth, trying to relieve the dryness in his mouth. He took a stupendously big breath and let it out to the count of twenty. Well, Dr. Benson, he said to himself, guess what?

There were half a dozen other people in the restaurant, a fact which made Lionel neither happy nor unhappy. He knew this for sure because he had measured all the possibilities involved in there being exactly six people in the restaurant. That was enough for them to protect each other if something should happen, but not enough to cause a riot. Of course, he was not too fond of the looks of all of them. The old woman across the counter from him looked like Damon Runyon's best. Broadway Annie, nosegays and tipsy. The two businessmen down the end were about right, straight on the center of life and solid. But, on the other hand, you never knew the facts about anyone. They could belong to the Mafia or be a new style in pimps. And that man sitting there in a booth by himself. Lionel distrusted men who sat by themselves, especially when they looked seedy and kept their hands under their jackets, right about where a gun holster would be, if one were going to wear a gun holster.

Quit it, he said to himself, don't get fishy now.

His sandwich came and he tried to enjoy it. A couple walked in, two children, sour looks, and sat down in a booth. "Try not to order the whole store," the father said.

"You don't want them to go hungry," the mother said.

"Try it. For a new experience," the father said.

The seedy-looking man lit a cigarette and let it dangle from his lips. "Knew he would," Lionel said to himself. The man got a bowl of soup and when it came he flipped his cigarette on the floor and ground it with the heel of his shoe until the tobacco was shredded. Lionel felt as if he had E.S.P. The man put his hand under his jacket with a fingering motion and Lionel felt the sweat break out on his neck.

I will not think those thoughts, he said to himself. But, God almighty, doesn't he look the type. And what would I do if he were? Imagine if I said to the waiter, say, that guy looks suspicious. I have a mild form of E.S.P. and that guy looks brinky. Who do you think they'd arrest? Lionel tried to keep his eyes down, but every time the man's hand went under his jacket his eyes flipped. He's a killer, he thought. He felt nauseated. No, he's not, he said to himself, he's just a plain, ordinary person and I am being treated for mental illness because I think such thoughts and have such worries. Dr. Benson, please help me. Help me to be good and not have such thoughts. Help me to live in peace with my fellowman. I mean in an everyday way so I can take a walk by myself. Help me to enjoy a tuna fish sandwich or egg salad and a Sunday out.

The food arrived for the family in the booth. Cutlets and mashed potatoes for the father. Mother looked at it with anger. "Thought you said you weren't hungry."

"That was before."

"Before what?"

The waiter put down an assortment of hamburgers and bowls of French fries. Father said, "Thought you said last Sunday you'd never eat another hamburger."

"That was last Sunday."

The waiter said, "What'llya have to drink?"

"Two Cokes and two coffees."

"Make mine orange," the girl said.

"Me too," the boy said.

"I'll take tea," the mother said.

⎣The seedy-looking man finished his soup and pushed his bowl away. He sat limp on his chair, his chin hanging over the bowl as if he expected his head to drop into it. Lionel's eyes flipped up and down. The man stared out the plate-glass window in front of him. He swallowed. His Adam's apple floated in the skin of his neck. He put his hand under his jacket again and fiddled with the something there that was getting on Lionel's nerves. Lionel felt his skin crawl. Eat fast, he thought, and leave. But he couldn't think of where he had planned to go. He wondered if he should call Franklin. His eyes drifted to the telephones and he measured the distance from them to the seedy-looking man.

All right, heads I will, tails I won't, he thought, fishing in his pocket for a coin. "Look out," he screamed. There was a blaze of gunshot over their heads. He slid off his stool so fast it twirled after him for thirty seconds though he never counted it. Broadway Annie slumped forward like a broken flower. The two businessmen fell to the floor, one groaning. The little girl and boy screamed. Their mother flung herself across the table, covering them with her body and shrieking to God.

Lionel pressed himself against the wall of the counter. "Dr. Benson," he whimpered. The gunshot continued overhead for another eight seconds like a staccato of truth. There were three seconds of silence, then a final shot and the seedy man's head burst into blood. Lionel peered over the edge of the counter, his eyes bulging. Dr. Benson, he said to himself, you're never going to believe this. I mean, but you're never going to believe this. I mean but, boy, you're going to think I'm nuts. He raised himself up slowly. His heart tore apart with terrific turmoil, but his soul floated out like an intrepid butterfly.

REBECCA KAVALER

The Further Adventures of Brunhild

(FROM THE YALE REVIEW)

LET'S INVENT TORTURES, George said in bed. Exotic tortures. Margaret groaned, having found James Bond in double-feature dose torture enough for one night. But George went on, laying down ground rules: slow and mind-bending, with always the promise of worse to come. How about this, he began, first you fill a tub with Jell-O —

But Margaret had Hilly on her mind. She said she didn't want to play and patted his rump good-night. Joanna, how she would sneer at that. Margaret defended herself from that and other accusations Joanna transmitted to her through the long-distance, short-wave night: she had not been scared away when the truck blew up. Three days on that kibbutz was enough. It was the indecency of the tiny bungalow she couldn't take, vibrating all night as if a subway ran under it. Joanna stretching before her in the morning, her body bragging. But after thirty years of marriage, there was a great deal of comfort in a man's rump.

With children, you laughed or you cried. Joanna — Margaret laughed. Conversion to Judaism, life on a kibbutz, and all. Slinging the baby on her hip and the rifle over her shoulder. As if she were the first, as if she didn't have great-grandparents who had done all that already in Nebraska. Their granddaughter was a living doll, Margaret reported back to George, blond and blue-eyed with a nose just like yours — George would be relieved about the nose, she knew — and Margaret had laughed about the day-care center for the children.

Joanna explained it so patiently. The tone of voice Margaret had once used herself, squatting on her heels in a sandpile. One doesn't throw sand at another little girl, dear. No babysitting allowed for this grandmother, George. Check her in with all the other kids, pick her up at night. Emotionally healthy environment for learning. Free of the festering sores of family life and oedipal rivalries. Her own career fifteen years in cold storage while she stayed home with three little girls. Major in fine arts. By the time she met George she had abandoned oils, was apprentice to a sculptor. What great biceps you have, George said, like Little Red Riding Hood admiring the wolf. Into the maw of marriage and fifteen years, three daughters later, a designer of furniture. International awards. Museum exhibits. The Cannon chair now mass-produced, a household word. Not less a work of art because you can sit in it.

We're festering sores, George, Margaret reported back and laughed. Yet proudly. Proud of the rifle and the baby and the strong thighs, olive-brown, in British-style army shorts, and the joy of being up and about that made it seem always early morning of what promised to be a beautiful day. Nelson Eddy, that was Joanna. Leading a chorus of scouts through the forest, sneaking up on the Indians by blasting away with a blandly stalwart baritone. *Tramp tramp tramp* along the highway. That's Joanna. Now Carol was a different story.

My daughter the astronomer. Margaret said it like a Jewish mother and even George laughed. The smartest of the three — Hilly wasn't smart so much as — Now that's Hilly, all right, Margaret thought furiously, twenty-four years I've had her, my own child, and still groping for the word. And pretty. Margaret shut out the thought of Hilly, concentrated on a picture of Carol's prettiness. Tall willow of blondness, comforting to a mother as a sniffing blanket to a child. In the small Midwestern town of Margaret's childhood, the public library had had a life-sized Grecian marble. The first piece of sculpture she had ever seen. Gleaming palely from a corner darkness in the lobby, a woman sat, long robe falling over her knees in soft intricate folds, and over her bowed head the thinnest of veils, and under that, cut in clearest perfection, the beautiful sad face. Child Margaret had stood before it and shivered with awe: a veil carved out of rock. Carol was like that. A gossamer sheer veil carved out of marble. She and her husband, astronomer too, wrote papers no one in the family could read — not even George — covered all over with the chicken-tracks of mathematics. And stood in line for years awaiting their turn to peek through that big telescope in California. For Chrissake, you don't peek through a thing like that, George kept correcting her, not understanding that she used just such coy phrases to conceal the vastness of her pride.

Hilly. She was back to Hilly. And where was that? We'll see Hilly tomorrow. She must have said that aloud. She heard the firm, no-nonsense, now-go-to-sleep voice, as if she were putting the girls, not herself, to bed. But where was Hilly? Who had always known where to hide, even in a city apartment, so that no one could find her. No one. Nowhere. There were the police, searching the city streets for a five-year-old, there Margaret was, sitting by the telephone chewing the knuckles of a clenched fist, and George rushing home from the office. And there was Hilly, squatting in the laundry basket, camouflaged as dirty underwear. All those hours, motionless, not a sound. Flushed out in the end by the TV cartoons when Carol came home from school.

Margaret called out, "George!" Catastrophe in the middle of the night. But George only grunted in his sleep.

"I'll bet you didn't phone Hilly we were both coming down tomorrow."

She kicked him tentatively and got another grunt, which could have been yes, could have been no. When she called Hilly last week to tell her the news, she had said she would be over after the lunch at the White House. That was so Hilly could hear all about it — after all, it was not every mother who lunched with Lady Bird, along with twenty other Women in the Arts — a pride of females, George called it. Margaret had warned Hilly, "Clear everything off the floor, I'll need the room to drop names." Now George had to go down too, only the day before, Thursday.

"Couldn't you see that guy in the State Department Friday, so we could fly down together?"

She should have known better. George felt it a man's role to be unaccommodating. His counterproposal was that she should drop in at the White House on Thursday. "Say you'll take pot luck." She had admitted defeat gracefully. It was worth going down a day ahead to have George with her. Things went smoother at Hilly's when they were both there. Cancel appt. with Kenneth, have hair done in Wash., she memoed herself. George, phone Hilly, she had memoed him. And he hadn't — that had been a no grunt, she was sure. She would arrive a day early, and to Hilly she would be presuming all over again to "drop in." As if she ever made the same mistake twice. With Hilly, you didn't have to. With Hilly there was an inexhaustible supply of mistakes waiting yet to be made.

Margaret could hear George in the morning: "For Chrissake, I've got to make an appointment to see my own daughter? She'll *be* there, won't she? What is there to barge in on, except the kids?" George wouldn't see it. Nor had Margaret when last year, coming back from North Carolina, she had gotten off in Washington, on sudden impulse, just because the plane made a stop there. It had seemed so simple: spend the afternoon with Hilly, see the babies, take the Pennsy up that night. Margaret felt irresponsibly gay, all spur-of-the-moment, and warmly affectionate at the thought of being a delightful surprise. Hilly's phone didn't answer, but Margaret took a cab and drove out to Bethesda anyway, figuring: she's just outdoors with the kids. And she was, in that grassy square where all the backyards of the development block were thrown together in a kitty and called the Commons.

"How did you know I was here?" Hilly gasped.

"I just took a chance, darling. Surprised?"

She was that, all right. Hilly in a rage. Like the sudden starting up of a powerful engine, a dynamo threatening to shake apart its too frail housing. Hilly with her arms crossed, containing herself, but her nails picking at the yarn of the sweater sleeves. Unraveling the sleeve of care. Joanna, Carol — that combine from the past — were hurled at her. Margaret didn't just drop in on them, Hilly bet.

"Whenever I'm flying from North Carolina to New York and the plane makes a stop in Israel or Arizona, I do just that," Margaret snapped back.

"Even if I *were* here," Hilly said — as if that were a matter yet to be settled! — "how do you know that I'm not busy, maybe Ed and I are going out tonight, and I have a thousand and one things to do, maybe I haven't got time to sit down and have one of your nice long chats." So the nice long chat turned out to be a nice long sulk, because Hilly wasn't going anywhere and couldn't, on such short notice, think of a thousand and one things to do.

I will call Hilly in the morning before we leave, Margaret decided, and pulled the covers up to her chin, as if the decision had laid her permanently to rest. Then decided again, pushing the covers off, to let George call. From him Hilly might accept it as sufficient notice. Dealing with Hilly was like being ensnarled in some terribly complicated legal document, with innumerable clauses appended in fine print.

George cried out in his sleep. Automatically, Margaret reached out and shook him down to a mumble, and the mumble subsided to a faint fluttering of his lips marking the passage of his breath. The idiot sound Hilly used to make as a child by fingering a loose lower lip. Daytime George, solid and stolid, imperturbable, let's-reason-this-thing-out Geroge, as if life were just another hydro site, and all you had to do was locate and design the dam properly, determine the peak load, install pump reservoirs. But nighttime George, whining, whimpering, groaning. A mad laugh ha-ha-ing her awake at 3 A.M. Or a scream of pain escaping from some dungeon of torture. (Let's invent tortures. Fill a tub with Jell-O — what came next? She had never let George finish.) Hilly. Joanna and Carol had nightmares. Hilly slept like a rock. Daytime Hilly and nighttime George — there was a pair. They would have known each other. But daytime George refused to worry.

"It's a good thing she got married when she did, and had kids one two three. She'd have been a natural for the beatnik scene — hair down to here, skirts up to there, pot, LSD, the works. All I worry about now is kid number four. Somebody in this family is bound to come up with a boy."

More of the same from Joanna and Carol. A general all-round sighing out of relief. As if a nice steady job had been found for a weak-minded member of the family they had all been afraid was unemployable.

Fiercely Margaret boxed her pillow back into shape, answering that calumny with her fists. Hilly had more in her little finger than the other two put together. True confessions at 2 A.M. More than I. Margaret had known the painful boa-constrictor squeeze of envy when she first saw Hilly's paintings. Oils. Don't touch my oils, Margaret was always saying, the girls being too young. She gave them pastels and tempera, watercolor, clay. The mess they made. So Hilly saved up from her allowance, secretly, always secretly, hiding everything but the smell of turp in her room. Margaret sniffed, but nothing ever showed. (Which showed Hilly *could* be neat, and Margaret felt resentment fresh as if just then, once again, she had picked up Hilly's litter.) The chest seemed too far away from the wall, Margaret had pushed it back a little askew, and the still wet painting behind it had slid to the floor. The dry ones were in the

closet under a raincoat. Good hiding place for secrets. Half of
Hilly's clothes were always on the closet floor. I will not pick up
after you, Margaret kept saying. Who taught her to use oils? Secret.
Who stretched the canvas for her — that she couldn't have done
herself, not at that age. Secret. The wet one went back behind the
chest, but Margaret stole one of the closet cache — beautiful beautiful Chagall-like thing — and submitted it for the children's show
the Modern was holding that spring. Second prize, a full scholar-
ship, and Hilly the youngest entrant. If she hadn't won, she needn't
have known anything about it. None of the agony of waiting, the
fear of rejection. Just the wonderful surprise of winning.

Margaret folded the pillow around her head as if she could still
hear that raucous yell of rage — the heel-kicking, breath-holding
kind of rage Hilly had yet to outgrow. Take them, take them all,
they're yours, all of them, they're yours. Stalking out of her room
into Margaret's with each one. Take that, and *bam* on the floor, it's
yours. And Joanna saying, but you won, Hilly, you won — Joanna
who only went into rages when she lost — and Carol, whose sisterly
love had jumped over Hilly — like those family traits that skip a
generation — to cherish exclusively the third-born, her arm around
Joanna, drawing her out of range, explaining Hilly as if she were
a natural phenomenon, like lightning and thunder or falling stars:
she's having a tantrum, that's all, you can't reason with Hilly in a
tantrum (or lightning or thunder or falling stars).

So later all that furious secret scribbling had ended, just as suddenly, but not so loudly. Hilly was older then. Quieter. As if she
had installed one of those catches on her temper, so that she might
continue to slam doors with the same heavy brutal force, but they
would close with just a quiet hiss. Good grades, not so startling
as Carol's, but still she must have been applying herself. "She's applying herself," George said, looking pleased, his advice finally
taken, "she's settling down."

"You can say that again," Margaret said, handing him the tele-
gram. Not even to finish college, to drop out in the middle, to
marry what could only be called a nice young man. Who became a
lawyer, a nice young government lawyer in Washington, D.C. A
Catholic. What had happened? Was it a failure of nerve? With
women it was hard to tell. They just got married.

A *practicing* Catholic, Margaret complained to George as the
babies came one two three. George said she was bigoted. But she

didn't mind Joanna's husband being Jewish. She could have accepted a Hindu, a Buddhist, a Muslim — anything exotic and unheard of (that is, not heard of in the Methodist-Baptist enclave of her youth). Religions of bright shimmering colors, strange off-key music, unreal as those setting-sun travelogues of Lowell Thomas. Not connected in any way with the black bugaboo of her childhood. The old Gothic-Victorian mansion that housed some unknown order of nuns. The overlush tangled garden in front. The iron gate that so rarely creaked open and shut. The warnings whispered to little girls: don't walk past at night alone, don't ever go through that gate, no matter how sweet the blandishment, no matter how kind the face. Little girls vanished, were never seen again. Like those stories of ritual murder by Jews, George commented in disgust. No, no, Margaret corrected him, the little girls weren't eaten — although if you were little enough, there might be some confusion — they were kept prisoner, never let outdoors, underwent some strange black-magic metamorphosis to reappear, years later, as a new recruitment of black-robed nuns.

"I think she did it on purpose," Margaret told George, "married a Catholic so that she would have all those babies and not have time for anything else, not even to think."

"Forget it," George advised her, "she seems happy enough. Ed's a nice guy. He appreciates *you*, you've got to admit, so why don't you take the knife out, leave them alone."

Ed paid her compliments, if that was what George meant. Compliments never delivered direct. Via George. Or if George were not there, via Hilly, which was worse. Your wife's one dame who can wear these short skirts, George, legs like Marlene Dietrich. And, bared in a swim suit, her shoulders were pointed out to George as looking like Rosalind Russell's. Did you ever notice, he cross-examined Hilly, Margaret looks like Claudette Colbert — look at those cheekbones, that pointed chin. A collage of old releases on "The Late Late Show," Margaret summed up grimly, but did not really suspect him of evil intent. He was not so subtle. The compliments were mere counterpoint to the insults he paid Hilly.

A wonderful meal, Margaret took pains to tell Hilly, the cassoulet was superb. And Ed said, "Took her two days to make, it ought to be good, she gets it out of a book, and you know Hilly, she's a slow reader." The new short haircut was even to Margaret a shock, but its severe asymmetrical lines did somehow unclutter Hilly's face, and

Margaret discovered, My God, she's got a jaw of iron. But Ed said, "Reminds me of a Euclidean proof, you know the part that goes, 'which is absurd.'"

Why doesn't he ever say something nice to her? Margaret demanded of George. George said it was just Ed's way of showing affection — the way two old army buddies meet and call each other bastard. Margaret pointed out a distinction that George — and Ed — seemed to have missed. Hilly wasn't an old army buddy.

And sometimes at his most loving, he still called her Brunt. Margaret ground her teeth. Brunt. Little brown runt, Ed the new husband introduced his wife, their daughter to them. A Linnaeus, with a new system of classification, neatly fitting in a new weed. So you shouldn't have named her Brunhild, was George's defense of his son-in-law, and Hilly *is* silly. Margaret hated him for grinning, for making her grin. Carol's favorite chant — blond venomous sprite dancing around the little brown intruder, rite of exorcism, guaranteed to shrivel up a rival. Hilly is silly Hilly is silly. George had introduced the new baby to their friends with a dictum: never take a pregnant woman to the Ring Cycle. Margaret herself could not remember — even then, by the time she got home from the hospital, she could not remember — just why that name of all names had seemed the one for the new baby the moment it was delivered into her arms. Brown, not red like Carol. Not bald like Carol, but with dark long thin hair brushed by the nurse into the vanity of an old man's tonsure to hide its sparseness. One for me, now one for you, fair enough, George had said equably. Carol was him. This one was her — dark and brown-eyed, eyes truly brown, not the brown of muddy water that changes soon. And tall, too, George, Margaret had predicted, you can tell by the feet. Something had gone wrong there — just what was a mystery, with George six-two and Margaret five-nine and Carol and Joanna both flat-footing it to dances in fancy ballet slippers and scrunching down to fit their partners. But you couldn't call five-four a runt. Not unless you lined her up with the rest of them.

I loved you best of all. More true confessions. Margaret lying flat on her back still awake at 3 A.M. It had been different with the first. No examining, no scrutiny, no questioning of love at all. The love for Carol had come in an oceanic wash, in which Margaret and Margaret's mother and now Margaret's child and her mother's mother and her child's future child all bobbed about, indistinguishable from one another, little pinpoints of life floating like plankton in a sea of love, unpent by the great breaking of waters.

(Hilly had known that with *her* first-born. Margaret and George had been ushered into the hospital room with an enormous bouquet of flowers, in the center of which George had so cleverly hidden the bottle of champagne. A Catholic hospital, of course, all alcoholic spirits forbidden, those unhygienic black robes swishing through the corridors. Hysterical laughter at George's frantic efforts to silence the popping of the cork. And trying to click together soggy paper cups. Then suddenly Hilly put her cup down and reached out her hands to Margaret. *Reached out.* Like those newspaper stories every now and then of a child run over by a car, in a coma for years, with wide-open unblinking eyes, fed intravenously, recognizing no one, then suddenly one day the eyes blink and she no longer stares at, but sees, the woman bending over her and she wets her lips and tries to speak and at last she says it. Mother. Hilly cried and Margaret cried, softly they cried together, like two women at a wedding. George said it was lousy champagne.)

That's with the first-born. But ever after, you pick and choose. Joanna, now, had left Margaret cold. Another replica of George, a little less fair, a little more weight. She sucked at the nipple stolidly, even then *tramp, tramp, tramp*-ing along the highway. "You've got to be fair to Joanna," Margaret kept demanding of the two older ones. George must have noticed. He picked Joanna up more than he had the other two, played pit-a-pat with her to "Yes, Sir, That's My Baby."

But Hilly Margaret had chosen. Brunhild she had named the brown little female thing. A magnificent woman guarded by a circle of fire. And she had turned out to be Hilly. And Hilly was silly. But Margaret had consoled herself: somewhere a Siegfried awaits. The sleep is but a trance. The gods are conferring, arguing, striking their bargains. And Todd appeared. In the middle of the night, Margaret laughed.

George was right. Quite often, in the middle of the night, Margaret admitted George was right. They shouldn't have gone down to Hilly's last Christmas. It was Carol's turn to have them, and George couldn't wait to lap up that Arizona sun. Margaret had to twist his arm. "We could just stop off for the weekend, it's really on the way, and make a big do out of tree-trimming, and then I won't have to mail all these packages." So, not having wanted to be there at all, George had no right to enjoy it. "You seem to be having a good time," she said, when he came upstairs with his drink to see what was keeping her. It was an accusation. He had a glow on already and she was still unpacking, dying for a drink.

"Come on down," George said, sitting on the bed on top of the dress she had just laid out. "I want your professional opinion." Professional? Margaret hadn't noticed any new furniture. And if there were any, it would be Colonial, because that's what Ed liked, the whole damn development being Colonial by virtue of thin white matchsticks stuck in front of each pile of red brick. What they ought to do, Margaret said, is call it Williamsburg, and wear mob caps and knee breeches and sell souvenirs. No, it was Hilly, George said. "You're the expert on Hilly, there's something different about her. Besides the hair."

"She's not pregnant at the moment, if that's what you mean."

She was thinner, George agreed, but that wasn't it. She was euphoric. Yes, that was it, euphoric. She wanted to know if there was anything special Joanna needed for her baby, she was going to send a little Care package, it looked like. And she wanted to borrow their copy of Carol's last paper, she thought she'd like to try to read it. That was hard rock going full-blast downstairs, Margaret could hear it, couldn't she, and Hilly was shaking up and down and sideways and Ed was asleep again on the couch, and all Hilly did about it was sprinkle her martini over the length of him. "She said," George reported, "you have to water them occasionally or else they don't grow."

While she put on her make-up, Margaret developed a new theory. Maybe, she said, testing it on George, it's not really as boring here as Hilly makes out. Maybe she lays it all on, just for us. I can sort of see her, the minute she hears we're coming, canceling all kinds of madly gay events, warning off her real friends and rounding up those neighborhood hausfraus and government clerks. She makes Ed swallow some beddy-bye pills, then she drags out those awful blue jeans and T-shirt with baby-food stains, bites off her nails, rats up her hair, the doorbell rings, and there we are and she's ready just in time.

George seemed to think it worthy of some consideration. "You mean," he said, after thoughtfully finishing his drink, "something like my Aunt Teresa. Whenever she heard anybody was coming over, she rolled up her Oriental rugs and laid down old linoleum, because she figured they were coming to case the joint and there was nothing like old linoleum to convince them you had nothing worth stealing." He laughed, remembering Aunt Teresa. "She kept it ready, rolled up and standing on end, on the landing halfway up the stairs and God, what it took to get it to lay down again. God, it was funny. You'd let go and the whole thing would roll back up like one of those party ticklers. She had to plunk a heavy chair smack on each corner. You walked in and it looked like the furniture was arranged for some weird kind of parlor game. There we'd sit in the four corners of the room, shouting across to each other. God, it was funny."

By the time George had stopped laughing, he was asleep. Margaret corrected her theory: beddy-bye pills for any husband was gilding the lily. I'll water *you*, she threatened, and put her dress in the bathroom to unwrinkle in the steam, wrapped herself in George's robe, and headed downstairs to get the right liquid. Because of the robe, she stopped halfway down and peered over cautiously when she saw Hilly open the door. She hadn't heard the doorbell ring with the music blaring like that, how on earth could Hilly and how on earth could those babies still sleep, or Ed for that matter — she could see him on the couch, mouth open, shoes off.

Hilly seemed to be taken by surprise. She backed up when he came in — a startlingly good-looking man, Margaret saw that right off, and was startled even more when he took both of Hilly's hands in that movie-lover's gesture signifying don't struggle, you're helpless, and leaned forward, surely to kiss her, but if so, in mid-air the kiss changed direction and landed on Hilly's forehead in a smack of Edwardian gallantry. He saw me, Margaret thought, and continued her descent, making sure her sash was safely knotted. She couldn't hear a word they were saying, but they were hovering indecisively in the doorway, and she joined them there, detouring by the record player to turn it off.

Hilly looked flushed, but that might have been from dancing. Margaret waited to be introduced. Hilly stammered, oh Todd, this is my mother, and made it sound as if Todd had caught her with Margaret instead of Margaret catching her with Todd. One of those mix-ups, Hilly explained. Todd had been going to take them out to dinner that night, and Hilly said politely it was all Ed's fault, she had been at — out, the night Todd called (and Margaret remembered then she had been out several nights the past year when she had called and wondered at the stammer clipping out like a censor's scissors just where was out). Ed had forgotten to mention the date. Just like Ed. But Margaret understood quite clearly — from the way Hilly flicked her eyes everywhere but on Margaret's face — that the fault lay with her: she should have been in Arizona.

Todd who? Who Todd? Hilly was treating him like the most casual of acquaintances encountered in the full stream of street traffic, with whose full name Margaret need not be burdened. As for hers, he had to ask for it himself, which he did by advancing in so far Hilly had to shut the door, and reaching out for not one but both of Margaret's hands (so perhaps there had been nothing in that, although Hilly he had pulled forward, and her he thrust out, the better to examine at arm's length). As if the answer were Sylvia, he asked who is Hilly's mother, what is she?

"When I travel incognito, it's as Margaret Cannon," she told him, almost unwillingly, for he was stamping her with his seal of approval a little too effusively, considering that she was in George's robe. He had a penetrating eye — or was it just the anomaly of bright blue under such black hair. Nevertheless, Margaret decided, if he had looked at Hilly that way, no wonder she had cut her hair and tonight even wore a dress. A man looked at a woman that way, and up went deodorant and depilatory sales.

But he had good manners, this Todd. Refused to accept the reluctant invitation to stay for dinner. Not even for a drink. But insisted on a rain check the next night. Dinner at his place, and Mr. and Mrs. Cannon too. He looked forward to it with a pleasure that would not be denied. Margaret itched with an old impatience. Hilly was so inept at saying no. Her way was to say yes and then not show up. I'll have to check with Ed, she said, groping weakly for a way out, but Todd did not leave until she had done so, raising his black brows in heavy surprise at the revelation of Ed's presence when Hilly went over to awaken him. But Margaret wondered how long he had been aware of Ed's feet, in black hose, slim, elegant and sadly funereal, protruding from the end of the couch.

Do you really think Hilly is having an affair? Margaret asked George, but he was too grumpy about being awakened for dinner to be interested. She sent him down with instructions to pump Ed about their host for tomorrow. Hilly hadn't said a word, busying herself with setting the table. But very light on her feet now. George was right, she had lost weight. Just who is he, dear? What does he do? And where did you meet him? Margaret had once asked questions like that, but no more. Not of a woman married five years who had three daughters of her own.

Still Margaret was glad when Hilly went upstairs early — to check the kids, she said, but she didn't come back down — and Margaret said she was pooped too and would say good-night, making sure George was reminded by one of her "looks" that he was supposed to find out about Todd. Undressing, Margaret heard the first of several episodic bursts of typing from Hilly's room. She couldn't help wondering. Anyone would wonder. So far as Margaret knew, Hilly hadn't touched a typewriter since her seventeenth birthday. Even her letters were handwritten, a Lord Chesterfield touch in this day and age. Joanna complained: she writes me once a year and then I can't read it. Margaret waited until the typing stopped, not wishing to disturb her.

"Do you have any laundry soap in here, darling?" Margaret asked. Hilly was in the tub, the bathroom door open. Margaret heard the shower rings slide along the rod. "There's some in here, under the sink," Hilly admitted, and Margaret went in, forbearing to look, forbearing, with greater effort, even to smile at a girl hiding her private parts from her own mother. "There's a draft, dear," she said, and closed the bathroom door when she went out.

In the corner of the bedroom, the typewriter. Out of the corner of her eye, Margaret surveyed it. It was the same one, she was sure. The sleek modern portable she had given Hilly on that birthday, looking as good as new. Reams of Hilly's writing on sheets from yellow scratch pads, from loose-leaf school notebooks, on the backs of mimeographed engineering reports salvaged from George's wastebasket. Hidden in the camp footlocker Margaret had decided to give away. Margaret replaced .the lid, taking nothing, saying nothing, thinking only of the perfect birthday gift, to replace the ancient L. C. Smith which had been around the house for years, whose keys must all be sticking to judge from Hilly's typing. Happy birthday, with a little card rolled into the carriage, in the format of an office memo. To: my favorite author. From: Mother.

As good as new, never having been used. Margaret detoured over the soft carpet to check the make. Straightened the pile of three-by-fives on the rickety little table. Opened the cover of a book.

When George came up to bed, Margaret gave him no chance to report. Her news came first and she bounced on the bed like a girl when she told him. Hilly's going back to school, the books were stamped CATHOLIC U., that was Ed's doing, of course, but still back to school. She was writing a term paper, which must mean it was for credit, which meant she wasn't playing around but getting her degree at last. "She's doing it at night," Margaret told George and hugged him, as if to conduct the voltage of joy from her body to his. "If only I could help her in some way. She must be so tired, after all day with the kids and the house. This will shut Carol up, you know how she sniffs: What does Hilly *do* with herself? I tell her, wait until you have kids of your own, but she doesn't believe it, no woman without kids does." And Margaret wondered if they could give Hilly a maid. If Hilly would accept it now, a lump sum every year to pay at least a cleaning woman once or twice a week.

"Leave it alone," George said. "And don't tell Carol. Or anyone."

George was absolutely right. Not a word. And especially Hilly mustn't know they knew. You know Hilly, George, Margaret said, she'll wait until she's got the degree in her hand, and then she'll let it drop casually, or there'll be this picture of her in cap and gown — they *do* wear caps and gowns when they graduate, don't they, even though it's night school? Night school, to Margaret, would always sound like a settlement-house course for immigrant workers, but George was reassuring.

"Don't you want to know what I found out about this guy Todd?" George asked. But he hadn't found out much after all. According to Ed, a mystery guy, plenty of dough but no one knew from where or exactly what he did. C.I.A. Hilly liked to think, because he attended so many embassy parties and was always just back from Morocco or just off to Afghanistan. More likely a lobbyist with that kind of money, Ed thought. Kept his own horse at the riding stables Hilly used — she had gone back to riding on Saturday mornings, which was how she had met him, and the secret of her weight loss. It was no secret he had this thing going for Hilly, Ed practically bragged about it, certainly wasn't worried. It seems he makes it a threesome when he takes her out, George said, and supposed that made it all right, but he looked at Margaret with some doubt.

Where Ed was concerned, Margaret couldn't care less. Whatever was going on, it was good for Hilly. The girl was coming back to life. But Margaret did wonder which came first, the chicken or the egg. Todd or Catholic U. George couldn't care less about that, so long as Todd was chicken. Otherwise it could turn out to be a holy Catholic mess, or had Margaret thought of that? And Margaret agreed, looking very sober, the better to conceal the little licks of pleasurable excitement with which her thoughts were tasting the future. A pretty kettle of fish. Out of the frying pan into the fire. A circle of fire.

"Ed may be just a little too complacent," Margaret said with satisfaction. "If it means nothing, why does she want to keep him secret — she didn't really want us to go tomorrow night, she didn't want me to meet him in the first place. And she's kept us secret from him — it was pretty obvious she had never told him who I was."

George looked surprised. "He didn't know you were Hilly's mother?"

"You know what I mean," Margaret had begun before she saw his face. Okay, George, she said, getting into bed, that's one for you. Married thirty years, they kept score. Suddenly Margaret felt a great fatigue, sleep coming like a blacking out. Joanna, was her last thought, keeping a different kind of score.

What made you suspicious, George wanted to know, what made you open that door? No, the door was a mistake, that's all, she thought it was the bathroom. Nonsense, said George, you were prying, Margaret. You do pry, Margaret. Carol made an observation once, which, George said, even he could follow. You are always discovering Pluto, Carol said, confirming the existence of something you have already proven in your mind.

Margaret didn't admit that. The door was a natural mistake in a strange apartment. Besides, she argued, don't they say the victim of a murder is as much to blame as the murderer, that he attracts the murderer, impels the murderer to do his deed. Come murder me, me whose life cries out? "Certainly with what you call my discoveries, George, it's the same thing. What I discover is laid out before me, calling out, discover me, discover me. Take Hilly. She could have tucked away her notes and her books and put the cover on her typewriter for the two days we are here. Instead she leaves it all lying out in the open where I'm bound to see it." (As George had left that letter from his girl friend in his jacket pocket — but only when he was ready to break it off anyway. For two years he had been admirably discreet. Margaret never knew a thing.)

"Well, I had no idea," said George, "nor did Ed. Poor Hilly."

Not that anyone would have thought poor Hilly when they first arrived at Todd's. It was as if, her secret life fortuitously revealed, she was free to revel in it, to flaunt it, to strut about wearing Todd's gallantries like some garish feathery adornment to the simple black costume of everyday life. Todd had opened the door to them all, in equal welcome, but Hilly had advanced and taken over, him and his magnificent apartment, and the evening. It was hers. She was dressed to kill, as George put it. The short beaded dress shimmered like a sentimental recall of the twenties as she led the way to the unbroken wall of windows and flung wide her bare arms and said, look. Before looking, Margaret thought yes, she shaves now under the arms, yes for a man like that, one must shave everywhere.

But then Margaret looked, they all looked, and it was a view that stopped all thought. The apartment was cantilevered over a primordial jungle, a deep ravine of what seemed virgin American forest. Even in midwinter, without as yet snow, a thick stand of evergreens kept it fleshed out. Inside the luxury of modern furnishings, outside the luxury of life itself. "Now is that a view or is that a view?" Ed asked, in somewhat secondary proprietorship. It was a view, Margaret and George agreed.

Todd put in a modest disclaimer. "At any rate, a conversation piece," and with the accomplishment of a good host led them to sociable seating. Only Hilly hung back, still looking, and when she turned, she shuddered. "You should see it in summer. As if all this inside were a Mayan temple waiting to be overtaken and strangled and destroyed by that — that green outside."

Todd saluted her with a "darling," informed her it was only Rock Creek Park, informed husband and mother and father that he loved this girl. "The only woman I know who can find in a still-life the suspense of a Pearl White serial."

No suspicion then, but yet an unease. He had an unusually good-looking face with deep clefts in cheeks and chin that made for interesting terrain. Hard to shave, though, Margaret thought, seeing already a faint dark bloom. The drinks were refilled, the conversation hummed without a jolt or a jerk or an ungainly silence. Double-entendres for Hilly, man-to-man talk with George and Ed, for her polite attention. He was agile, Margaret granted him that. You are hopeless, all of you, she had said on the way over, I shall find out all about him. But she hadn't. How do you keep yourself busy? That was her favorite piece of Jamesian archness — What do you do? she always maintained was a brutal question. The Sunday *New York Times* occupied a large part of his week, he told her, and he always worked the Double-Crostics. It was impossible to place him. Vietnam flared up, mean and explosive, like those dirty cherry bombs the kids threw in the street, and Ed and Hilly began to shout at each other. "You mean we don't have a moral obligation to help them?" Ed threw at her, and Hilly answered him bitterly, "It's the people who want to help you have to watch out for." But even then Todd took no stand, except between the two of them, one arm around Hilly's waist, the other over Ed's shoulder, a gesture of United Nations grace.

A Negro manservant appeared in the arch of the dining area, not to announce dinner but to signal for help. From the depths of the sofa down, Ed opined, when Todd went to the rescue, "The best cooks are all men, you know that, don't you?" Margaret eyed his posture with distaste. If he slumped any more, he would be sitting on his shoulder blades. And she noticed when Todd returned how well he held himself, a man who could get away with wearing a cummerbund. He was rolling down the sleeves of his silk shirt, and his arms, strangely white under the silky coating of black hair, looked aseptic. He comes from the kitchen like a surgeon from the operating room, Margaret thought. It was straight to her he came. His next operation. "And how do *you* keep busy," he asked her, "now that your little ones have flown the nest? You must be doing something right, to keep so fit."

I have passed the physical, Margaret thought, and stretched her long legs with the confidence of middle-aged virtue free of varicose veins. I have been admiring my chair, she told him. He followed her glance to the black leather slung on stainless steel. "That's a Margo Cannon design — pure sculpture, isn't it?" he said, and it was not until then that the name struck him. You? He was impressed. "Hilly, you never told me," he accused her, and Hilly shrugged. "Why should I?" she said, and began to eat voraciously from the platters of hors d'oeuvres.

It was then he took Margaret on the Grand Tour. They always did, Margaret was used to that. You design furniture so they show you their drapes. But it was then her unease surfaced. Lovely, delightful, very nice indeed, she said, and every room was very nice indeed, but he was anxious. Too anxious. The nervous housewife, Margaret recognized, who has done it all herself, without calling

in a decorator. As if all that he was hung on whether he had good
taste.

And the one room she didn't like was his bedroom. Without
knowing why. Perhaps because the bed was round and she hated
round beds, liking a head and a foot and a special side marked as
hers. A malignant mushroom it looked, with its tufted burgundy
velvet cover. Something made her look up at the ceiling, but the
ceiling was white and blank and reflected nothing.

So George said that after that tour she should have known where
the bathroom was. They had had dinner and she needed to go. By
mistake, Margaret insisted, she had opened the linen closet door.
She went back and got George on the pretext of showing *him* the
place. She stationed him by the closet and flung open the door and
said, "There." And when he said nothing, "Don't you see?" George
said it was all very pretty, tied up in ribbons and all, but he was
fumbling as for the right answer on a quiz show. "Come off it,
George, if you lived alone and weren't married, would you have
things like that in your linen closet, now would you?" George said
he wouldn't have much of anything in his linen closet, it being all
on the bed or in the laundry. Margaret lost patience. "Well, if you
won't say it, I will. He's a homosexual, I don't know if he's a practicing one, but — "

And it was at that that George began to laugh. That booming
big-bertha laugh of his. Because, he explained later, it reminded
him of the way she spoke of Ed as a practicing Catholic. It was the
laugh that brought Hilly weaving down the hall, too much to drink
before dinner and then joining the men for brandy afterward. A
smile was lurching all over her face. "What's so funny?" she asked,
and snuggled in between Mummy and Daddy.

Whenever George thought of that evening he still laughed. He
had never seen Hilly really drunk before. It was disgusting, Margaret said, but George laughed. As if Hilly were still a little girl
and showing a cute precociousness. To be discouraged in her presence with a disapproving frown, but alone, with Margaret, to be
laughed at. "That touch football she started up, I guess we were all
pretty looped, Christ, jumping all over *that* furniture — what was
it that broke? A Savonarola chair, you called it?" Once started,
George couldn't stop laughing.

"Those Kennedys have a lot to answer for," Margaret said grimly.
"And *I* wasn't looped and *I* didn't jump over furniture."

"Okay," admitted George, "just us guys and Hilly. I could have broken my neck slipping on those damn beads from that dress of hers."

So you could, Margaret agreed with equanimity. The climax had come with Hilly's kick. Do you suppose, George asked Margaret, she meant it to land there? Never mind Margaret's answer, he winced in sympathy. Poor Todd.

Poor Todd? Poor Hilly. Ed managed to land one where it hurts too. Ed called up to give them the good news. "Guess what's with Hilly," George said when he hung up. Margaret didn't have to guess, she knew.

"What would you say the odds are, that this one's a boy?"

"You see what it means, don't you," Margaret answered him, "she'll drop out of school. She'll never finish now."

Head hanging over the bed, Margaret dosed her clogged-up sinuses. Drop, drop, drop the drops went down, tasting bitter as gall.

"And how did he sound, Ed I mean?" she asked when she was right side up again.

"Pleased," said George. "One thing you have to say about Ed, he's a good father."

"I could kill him," Margaret said. "I could kill you all."

And George said, "Good, dear." He hung up and told Margaret she was all wet. There had been no need to call Hilly again in the morning.

But in the cab Margaret still felt the beginning of tightness at the back of her neck. Not because she was going to Hilly's, she assured herself. The old fear of going up in a plane came back, for no reason, every now and then. George had the driver stop and picked up a *Times* before they entered the midtown tunnel.

"That's interesting," he said, neatly folding the paper into four longitudinal slices, an art she had never been able to acquire. "It says here soldiers are being returned from Vietnam at such jet speed there isn't time to diagnose their malaria, and it could become a reservoir for our native mosquitoes."

George had a knack of finding little anxiety-provoking items in the paper. She should worry now about malaria. It was not until they had buckled their seat belts in the plane that she remembered what had kept her awake all night and asked him.

"Okay, George, first you fill a tub with Jell-O. Then what?"

JOHN L'HEUREUX

Fox and Swan

(FROM THE TRANSATLANTIC REVIEW)

IT SEEMED THE COLD would never let up. For over a week the temperature had been below freezing and for most of that time it had hovered around zero. Francis hated cold weather, his long stringy body responding to it with unmanly shivers. Nor could he afford the winter coat he needed.

Christ, will it never end, he asked himself, and he pulled his scarf tighter. It was a long striped scarf worn like a college student's — outside the jacket, hanging down in front and in back — even though he knew he was too old for that sort of thing.

A girl turned to stare. A winter hippie, a rarity, she wore an enormous black cloak with silk frogging and fur buttons. Over this her blond hair hung in ropes almost to her waist. She squinted at him through tinted granny glasses.

"Groovy beard," she said, raising her hands to her face. "You look like a fox, man." And then she added, "Sexy!"

He smiled at her. In Harvard Square you could expect anything. He felt at home here, anonymous.

Francis Xavier Madden, Stud, he said to himself and shook his head a little at the mockery.

It was not altogether mockery, however, even though he himself was oblivious to his looks. His beard had made the difference. Because he had no money to throw away on haircuts, he wore his hair long, the thick straight copper turning a ruddy brown at his mouth and chin, with a strand of gold here and there. His beard emphasized his heavy lips and his curiously protruding teeth in such a way that girls — at least the ones he met in Harvard Square

— found him unusually attractive. They often stared at him, many even spoke. Still, he was always astonished whenever anyone referred to him as sexy. Sex had never been one of his major concerns.

A sexy fox, he thought. A nice image. He had spent the entire afternoon turning over in his mind ideas for a story about a fox and swans. He had not thought of introducing sex. A sexy fox.

He recited the clipping once again. "At Southampton, fish were caught and frozen in the ice, their heads jutting out. Starving seabirds swooped down to peck at them. And swans froze in a river at Christchurch, Hampshire, their legs trapped in ice. Foxes glided across to devour them."

He had found it in the morning *Globe* and, for some reason he could not specify, he was deeply moved by it. In the human reaction to such inhuman cold there must be a story, he told himself. By the end of the afternoon he had the beginnings of a plot. A woman, a perfect Catholic, would be on her way to perform a "charity" and thereby wreck a reputation. She would pause at a little footbridge over the river — Christchurch River, since the story was to be heavily ironic — and would watch while a fox crept from among the trees and devoured the trapped swan. She would then continue on her way as purposeful and righteous as before. Or perhaps she would be changed by what she saw? No, people never were. He wondered if the "Christchurch" part might be too much. Well, he would work that out later.

He passed the Coop and deliberately looked the other way. No sense checking out overcoats he couldn't afford. That would only set in motion his endless mental book-balancing: possible income measured against definite expenses. He had not realized about money. Well, first sex, then money. You've got to have priorities.

If only he could sell the story. Christ, if only he could *write* it. He told himself to stop worrying, it wasn't healthy. Besides, this story was going to write itself. He had begun it with ease, and would have liked to continue writing but Caryl was expecting him and she needed . . . well, at least he could read her the first page, which she would like, and tomorrow he could begin work with, with what? With . . . He paused, waiting for a car to turn out of Church Street.

"Cold, sweet Christ, it's cold," he said aloud.

"It's too cold even to snow." The girl in the cloak had followed

and stopped with him now at the street corner. She was hopping
from foot to foot to keep warm. "At first I thought you were a young
guy."

"So did I. At first."

"But you aren't. Funny, you got a groovy beard."

He smiled, and immediately wished he hadn't. He knew she
would ask for a quarter.

"Got a quarter?" She squinted at him with little pig eyes. They
were pink. Or perhaps it was the glasses that made them look pink.

What's the use, he thought. A gust of wind swept around the
corner as he tugged at his glove. He could feel the ice seeping up
his arm and spreading across his chest. He wanted to cry.

"Here," he said, dropping the quarter into her red mitten. He
could never refuse anything he was asked for.

"You're a groove," she said. "See ya." She did a strange little
pirouette that made her cloak billow out and then swirl, snug,
around her body. She returned to her position at the Coop.

It would be something to tell Caryl. She would enjoy it, but then
she enjoyed everything about him, most of all sleeping with him.
What a crazy situation, he thought.

The crazy situation had begun normally enough a year earlier
when they were graduate students at Harvard.

Caryl Henderson was a tall plain girl who at twenty-eight decided
her chances of marriage were slender and that if she wanted to
have any kind of fulfilling life, she had better set about making it
herself. And so, once she was accepted at Harvard, she quit her
teaching job at Cambridge High and entered the Ph.D. program
in English. She had resolved upon intellectual happiness, the doors
to other kinds being closed to her.

Francis Madden had long since chosen his vocation when he came
to Harvard. He was a Jesuit. After three years studying theology,
in the year he was to be ordained, he began to ask himself — as he
often had before but this time with peculiar insistence — if this
were what he really wanted to do with his life. Too many of his
Jesuit friends had been ordained to the priesthood only to leave
and get married within a year or two. Not that route for him. And
so he postponed his ordination and, after a great deal of ecclesias-
tical maneuvering, arranged to work for his Ph.D. at Harvard while
making up his mind about the priesthood.

Caryl and Francis became friends by the accident of sharing classes. She was in her fourth year of studies but, as teaching assistant to Professor Barker, she regularly attended his lectures. Neither Caryl nor Francis was in love with the other, nor with anyone else for that matter, nor did they think of falling in love. They were just friends, older than their fellow students, and they shared common interests. The difference was that Francis hated graduate studies and Caryl loved them.

At the end of his first year, then, Francis decided to quit school altogether and, almost as an afterthought, to quit the Jesuits as well. The academic game had brought home to him a truth he had only half suspected: all his life he had done what other people thought he should do, whether or not it was the right thing for him. He had begun work on a Ph.D. not because he wanted it but because in the Jesuit Order a Ph.D. was the only criterion for intellectual acceptability. For similar reasons — because it was in itself a good and difficult thing to do and because Catholic families could aspire to no more blessed state than having a son who was a priest — he had very nearly been ordained. Now, realizing what his motives had been, he turned his back on both and walked out free, he was sure, into a whole new life.

Caryl was delighted that he had found his freedom, she said, delighted that he could now spend all his time writing. She was in fact more delighted than she could reasonably explain to herself. She was a devout Catholic and a plain woman and he was practically a priest; it had never occurred to her until now that during their frequent lunches and their walks through Cambridge Common she might be falling in love. She had cut her hair, it is true, and wore it in a soft halo about her face where before she had pulled it back into a tight little bun. And that because he had once admired that girl on television, Mary Tyler Moore, or somebody. And she had begun to wear lipstick, too, which he liked. But that wasn't the same as falling in love, she told herself.

Just before he left the Jesuits Francis sold his first short story to *The New Yorker*. Having never before published anything, he was more elated by the acceptance than by the money and so it meant little to him that Superiors let him keep the five hundred dollars and bettered their gesture by giving him two hundred more. When he phoned Caryl with his good news, she cried with pleasure. She had good news as well — she had just passed her comprehensive ex-

ams and could now begin work on her dissertation — but with
a tact that was as natural to her as giving, she postponed telling him
until later. She invited him to dinner to celebrate.

"A coming-out party," he said.

"A recognition party," she said.

The dinner was an unqualified success. Caryl was not a good cook
and, having the wisdom to recognize her own short-comings, had
concentrated her efforts on preparing a few simple dishes well; she
served him steak and baked potatoes and a colorful display of fresh
vegetables. Francis had thought to bring wine, a good Pinot
Noir he would not be able to afford in the future. And she always
had Scotch on hand. Furthermore Woolf remained in the bathroom during dinner. Woolf — at first called Virginia until his true
sex had made itself known — was a dingy alley cat Caryl had
adopted for the purpose, she said, of destroying her furniture.
Woolf resented newcomers and generally sulked in the bathroom
when company came.

They laughed a great deal and toasted Francis' story and
The New Yorker and the story again. They drank more than they
were accustomed to, feeling adventurous and successful what with
her Ph.D. exams completed and his writing career begun.

After dinner Francis read his story aloud, as later he was to read
everything aloud to Caryl. It was less a story than a slightly fiction-
alized reminiscence of his days in the novitiate, but it had a certain
amount of action and made some telling points about how the
religious life shapes a man's character. Caryl was enchanted.

They toasted the story again and, when they were about to toast
The New Yorker, Francis kissed her instead. It was a light kiss on
the mouth, but he lingered there a moment and was astonished
to feel Caryl's lips part and her arms slip away from him and
tighten around his neck. He felt it was time to loosen his
hold on her but she seemed content where she was and so, rather
than appear rude, he began to explore her teeth with his tongue.
He began to feel feverish.

"No one kisses like you," she said, gasping, as she pulled her
mouth away and clung even tighter to him. He smiled to himself. Never having done this before, he was glad he had done it
right. Then he reflected that perhaps she had never done it before
either, so how would she know? Somehow, he found that encouraging. He turned off the lamp.

"I don't know what I'm supposed to do," she said. "Just tell me what to do."

They slumped in each other's arms. Pushing the pillows about and nudging hips and knees, they managed finally to get into a semireclining position. They kissed again and then once more. Francis began to discover that a certain finesse was required, force and enthusiasm being insufficient to sustain the sweetness of the pleasure.

"It's like a symphony," she said, and he laughed loudly until the couch, which at night doubled as her bed, shook with his laughter. He was pleased with his newly discovered expertise. "Stop it," she said. "You're laughing at me."

"No, I'm laughing at me." He kissed her lightly on the neck. "Biology is fun."

He removed his tie and his shirt, he explained, because it was too warm. He drained his glass while he was up.

"I'm a little drunk," he confided.

She said nothing, only slipped her hand beneath his T-shirt, and felt his body grow tense. "What?" He didn't answer. "Shouldn't I do that?" She began to remove her hand just as he slipped his own under her sweater and began to caress her breasts. She unhooked her brassiere for him.

What in God's name am I doing, he thought, but even as he thought it, he got out of bed and began to remove his trousers.

"What are you doing?"

"Don't worry, I won't hurt you, I promise. I'm just going to hang these on the chair. They're my best suit and I don't want to get them wrinkled."

Francis folded the trousers neatly and was about to place them over a chair back when Woolf, who had been curled comfortably in the seat, arched his back enormously and hissed. The cat sprang from the chair and disappeared into the little kitchen.

"Damn cat scared the hell out of me."

He turned and found that she had removed her skirt and sweater. She was sitting on the edge of the bed, looking at him, trusting him absolutely. Though she had always been unusually modest, she felt no embarrassment whatsoever with him. She did not think of that then, but she would later.

"Woolf is jealous," she said.

Francis felt suddenly awkward. He took her hands in his own and she began to rise just as he began to ease himself onto the couch. They collided and, in her attempt to sit down again and in his to stand, they plopped to the couch in a tangle of arms and legs, Francis rapping his head soundly against the window frame.

"Ouch," he said, his confusion localized for the moment. "I banged my head."

"It's the window frame."

"I know it's the window frame."

She rubbed the back of his head which he lowered to her breasts, incredibly white and smooth, just as he had imagined breasts would be, though until then he had never imagined Caryl's. It's like a novel, he thought, and kissed her breasts the way they did in novels. He moved closer to her, his knee between her legs, his right arm a clumsy lump under her shoulders. There seemed to be an awful lot of arms and legs around.

From his study of moral and pastoral theology, Francis knew a great deal about sexual play. Books, however, differ considerably from experience and, as he slipped off her panties, he was totally confused as to what went where. Caryl had not had the benefit of theological training and so she lay there, passive and grateful.

"Move this leg here," he whispered.

But as Caryl moved her leg and Francis edged closer to her, Woolf with a terrible hissing sound sprang from the desk onto the bed.

"Christ!" Francis was terrified. Recovering, he reared back to push the cat from the bed, but as he did, his arm caught the window curtains and pulled. They came tumbling down on the bed, the curtain rods with them. Woolf screamed and tried to bolt, but he was trapped in the curtains and his struggles only entangled them all further.

What an idiot I am, he thought, wrestling his feet to the floor where at once he tripped on the cat and landed on his hands and knees. Caryl's delighted laughter made him feel even more foolish. He vowed this would never happen again.

Caryl spent the next day waiting for him to return. The experience had been the most beautiful of her life, except for the funny part, but even that was good. Everything with Francis was good. That morning, as she did every morning, she received Communion, having first considered that her catechism said last night was sinful and having reconsidered that her catechism was wrong. Love is good and beautiful, she told herself, and she could not in conscience confess what they had done as sinful. Sin had no part in this whatsoever. She waited for him, then, to return in the evening.

Francis had stumbled home confused, and a little pleased with what he took for his sexual prowess. The next morning however he went to confession, resolving to see Caryl that same evening to explain that if this ever happened again, they would no longer be able to see one another. That day was a Jesuit feast, however, and when Francis arrived at Caryl's apartment he had already had three Scotches, two wines, and a brandy. His opinion of himself had improved measurably and he was feeling very consciously male. He kissed her as she opened the door.

It was exactly one hour and seventeen minutes later that, in bed once more, he eased his body away from hers. They had found the act of love easy and natural, once Francis had put his textbook knowledge aside, and they had rejoiced in it. They lay there, smiling at one another. It was only much later that night that the possibility of Caryl's being pregnant occurred to them.

For the next two weeks they lived in a state of continual panic.

Papers came from Rome dispensing Francis from his vows and freeing him from all obligations to the Society of Jesus, but Francis scarcely noticed them. He moved from Jesuit life to the life of a layman without noticing what was happening to him. His entire consciousness, like Caryl's, was focused on one event: her next period.

He would marry her, he thought, and legitimize the baby. She would have to drop her dissertation, or at least hide out in the late days of her pregnancy. He would have to get a job. That took care of his writing career, God damn it.

She wanted more than anything to marry him, but not in this way, not with the knowledge that if he had to give up his writing, he would always resent her. She wanted him to be free to write and free, if he chose, to marry her. But what about the baby?

The two weeks passed, a psychiatric study in guilt and responsibility for the two of them, and then — just when they had all but named the baby and provided for its education — they found she was not pregnant. Terrified at their new freedom, they celebrated her period with dinner at Barney's. Afterward, they returned to her apartment where she wanted to make love again, but Francis would not.

"Can't we just go to bed and lie there together?"

He frowned and said nothing.

"We won't do anything bad. It isn't as if we would do something bad."

He was about to ask her if she realized he had a vow of chastity when he himself realized he had one no longer. So instead he told her, "We can't. You know what will happen."

"We won't have . . . you know . . . intercourse. I hate that word. It's the most beautiful thing in the world and they call it that awful word. But we won't do that." She pleaded. She was like a child asking for a candy cigarette.

"It isn't intercourse that makes it a sin. It's the whole thing. It's what you're saying about your feeling for the other person when you go to bed together. It means you give yourself to that person and to no other. No other at all."

He was trying to remember his theology, the carefully elaborated reasons which demonstrated even to the unbeliever exactly why premarital sex was sinful. Hearing himself now, he was not convinced.

"Well, you aren't giving yourself to anyone but me." She did not see the problem.

"But I can't. I can't stand the guilt the next morning. And in confession they'll just tell me I have to break off. That's what they always do."

"I don't feel guilty at all. I feel wonderful. And I don't tell it in confession. I would if I thought it was wrong. But I don't. Not if we don't have intercourse."

And so that night they went to bed together and did not have intercourse. Francis, who had roamed her body and enjoyed emissions three times, dutifully went off to confession the next morning. Caryl, however, was blessed with an astonishing dispensation of conscience, or so it seemed to Francis, and she rose bright and holy, ready for Mass and Communion.

Their relations continued in much this way throughout the summer. As Francis' love for her had changed Caryl into an attractive woman, his physical affection for her made her a free one. Her years and years of strict Catholic upbringing fell away in that one night. She was liberated. She had always given away things she owned but now she was able to give herself and she gave lavishly. Surprisingly, her sense of freedom extended beyond herself and, where she had wished for nothing better than to marry Francis, she now wished his happiness above all else. It was this selflessness, though he would never have guessed it, which made him most uneasy.

Francis, on the other hand, felt daily more constricted, more obliged. The Catholic training, the involuted mental discipline of the Jesuits, which he had happily and with ease cast off in his first love for Caryl, returned to him now and possessed him completely. He was haunted by a sense of sin he had not known in years. He felt he should break off with Caryl, but she was all he had, and he was not sure that perhaps he might love her almost as much as she loved him. Still, he felt obliged to visit her often and to call each day, and this worried him. It seemed to deny his freedom. And when he was with her they would invariably begin kissing and petting and then that would mean another guilty morning and a trip to the confessional. By this time he was rotating priests, but they all told him the same thing: unless he planned marriage, he should end the relationship. Furthermore, she seemed oblivious to his maddening need for something more than just being naked in bed with her. This, he thought, is what they really mean by the frustration of a faculty. He had left the Jesuits for freedom to be himself and he was being something he could not even recognize. He had quit graduate studies to write and he spent most of his time worrying about not writing. Summer passed this way and now much of the winter.

It was, he thought, a crazy situation. He pulled his scarf tighter as he left the Cambridge Common and approached her apartment. It seemed the cold would never let up.

"Sweet, hello," she said, stepping into his arms. It amazed him how beautiful she had become.

He held her tightly, half aware of her breasts warm against him, half aware of the door still open at his back. I can never enjoy anything, he thought.

"Hello, hello," she whispered. It was what they said nights when they slept together.

"Hi." He whispered the expected response and closed the door. "Wow, it's cold."

"Sit. I'll make you a drink." She caressed his beard for a moment before she disappeared into the little kitchen.

"Hey, you know, there was this girl who asked me for a quarter,

followed me actually. She had funny little pig eyes and a wild
cape . . ."

"That's Magdalena," she said from the kitchen. "Don't you know
her? She makes a fortune in the Square."

"Magdalena?"

"Her name's not really Magdalena. It's Margaret Ann or something, but she fancies Magdalena so everybody calls her that."

"How do you know her? How do you know all that?" He was
vaguely offended. He had hoped to please her with his description.

"Oh, I know a few things."

Handing him the drink, she posed for a minute with one hand on
her hip and her breasts thrust forward, a new thing with her,
a thing that annoyed him since he found her breasts distracting
enough anyway. He pretended not to notice.

"Well, tell me about your writing," she said, suspecting she had
annoyed him. "Did you write today?" She gave him her total attention; for her nobody, nothing else, existed at that moment. He was
so beautiful, so perfect.

He sipped his drink. "Good Scotch," he said. He could not afford
good Scotch himself, his seven hundred dollars having been con-
sumed by rent for his shabby two rooms on Green Street and by
restaurants he could not afford and gifts he should not have given.
But he was learning all that slowly.

"You did write, I can tell. You're like a cheshire. You're like poor
old Woolfykins when he had caught a mouse." She had had Woolf
put away once it became clear that he and Francis were incompati-
ble. "Tell me. Read it to me."

"It's kinda good, I think." His readings always required a spoken
introduction. "I think I'm really on to something."

He recited the news clipping about the cold on Christchurch
River, the fish and the seabirds, the swan and the fox. He told her
that there would be a woman, a very particular kind of woman, who
would witness the murder and then go away unchanged. Or maybe it should be a priest; he wasn't sure. And the tone would
be heavily ironic, light on the surface but deep irony.

"Read it," she said. He wrote better than he explained and she
wanted very much to like the story.

"You don't like the plot?"

"Read it."

"You don't like something. I can tell."

As it happened, she did have reservations about the story. He had never been to England and there were no swans at Harvard. Besides, why so artificial a contrivance? But she refused to let herself think about these things.

"I love it. Read it."

"O.K." He cleared his throat, sipped his drink, cleared his throat again.

"'She was a perfect Catholic. In nineteen sixty-eight few Catholics were perfect, but she was perfect. She went to Mass every Sunday of course — which everybody did — but besides that she talked to Lutherans about religion and organized card parties for the Passionist retreats and staged, at considerable expense to her nerves and to her family, fashion shows for the benefit of the Stigmatine Fathers. She was a perfect Catholic at a time when few Catholic women were.'"

He looked up, dissatisfied at the writing. It had seemed to work before, but now it seemed all wrong.

"You don't like it, do you," he said.

"Frank, I love it. I like the 'at great expense to her nerves and to her family.' That's really good."

"What is it that you don't like? Is it the Catholic business?"

"Well, you might eventually want to write about something else." She spoke apologetically. "You do keep returning to that over and over."

"I happen to *be* Catholic, is all. And I don't like screwing around unless I'm getting married."

"Read the rest of the story, Frank." She had never argued with him, knowing somehow that she must be in the wrong.

"It isn't that I don't love you." He wondered if he did love her. She was lovely and intelligent and utterly selfless. And those fabulous breasts. Marrying her was not the problem; feeling he *had* to was the problem. Or did he imagine it? "It isn't that."

"What is it?" She asked the question simply. It was not a challenge.

"It's . . . I mean . . . *you* want to marry *me*." He waited. "Don't you?"

"Yes, I want to marry you. But only if you want to marry me. I want you to be as free and happy as I am."

"Free! Christ, this is impossible." He stood and looked around for his jacket. "I'm going to go, Caryl. I'll come back some time. I

shouldn't have come tonight. It was a bad idea, the whole thing.
I'm preoccupied, I guess, with that goddamned story."

He brushed his lips against hers and left.

The wind across the Common cut his face and neck. Francis
tugged at his scarf, but that did no good. The cold would never end,
he thought.

And what on earth had propelled them into such an incredible
argument? Who had first mentioned marriage? He tried to recon-
struct the scene. She hadn't liked the story because of something
about the swans. Had she actually said that or was she just thinking
it? No, she hadn't said it. But he knew, he knew. He could change
the swan to a fish and the fox to a seabird; that would be more
plausible. And he could locate the story on the Charles instead of
Christchurch River. What had come over her anyway? Why should
he feel so obliged to her? Trapped, almost.

"Got a quarter?" Magdalena squinted up at him, not smiling,
merely making her request.

"Why? Why should I give you a quarter?" Francis was amazed
at the sound of his own voice; it was raw with hatred.

"I need bread, man."

"Why don't you go work for it instead of pestering people in the
street? What makes you think the whole world owes you a living
just because you've got the brass to ask for it? Who the hell do you
think you are, anyhow?"

"Look, man, I do my thing. You do your thing, right? I ask for
a quarter, you don't want to give a quarter, so say no. Who needs
a speech?"

She stood there, having somehow confounded him with her logic,
while he strode angrily away, not to Green Street but to the Charles.

"Sexy beard," she said. "He's a fox."

His anger made him forget the cold and he walked rapidly down
Boylston Street to the Anderson Bridge. He did not know why. He
glided out on the ice, easing himself along gingerly at first, and
then walking firmly once he discovered it was safe. He had not
known that rivers freeze.

Only after he had walked half the distance to the Weeks Bridge
did he become conscious of what he was doing; he was searching for
a fish frozen in the ice, "their heads jutting out," he recited. But
that was absurd. What on earth would a fish be doing with its head

out of water? Still, in the story it would be a wonderful Christ symbol. He smiled to himself. She was right, he thought.

When he reached the Weeks Bridge, he left the ice. With a feeling that he was shouldering the inevitable, he retraced his steps to Harvard Square where he waited impatiently for Magdalena to make her appearance. He looked in the newspaper store, but she was not there, nor was she in the theater lobby. She was probably home by now, doing her thing. It was too cold to wait any longer.

He set off quickly up Boylston Street. At the corner of Church, he paused. There was an ashcan standing next to a mailbox. He took out the folded page of his story, dropped it in the ashcan, and then for no particular reason took it out of the ashcan and dropped it into the mailbox. The gesture would be something to tell Caryl.

He shivered in the unnatural cold as he crossed the Cambridge Common.

RALPH MALONEY

Intimacy

(FROM THE ATLANTIC MONTHLY)

THE XEROXED MAP was wrong; the boy was right. When they reached the fork where an arrow on the scoutmaster's rude drawing pointed left, Harry started left. Brian cried out in a loud panic, exactly as his mother gave driving directions. "Straight ahead! Straight ahead!" He was very nervous. It was enough to arrive in a funny-looking car with a father who was not private property, whom people could see on television. But to get to the camp-out last, with presumably a scouting civilization erected and waiting for them, and with no excuse for being late but the folly of getting lost, was all too much. Harry could smell the nerves on him. "We hiked it last winter," Brian said, less loudly.

They stopped. Harry smoothed the map on his knee. "Here we are," he said, pointing, "and here's where Charlie Citizen says turn left."

"The camp is straight ahead," Brian said. "We *hiked* it."

"Tell you what," Harry said. "Maybe he took you a long way around on the hike, for the exercise, you know?" Brian nodded, not believing at all, but agreeable. "Maybe this is a shortcut. We'll try it for five minutes. If it all looks silly or impossible, we'll come back and go your way."

"O.K.," Brian said.

"Well, Jesus Christ, kid, I didn't draw this map." Harry put the car in gear and turned left. "I mean if I drew the map it would have naked ladies in the margins, right?" Harry always doodled nudes, on the telephone pad, on scripts.

"Right!" Brian said, and he laughed. Naked ladies made him laugh. He was that age.

They drove on the scoutmaster's route until the road petered out, narrowed to a track beside a swamp. They asked directions of a man gardening at the edge of the swamp, a man so purely Greek of feature that Harry was surprised he spoke English. He directed them back to the main road, Brian's route. "You were right all the time, kid," Harry said. He did not add that the scoutmaster was an overpowering jerk because Brian deeply admired the man. He formed odd loyalties, Brian did, but they were strong loyalties, and he would not have them stepped on.

They arrived at the camp-out site among the first half-dozen of some thirty father-son groups expected. "We're early!" Brian cried, shrill as a girl, delighted to be safe from ridicule on that score. As they were unloading the camping gear from the back seat and the trunk, Harry said, "I wish you wouldn't . . ." and stopped. They climbed a muddy rise toward a monster cookout pavilion, all cement and fireplaces. "Wouldn't what, Dad?" Brian said.

I wish you weren't prettier than the prettiest girl in all your schools. I wish you wouldn't be embarrassed because a Citröen is not a Ford station wagon. I wish you were not so vulnerable to ridicule.

"Wouldn't what, Dad?"

They entered the pavilion. "What I was going to say, I guess, is I wish you wouldn't let things bother you like this, wouldn't let . . ."

"Like what?"

"Well, like you were afraid we'd be late and everybody would make fun of you because I got lost."

"I wasn't afraid," Brian said.

"I don't mean exactly afraid. That's not quite the word."

"I wasn't."

"O.K."

The scoutmaster, Hyatt, a great stone block of a man, greeted them. His baritone boomed and hammered off the cement floor and the vast, low ceiling. "Everybody put your gear here. [He was addressing only Harry and Brian.] We'll all camp in the shelter. Looks like rain. Hello, Brian."

"Hello, Mister Hyatt," Brian said shyly.

Harry shrugged the pack higher on his back so the tent roll
cushioned his neck. "We have a tent. I think we'll make our camp
up on the hill. Come on, kid." He was jealous of Hyatt. They went
out of the pavilion and across a clearing with a bonfire stacked
in it and up a path, Harry leading. It was a steep climb on a rough
path, and Harry was soon winded. "Hey," Brian said, as a sort of
beginning. Harry's knee hurt anyway, and he stopped. "What's
on your mind?"

"I wish you wouldn't be so tough on Mister Hyatt."

"Tough on him? I didn't *men*-tion his goddamned map. Wait
till the other fathers get through with him."

Brian climbed on past, head down, watching the trail. "You were
pretty rude."

"Well, he's a horse's ass! Everybody sleep on the concrete!
Christ!" But the boy's choice of word hit him where he felt jealousy.
Rude. Harry started climbing again. "But he likes you and you
like him, so he can't be all bad. I'll mind my manners." They
camped high on the hill, fifty feet above the last fireplace. Harry
pleasured himself and apparently interested his son recalling camp
facts he had learned in the army. They put their tent up as an open
shelter with one flap straight out and the other closed to the wind.
Brian blew up the air mattresses while Harry dug a shallow ditch
uphill of the tent in case of rain, all the while explaining the why
and how. They put the air mattresses under the tent and spread
their sleeping bags on them. They built a fire against a big rock,
above which the trees opened to form a natural flue. Harry pointed
out the flue, and Brian, looking up, said, "Tough." They collected
flat rocks and put them around the fire for safety and to heat, so
they could be cooked on later. Then Harry led Brian along a logging road in a search for a running stream. "We can drink from it
and wash mess kits in it, and we won't have to drag water up from
down below." There was no stream, although there were old stream
beds that Harry pointed out.

After a mile mostly downhill on the logging road, Harry turned
them around. His knee hurt. "Be nothing but still water down from
here. Ponds and puddles. They're not clean. Looks like we'll have
to haul water up the hill."

"I'll bring it up," Brian said. "I don't mind." They started back
uphill. Harry's knee ached, but he did not favor it. The love of a

beautiful woman is supposed to cure everything, but having a son who is a hell of a nice kid cures a lot, too.

Back at camp they had ham-balogna sandwiches and Cokes. Brian decided to try out his sleeping bag, just for size, and was asleep before he had the bag zipped. He had been too excited to sleep much the night before, and the morning had been a time of terrible anxiety for him. Harry liked very much to think that Brian had at last relaxed when he saw his father knew about, could cope with, woods and fire and water. While the boy slept, Harry took the *Times* from the knapsack hanging on a tree and read the reviews and the sports pages and watched his son sleep. The boy was a beauty, and he was very bright, and he had been blessed with his mother's courage. He was marked exceptional at birth, but he wanted so to be ordinary. *It will all fit together when you're about nineteen,* Harry told him, but you got a lousy seven, eight years ahead of you. Good luck.

He woke Brian in midafternoon, so the boy would not sleep himself out. They played catch on the road, then gathered a great heap of deadwood for the fire. They were sitting with their backs against the same tree, splitting a Coke and watching the sun go orange on the next ridge, when Hyatt's voice boomed in the forest. "All Webeloes! A meeting! On the double!" Brian jumped up as though stung. "Webeloes! Meeting! On the double!" Hyatt boomed again. "I'd like to go right now," Brian said, actually pale with urgency.

"O.K. Go right now," Harry said.

"You'll be all right?"

"I'll be fine, handsome. You get on down."

Brian ran down the steep trail in breakneck double strides. Other boys joined him on the trail, running the same heedless downhill way. Harry walked back to the tent, feeling and recognizing and discarding a jealousy of Hyatt's power, and he was hit by a tremendous thirst.

On the drive up to the camp-out, Harry had seen, out of a corner of his eye that would not close, a roadhouse. He remembered with the touring alcoholic's keen precision where the roadhouse was and how long it had taken to get from there to the camp. He stood now and took stock. He had money, forty dollars he had brought along "in case we have car trouble." (In case we have car trouble near a liquor store.) He had also to consider his honest intent, fortified

by a private and therefore sacred vow, to stay dry, as dry as the boy,
for this single, simple overnight in the woods. And he considered
the howling in his belly and bloodstream, in the hollow hours of
the day, for his customary swift sundown overdose of alcohol. He
eased down the trail to a turning, not yet committed and quivering
with indecision. All the boys were gathered in the pavilion. Beyond
the pavilion was the parking lot, where Harry's car, certainly by
design, blocked traffic. He had the gift of unconscious foresight.
There were forces now in motion he could not control. He *had* to
go down and move the car. He continued down the trail with a
stately tread he had learned doing Lear in Canada, but with electricity in his knees. He made a wide circle around the pavilion,
down to the car, and got in the front seat and shut the door softly.
The starter made a great racket in the stillness, and Harry looked
up and saw Brian watching him from the fringe of the group of boys.
Harry in dumb show indicated he was only reparking the car. Brian
looked away. "It's blocking traffic," Harry said aloud to the window, "I'll be right back." He drove off.

Harry had three martinis at the roadhouse, as fast as his stomach
would accept them, and drove back toward camp. At the crossroads,
in the gathering dark, he saw the Greek gardener of the morning
smiling and pointing to the right. Perhaps the man had had so many
visitors during the day he had given up gardening and become a
signpost. Harry waved and drove on. He parked the car solemnly
at the very rear of the lot, shut off the engine, and broke a spectacu-
lar sweat. In all, he had been gone less than forty minutes.

At camp, Brian had a big fire going, much too high to cook over,
and he had mess kits and utensils spread about him and hamburg
in aluminum foil in his hand, and no place to go but up. Forlorn.
Harry plunged into the making of dinner with skill and great cheerful energy. He taught Brian to cook on the open fire, and they ate
hamburgs and beans until they stalled. There were dishes to be
done then, and pleading his aching knee, Harry sent Brian downhill with a tangle of mess gear in either hand and a flashlight clipped
to his belt. To do his part, or seem to be doing his part, Harry hung
both sleeping bags before the fire. Almost suddenly Brian was back,
the mess kits, astonishingly, immaculate. "Mister Hyatt helped me.
He's going to light the bonfire now. We're going to sing and everything and tell ghost stories. Will you come down?"

What sweet urgency. "Sure," Harry said. "Let me get my flash-light." There was a great leaping bloom of yellow fire in the valley, followed by a dull explosion. At the tree, getting his flashlight from the knapsack, Harry felt a blaze on his cheek like a great sudden shame. "Napalm," he said. They started downhill in the glare of the new fire. There were shrill screams below, then cheering and young laughter. Brian surged toward the noise and stopped at the turning. "All the fathers are in Mister Marcucci's tent," he said. "I'll walk on down with you anyway," Harry said. He was thinking that the only water came from a frail solitary spigot, that his car was parked now so deep in the lot he'd never get it out, that he and Brian were too high on the hill if the wind changed. And he was thinking that if fifty thousand acres of forest went up in flames in the night and he, Harry Hall the actor, were found charred and spastic in his sleeping bag, he would be blamed for smoking in bed and Hyatt, with his homemade napalm eruption, would be awarded perhaps the Carnegie Medal for alertly pissing on the pavilion roof.

When they got to the clearing where the great fire was, Harry discovered that the shrill noise came from boys who had lost their eyebrows or lashes or forelocks in the explosion. Hyatt, with stout baritone laughter, was incorporating his judgment error into the camping mystique. "It'll all grow in again boys," he called man-fully. "Not like mine!"

Fire has been exactly described as greedy, and this fire reached, reached, for the trees in the dark beyond. Harry gently pushed Brian down on a log far from the blaze. "Horse's ass," he said.

"Don't say anything to him, will you?"

"No. I'll go up to Marcucci's tent with the other fathers. Have a good time. I'll see you back at camp."

"Good night," Brian said absently. He surrendered his perfect profile agape to the fire and the Webeloe-camp-out-singalong-ghost-story camaraderie he had been promised.

The Marcucci camp offered more comforts than most standard housing. Marino was on his sixth Boy Scout son and had camping equipment sufficient to a Corps headquarters. A yellow tarpaulin secured to four trees roofed a central area, with pup tents around it and a vigorous fire beyond. Men sat or stood, drinking from beer cans or plastic cups. Harry knew them all from Little League, Scouts, PTA, swim team, adult basketball, and related suburban frolics. They truly didn't like him because their wives truly did, and because he was an actor and didn't *do* anything. Yet they greeted Harry with a fireside grudging gruffness that said, flako or otherwise, he was another daddy and welcome. "A drink, Harry," Marino Marcucci said, holding up a bottle in a striped ditty bag.

"No, thanks," Harry said. "I thought maybe I wouldn't drink until my kid did. Just today, anyway."

A big red-headed lieutenant of police named Sullivan laughed in his face. "We saw you scoot down the mountain in that Citröen. You came back up smilin'."

Harry laughed, too. "You got me. All right, Marino, I'd love a drink." Marcucci filled a green cup with whiskey. Harry saluted the gathering and drank. He sat on the floor, and the conversation went back to what it had been, which was lousy.

"They're movin' up this way," an accountant named Auser said. "It's a shame, too. Everything they touch turns to shit."

"We got total war goin' on uptown," Sullivan said. "Cops go out in threes, always in cars. Pretty soon we'll be sending them out in squads with tommy guns. There's a fire alarm, we hafta empty out a precinct to cover the firemen. Snipers with rifles. Bricks and bottles from the roofs. They're fuckin' animals."

It went on like that. Harry sipped his drink but otherwise kept his mouth shut. He felt physically small, as he often did in the company of men, except when he was working. However, man talk has its mystique, and there are rules, and one's turn to speak revolves like the bidding in bridge. Harry passed two or three times, drinking whiskey to stop feeling small, until he felt Sullivan staring at him.

"Don't look at me," Harry said. "I've been in show business since I was eight years old. Negroes taught me to dance, juggle, get on and off, half of what I know." It was a simple enough thing to say, but Harry found that it drew on his courage to say it.

"You're lucky," Sullivan said, nodding mysteriously. "You don't have to live with it. You don't see what we all see." He waved his beer can to include the other men, the workers, men who *did* things. "You're lucky."

The concept, commonly held, that what an actor earns and builds for himself is due to good looks and dumb luck infuriated Harry Hall. And, of course, there was whiskey in him. "Lucky because I was doin' three a day when you were playing ring-a-lievo?

What the hell is lucky about that?" Harry stood. "Marino, give me another little taste, will you?" Marcucci came forward with the striped ditty bag and poured only a taste into Harry's cup.

"Belafonte, Poitier, Sammy Davis, Junior!" Sullivan said. "What the hell do you know about Harlem or who's moving in up here next month, next year?"

"Hey, Red," Harry said, calling from his diaphragm to kill any quaver. "Who'd you hate before niggers? Who you gonna hate next? You got any plans? What if they work and learn and fit in and make it? Who you gonna hate then, Red?" He saw clearly that Sullivan would hate Harry Hall next, and had already started.

"That's enough. Not in my tent," Marino said.

"I don't worry about it," Sullivan said. His eye was hard on Harry, his hand with a cigarette in it steady before his face. "It won't happen in my time or my kids' time or their kids' time. You can fall out of a tree any day, but it takes a hundred years to walk like a man."

"O.K.," Harry said. "I'll see you around." He drank off his drink and handed the cup to Marcucci. "Thanks, Marino. Next year I'll bring up whiskey and you can come drink with me."

"All right, Harry. I'll remember that."

Nobody asked him to stay. Harry walked rapidly off in the dark, out of earshot. He didn't want to hear what Red Sullivan had to say next. Down the hill boys shrieked in mischief, and Hyatt's voice boomed. Harry turned on his flashlight and started up the path. Above him on the path there was another body with a flashlight before it. While Harry's heart did not leap up, it gave a small jump. "Who's there?" Brian said, scared in the dark.

"Cyrano de Bergerac."

"Hey, Dad," Brian said. "I thought you were still at Marcucci's."

They went on up the path together. "Didn't work out," Harry said. "How come you left the bonfire?"

"Didn't work out either," Brian said. "Mister Hyatt told a corny ghost story, scared nobody, then we all sang 'Workin' On the Railroad' over and over because it was the only song the man with the ukulele knew the chords to."

"You should have played."

"Come on."

"I know." At the camp, Harry put the want-ad section of the

Times on the coals of their fire and laid deadwood on top. A blaze jumped up at once. Harry held Brian's sleeping bag open to the heat until it steamed with some forgotten moisture, then he closed it and put it on the boy's mattress. Brian took off his sneakers and got in. "Wow! Hot," he said. "You know, Dad, can I tell you something?"

That meant solemn time. "Sure." Harry held his own sleeping bag open to the fire.

"The thing is it was all right down there. Everybody was having a good time. I was having a pretty good time, too. I guess. But I really wasn't. The kids were running around and goosing each other and screaming. Mister Hyatt couldn't get them to settle down and have a real, you know, camping party."

"That's too bad," Harry said, beginning to like Hyatt a little, in spite of the jealousy. "That's a shame."

"Then all the kids started to sneak off to raid each other's camps. They were all around, screaming in the dark. That's why I came up here. To guard our camp."

"Good man." Harry spread his sleeping bag on the mattress and knelt on it.

"Boy, I'm tired," Brian said.

"Been a long day. Go to sleep." There was no need to say it. Brian fell asleep like a ball rolling off a table. Harry watched him. A beauty. His mother wanted him to model, do commercials, put the money in trust for his education, his marriage. Harry wanted him to have a childhood. But his extraordinary looks, and people and events, seemed to conspire against a childhood for Brian. Perhaps some of us are not meant to have childhoods. I wasn't. Christ wasn't. Maybe childhood was another dumb mystique, another lie.

With a pang like being skewered on a ragged stick Harry wanted to get in with the boy and hold him as he did in bed when Brian had flu or a bad dream. To smell his cleanliness before it was gone, to feel the fragile, warm back buckled to his body. To hold, to hold him, one more time, while he was still a child.

Harry got into his sleeping bag and zipped it up. Then he reached and zipped Brian's bag shut. He kept his fingers in the great plastic loop at the top of the zipper and lay back and waited for sleep.

MARVIN MANDELL

The Aesculapians

(FROM EPOCH)

How I — a mathematician scrupulous about keeping the disorderly, the unexpected, the uncontrollable from worming into my Eden — ever got raveled up with Marcy, I guess I'll never fully know. Maybe it was my Social Debt: her father had been killed in the Spanish Civil War before her birth. Maybe it was her breeding: she had been brought up by what I thought were the Right Principles, that is to say, no principles at all except those of Mother Nature, who in those days, it seems, had gone into hiding or else got herself arrested somewhere (no doubt for soliciting!). Most probably it was her beauty: when I first met her I was taken with her serenity (she was only fourteen) ; her mother seemed more the unsettled adolescent in movement and voice, if not in body. Long-faced, skin glowing from more than summer, large dark eyes sparkling and widely spaced (late summer in those eyes sedately looking out over a body of early spring ripeness), sensuous but delicately curving lips, hair streaming all the way down to her thighs, a silky black, a surprisingly broad forehead and a bold chin (Gibraltar guardian to all this Riviera?) — Marcy stood there before me — I can see her still — a youthful Queen Nefertiti poised before Life. As I look back over eighteen years now, I remember best the serenity in those dark eyes; I am aware enough of the restlessness and shiftiness of my own eyes to recognize that hers were self-contained. But oh my soul! What a lovely and fierce creature beyond this serenity. Her mother pressed my hand very meaningfully that night when I left, but she didn't seem to mind it when I went after Marcy and not her.

She was too young then, in 1952, or so I thought. Anyway I was.

At twenty-five I saw myself as too old to fumble around with her and too young to initiate anyone else into anything. At that time I was Learning About Life from an older woman myself. So beyond the deep empty abstractions, the kisses, and the usual vows, nothing much yet. Once we sort of played around with each other on her couch after returning home from a show, but I heard a cackle and just knew her mother was nesting around somewhere in the apartment, though she was sure she wasn't. The other time, on Fire Island in September, we lay beneath the stars; but when I undressed her the moonlight showed me a bruise on her knee — the kind someone gets playing children's games — and I quit, or, to be honest, deflected my passion into the sand. That's it, or all you could call "it." By the end of the year, her mother, chasing or being chased by a lover, took her on her first European jaunt.

They returned two years later, Marcy's having been a year at A. S. Neill's Summerhill School and I don't know where else, and I soon learned that Things Had Changed. She gave me the key to a Port Authority Terminal locker and asked me to pick up her luggage. I had no sooner pulled out her suitcases than I found myself hustled into the men's room by two fellows, both young, one with an unbearable hair grease, the other with a huge knife, the flat part pressed against my side, and eyes that told me he wouldn't hesitate to slice me up and throw me into one of those lockers.

"Where is she?" Knife asked. He didn't need to, since, in shoving me into the men's room, they ignored the luggage and left it right in the middle of the busy terminal, which bothered me even though I was a wrist flick away from death. (I'm courageous with my life, I guess, but I'm squirrellike about not caring to lose things, especially pens and luggage. Figure it out.)

I gave them the address of that older woman, who had tired of draining me four times a week and had kicked me out not long before. For one thing, she didn't know Marcy, and, for another, she could handle anything. I wonder if they ever found their way out of the Bronx.

That night Marcy showed up at my apartment and I gave her Hell, along with her luggage. "Why me?" I asked her. "Why did you want me killed?"

She threw back her head and laughed. "No one wants to kill you." She rumpled her hair, hiding my eyes from her with a lock. "It's that darn Gregory. He just won't leave me alone. I couldn't

ask anyone else to get my stuff, could I?" Then, smoothing my
hair back and fixing her big eyes all over my face: "I trusted you."

"Why didn't you at least warn me that I might get murdered?
I mean the Port Authority Building isn't Istanbul. Why not warn
me?"

"But now you got the stuff and you're here," she said. She re-
sisted any effort to drag her into the past and future; she preferred gracefully to skim the light surface of the present and ignore
whenever possible the depths of causation, with its recall of roots
and prediction of blossoms. Then, without asking about Gregory
and his friend — just assuming, I guess, that they would always
be knifing around for her — she put her arms out to me (or at
least in my direction) and dropped her head back to offer me that
long slender neck. For a sixteen-year-old girl she knew which parts
of the body to move, which buttons to press, or rather which
buttons to offer to *be* pressed. We're all made like that, of course;
only most of us are at least aware of others' needs, if not of the ways
to satisfy them. Not Marcy. Once we started she never looked at me
or spoke to me, never touched me except to hold or to direct my
hands, my mouth, my legs, my penis where they would do her the
most good. I realize now that in my inexperience I probably
misjudged her then. She was not offering battle when she clawed
my back — I can still feel those nails! — nor when she rammed her
jaw and her knee against me: she was a tiger cub holding
on against an energy that must have been swirling through her; her
body may then have been too frail for such a force, and, holding
on, she may have been trying to induce me to disarm her. But what
did I know of the difference between subduing and disarming?
What did I know of tenderness? When I tried to thrust and felt her
nails digging into me and her other two weapons ramming my
cheek and my leg, I foolishly fought back. Fought back when I
could have surrendered and triumphed. Our clothes had slid off
us, but our muscles stuck fast, and so not much rhythm grew between us. When I came it must have been as much out of escape
from struggle as it was out of pleasure. I can't honestly say if she
came. Soon she was on the phone chatting with her mother. Later
she showered, picked up her hard-earned luggage, and went home.
I guess she went home. Who knows?

After that night Marcy must have decided to adopt me, for my
involvement with her seemed to become inextricable. Only not

sexually: having laid our aces and deuces of expectation and performance out on the table — or bed! — we saw that we were not
Meant For Each Other. What I wanted then — I think in retro-
spect — was someone to soften my edge, to anchor me on earth
after eight or ten hours flying around in IBM program abstractions,
to give emotional color to my forms. What she wanted — who
knows? Beauty, God, maybe Devil? Perhaps she was shooting for
a shore beyond desire. I don't know, and with my very material
needs, fears, and perceptions, I surely offered her no launching pad
for it. But I became useful to her probably because I was her only
male acquaintance of between thirteen and seventy who did not
go knifing around for her, who lent her an ear and a little money,
and who did not presume to judge her — except when she subjected me to mortal risks or hardships beyond the loss of a peaceful
evening. And useful to her because all who live on the precipice of
a flat world of the present need someone who sees things as they
are and calls things by their right names. Or tries.

Her mother picked her up again, and, once more goddesslike
in pursuit or escape, took her off to East and West Europe. I didn't
see her again until late 1956. Though her experiences proved to
be of the kind that jagged metal carves out of life's tissue, she
seemed to be unchanged. For a girl who reacted intensely to every
look and gesture to her, she was not very impressionable; she was
like one of those little turnabout sailboats which respond to every
puff of wind by nearly capsizing, yet never seem to get anywhere.
Maybe she was already there. In East Berlin she had become involved with a married former boy friend of her mother's; his knowing a Party official enabled her to get an abortion. In Budapest she
escaped the knife, but two young men, she told me, actually fought
with long knives to see who would join her in bed, where she lay
waiting.

"Did you make love . . . while the other one bled?" I tried to
ask dispassionately.

"No, it was nothing like that," she replied. "Ferenc took off before getting cut." Then she added: "I hate them both."

If she were a man-eater, she could notch one or two, but I don't
honestly think she was. Later you will wonder at this, but I am
convinced that I am correct. It was all too matter of fact. Men died
for her, perhaps, but she didn't kill them or relish their deaths. If
she had animus, she would be easier for me to understand: this

recital would be shorter. It would be easier to put it together and to sound its depths; since I can't do either coherently, I'm going to continue telling what I know about Marcy as it happened. Maybe, like Marcy, I'll end up denying causation, though I doubt it.

As you may have guessed, Marcy was not political — who was in those days? — but imagine the reaction of her father, who, I've heard, may have been killed by a GPU bullet, had he been alive to hear Marcy's flippant reply to my questions about what she knew of the Hungarian revolutionaries who had just been suppressed or murdered after her return: "Serves them all right; they're an evil people."

But not only people were evil: Marcy suspected snow crystals and cloud formations, among other things. Back in my undergraduate "Condorcet" days I would have tried to explain such phenomena to her scientifically; but by 1957 I knew a little more about human science. Enough not to try, anyway, and, as I said, that's why she stuck with me.

Marcy moved into her own flat on the Lower East Side, although now she saw more of her mother than before, I think. They killed whatever fun parties had for me in those days because I always suspected them — perhaps unjustly — of zeroing in on some poor fellow or two; anyway the momma was Marcy's only worldly care, so that if she was ditching her appointments with God it would only be in order to help her mother stuff her craw. (Surely whatever strategy that was used must have been tacit and not even conscious, for Marcy was incapable, as I have said, of wiliness.) Maybe I'm too hard on middle-aged women's inability to disguise their hunger; chalk it up to that one who initiated me.

Around this time Marcy picked up Peter — don't ask me where. Peter's the right name for him, too, because it was on this rock that Marcy established her church (although, in fairness to Peter, his faith in her did not waver in the usual sense). Peter was more sand than rock, I suppose, but, remember, Marcy, too, was evanescent. Peter would have done anything for Marcy, and he ended up doing just that. Peter was a Greek seaman who had jumped ship and then supported himself by washing dishes. I didn't then know where he lived, but it was easy to find him: hovering somewhere near Marcy's flat, a brooding young presence amid all the clothing hucksters — while they bought and sold, he searched and feared.

Until the last days of her pregnancy, Marcy worked on a job

that harvested the maximum amount of suspicion for a young immigrant dishwasher worried about losing his visa, his girl, and his
wits: she became a solo dancer in Village coffeehouses. Next door
to a pizza maker who tossed dough into the air, Marcy slithered
through her "liberating dances," as she called them, for five or six
hours nightly. I went with Peter to see Marcy perform once and I
can understand his fear. What he failed to see, though, was that
her dance — whether liberating or not — was free of the context of
the coffeehouse: if her sinuous movement corresponded to what the
audience wanted, this was coincidental. All Marcy's movements
flowed about her but back to her. She was moving in a dimension
other than the audience's. Old-timers in those places probably
think of her now as a precursor of go-go girls. As I have suggested,
there was some flickering — some unsteadiness — in her movements,
but this was not the slick, mechanized bump-and-grind go-go.

I doubt if any kind of sexual proposition — including that which
packaged a Hollywood contract — could have touched Marcy; but
perhaps if some wild fellow were to stagger along and tell her he
was the Messenger, that would do it.

God knows, men tried all the gambits. She refused most, not
because of any special loyalty to Peter, I'm sure, but because of a
kind of System she had devolved. An all too simple system: Queen
Nefertiti looked into your eyes; if you were owllike, you were In,
at least for a night, provided Peter didn't stick you on the way. If
you wore glasses, if your eyes, like most people's, were narrow or
shifty — and don't ask me how I passed — you, rat, were Out. Whatever your other Labors or credentials. That key was all Marcy felt
she needed to open the vault of Mother Nature; on such a science
did Marcy stake her trust. The trouble was, if your eyes told true
and you really were so simple, or as she said, HONEST, then how
were you to get by St. Peter lurking somewhere around the gate?

Poor Peter's moony eyes must have been getting bigger and bigger with what he had to look out for. One night he came to my
place to get out of the rain, refused food and drink, and sat in my
big chair to weep, tremble, pray, curse, and sulk.

"Izzat where you . . . did it . . . to her?" he asked, pointing to
the couch.

Shocked, I didn't try to deny anything, but just to fend off the
other questions, I convinced him that it was not very successful, that
we were not laughing at him at the time, and that neither of us, in

fact, had even met him as yet. All this was true, even though I felt somehow that I was lying. I erred in offering him a bathrobe and blanket, for he suspected both of being seductive implements. The whole thing felt ironic to me since, despite the fact that he and not I had had any kind of relationship with her and that she was in all probability carrying his child — certainly not mine — despite these facts, the only way he could see me was as her seducer. Perhaps he was worried also that I had more than he and that when her baby arrived she might retreat to my better furnished and more spacious apartment. I don't know. He had worried about losing her before she was pregnant, now that she was pregnant; and he would hold on to his worry until his death. It was this worry that not only transported him to that death but also somehow buoyed him through life.

If there was another subject to discuss with Peter, I never found it. He sat there in his wet jeans and sweat shirt and dribbled out his misery, while I — I must admit — alternated between forced sympathy and boredom, with an occasional twinge at witnessing the possible soiling of my only good chair. When I contemplated being responsible soon for *three* of them (her mother had disappeared), I thought of changing my employer, my friends, and my address and taking out an unlisted number.

Finally I gave up trying to accommodate him one minute and resenting him the next, and I went to bed. At three I was awakened by the phone and by things slamming to the floor in the other room, where Peter must have begun scraping around on the first ring.

It was Marcy and she wanted Peter. He groaned an answer before the receiver touched his ear so that I could hear what she had to say so loudly and matter of factly: "Peter, I'm with a boyeee."

Peter could barely get something out. I believe it was in Greek. He also managed to ask her who and where and received a horrifying little click in response. He started to run out of the room, knocked down an end table with a lamp whose crash adequately voiced my feelings, then ran back, tried unsuccessfully to dial her number, finally let me do it, received no reply, and tore out of the apartment. I heard him bounding down the stairs as I was brushing pieces of glass off my bed. Sleep did not come for over an hour, and, when it did, brought eschatological terrors which I managed to forget.

It could not have lasted long, either. I woke up upon hearing my name called out and saw Marcy sitting on the bed beside me. "You're hard to wake up," she said. I charged out of bed naked and ran to the door. "Don't worry," and she added, smiling, "Peter's not here."

"Ow!" I cried. I had stepped on a glass splinter. I wrapped a blanket around myself and got a Band-Aid from the bathroom. "Where is he then?"

"Who?"

"Peter, of course, Peter!"

"In the police station."

"God, what for? What happened? What did he do?"

"He cut Quincy last night with his knife. I signed a warrant for his arrest. He's crazy if he thinks I won't testify against him, too. I will, I will."

He had found them together at a friend of Marcy's place and had knifed him along the thigh. I hate to think of where his knife would have gone had he had his wish. The fellow was now at Bellevue, although Marcy said she had been told that he would be released in a day. I looked at the drops of blood I had trailed from the bathroom: then he was armed last night at my place; I could have been killed by him. Marcy was hungry and went to the kitchen to fix herself something.

"Marcy, why did you do it?"

"Why did *I* do it? What are you talking about?"

"Why did you call last night? Why did you have to tell Peter anything?"

"Because I am honest," she said, as she arranged cheese and fruit on a platter, after having washed them thoroughly.

"Not true!" I cried out, finally getting her to look at me and then not knowing what to do with those eyes once they were on me. I looked away. "Not true! That's just a mask and you know it. You were cruel to him."

"Ridiculous!" Marcy said. "I have no reason to be cruel to anybody. Why would I want him to suffer?"

"Marcy, you must know that there is more to you than you know." I knew this was hopeless before I had said it. Just as impossible of convincing a child. But I had not prepared myself for her fury.

Marcy strode around to face me; her jaw thrust forward, she

was reddening and glowering: "Who are you to tell me what I am? Your voice sounds like a typewriter. Look at yourself, Mr. Jesus."

I felt more like crawling back under the covers or protecting myself from those eyes than examining myself, for Marcy's fury was burning me and, naked, I felt vulnerable. My Marcy's eyes are indeed like suns, burning black suns. I'm a slow riser, never at best in the morning; all this was a shock to my nervous system.

Marcy patted her belly. "My child is not going to slink around; he is going to be honest with everyone." She seemed too childlike herself to be having a child. Who was I to be judging her, anyway, but if this was the way Mother Nature had designed us, I was glad that I had been let out for adoption so early. When she saw that I wasn't going to threaten her any more, she served us some food and asked me in an ordinary voice for bail money for Peter. She was ready to set things up in the next alley. Testify against him indeed! So much for her toe dips into the future!

So we sat and ate while I should have been hustling down to the bank to cash a check to spring Poor Peter. I admit I had other thoughts, too, but nothing came of them. Be disgusted, but don't judge me unless you've sat, dry as kindling, wrapped in a bathrobe on the edge of the bed a few inches away from a very nice fire. Even while your mother was dying. She had propped pillows on the bed to make herself comfortable, dangling her legs over the side. She was wearing a snug beige knitted dress, her most formal clothes, probably because she had just come from the hospital and the police station. Marcy had no use for bras at least a decade before that became the fashion, so that when she laughed or moved about, her curves trembled and I kindled. Marcy cupped a plum and some cherries in the palm of a hand and indolently chewed, using her tongue to roll a piece of fruit along the roof of her mouth before surrendering it to her teeth. She let cherry juice dribble out onto her chin; then her tongue swished out, not to wipe it but to play with it, as children do with lollipop smears. It's a good thing the fruit was cold enough to douche me, or, when finished, she could have swept me off the bed, a heap of ashes. I touched her legs, but they stopped moving and stiffened against me. Unsure whether that was part of the love-strife of before, I turned to her, but her scowl was enough to send me into the other room to dress. She poured herself some milk and we left.

If Peter was happy to get out, he was careful not to show it.

What an anomaly that to keep Marcy you needed so much cunning that you dared not show in trying to win her! Maybe her only fit mate would be one of those yogis that could turn his blood pressure and his pulse on and off. Worried as he was about his job, Peter didn't want to get off at the restaurant; perhaps he was afraid of leaving her with him. I wished then that Marcy would find some way to see the rest of her pregnancy through — maybe three months — without further shafting Peter; but then I remembered what I myself had been Up to an hour or so earlier, and I quaffed the moralizing. It's usually the man — isn't it — who gets Wander Lust during pregnancy? With Marcy, of course, she followed not a yen but Nature Herself.

"How would you two like to apply for a marriage license?" I asked, perhaps to reassure Peter of my Good Intentions. Hearing a raucous laugh from Marcy's side of the back seat, I realized that I had only hurt him more. Marcy was in a good mood, though, despite the fact that she hated cars and car rides and that I wouldn't let her smash my radio once and for all. I doubt if she was worried about getting any guff from Peter later: for one thing, she didn't think much in the future tense, as I have said; and for another, she wasn't used to taking crap from anyone, even her mother.

"I gave my love a cherry that had no stone . . ." She was singing folk songs — I don't think she cared for any other music — and once in a traffic tie-up she hopped out of the car and lightly as a sandpiper skittered atop the hood of the car to dance and sing. Pregnant and all. Marcy could move and move and with so little space, the smallest platform. Her body, frilled by beige knit, swayed and whirled, never repeated itself, almost made you forget that it rested on arms and legs, that it was tied to Earth by the same Law that governs us all. For those of us who do not flow so easily with Nature (my sickness, my sickness), such movement is Grace. The honking increased either to blame her for the jam or to encourage her. One or two fellows with ideas in their eyes walked over toward us, but Peter shook his fist at them and she finally returned inside. In the Depression I remember fellows got big pay for toting dynamite. Here was no Depression, less than no pay, but there I was. I say this, but I felt different: snarled in a jam on Second Avenue, we — Peter and I — had been given a moment of vision of the Golden Girl. Even though Peter faced prison because of her.

Nothing came of that, though. We went to Bellevue to ask

Quincy not to testify. There was no way of keeping Peter out of Quincy's room; I guess he wanted to see just what there was between Marcy and this fellow. As we walked through the hospital corridors, Marcy seemed to hang on me and Peter asked too many questions. Both were afraid — of facing Quincy, I thought at first; but after our visit I decided they were afraid of the hospital itself.

"I'm going to have my baby at home," Marcy said. "This place is full of sickness."

Quincy was waiting for an examination so that he could leave. He did not seem alarmed to see Peter; I suppose he thought apologies were due. How protected these kids are; they think the world is arranged for their own good. We had no trouble in convincing Quincy not to testify — he was a pacifist and a noncooperator with the Establishment — but Peter had come for a different purpose: he warned Quincy against seeing Marcy again. Marcy insisted that it was none of Peter's business, that she would not be chained down. What struck me was how little calculation there was in each of these people: Peter didn't know enough to suppress his threats, at least temporarily until the charges might be dropped; Quincy didn't know enough to use the charges as a lever; Marcy didn't know enough about promise or threat to gain clear passage for all. I'm not exactly a conniver myself, but compared to these shiny-eyed children, I was Machiavellian. How to keep them from harm?

A nurse came in to warn us about the noise and henceforth I acted as a liaison between the Outer World and them, but they paid no more attention to my hushing than to a hissing radiator. Quincy did not mention the attack or his suffering and seemed not to blame Peter for it all; what bothered him was what bothered Peter — both accused each other of trying to "fool" Marcy. Marcy scolded them for trying to manacle her with claims of the male. Finally the inevitable question: "Who's better with you?" Peter asked it. I don't think Marcy heard.

"Come on, Marcy, let's go," I said quickly. "We've got to go now." I got up.

"Shut up," snarled Peter. "Tell us, Marcy: who's better with you?"

I held my breath and tried to stop my right eye from twitching. Marcy wouldn't lie, nor would she twitch.

"Quincy's more gentle but — "

"Marcy," I cried out.

"Peter's more forceful."

"Who do you come better with?" Peter wouldn't let go. With his hands he held the rail of the bed; with his eyes he held Marcy.

I thought this was winged confidence until I saw that the whites widening around the pupils of his eyes were openings to terror, only terror; the true gambler rides out all the way to a fall.

"It doesn't matter."

"Sure it matters! Tell us!" growled Peter.

"I told you: it doesn't matter who I'm with."

"You went to pieces with me. That happen with him?"

Quincy sat like me, mouth open, eyes fastened on Marcy, whose jaw was as firm as ours were loose and who seemed to be dying to stare Peter down, the way kids do. I was too speechless to stop the scene, and I guess Quincy was too; Peter's words floated in like surgical jabs, and we must have frozen there, as if anesthetized for them.

"Yes, it happened with him."

We were at least ten flights up. Peter could have dragged both of them to the window and thrown them out, although, given the equanimity of those two, probably only I considered this possibility; he also could have jumped out himself. Instead, he shoved the bed with Quincy sitting on it and stumbled out of the room warning Quincy: "You better stay 'way from her. I no kid."

Not long after, Marcy and I also left, as neither of us could think of anything to say to Quincy. Quincy's a very quiet and passive pacifist, I thought on the elevator; either that or he's drugged. (Yet he must have hung in there with her that time. Would I have been driven like a leaf before that storm?)

I wish I could leave this narrative here — where my lawyer gets them to drop the charges against Peter — and skip to the end, where Marcy, as you might guess, falls into the late 60s like a mouse into soft cheese and becomes a leader of a religious-drug-diet-touch-therapy cult somewhere in California. But I can't skip the Heavy Breathing Stuff, as some programmers I know at the office would call it, much as I'd like to.

Seven months pregnant, Marcy gave up her job and, when her mother still did not show, allowed Peter to move in with her and — I guess — help support her. A midwife delivered Marcy's boy without complications at home. Marcy would not permit even the placenta to be thrown away. She wrapped it and kept it in the refrigerator and gave it to Peter and me to burn only after an artist friend painted it for her.

Whenever I saw them, Marcy was breast-feeding or fondling Didi, one baby who would never die of marasmus. Peter kept — more likely was kept — at a little distance. He looked on with what I thought was a familiar look: he was jealous. I guess the journey from pride to jealousy is not long. If Didi cried when you approached him, Marcy would be convinced that he sensed your sickness, your dammed-up energy, and that he disliked you. I radiated warmth, that is, I never approached him until he had burped.

Marcy threw out, before my eyes, most of a layette that I had bought for Didi during his first week. She would not confine her baby with pins and diapers. It took me days to convince her of the need to keep Didi clean; I bought a lot of rubber sheets and Peter spent much time pacing around a laundromat.

For the first time in the six years that I had known her, Marcy lied. She was driven to it by a sensible public-health nurse who hounded her for over a year for not circumcising, immunizing, or vaccinating Didi. I don't know what the woman told her, but Marcy was terrified of losing Didi. She had begun to anticipate, to live in the future. So finally she invented a past: she convinced the nurse that he had had the shots.

Marcy's mother was killed in a plane crash. She had never seen Didi; I'm not sure if she knew of his existence. I rushed over to see Marcy when she phoned. She met me at the door to calm me down and warn me not to upset Didi. Though self-possessed, she was helpless, as was Peter, about details, so that I stepped in and made funeral arrangements (there were no remains). All this was wasted motion, however, as I was the only person who attended the services. I had contracted a babysitter for a few days to no avail: Marcy would have nothing to do with death. She gave the Salvation Army the trunks her mother had left with her without even opening them and I doubt if she ever saw the small monument I had put up in the cemetery. I just wish I had been with her when the airlines insurance adjuster came around. Nothing I had said did any good: she was an easy mark for him — I'm sure she ended up with the smallest pittance of any of the victims' heirs. But then money annoyed her as much as death. Nature's children must be foolish for they never even see that money that's soon parted from ordinary fools.

After a year or so Marcy weaned Didi, got back her dancing
jobs, and tossed Peter out into a furnished room somewhere and
on to his usual stalking post by the Orchard Street clothing hucksters, who must have taken him for a conscientious price watcher
from uptown. Marcy often boasted that she had good rapport with
the neighborhood toughs and that, her late hours notwithstanding,
she would never be molested by them. "Girls who get raped are
looking for it," she would say. Marcy took no shit.

Until this time, Marcy had no use for studying or teaching, her
formal education having mostly stopped at age fourteen. (If eye-
glasses aroused her suspicions, books confirmed them.) But now she
seemed to need a coterie of adolescent disciples around her, friends
of Marcy's babysitter, kids who had dropped out of school and
who either lived off their families or hustled a living even more
marginal than Peter's or Marcy's. Education had led them only
to the location of bathrooms, lunchroom, and the assistant principal's office; on the other hand, for Marcy, education was merely
a citadel against nature, like religion or war. But where the kids
had learned only of their inferiority, Marcy claimed the opposite,
and I suppose this drew them together. I don't know what she
taught them or what they did, except consume many hours smoking pot and probably consoling each other. Peter suffered. Once
he tried to invade, but never tried again, and resigned himself
to being the yo-yo at the end of Marcy's finger to return to her only
on command. His vigil he intensified, though I don't know for what
purpose, since he knew they were there. It's hard for me to imagine
Peter eating or working; he must have done those things mechanically, without using his eyes, which never really became unstrung
from his vigil and which grew more and more vacant and stark.

Early on August 22, 1962, my wife — I was married now —
awoke me and gave me the phone. Before taking the receiver I saw
that it was 3:30 A.M. and knew it was Marcy.

"I'm at St. Luke's Hospital. Can you come? I'd like you to
help me." Her voice trembled. "Bring a bottle for Didi. Peter's
not well."

I grabbed some milk, found an all-night drugstore, and really
flew to the hospital. People were cramming the Emergency Ward,
but Didi's cries led me to the right room. Marcy would not talk
about anything until she had settled Didi, some several minutes.
Didi was dressed in a hospital gown beneath which I saw bandages;

Marcy appeared unscratched. For a few mad moments, I imagined that Peter had harmed Didi; those moments will always travel with me, I guess, like deadweights around my not-very-winged vision.

"I just hope Didi's not scarred for life, or anything. He should have got Didi first." Marcy held on to my shoulder as if it were a life preserver. Didi lay on her lap and finally took the bottle, although Marcy had not been able to get it warmed.

There had been a fire in Marcy's apartment shortly after her working hours. Peter saw smoke and came tearing into the flat. Smoke and heat were so intense that he got Marcy and her young friends — probably stoned although she didn't say so — to form a chain, and he led them down three flights of stairs and outside. By this time the Fire Department had arrived and the whole tenement was spitting fire and screams. Marcy said she rushed up to Peter and yelled into his ear, "Didi! Didi!" Peter charged back into the building and soon appeared with Didi in his arms at a window that he had just broken. "I was afraid then that Didi was dead." Marcy moaned. The firemen had raised a safety net toward the second floor for other people, but they didn't see Peter, who, nevertheless, managed to throw Didi on to it — maybe a fifteen-foot drop I would guess — before collapsing himself. He never shouted, Marcy said. Some minutes later, firemen pulled a burning beam off his chest and picked him up. He had been crushed and badly burned — no one knew yet how badly. Now he was in an oxygen tent, having received first aid from the firemen's respirator. Marcy stopped her narrative to buttonhole a doctor, who angrily shook loose.

"I've told you, ma'am, your baby only has minor lacerations — just rope burns. Please, I'm very busy. Can't you see?"

Marcy couldn't see. She sat down again and sputtered her contempt: doctors were pretentious butchers who hid their incompetence behind their bustling. Suddenly she arose and said, "I hate this place. I must get out. Help me."

We strode out without taking the child's few things and without telling any of the busy staff. When we were halfway to my place, dawn broke and sort of woke me up. "What about Peter?" I asked.

"I can't stand that place," she said. We would return to see him after she had recuperated. There was nothing we could do for him now, anyway.

The afternoon paper carried the fire, big news even for New York. Some had already died, many more, including Peter, were severely burned. The fire began "of undetermined origin" the paper said; to my knowledge, this was never amended. I had thought Marcy had said the fire had begun in her flat, but she never repeated this, and I don't think she really knew anymore, if she ever did know. The paper said nothing of Peter's exploits. (Days later, hoping that it would somehow help Peter, I related the story to a news editor, who listened but never used it. The fire was all but forgotten, and I guess everyone's eyes were on Cuba.)

My wife took over Marcy and Didi, and I returned to the hospital in the evening to find out what I could. I filled out forms for Peter and finally saw a doctor. I felt myself shrinking within as I heard shock, fractured ribs, puncture of the lung, internal bleeding, probable brain concussion, extensive third-degree burns of the skin, possible loss of sight and hearing, on and on. "God, he would be better off dead." The doctor nodded and left.

That night we sat around the fire — my wife and I drinking gin and smoking too much, Marcy, who never smoked or drank, nursing a cocoa — and I tried to tell Marcy the Worst in The Best Possible Way. Perhaps I succeeded too well, for Marcy, no longer trembling, coasted through my stuttering on a rather even keel. Unused to traveling on the rail, she rights herself quickly, I thought; then I corrected this with the assurance that Nature's Child just cannot imagine such carnage unless spang up against it. I was to correct this many times more; I guess I'll never find the final revision. Marcy fell asleep and, unable to wake her, I picked her up and gently carried her over to the bed where her child lay. Seeing her beside Didi, I noticed then that Marcy breathed in short breaths, just like a child. Had she always? I felt protective.

In the days that they stayed at our apartment, Marcy and Didi clung to each other and whispered to each other as if setting up their own enclave in foreign parts. I liked the direct way she talked to Didi about everything, although I admit that I shared my wife's pique at their eating none of her cooking; they would take only fresh produce; they would keep their bodies from becoming "chemical factories." This time when the landlord's insurance man came, I managed to handle him and got Marcy at least enough to set up another apartment.

During her stay at our place Marcy did not voice any desire to visit Peter, and neither of us suggested it to her. I saw him and knew that there was nothing beyond bandages and tubes to see, a sight that would surely frighten Marcy, who might even feel — who knew? — responsible in some way. They moved Peter, as an indigent, to Bellevue, where he was pushed from ward to ward and finally brought to rest in the burn ward. Peter survived. The tent, machines, tubes, a cast, all were gradually removed — all but the bandages. Through these were visible only his big dark eyes and his mouth. Those eyes no longer searched; it was as if they had found what they were seeking, and then froze in a flat trance. I was frightened when week after week brought no change: they expressed nothing, not even recognition. I should have preferred anything — terror or furor — to that dark flatness. They were like craters of the moon.

Perhaps Marcy could change this, could heal. She must see him. I went over to her new place, near the old, and we sat down to tea. She knew why I had come and disarmed me by telling me so right off. Her jaw thrust so far forward that she could almost balance her cup, but her defiance was undercut by a boredom curled around the corners of her mouth; how tedious it must have been for her to verbalize what she had already decided, to go over ground already worked.

"What you don't understand is that I didn't *love* Peter *before* the fire. I wanted him to leave me alone. I didn't ask him to keep watch over me."

"Marcy, aren't there some things that we don't ask for but are given to us, things which we must repay? Our life, for instance?"

"Mr. Jesus, you ought to be a minister," she said. Then, simply, "I'll go."

Who knows, it may have been the first time she ever weighed anything; if not, it certainly was the first time she had ever chosen the lighter half of the scale. Then, as if to compensate for being deflected a few millimeters from her instinct, she growled playfully, pushed me in the face, and wrestled me down to the floor. Did she want to make love? I think she would have enjoyed pinning me more. Neither happened. She got a babysitter for Didi and we went to Bellevue.

We walked the two or three miles. Marcy had convinced herself that "machines" had caused the fire and most other miseries, and she was trying to forswear their use. As soon as we arrived in the lobby and saw stretchers and wheelchairs and some aides and nurses among the crowd, I must admit that I felt the impulse to bundle my Marcy out of there. She, too, gave a start when some doctors in green fatigues passed close by; she clenched my hand in fear, or maybe in reproach. When we reached the elevator she drew back and I thought it was all over, but she turned toward the stairway and I found myself panting behind her, wondering, as we reached the sixth-floor landing, whether in all the universe this was the right place for us to be, hoping, as we approached the eighth, that this gyre we were ascending would spin us into something other than a burn ward. I was a little giddy when we got to the ward and I fancied that Marcy was floating before me with her streamers of long black silky hair.

Suddenly she stopped. We had arrived at the burn ward. I looked but there was nothing but bandaged patients to see. Almost everything unpleasant in a hospital is covered up with bandages and linen. Nature reveals; civilization conceals. No, what stopped her and made her pause to lean on the wall were sounds rather than sights, sounds I guess I had blocked out in my weeks of visiting, sounds of human agony and helplessness. One voice kept repeating, "Kill me, you cowards." The rest were not so distinct. I noticed later that every time someone entered the sounds increased, as if every visitor or doctor were a god to whom one might communicate some memory or hope, some plea or curse.

I touched her elbow; maybe she thought I was pushing her on rather than trying to help her, for she shook loose and we entered, her jaw in the lead. I brought her to where Peter had been — we even started talking to the man — but a nurse who must have recognized me came over and led us to Peter, whom they had moved again.

An aide was feeding him — he was fed at odd hours, even during the visiting period — and I thought he reared up a little on seeing Marcy and maybe would have stopped eating but for the fact that all his system had been geared to keep up with the aide, who was very mechanically feeding him. He had triumphed in shedding some machines, I thought, only to get hooked on to other ones.

I talked to Peter, or rather at him, for some time while Marcy stood by speechless. I kept watching her, for I could almost feel this new scene embossing itself upon her consciousness, like acid eating

away at something smooth. I remember wondering then if this horrible scene would at least shake her invincibility, yet — who knows
— maybe it only reinforced it, braced that jaw; for, after all, luck
had snatched her from the fire unscratched.

Peter could see and hear and could now move a little; no one
knew yet what harm had been done to his brain or his nervous
system. I had been hoping that Marcy would start helping him on
his long journey back to life. (I had so little time myself even for
these visits.) But I knew now that she did not have the stuff to live
with this. She might tighten some joints, but she was too inex-
perienced an armorer to lock out the scene; she would neither
dehumanize herself nor the victim, and how else does one live with
this? If she was a nature plant, she was not the hardiest, so that
her lack of civilization guilt would not be compensated for by any
toughness of nature. Far from mobilizing Marcy, this visit might
indeed shatter her. I had only to glance at this poor hapless creature in this alien setting to realize how inadequate I was at pro-
gramming people.

I talked on and on about Peter's job and his few belongings that
I had taken from his former room to store for him. I'm the luggage man, remember, the squirrel always ready to save someone
a few nuts. People entered and left the ward, but I waited in vain
for Marcy to intervene and announce herself to him. He must have
seen her standing there. I felt I was caught between two trances, so
I just kept on talking.

All of a sudden, as if she had been wound up to an unbearable tension, Marcy uncoiled. She sprang out toward the center of
the floor, her hair flashing about her, her arms splaying out. Her
long body began bending and turning, now swooping low to the
floor, now spiraling upward, cascading backward, and then swirling around. Motion flowed into motion. The body delicately fluttered, then flared, became a flame, then just a curve, always moving, moving.

I had put my hand out to stay her, but that was futile, and
somehow she electrified so with her vibrant energy that the moans,
the bandages, all the grotesque setting to her dance receded from
my consciousness. I don't know how. This was her triumph.

More than that.

She was skittering just as lightly as that last time I had seen
her perform at the traffic tie-up, but now instead of gravity she was

defying matter itself. It was as if her energy had escaped from its
mortal sack and was streaming out. No unsteadiness, no flickering
now, but a shimmering, a radiant shimmering, a glow of the curve
of life and beyond life, the curve of the infinite. The dance had
begun by outraging my sensibility with its inappropriateness; went
on to charm me with its youth; and finally had transported me,
as if it were a bird of paradise, to a shore beyond life and death,
that shore beyond desire. I who sought only the earthly. I noticed
that there were tears on my face, but I felt lighthearted, healed,
and I wiped them away joyfully. Had Andromache seen the same
thing when she smiled through her tears at her baby and her doomed
husband? We could live or we could die, but we could not lose,
because at the core flowed all that energy, as the dance had revealed.

Then she disappeared. I suppose she ran out of the ward, but
I was too blinded by vision to see. It's difficult for me to imagine
her negotiating the steps and passing through the revolving door.

I never saw her again.

I wonder how Peter and the others under gauze saw the dance,
whether it delivered them, as it did me, from the flesh-coffin or, in
fact, charred them more. When he could talk some weeks later,
Peter never mentioned Marcy, yet if I can read eyes at all, that's
all I saw in them; his soul could not hold more than Marcy, not
then, anyway, or for the rest of his life.

Week after week I returned to the hospital. He never liked me,
I suppose, but he had no one else. When the bandages came off —
well, that's another story, but I hung in there, I guess that's what
friends are for. No, moralism aside, Marcy just could not have
done this. You could not say that he had a mouth, ears, or a nose,
but he did have those large eyes, no longer haunted or blank but
now locked into a permanent, futile yearning. My wife came with
me to visit once and said that she had been prepared for everything except those eyes. (She made it to the women's room before
she broke down.) Over the years they tried many times to graft,
despite the small area of his body that had not been harmed, and
they must have spent as much time on him in Cosmetics as in Surg-
ery, giving him a wig, eyelashes, eyebrows, lips, nose, ears, God
knows what else. Nevertheless he looked hideous beyond hope. By
late 1965 they would not keep him at Bellevue any longer, though
he was to return semiannually for checkups or more grafts. He

did not want to leave the hospital, and I don't want to tell you the ruses we used to get him out of there. The only hospital possession of his we took with him to my place was his identification card, on which his name had been misspelled. He wouldn't part with it.

It was like sheltering a criminal. He would leave our apartment only at night and only after my wife or I had guaranteed him that the hallways were clear. The only thing he wanted was a cloak, which I got him from a theatrical supply store.

Oh, Marcy, if only you could have stayed!

We could not interest him in work or in any pastime. I don't know what he did at night with no money or friends, but during the day he did nothing, not even read. He cursed life and wanted to return to Bellevue. We finally acceded — with what relief — but he was admitted to psychiatric ward. Maybe it was in retaliation for not being allowed back into the burn ward that he began hiding behind Coke machines and disposal units and then leaping out to frighten people, cloak and all. In August 1966, he was found on the floor of the men's room dead. He had managed to slash both wrists with the wire of his identification card.

Could I have healed him?

Recently I heard from a hitchhiker that near Big Sur Marcy had set up or found herself in the center of a drug-diet-touch-therapy cult calling themselves Children of Aesculapius. I wish her well.

CYNTHIA OZICK

The Dock-Witch

(FROM EVENT)

THAT SPRING IT FELL TO ME — as family pioneer, I suppose — to do a great deal of seeing-off. Which was a bit odd, considering how we are a clan if inlanders; for generations we have hugged those little southern Ohio hamlets that surprise the tourist who expects only another cornfield and is rewarded, appropriately, only by another cornfield — but this one marvelously shelters a fugitive post office and a perfectly recognizable dry goods store. We have long lived in these places contentedly enough, in summer calling across pleasantly through rusting screens from verandah to verandah, in winter warming our hands on hymnals in the overheated church. We have little dark lakes of our own, and we can travel, if we wish, to a green-sided river for a picnic, but otherwise water is not in our philosophies.

My own lodging is a seventeenth-floor apartment in a structure of thirty-one stories. I am a little low-down in that building, as you will calculate — perhaps there is still some adducent Ohioan matter in me that continues to seek the earth. The earth, however, is covered over with a stony veneer and is paced by a doorman costumed like the captain of a ship. There is something nautical about my house — from my windows I can see the East River, and I know that if I follow it downtown far enough I will find the mouth of the wide sea itself.

I am the only one of my family to turn Easterner. At first it was shrugged off as rebellion, then concentrated on ferociously as betrayal, and finally they wrote me long letters about the good old dry heat of home, and how I would surely get rheumatism up so high at night in the damp air, and about how this or that farm was being taken over for "development." There were progress and prosperity to be had at home, they wrote, and girls of my own kind, and, above all, the clear open purity of the land. I always answered by telling my salary. In those early days I had what the partners ritually called promise, and was paid in jagged leaps upward, like a graph of our national affluence — I was only two or three years out of Yale Law, more dogged than precocious, a mad perfectionist who chewed footnotes like medicinal candy. The firm I worked for in turn worked for a group of immense, mystically integrated shipping companies. We younger men grinding away in the back offices were all from landlocked interior towns; the cluster of our lawyerly heads slogging over our crowded-together desks looked like a breezeless patch of dun wheat. In the lunch-jokes we traded (pressed hard, we mostly ate out of paper bags at our desks) we snubbed landlubbers and talked about the wondrous Queens, whose formidable documents passed through our days like tender speckled sails. We all said we felt the sea in those papers more intensely than any sailor below decks; we toiled for the sea through the conscientious tips of our ball-point pens. Of course we said much of this in self-mockery, and some wag always found the opportunity to hum "*po*-lish up the *han*-dle on the *big* front door" from *Pinafore*, but there was a certain spirit in which we really believed it. Those fabled white-thighed ships in the harbor not many streets west of our offices meant commerce and passengers, and *we* were the controlling godlets of commerce and passengers. Our pens struck, and the ships would begin the subtile, gigantic tremor of their most inmost sinews; our pens struck again, and the engines would die in the docks. Talk of being lord of the waves! Curiously, I never had any desire to journey anywhere at all in those days. On the one hand, I didn't dare; to take a vacation and go blithely off to look at the world would have been to lose my place in line, and if I knew anything at all, I knew I was headed for the captain's table, so to speak, of that firm. And on the other hand, it was enough to smell the salt scent rising out of the mass of sheets on my blotter, each crowned with a printed QUEEN MARY, QUEEN ELIZABETH, QUEEN WILHELMINA, QUEEN FREDERICA, QUEEN EKENEWASA — it was the salt of my own loyal sweat.

The ships themselves, of course, we never saw; they were brawny legends to us. Now and then, though, we would get to hear what

we supposed was an actual captain. Whenever a captain showed
up in our offices he was sure to be heard, and he was sure to be
angry — usually at one of us. He would spend half an hour bawling
at some tangled indiscretion of ours perpetuated in triplicate
sheafs, and we could catch his vibrations through the partners'
Olympian oak doors — shouts of wrath; but the shouts always disappointed. If you didn't understand to begin with that it was a captain in there, you might think it was the head of a button manu-
facturers' union, or a furniture company, or a cotton farm. All that
monsoon of rage was only about cargoes delayed on trains, or cargoes arrived three weeks too soon, or cargoes — mostly this — un-
paid for. Or else it was a complaint about registry or tariffs, or a
quarrel over tankers. It was no use visualizing commanders of
triremes or galleons — almost all the captains we heard yelling
through those oak doors were tanker-types, and when they came
out, still vaguely snarling but mainly mollified (it was hardly coin-
cidence that afterward one of us would feel the threat of getting
fired), they all turned out to be rather short, flabby men wearing
business suits and not very shiny brown shoes. My doorman had
more of the salt about him than any of them.

Ah, well, the secret of it all was this: they were captains in our
fancy only. What they really were, those furious ordinary men, was
executives of the shipping line come to unravel a mix-up in the
charter contract. It was nothing but contracts, after all — land-
lubber stuff. The farmers down near Clarksburg used to growl just
that way, no different, over market prices, subsidies, transport. And
the captains — this was the worst of it — the glorious captains,
those princes and masters whom we never saw and whose ships
we only imagined, were, like us, only employees. They had no sway
over the schemes of the sea, which belonged to our calm partners
behind their doors and to the plain former-tanker sorts who ran the
lines with their brown-shod feet set squarely on a dry expensive rug.

But if you avoided the shipping executives and the freight for-
warders and stuck to the names of the Queens and kept your pen
charging through that stupendous geography of paperwork — Porto
Amélia, Androko, Funchal, Yokohama, Messina, Kristiansand,
Reykjavik, Tel Aviv, and whatnot — you could preserve your sea-
sense and all its luminous briny tenets. There was a period one
spring when, I remember, I used to read Conrad far into the night
and every night, novel after novel, until I felt that, if I had not been

a seaman in my last incarnation, I was sure to be one in my next. And when, in the morning, groping groggily at my desk, I confronted a fresh envelope full of contradictory demands and excruciatingly detailed subclauses, it seemed like a plunge into the wave of life itself: Aruba, Suez, Cristobal, and all the rest crept up my nostrils like some unbearable siren's perfume, all weedy, deep, and wild. Those days a hot liquid of imagination lived in the nerve of my joy.

Still, I never actually boarded a ship until my uncle Al, a feedman in Chillicothe, decided the time had come for Paris and Rome to experience him. He was a thrifty person, but not unprogressive; he had opted in favor of sea travel and against flying because Aunt Essie had always thought the Wright brothers blasphemous. "If God had wanted people to fly, you and I would be flapping this minute," Al quoted her. She was dead three years, and my uncle's trip was a kind of memorial to Essie's famous wanderlust. She had once stayed overnight in Quebec, and it seemed to her it would be interesting to spend a week or so in a place where everyone acted insane; she meant the effect on her of a foreign language. Al said he himself wouldn't mind if he never set foot out of Chillicothe and environs, but it was for the sake of Essie he was going out to look at those places. "She would have wanted me to," he said, squinting through my windows at the river. There were no children to leave the money to; he was resolved to get rid of it himself. "Is that the ocean out there?" he asked. "It's the East River." "Phew, how can you live with the smell?" he wondered. The next day — it was a Saturday — we took a taxi to the piers. Al let me pay the fare. There was a longshoremen's strike on, so we had to carry the bags aboard ourselves. The ship was Greek, compact and confined. The patchy white paint on the walls of the tubular corridors was sweating. "Why, the downstairs powder room at home's bigger than this," Al said, turning around in the box of his room. He was sharing it with another passenger, who had not yet arrived; all we knew of him was his name, Mr. Lewis, and that he was from Chicago. "Big city guy," my uncle said in a worried voice. Mr. Lewis came so late that the visitors' leaving-signal, something between a gong and a whistle, had already been blown twice: he had only one little canvas bag, with a sort of tapestry design involving roses and a calligraphic letter L on the sides — he swung it between a pair of birch crutches. He told my uncle he was a retired cabinetmaker, and had arthritis.

His true name was Laokonos, and he was going to Patrai to meet his brother's family. Mr. Lewis had an objectionably strong accent, and I could see my uncle meant to patronize him all the way across. "Good-bye, have a good trip," I said. "Fine," my uncle said, "will do. You bet. Thanks for putting me up and all. I'll remember you in my will," he joked. The signal hooted a third time and I went down the gangplank and onto the covered pier — it was really a concrete roof with a solid concrete floor and open sides. It felt like the inside of a queer sort of warehouse, not like a pier at all. You could not even see the water — the bulk of the ship, pressed close against the margins of the sidewalk, obscured it — but the wind was tangible and shot through with an ecstatic gritty taste. I thought I would wait to watch the ship move off into the water. It was a small, pinched, stingy, disappointing thing, apparently without a single sailor anywhere on board; then it occurred to me that the owners might have been too poor to afford proper sailors' dress, and passengers, visitors, and mariners were all indistinguishably civilian. Anyhow most were Greeks. On the pier all the people waiting for the ship to shudder into action and farewell were talking Greek. There we stood in a patient heaving jostling bunch, raggedly crushed up against the barricade at the end of the sidewalk under that warehouse canopy, staring at a long piece of peeling sunlit hull. The top part of the ship was hidden by the roof of the pier, the middle part was cut off by the sidewalk, and what we had framed for us was a quarter-mile of flank, without even the distinction of a porthole. The Greeks went on strangling themselves with their jabber, which seemed to knock them in the teeth as they spoke; meanwhile the ship did not stir. It was not what I had imagined a dock-scene to be, and after half an hour of that mute vigil it struck me that the intelligent thing to do would be to vanish. My uncle was irretrievably encased somewhere in the marrow of this grimy immobile crab, and in any event there was not even a deck with a rail for him to lean over while we mutually waved and mouthed — nothing of the sort. "You think something's wrong? The engine?" one of the visitor-Greeks beside me asked in perfectly acceptable New York English. "My mother's on there, going to see relatives, you shoulda seen her cry when I brought in the fruit. Who you got on?" "My uncle," I said, reduced to a Greek with relatives. "Ever been down here before?" the Greek asked — "how come they take so long to get going?" "Bet they sprung a leak," someone volunteered. "The cook's got indigestion, by mistake he ate what they serve the passengers." "There was a mutiny, they found out the captain ain't Greek." "A Turk, they threw him to the sharks." "Believe me, when you get back over there in a clean suit of clothes, they're worse than sharks, they think you're an American you're a millionaire." A local segment of the crowd gave a cheerful howl at this: there was camaraderie of seers-off I had not suspected. "Excuse me," I said, attempting a passage through. "You leaving?" "What you want to leave for?" "She's gonna take off!" "You'll miss when she starts!" they cried at me from all around. And then, dropped with a startling clarity among the duller voices, a voice unlike the others: "Don't go. It's a mistake to go so soon. There's always a delay, even with the Queens, and if you go you won't see the milky part."

The cocky tone of this — and then the shimmering word "Queens," which secreted all my private visions — held me. I looked and looked. "Milk?" I called like a fool.

"The wake. It's like a rush of milk expressed from the pith of Mother Sea."

She was two yards from where I stood clamped by the laughing mob, a woman of forty or so, small, puffed out by an overstarched dress. It was gray but a little childish for her age and face. Her slivery eyes were darkly ringed like a night-bird's. "If you see someone off you should see it *through*," she chirped back at me.

I said helplessly, "I've waited — "

"So have we all. You're *supposed* to wait. It's part of the sacred rites of the pier. And when she heaves off you're supposed to give a great yell. I'll bet this is only your first time. I'll bet you're a dryfoot. Midwesterner?" she wondered from afar.

A growl was preparing under our feet. The concrete rumbled like a dentist's drill. "She's starting!" "She's going!" "I can see her move. She's moving!" The mangy rectangle of ship-side glared back at us without a sign of motion; as if to set it an example, the mob began to mill. Then, with a kind of gentle hiccup, the hull commenced to tingle visibly, almost to twitch, like the rump of a horse. A jungle-roar came out of her and struck our faces. "There!" "Can you see anybody?" "The deck's on the other side." "There ain't no deck." "Look for a porthole." "Porthole's too low down." "Oil, that's what it is. I told you oil."

A metal smell, the fragrance of some heavy untrustworthy machine, assaulted the wind. The water was all at once revealed, a vomit of snow. It piled itself on itself, whorl on whorl, before it melted into a toiling black, like an ominous round well or dark-blooded eye. The creamy wake ran swiftly after the stern. Without warning she was off and out, and we saw the whole of her, stacks, strakes, and all, grumbling outward. The farther she went the better she looked. She smoothed herself down into an unflecked un-soiled whiteness; she rode with her head up, like something royal, and the Greeks shrieked and waved. Then she made a wide turn, trailing out of the harbor into the shining platter of openness, and we could spy, on her other haunch, a tiny deck filled with tiny figures. My uncle and Mr. Lewis must have been among those wee dolls. But I had had enough, and walked the long dim concrete route out to Canal Street for a taxi, peculiarly saddened.

It was only a week after this that my young cousin's senior class came through, thirty fastidious crew-hatted girls from Consolidated High, headed for a tour of "Scotland, the Hebrides, England, and Wales": thus spake the tour pamphlet. "Not Ireland?" I said. "George, *no*body's interested in *Ire*land," my cousin said (she was really my first cousin once removed); "we're going to see an actual *stool* that Robert Burns sat on. It's in a museum in Edinburgh. Did you know there's a big castle, like an old king's castle, right in the middle of Edinburgh? It's in the catalogue, want to see its picture? I don't know how you can stand New York. Mama thinks you're crazy to live in such a place, full of killers with daggers." She made a pirate's face, and handed me a goblet of champagne. They were giving themselves a party. All over the ship — it was a students' ship, and German — there were parties. A gang of boys had hauled the canvas off a lifeboat and were drinking from green bottles, their knees flattened under the seats. The ship smelled of some queer unfamiliar disinfectant, as though it were being scoured desperately into a state of sanitation. The students did not seem to mind the smell. Their bunks were piled with suitcases and stuffed knapsacks. "We're landing at Hamburg first, and then we have to go *back*wards to Southampton," my cousin explained. "It's cheaper to do it backwards. The champagne's all gone, you want some beer?" She went to get me some, but forgot to come back. The senior class of Consolidated High began to scream out a song. They screamed and screamed, and though I had promised my cousin's mother I would take care of Suzy as long as she was in New York, I felt suddenly

superfluous and wandered off on my own. The disinfectant followed
like a bad cloud. In a corner of a cabin two levels down, jammed
into the angle of a bunk, I saw the starched woman. She was eating
a piece of orange layer cake, and there were four shouting students
squatting beside her. "Who're you seeing off now?" she addressed
me out of the din. "Your sister?"

"Don't have a sister."

"Brother? Don't have a brother. Have some cake instead?"

I squeezed into the cabin and accepted a bit of icing on a paper
plate. "Who're *you* seeing off?" I asked her.

"The sailors. What do you do?"

"Fine," I said.

"I didn't say how, I said what. I can see you're fine — you have
very fine skin, you're not a sailor anyhow. My God, it's noisy on this
one. I'm about ready for the dock. Will you wait till the end today?"

"The end of what?" I said; I thought her too friendly and too
obscure.

"Of the dock part. You've got to see her go."

"I saw her go last time."

"You don't talk of time when you talk of Greek sailors. Greek
sailors are timeless. Greek sailors are immortal. I bet you work in an
office. Something dry, no leaks."

"A law office," I admitted.

"Makes sense, but I don't like lawyers. Wouldn't be one for anything. I'd be a sailor if I were a man. I suppose you're thinking I'm
an old maid — well, I'm not. I've got a couple of married daughters, would you believe that?"

I politely muttered that the fact was hardly credible.

"I know," she agreed. "I've kept my youth." We struggled
through the ship together, and finally out of it and down the
gangplank, while I observed for myself that this last remark of hers
was almost justified. "If you see someone off you should see it
through," she said emphatically, in the same confident voice as last
time. She had a long but all the same jolly face: long earlobes
stuck through with long wooden earrings, a long square nose, a long
hard chin. She wore her hair too long. The first quick look you
gave her took off fifteen years, and turned her into a girl, not pretty,
but rather of the "interesting" category, which I had always found
boring; the second look, not so quick, put the years right back on,

but assured you of something wise and pleasant. We waited for the ship's wake to form, and then waited for her to find a dairy metaphor that did for it. "Butter-churn," she said at last — "the ocean's butter-and-eggs route. I *don't* like adolescents. They can't concentrate. Sailors can concentrate — well, maybe it's because they *have* to," she conceded. "Do you have to go back now?"

"I'm past my lunch hour."

"Poor you. A little drudge. Do you see that drugstore down there — no, the one across, over there." She pointed along Canal Street. "That's my husband's. He's been a pharmacist around here for just about forever. A drudge worse than you, and been one longer. I doubt whether he's ever walked two blocks to the piers for the thrill of the thing. *I* do it practically every day. You like the water, don't you?"

This startled me. "Yes," I said.

"Well, law leaves *me* all at sea too," she cracked, and fell into a tumble of laughter. She darted into the dark little store when we came to it. "In the afternoons I help out sometimes," she piped from the doorway.

After that it was a neighbor from home I put up, and then two members of the Clarksburg Post Office; and the Mayor actually. It seemed to me the whole timid town was emptying itself out, via my apartment and the docks, to throw itself on the breast of Europe. I could scarcely account for the miracle of all that fit of traveling that had fallen on the state of Ohio. As for the traffic that passed through my hands in particular (and my towels and my sheets), I soon began to understand how word had gotten back that I was, though crazy to live in such a place, cheaper than any hotel in the same place, and that I could "afford" it. This was the price I paid for having boasted so frequently of my grand salary, which now — after a weekend of restaurant dinners and taxi fares for a pair of honeymooners, children of the brother-in-law of a treasured friend of my great-aunt-by-marriage — hardly seemed so grand. The price my visitors paid was something else, and perhaps worse — word got back to *me*, ever so mildly, that in Ohio I was considered a dull unlively half-dead sort, a snob, preoccupied with my own vanity, a New York careerist. They wrote me off as a lifelong bachelor-to-be, without a heart.

On my side I thought them all wretchedly ungrateful, and if I kept my threshold open for them it was to study their ingratitude.

They streamed in, earmarked by every cliché of inland dress, the men's trouser-legs ludicrously billowing, the women very large in their backward-brimmed hats and tunicked flowered rayon suits and chalky white shoes, all of them gloved and looking out cautiously from narrow-nosed, sun-fearful, flaky faces. I despised their slow voices and I was certain they privately jeered at mine, with its acquired pace hard-won at Yale. We made briskly poisonous parties of it; I had the satisfaction of noting plainly how the headwaiters shared my contempt for them. The truth was, I suppose, that I courted and fed on my contempt, glad to see what I was well out of. The women asked pityingly whether I had never been abroad, and when I admitted I hadn't, the men laughed through cigar mist and said, "Now then, y'see, I've always maintained there's no one more provincial than a New Yorker. Never seen the Eiffel Tower? Never seen Rome? Well, I tell you, George, go ahead and have a look at Rome. One thing about Rome, it's worth a whole roll of film."

That spring I saw the inside of all sizes and varieties of ships and ship cabins, the greasy and the glittering, wherein I nuzzled elbow-to-elbow with my recent guests, all of us gripping our modest drinks in an unconfident little group and sick to death of one another's shafts. By then they had stopped asking when I was going to get some sense into my head and come back home to live in the real America; but by then the relief that always followed the self-indulgence of my scorn for them had begun to take hold. Standing, secretly frightened, in their narrow traveling-closets, they stood for everything I had escaped. They went on their foolish ritual tours and thought themselves worldly, and by Christmas would have forgotten it all if it had not been for the ritual color slides they showed as ritual proofs of the journey. And I, meanwhile, took *them* as ritual proofs of my own journey — of how perilously near I had been to becoming a boarder of ships, instead of a seer-off. The passenger inexorably returns to his town in the stupid marrow of the land; the man on the dock quivers always at the edge of possibility. What I had attained, in my short stride from midland to brink, was width, endlessness. Waving vainly on the pier, I waved good-bye to all my dead ends. When at last the ship ground vibrating out through the scribble of spume, headed not really for its destination but more essentially for the way back, something like prayerfulness ascended in me. I thought at first it was only pleasure that the burdensome visitors were gone; but then I knew it was the peace of clinging to the rim of infinity, without the obligation of resuming the limits of my old land-sewn self.

Through it all I never missed glimpsing the starched woman, with her long head and her deceptive long-haired girlishness; it was like being startled by a constantly yielding keyhole; sometimes I caught a curious view of her in someone's cabin, noiselessly clinking her earrings in an abyss of noise, and now and then I saw her leaning, always in a festive mob, holding on to a cookie, over a deck-rail, or threading in rope sandals through a slender corridor with a slender searching eye. Then the leaving gong would clamor, and often enough I would find her beside me in the dock crowd, thirsting downward into the white whirl excreted by the outgoing ship. She was always dressed with a noticeable cleanness and stiffness — her sleeves and skirts were as rigid as a dark linen sail. "Whipped cream," she said of the wake, and then as usual we walked out with self-gratified wise sadness into the noon glister of Canal Street, until the black doorway of the drugstore sucked her suddenly in.

Or she would not be there. And then — the day after I had seen someone off and she was not there — I would leave my office at lunchtime and take my sandwich in my paper bag with me and walk west to the docks, along Canal Street, past the hardware marts spread outward on all the sidewalks, and choose a pier alongside which lay a white liner, and look for her. And there she would be, laughing seriously among strangers, eating cake, stamping her feet with their visible clean toes on the concrete, all for farewell to the departing voyagers. Or else would not.

She would not be there more often than she would be there, and on those days I was always disappointed. I circled the cement dock-floor a while, chewing my sandwich at the side of an idle Cunarder, and tramped back, inflamed by regret and belching mustard, to my desk and its spotted documents. The Queens did not satisfy me then; I had the itch of curiosity. She was never there to see anyone in particular off, I had learned; no one she knew ever went abroad; she was there for the sake of the thing itself — but I never could fathom what that thing was: was it the ships? the sailors? the polyglot foreignness? Was it only an afternoon walk she took to the nearest bustling place? Was she a madwoman? I began to hope, for the colorfulness of it, that she might really be cracked; but whenever we conversed, she was always decently and cheerfully sound — though, it must be said, not like others. She was a little odd.

She asked me one day whether I was good at cross-examination.

"We don't do much of that in our office. Mostly it's desk work. We don't go to court hardly at all — the idea is we try to keep the clients *out* of court," I explained.

"Haven't you ever been to a trial?"

"Oh, I've *been* to 'em."

"But never broke a witness down?"

I smiled at this brutality of hers. "No. Really, I'm not a trial lawyer. I just sit at a desk."

"You're a passive intellectual."

"No, I'm not. Not really."

"Well, I'm glad you're not the sort who tries to get things out of people — admissions."

"You don't have to admit anything to me," I promised.

"I wouldn't anyhow," she said. "I'm the sort who doesn't tell things. If you tell things you don't get to keep them."

"*I* don't like to keep things," I said.

"Do you like to keep people?"

"I guess not. If I did I wouldn't always be sending them off."

"You're not sending anyone off today," she observed. "And you were here day before yesterday, and you didn't send anyone off then either."

"True," I said.

"Are you keeping someone back?"

I had to laugh, though not pleasantly. "I guarantee you my apartment's empty right now."

"I want to see it. Your apartment. You said you can see the water from it?"

"Not this water — just the river."

"All water is one," she announced. "I want to see. No one's there at all?"

"I don't keep anyone. Really. Not even a mistress."

She looked offended at this. "I have married daughters, I told you. And a husband. They're my wake. You understand? When you live you leave a wake behind you, and it always follows you,

whatever you do. What you've been and where you've been are
like a milk that streams out past you all the time, you can't get free
of them. Mortality issues its spoor."

I was suddenly angry; she was lecturing me with platitudes, as
though I were a boy. "Well, don't worry," I said. "I haven't invited you to be kept!"

"You haven't," she agreed. "But you will. Oh, you will, you will."

I said, exasperated, "Are you a clairvoyant?"

"Don't sneer. Everyone is who goes along with Nature. You're
not made of wood."

I touched the side of her dress, which extended as crisply as the
hide of a tree. "No," I said, "but *you* are. Why do you dress like
this? Why don't you ever wear anything soft?"

"To armor myself. If I were soft you'd want to keep me."

"Oh, go to the devil."

"And the deep blue sea," she said, turning her hard back on me.

I stayed away, after that, for almost a whole week. I did not
even know her name (though she knew mine), and still I disliked
her. She was a triviality, a druggist's wife, a crank who hung around
the docks, and I thought myself absurd for having given so many
lunch hours to her queer company. I kept my sandwich on my desk
and rattled papers while I ate it; my colleagues did the same; I had
already, as a consequence of having sacrificed all those bright noons
to the docks, fallen a little behind them. We were in an unacknowl-
edged race. The more documents one digested, the more one was
digested by the firm: I had to remind myself that my whole ambition was assimilation into that mystical body. But I felt vaguely
enervated. The race seemed not quite to the purpose; yet I hardly
knew what was more to the purpose. My colleagues struck me as
silly now when they whistled *Pinafore* or snickered out their little
jokes about tanker-types. I withdrew from them — I don't think
they noticed at first — and immersed my unexpectedly bored brain
in the Queens' sheets. But now they seemed not so much like sails
as — well, sheets. They fluttered under my hands with the limpness
of unruly bedclothes. Their salt emanation I knew to be no more
and no less than human sweat. I gave up reading at night; I gave up
sticking at home nights. I put on my oldest pair of shoes and scuffed
along the riverside — to reach it I had to dare the Drive that
swarmed on its ledge. The car lights smacked my eyes and I ran for
my life across that wild road with its wild shining herds. Up from

the stinking water came the noises of melted garbage sloshing against the artificial bank. Rarely I saw a barge creep by. The river was not enough.

On Friday night — the end of that same week of abstinence — I walked crosstown and took a bus that sliced inexorably toward the lowest part of the city, where the harbor lay pining. A pungent mist crowded the air. It was dark down there, a dark patrolled by the scowls of guards. They would not let me out onto the piers, so I prowled the cobbled sidewalks, looking down alleys; once I saw a pair of rats the size of crouched penguins, one hurrying after the other in a swift but self-aware procession, like a couple of priests late for divine service. The docks were curiously uninhabited, except by a row of the smaller sort of ship, bleak cut-outs with irregular edges as if chewed out by bad teeth — the mammoth prideful ones were all out at sea, or else dispersed among the world's more fortunate ports. I longed sorely for one of these: one of the radiant Queens — it was for these I had made this nighttime pilgrimage, hoping for the smell and signal of deep deep ocean. The loneliness of that place was excruciating; now and then a derelict lurched by, or a hushed criminal sliding forth on an errand of rape. For the first time I had an unmistakable desire to go on a voyage — I was aware of it as surely as of a taste: I had to have the marrow of a fleck of salt. I had to search into the inmost corridor of my urgency. I scurried eastward, then south (imitating the pace and gait of those sacerdotal rats), to the death-lit Battery. The terminal was as brilliantly electric as some hell. A ferry stood panting in its slip, and I boarded it on the run, just as the gate began to close. The dock and the stern split apart and the tame water dandled and puddled between them, nearly under my feet. A froth spit up all the way, stronger and stronger. The wind on the deck was harshly warm. I sank my gaze into that harbor-pool, and pulled a rope of sea smell into a gluttonous lung; it was not enough. It was not the Thule of depths, it was not ocean enough, it was not savage enough. It was not salt enough.

Returning from Staten Island I slept on one of the side-deck benches; a drunk and I tenderly shared shoulders. The ferry was as bright as a wedding-palace or carousel. It was full of music borne by lovers embracing transistor radios. Once when the drunk's head fell from my shoulder, I awoke and saw in the blackness beyond the ferry's aureole a fantastic parade, majestically decorous — I thought it was a galaxy of rats riding the top of the water; I glimpsed pointed alert ears. But it was sails. I saw the sails of galleons, schooners, Viking vessels, floating full and black; dark kites.

On Saturday morning I kept away; it seemed to me I had a fever, though my thermometer registered normal. All the same I wallowed and rooted in my hot bed all day, rising out of it only to drink ice water. I drew the blinds so as to shut out the river; I was frighteningly parched. In the evening I poured whiskey into the cold water, and then a little water into much whiskey. On Sunday, though feeling no better, in an atavistic fit I went to church. The text was Jonah: "For thou hadst cast me into the deep, in the midst of the seas; and the floods compassed me about: all thy billows and thy waves passed over me." Afterward I vomited in the vestry.

The next day, at noon (but I had brought no lunch), I was too impatient to walk, so I hailed a taxi for the piers, but leaped out of it in the middle of Canal Street, within a block's sighting of the wharf buildings. We had been halted by thickening traffic; I could not endure it. The rest of the way I ran. I ran up the stairs and into the long concrete hall. Everything was as usual — the mob, the noise, the familiar screeches of good-bye. Dimly from the bowels of a dim-gray ship I heard the leaving-gong. It was a Jewish ship heading for the Holy Land — it had an unhealed gash in its prow and along part of its visible side. All around were Orthodox sectarians wearing black hats and long black coats and antic beards, some of them clownishly red. They were weeping as though the broken wall of the ship were some ancient holy ravaged mortar. I flagged my arms like a fleeing ostrich through their cries and forced myself into the stream descending the gangway. A huge-breasted woman in a robust white uniform, robustly striped at the wrists, called to me to desist, but I pushed harder against the breasts pressing downward against my climb. Still struggling I was freed into the ship, heard a wired voice command departure, and began to comb the passageways for my stiff prey. Almost instantly I found her: she was leaning against the door of a public lavatory, gleaming with splendid tears: her long face looked varnished. The gong struck again, the voice in the loudspeakers hoarsened and coarsened. "Why are you crying, for God's sake?" I said. "Everyone else is," she said, "everyone all over the place." "Quick, let's hop off or we'll end up in Jerusalem." I pulled her by the sleeve — the starch of it scratched my palm — and we flew downward. In a moment the hastening ship be-

gan to moan itself loose from the dock. The onlookers sent out a
tremor of ecstasy. They joined themselves neck to neck and kicked
out, kicked in, spun: they were dancing the ship toward the sacred
soil. "Let's dance too," I said; I was overjoyed at the miracle of
having seized her in the pinch of my will. "No, no," she said, "I
don't dance, dancing makes me simply creak, I'm an antique for
goodness' sake, I'm not young." I lifted her in the air — but she was
as heavy as a beam — and flung her down again, out of breath.
"See?" she said. "I told you." "What's your name?" I demanded;
"all weekend I remembered that I don't know your name." "Undine." "Undine?" "Call me Undine," she insisted. "I will if you
want me to. What does the druggist call you?" "Sylvia," she replied,
"a name for a stick. A stick-in-the-mud name." "Undine," I said.
    That afternoon we became lovers. She peered down from the
windows of my apartment. "I like it up so high," she squealed —
"you said you could see the river, though."
    "There it is."
    "That dirty little string?"
    "All water is one," I said, mimicking her.
    She looked at me meditatively. "*I* taught you that." And then,
rattling the sash: "Oh, I like it up so high! I miss being up high.
Where I live now it's low."
    "That window's not made to open," I explained, "we're air-
conditioned, can't you tell?"
    "Sure I can tell. Air out of a machine. That's abnormal. It isn't
natural, I'm against it."
    "Come back to the bed," I begged, "it's all right here."
    "They'll miss you at your office."
    "They're all drudges at my office."
    "I taught you that."
    "Teach me, teach me," I said.
    "I'll teach you fashion first. You don't like my clothes."
    "I'm against clothes, they're not natural. You're not fashionable
anyhow — your clothes are like bark. I peel bark, that's what I do."
    "I know you do. I knew you would."
    "You're a clairvoyant."
    She laughed with an eerie autumnal clarity, like a flutter of
leaves. "No, I'm not. I just go along with the tide. If I see a tidal
wave I just mount it, that's all."
    "I'm the tide," I said.

"I'm a wave."

"I'm the crest of the wave."

"I'm the trough."

"We coruscate."

"Like a fish's back."

"We rock, we tumble, we turn."

"I can see all the world's water from here, it's so high."

"You stay down," I ordered her.

She stayed all that night, and all the next day and all the next night. Early on the third day I put on a business suit — how strange it felt on my liberated, my sharpened, skin! — and came into my office as in a trance. My colleagues looked oddly nonhuman, like some unfamiliar species of sea-animal; the papers languishing on my desk seemed to have rotted. "You didn't answer the telephone," they accused, "were you away? An emergency?"

"I think I was sick," I said, and at once believed it.

"You look thin," they said, "how thin you've gotten."

In the mirror in the washroom I examined my thinness. It was true, I had grown very thin.

"Are you staying in for lunch?" they asked me. "Or are you going out like week before last?"

"Sure," I said, unsure of either.

"We had a man over from one of the Queens the other day. You missed some real roars, boy. A tycoon."

"A typhoon?" I said.

"Are you sick? You look sick," they said, giggling.

"I'd better go home again," I agreed, and went. The apartment smelled of decay. She was gone; she had turned off the air-conditioner and the refrigerator. My pillow smelled of rot. The milk had soured; so had the wine and the cream; two or three peaches were black. A bowl of blueberries had been transformed into an incredibly beautiful flower, all gilded over with mold.

I lay in my bed, exhausted by desire for desire; spiraled in reverie, I dreamed our three days' love-making. I thought how she had slid from her parchment sheath and how all my pulse had mingled with hers. "Undine," I pronounced to myself, depleted. The belt of her dress was coiled on a chair; I reached out a languid hand and unfurled it. It was stiff, like frozen linen, like the side of a fossil tree. But her waist had been flesh, and as pliant as a tongue. I hid the belt under my pillow; she had returned to her husband — this made me spring up. In half an hour I was beating Canal Street with truculent shoe-soles. I stamped and scudded, afraid to go to the other side. Across the street, between two hardware vendors, the drugstore squatted like a dark fly. No one went in and no one came out. I wondered what sort of a living they could make in a place like that. A truck blinded the road and I ran in front of it; horns sang at me, for no reason I was still alive; I bought the first object my hand seized — a washboard. Clutching it like a lyre, I entered the drugstore. Behind a fly-flecked cardboard-crowded counter she stood holding (I thought) a real lyre, laughing her confident laugh. "We're working on a lipstick display. Isn't it nice? Look — " Her instrument turned into a tin tray fluted with golden tubes, each bloody at the tip. I read the names of all the lipsticks: Purple Fire, Crimson Ice, Silver Gash, Heart's Wound. "The pharmacist is out," she said; "I mean he's in the cellar. He's bringing up cartons. Cosmetics. Woman's weakness since Cleopatra. Nothing touches *my* face, let me tell you — only water. If you wait you can meet him."

"Please," I said, "come back to the apartment."

"Suppose your cousins are there? Or your brother? Or your uncle?"

"You know I don't have a brother. No one's there," I swore. "No one. No one's expected. The place is empty."

"I shut off all the fake cold, did you notice?"

"Come back with me, Undine."

"Sylvia. *He* calls me Sylvia. He used to be all right but now he's all dried up, he's practically not there. I don't love him. I don't know why I stay here. Where else would I stay? It isn't as though we had any children."

"Your daughters? Your married daugh — "

Out of a hole in the flooring in the back part of the store a big tan box floated upward; behind it (seeming to paddle up, as out of a whirlpool) Undine's husband emerged. "My husband's name is George too, did I tell you that?"

He was clearly disappointed that I was not a bona fide customer; we shook hands, and then he lifted the very hand he had given me and parted the fingers to make horns behind his head. "She met you down there?" he asked. "At the docks? She always hangs around there. Eventually I get to see 'em all. Don't think I mind, it's all the same to me, buddy." He glared at my washboard. "Did you pay for that thing?"

"It's his, honey, he bought it next door. We don't sell that item," Undine said.

"Well, then put it on the order book, I don't mind the competition. One hundred thousand items in stock. Hairpins to Sal Hepatica. Paregoric to pair-of-garters. We don't do much prescription business, though. They all go uptown to those cut-rate places. Robbers, they cheat on the Fair Trade Law, cut off their nose to spite their face."

"I hate my nose," Undine said. "It's too long. I look like Pinocchio with it, don't I?"

"Quit fooling around," George said. "You want to go out with him, go out with him. I got plenty to do here, I don't need help either."

"Let's see if there's a ship going off," she assented, "one with real sails," and I followed her out of the store.

"Why do you treat him like that?" I asked.

"Oh, I don't know. Because I want to. Because he looks just like the Devil. Doesn't he look just *exactly* like the Devil, I mean really and truly?"

I considered it; she was perfectly correct. He was all points, like the ears of a rat — he was the driest, thinnest man I had ever seen. For some reason I felt cooled toward her. Her toes in her rope sandals looked too straight, too rigid. The tops of her sleeves jutted straight up from her shoulders. Her hem was like a rod.

"All the sails have come in by now. Did you read about it in the papers? From all over the world. They train sailors on those old sailing ships. Replicas. That's how they teach them about ropes and things. There's a Viking one from a movie they made. Did you see about it in the papers? Every single country's sent a sailing ship into New York Harbor. It's a show, didn't you read about it?"

I said hoarsely, "I haven't seen a newspaper in three days."

"Well, they came before that. They started to come in last week. It's thrilling, don't you think it's thrilling?"

"I don't want to go to the docks. I want you to come home with me," I said, but I hardly knew now whether I meant it. Guilt over her husband ground in my throat. "Why did you say you had daughters?"

She stopped. "Oh, you're a liar."

"*I* haven't told any lies."

"You said you never cross-examine. You said you never pry. You said you don't try to *get* things out of people."

"What's that got to do with daughters or no daughters?"

"Of *course* I've got daughters," she said sullenly. "I have a husband, don't I? — They're married, I told you, and gone away."

"All right," I said. "I misunderstood."

"I don't want you anymore."

"I don't want you either."

"You're a drudge. You look exactly like the Devil yourself."

"I've lost weight," I said, defending my body.

"You might have a cancer. Cancers always begin that way. Look at the sails!"

We had come to the end of an alley opening on the water: a thousand dazzlements cluttered the sky. Sails, sails — it was as if some suddenly domesticated goddess had reached down to hang an eon's worth of laundry. Or it was as if a flight of enormous gulls had paused in silence to expose their perfect bellies to the equal perfection of the daylight's brilliance. The harbor seemed very still. "If it's a show," I said, "where's everybody? If it's a flotation museum, where are the visitors?" "Shush," said Undine, "it's just maritime business, who said the public was invited?" "Where are the sailors?" "*I* don't know. Ashore maybe. Asleep. Don't ask me, maybe we're having a hallucination. Look at this one!" Almost from the utmost stretch of our fingertips a great enameled bow rose, as curved and naked as a scimitar, shining wetly in the sun gaze, like a nude breast: above the bare cutwater stood thirty-seven white-clad sentries, stiff at attention in the clear air — it was a full-rigged ship under plain sail. "Look at the masts!" Undine cried — "they're like a forest. Big heavy trunks, then branches and twigs." "I don't like the hull," I said, "it looks too fragile. Potential sawdust. Give me steel every time." "Oh, that's wicked," she said — "steel comes out of a furnace, and then out of a machine, it isn't natural — " "Sawdust," I insisted, squinting upward at the empty prow. It seemed to me there should have been a figurehead there.

She stomped after me reluctantly, scowling, kicking heavily, banging at things with my washboard. All the way uptown she would not speak to me; she spat at the doorman when he turned his glorious captain's coattails; she scratched her nails savagely on the elevator's gray metal walls. She would not come into the bed. "I'm hungry," she said. "You switched off everything and spoiled all the food," I complained. She sidled out of the kitchen frowning with contempt, grasping a tiny silver coffee spoon — then she went to the bedroom window and stabbed the handle through the glass. It did not shatter; it only gulped out a little hole, like a mouth, with creases and cracks and wrinkles radiating outward. "Air," she said in triumph, and at last, at last, we made love.

But she was weighty as a log. The mattress descended under her, groaning. She raised her legs and thrust them on my shoulders, and it was as though I had dived undersea, with all the ocean pressing on my arched and agonized spine. I felt like a man with a yoke, carrying on its ends a pair of buckets under a spell — the left one held the Atlantic, the right one the Pacific. When I slid my hand under her nape to lift her mouth to my gasping mouth, it seemed to me her very neck was a cord of wood. Her hair oppressed the pillow, each strand a freight, a weight, a planet's burden of gravity. How heavy she had become! Her tongue lying on my tongue exhausted me. I toiled over her unrefreshed, unspeakably wearied, condemned to a slavery of sledging logs.

"What's the matter?" she whispered. "Don't you love me? Are you tired?"

With convulsed breath I told her I loved her.

"You satisfy me," she said.

She stayed the night. We ate nothing, drank nothing; we never left the bed. In the morning I said I would go out. "No, no," she commanded. She snatched her belt from under the pillow, where she had discovered it, and buckled her wrist to the bedpost. "I'm attached," she said. "I can't leave, and neither can you. I've got to stay forever, and so do you."

"My job," I said.

"No."

"Your husband," I appealed.

"I don't have a husband."

"Undine, Undine — "

"Come on me again," she said. "Come aboard, I want you."

"We'll starve. We'll perish. They'll find our bodies — "

"I don't have a body. Don't you want me?"

"I want you." I wept, and heaved myself into the obscuring billows of my bed. She made me sweat, she made me a galley slave, my oar was a log flung into the sea of her.

"No more!" I howled; it was already dawn.

"But you satisfy me," she said reasonably. "Don't I satisfy you?"

I kissed her palms, her mouth, her ears, her neck, for gratitude, for torment, for terror. "Let's go for a walk," I begged.

"Where? I'm welded here, I told you."

"Anywhere. I'll take you home. We'll walk all the way."

"It's miles and miles. Will you carry me?"

"I've carried you miles and miles already."

"I don't want to go home."

"Then wherever you want."

"I have no home. I'm homeless. I'm adrift."

"Wherever you want, Undine! Only to leave here a while. Air."

"But I broke the window for you, didn't I?" she said innocently.

"We'll go look at the sailing ships," I proposed.

She had hold of my hair. She licked my eyelids. "No. No, no, no."

"Never mind," I said, practical and purposeful. "Put on your clothes."

"I have no clothes."

"Where did you drop them?" I looked all around the room; they were not there, except for her starched belt, which still waggled stiffly from the bedpost. But on the chair I saw the washboard— she had brought it all the way from Canal Street.

"Here," she said, grabbing it. "I'll play you a tune. Can you sing?"

"No." For the moment I forgot that I had been in the Clarksburg church choir.

She drubbed her nails back and forth across the washboard.

"That sounds terrible. Stop it. Put on your clothes."

"I have no husband, I have no daughters, I have no house, I have no body, I have no clothes," she sang. "Your love is all I have."

I said in a fury, "Then I'll go out alone."

"All right," she said mildly. "Where?"

"To work. You know what I want?" I said. "I want to go to my office and put in a good day's work, that's what."

It was true: all at once I had a rapturous craving for work. In the street I passed a crew of diggers, sunk to their waists in a ditch, wearing yellow helmets. I envied them violently. Their backs were glazed, their vertebrae protruded like buried nuggets, under the lips of their helmets they lifted sweated wine-dyed lips. They grunted, quarreled, cursed, barked (a few yards away it all turned into a liturgy), and all the while their spines dipped downward, straining for the bottom of the ditch. They had nothing to do but devote themselves to the ditch. They were like a band of monks, ascetic, dedicated, their shining torsos self-flagellated.

The sight of them deflected my feet. I hated my office. I hated its swarming susurrant documents — they were all abstract, they were no more than buying and selling, they were only cadaverous contracts. The rest was myth and fantasy — the captains, the salt spray, the Queens. All mist, all nothingness. What I wanted then was work — shovels, pitchforks. I thought then of those inland towns and farms I had left behind, where the work was real and not a figment, where the work could be felt in the spine; work was earth and earth was work. I thought, for want of earth, I would go down to the docks and hire myself out for a longshoreman or, better yet, a sailor. I felt I had given myself out too long to fancies, and, just as I was meditating on this very notion — how passion is no more palpable than the spume's lace and lasts no longer — I came to the drugstore, and went in, and had the horrified sense of looking into a mirror.

"We got 'em now," said my double, "a whole new shipment. Arrived today."

"Shipment of what?" But I was shrill as a parrot.

"Them." The druggist pointed to a pile of cheap washboards. "I maintain if they got something next door, we got to take it in too, otherwise the competition smothers you."

"But you look like me," I said.

He was indifferent to this.

"Like *me*," I insisted, stretching my eyelids, exposing my face. I could scarcely believe I had grown so spare, for he was as dry as a length of hay, and his skin was blotched and fulvous, and his jaw was sharp as a pin. His eyes were at the same time shrewd and hopeless, like those of a man resigned to his evil, though he might covertly despise himself for it.

"Look at me!"

"Don't shout," he warned in a voice of dignity. "This is a professional pharmacy, ethical. Where's she at now?"

"In my bed."

"Don't be too sure of that, buddy."

"It's where I left her."

"You left her there don't mean she's still there."

"I don't like your looks," I said.

"Then how come you zoomed all the way downtown to check on 'em? Listen," he offered, "I got a glass in the back, Sylvia uses it sometimes." He led me past the prescription counter — it was scabbed with dust and antique droplets — and then down two steps to a small rear cubicle. A long piece of stained mirror clung to the wall. We stood side by side in front of it. "See?" he sneered. "Peas in a pod."

I was staring at two straw-like creatures with pointed chins and ears and flickering eyes. "A pair of Satans," I cried.

"Well, we got different occupations," he said soothingly. "What kind of work do you do?"

"A sailor," I said. "I'm going to ship out as soon as I get my papers." But at the word "papers" I suffered a chill.

"I used to be a sailor. Pharmacist's mate, S.S. *Wilkinson.* I been everywhere."

"I haven't been anywhere."

"With me it came out the opposite. She made me stick in one place. She got me rooted to this hole and I can't get out. I never get out. See that?" He waved a dry arm at a bundle in a corner. It was a narrow campbed tangled up in dirty blankets. "I even sleep here. It's like the hold of a ship back here."

"Where does your wife sleep?"

He gave a scornful smirk. "You can answer that one better than me, buddy."

"Look here," I said, all business. "I want to get rid of her. Get her out of my hair, will you?"

"Had enough? Too bad. That means she's only just getting started on you."

"Quit grinning," I yelled.

"I got to grin, why not? She runs her course."

"How long?"

"How should I know? Depends how long she gets something out of it. With me it was only a year or so — "

"A year? One year? But you've got children, daughters, grown children — "

"*She's* the one with the daughters, not me. *She's* got daughters all over."

"She said two. A couple, she said."

"A couple of thousand, for all I know about it."

"She said married!"

"Listen, she'll call anything a marriage. A blink, and it's a wedding."

"Isn't she your wife?"

"Why not?"

I fled.

It was late when I arrived, even though I had not stopped for breakfast. My colleagues were already immersed at their desks; their papers shimmered and shuddered. From the partners' office came whip-sounds of bleating winds: a quarrel. "It's over you," they told me. "They want to fire you. Old Hallet's holding out for you, though. Says your stuff's been very good up till now. Advocates mercy."

"The reason I'm here," I said bravely, "is to resign."

They tittered. "Now you won't have to."

"I have my pride," I said.

"You leaving? Where've you been? You look like the devil, my God, you look like hell," they said.

"If a woman comes here, don't let on you've seen me," I pleaded.

"Little old stout woman?" one of them said. "Youngish and oldish both? Nice firm breasts? Nice hard belly? Nipples like carvings? She's already been."

Terrified, I crept back from the door. "*Been* here?"

"Turned up an hour ago asking for you. Dishabille, so to speak."

"Please!" I said out of a burning lung.

"Naked. Nude. In her birthday suit, George. Fine figure, straight as a pole."

"Asking for me?"

"Asking for George."

"Where is she?" I whispered.

"Lord knows. We sent for an ambulance, y'know. Had to. Not that a law firm's no place for loons, mind you — "

The shouts from the partners' office swelled; I heard my name.

"She was carrying a lyre. She was covering her modesty with it."

"A washboard you mean," I said.

"*There's* a loon for you. Poor poor George — it's *pos*sible to tell the difference, y'know."

"It was only a washboard," I persisted.

"A lyre," they said. "It looked like the real thing, that's the nuttiest part of the whole show. Made out of a turtle-shell, green all over. Phosphorescent sort of. Could've been dragged up out of the bottom of the sea, from its looks. Think she swiped it from a museum? If they don't get her on disorderly conduct they'll get her for that. Poor George. A friend of yours?"

I ran from them, choking.

She was waiting for me in my apartment: I was scarcely surprised. "That was mean," she said; in a shower of her long hair she squatted on my bed. "They took me into a sort of truck. You let them do that! I had an awful time running away from them. They would've thrown me into prison!"

"You're out of your mind," I said, "going up there like that. You've lost me my job."

"What do you care? You didn't want it anyhow."

This was incontrovertible, though I wondered how she had guessed.

"Come here," she commanded.

"You can't just go up into offices stark naked."

"Who said I did? Oh, for goodness' sake, don't lecture, I only went up there to look for you. It's your fault, you shouldn't have gone away."

"You can't *do* a thing like that in a civilized country. You'll probably get us into the papers. For all I know the police'll be up here in a minute."

"I wasn't stark naked."

"They said you were."

"You believe everyone but me! I bet you'd even believe George, and George is about as steady as a leaf on a stem."

"They said you didn't have anything *on*," I said.

"I was in a hurry. Didn't I *tell* you I wanted you? You had no business running off. I couldn't find my clothes, that's all."

"A stupid stunt."

"Now you're in a rage again. Always in a rage."

"I'm not — "

"Besides, I was covered up anyhow."

"With what?"

"You're cross-examining again," she accused. "It's none of your affair. I covered up what's supposed to be covered up in a civilized country, that's all."

"Where's that lyre thing?"

"Don't be stupid. How should I know? Come here, I want you." She tossed up a smooth leg. Against my will I went to her. "They said you stole it."

"Where on earth would I get a lyre? A funny thing like that? You're insulting." She reached under my pillow, laughing crossly. There it was: the ancient little hand-harp. "On my way up to your office I passed a pawnshop and saw it in the window and bought it."

"Went into the pawnshop without any clothes on?"

"Oh, don't *dig* like that. Mind your own business. Look, I'll sing some more, all right? Do you know Greek? I'll sing you a Greek song."

"*You* don't know Greek," I said.

"Oh, don't I? I know all the languages. I know Greek, I know Walloon, I know Orangutan — "

But when she began to sing it was in German:

> *Meine Töchter sollen dich warten schön;*
> *meine Töchter führen den nächtlichen Reihn*
> *und wiegen und tanzen und singen dich ein.*

Her voice was coarse; it recalled a plank of fresh-cut wood thumped against the grain, and it was somehow blurred, like a horn heard from afar, or as if her lung had been afflicted by a fog. "You don't sound like yourself," I complained.

"A cold," she assented. "Don't interrupt."

"Stop," I said, "I don't like it."

"Are you one of those people who think every unfamiliar language makes a bad noise? You ought to have more sense than that," she said, "a man like you."

This shamed me, so I listened mutely. But now she was continuing in new syllables I could not recognize, very short and rough. "What language is that?"

"Phoenician," she answered.

"Oh come on, is it Arabic?"

"I just told you, it's Phoenician. It's about the sea when the waves are especially high and the rowers can't see over their tops."

I was annoyed. The dark queer burr in her throat had begun to arouse me, and I could not bear to be teased just then. I wanted to get rid of her. "All right," I said, "you found an old song sheet wrapped in an old scroll in an old jar in an old cave, is that it? Fine. Now go home, will you?"

"It wasn't like that at all. I just happened to pick up the words one time."

"On the docks, I know. From the current crop of Phoenician sailors. Go home, Undine."

"I have no home."

"Then just go away."

"You'll be sorry if I do."

"Damn it, I want to get some sleep."

"I won't bother you. Come into the bed."

"No."

"Come here," she insisted.

"Go away. It's *my* apartment. I didn't invite you here."

"Yes you did."

"Ages ago. It doesn't count."

"Last week."

"It feels like an aeon."

"Come here," she said again. She dipped two fingers into the strings of the lyre and provoked a vicious ripple. "Because if you don't, do you know what I'm liable to do? I'm just liable to throw this thing right through that window."

"I want to be let alone," I said.

She threw the lyre through the window. It penetrated sideways and cleanly, like the cut of a knife, with a soft clear click of struck sound — a thin pale note came out as it hit, and the pane and the lyre were gyrating downward to the street together; I was in time to glimpse the two objects still gleaming and braiding in air. They fell not far apart, between two cars in the road.

"You could've killed someone down there!"

"I warned you, didn't I?"

I went to her docilely enough then; it was as though she had broken something in me — some inner crystal, through which up to the moment of its shattering I had been able to see rationality, responsibility; light. I saw nothing now; her mouth became a wide-

open window, and I hurled myself through it, whirling my tongue
like a lyre. I stretched the strings of her hair and webbed them and
plucked at them; they seemed in my teeth as tough as rope. I was
blind and faint, but her body took me ravenous for it; no sooner
did I slip into consolation than a gong of lust pealed me alert. All
the same the dreaded faintness returned, it kept returning, I awoke
to her and it returned, I could not endure it, I was drained, behind
my heated eyeballs it grew ladderlike and dark.

It was night.

"I want to sleep," I moaned.

"Tired already? Ah, little man-darling." And would not release
me; and I had to tense again for the plunge. All that night it was a
dream of plunging and diving; the undersea of her was never
satiated, the dive was bottomless, plummeting, vast and vast. "Soon,
soon," she promised me, "soon you'll sleep, you'll see, trust me, always rely on me, I keep faith with everyone, don't I?" She crooned;
and the warp of her voice lifted me alive like a tree. "Aren't you
happy now? Aren't you glad I stayed?" she asked me. "Yes, yes," I
always replied, swimming in the wake of gratefulness.

At three o'clock — a blessed little nap had momentarily reposed
her, and she lay in my arms while my open scared eyelids flickered
like flies — the telephone rang. "It's nobody," she reprimanded
with a yawn, but she passed the receiver to me, wreathing my member with a cord to hold it captive.

"That you, George?"

It was my Uncle Al.

"Listen, George," he said, "I made it back sooner'n I thought I
was going to — didn't like it over there. Neither did Nick. You
wouldn't remember him, little gimpy foreign guy, this Greek I went
over with, same cabin and all? This fella Lewis? Fact is he's with
me now. I don't like to call you in the middle of the night,
George boy, that's the truth — "

"Where are you, Al?"

"Down at the docks. My God, George, you ought to see what
they got going down here — spooky enough to give you the creeps,
about a hundred of them old wooden tubs all over the place, out of
a goddamn story-book, sheets out like a pack of Hallowe'eners. Back
home we got bathtubs better-looking than some of that. Say listen,
George, the truth is I'd like to know if you could put up the two

of us for the night? Me and this Greek fella, he's not a bad little guy — "

"You mean you want to come up here right *now?*" I said.

"Well, yeah. Just stepped off the boat. Managed to get a spot back on this little Eye-tie job, accommodations a little on the spaghetti side, but you don't waste a cent — "

"Look, Al," I said, "maybe you could get yourself a hotel room around about there, it's pretty late — "

"That's the *point* kid, Nick here with his arthritis and all, it's kind of late to go looking around, couple of strangers in town — "

"I don't know, Al," I said, "this place is sort of a wreck at the moment. I mean it's sort of a wreck."

Undine pulled on the telephone wire. "Don't talk any more. I want you. Come back," she called.

"Oh, come on, it's all in the family. We don't mind a little mess. Unless you got a lady-friend up there?" he hooted.

"No, look, all right," I said. "That's fine. Sure, Al, you come on over," I said.

Her nostrils had turned rigid. Her neck twisted up like a root. "What did you do that for? *We* don't want anybody."

"I owe it to my uncle. He's bringing along that Greek too. You'll have to leave now," I told her.

"But you said I made you happy!" she wailed.

"I *tried* to put him off, didn't I? You heard me."

"All I heard was you said the place was a wreck. It's not, it's perfectly nice. I like it."

"It was a way of telling him not to come, that's all. *You* heard. I couldn't help it, he insisted."

She leaned her breasts against the bedpost, meditating; but her arms strove backward. "You don't want me really?"

"Enough is enough," I said.

"Enough," she said — and with an easy slap broke off the knob of the bedpost — "is enough" — and with a stray sliver of window-glass shredded the bedclothes. Bits of rubber foam twinkled upward.

"Undine — "

"A wreck, you're right, a wreck," she cried — she was solemn and slow. She cradled the shade of a lamp, tender as a nursemaid, then crushed it under her naked toes, and used the brass lamp-pole to smash the frame of the bed. Her blows were cautious, regular, and accurate. She hewed the arm off a chair and the arm demolished the bureau. Drawer-knobs in flight mobbed the air. In all the rooms the floorboards sprang up groaning. Vases went rolling, limbs of little tables disported. Piece by piece the air-conditioner released its diverse organs; in the kitchen the ice-trays poured and clattered, the stove-grates ground the refrigerator door to a yellowish porcelain dust, the ceiling was pocked with faucet-handles embedded like silvery pustules. She slashed the sofa pillows, and crowing and gurgling with fury and bliss felled the toilet-tank. Mound by mound she heaped it all behind her — barrows rose suddenly up at her heels like the rapid wake of disappearing civilizations. A cemetery grew at her thrust. She destroyed with a marvelous promiscuity — nothing mattered to her, nothing was too obvious to miss or too miniscule to ignore. She was thorough, she was strong. I waited for the end, and there was no end. What had been left large she reduced; what had been left small she pulverized. The telephone (I thought of calling the police, but reserved this for the neighbors) was a ragged hillock of black confetti.

Finally she went away.

I lay down in the wreckage and slept moderately until my uncle and the Greek arrived. There was no door for them to come through: they simply came in, trampling sawdust.

"Good Lord," Al said. "Sweet Jesus. Was it burglars?"

"A bitch," I said.

"A witch?" said the Greek, hobbling from waste to waste on polished crutches.

"We always say back home that this here's one dangerous city to live in," Al said. "If you had half a brain, George boy, you'd come on home. Practically all of Europe's just the same. No good. I saw that Mediterranean, and I didn't like the smell. You got to go deep into a country, away from the shore line, if you want decency."

"There is no witches," Mr. Lewis said boldly.

"The boy knows that," my uncle said. "Here come the police."

The neighbors came too; there was a confusion, in which the Greek forgot his English, all but the odd word "witch"; they took him off to the station house, and my uncle loyally followed to post bail. "Superstitious little runt," he explained, enjoying the crowd.

Morning was not yet; I ran through crepuscular streets, liberated. Now and again I stopped before a display window to pose and observe my reflection; it seemed to me I had none. How thin I must have become! I ran and ran, into the seeping dye of dawn. I felt an insupportable vigor. My feet scooped up miles — the miles themselves appeared to have been exorcised by my vigor and my glee, and grew improbably briefer. In an instant I was on Canal Street, half an instant afterward I was scudding past the drugstore — it looked intact, and fleeing it I wondered whether the druggist's mirror might deliver up my lost reflection. But I could no longer halt, I ran on, I ran to the gray piers, I ran to the morning-tipped sails wind-full in the harbor. All the way I jogged her name in my teeth.

I knew where to look for her.

"Undine!" I shrieked into that deserted alley I remembered.

"Sylvia!" howled the druggist. His bits of hair stood aloft in peaked tufts, his jagged ears bristled, his triangular chin poked the bone of his chest. He was so wafer-like that I feared for him to show me his profile; I was certain he would vanish into a line. "You too?" he said when he recognized me.

"She's left me," I croaked.

"And me," he informed me.

We hugged one another; we danced on the edge of the pier; we babbled at our luck.

"Will she come back?" I asked him.

"Who knows? But I bet not. Not after this time, I bet. She's all worn out, it looked like."

"Did she tell you where she's going?"

"To visit her daughters, she said."

"Where are they?"

"India, she said. Also Africa."

Triumphantly I took this in. "Did you ever see her off before?"

"One time I did. But after that she came back. She went on a Queen, that was the trouble — they caught her, scraped her right off. And anyhow he said she hated the thing, all cold metal, like riding a spoon, she said. Don't shoot me so many questions, buddy. I ain't your teacher."

"I only want to know if you can see her."

He squinted into the yolk-colored sky. "Not yet. Look for yourself."

"But there are so many ships, I can't tell — "

"She might not be aboard yet."

We skimmed up and down the alley, sniffing at the water. It brightened under the dawn; it spun out slavering columns of red.

"See that two-master? She ain't on that one."

"I can't — no, that's right, not on that one."

Down to the horizon, into the very bottom of the sun, the flotilla stood, bark after bark after bark, the galleys and galleons, the schooners and sloops, the single high Norsemen's vessel, the junks and the dhows and the xebecs and the feluccas, with their painted whimsical hulls and their multitudinous sails in rows and banks and phantasmal tiers, paper-white geometries clambering like petals out of the masts, and the water galloping and spitting beneath their tall arched bows.

The druggist's glance hopped from ship to ship.

Then I — too shy of what I sought to look so far — spied her: she hung nearly over our heads, she was an eave shadowing our heads, her hair streamed backward over her loins, her left hand clasped a lyre, her right hand made as if to pluck it but did not, her spine was clamped high upon the nearest prow. Although her eyes were wide, they were woodenly in trance: I had never known her in so pure a sleep.

"Undine!"

"Sylvia!" mocked the druggist.

"She doesn't answer."

"She won't," he responded with satisfaction. "You can go on home now, buddy."

"She won't answer?"

"Use your eyes, buddy. Does she look like she will?"

I saw the long and delicate grain in her thighs, the nodules in her straight wrists, the knots that circled and circled about her erect and exact nipples, the splintered panel that cleft her flank. (I recalled a mole in that place.) "Look at that," said the druggist, pointing to the notch, "she's getting old. More'n a century, I'd say. Want to bet she doesn't make it back? Falls right plump into the Atlantic? Her rigging's weak, she looks glued on, water'll wash her right off."

I pleaded with him: "She won't answer?"

"Try her."

I flung back my neck and shouted up: "Undine — "

A figurehead does not breathe.

"Go on back, boy," said the druggist.

"And you?" I asked him; but did not leave off gaping into the flock of sails that seemed to spring from her immutable shoulders like a huge headdress of starched fans. They gasped and vaguely hissed, and she beneath them strained her back to meet the prow's grand arch, and threw into their lucidities her stiff gaze.

"I got my business to take care of," he told me. "Build it up a bit now maybe. Hire somebody with better customer visibility. *She* never let me hire anybody."

"She wrecked my apartment," I confided. "She lost me my job."

"That's the least of it. Believe me, buddy, the least. That's the stuff you can fix up."

"I guess I can fix up my apartment," I said dejectedly.

"You are going for a sailor, like you said?"

"No." And spotted panic in me.

"Going back to wherever you come from?"

I considered this; I thought of the fields of home. "No," I said after a moment.

"Well, so long, buddy, I wish you luck with things when you find out."

I said in the voice of a victim, "Find out what?"

But he had turned his side to me, and, though I stared with all my strength, I could no longer see him.

JOE ASHBY PORTER

The Vacation

(FROM OCCIDENT)

I

IF I CUT ACROSS Moose Zacham's barnyard on my way to town, he won't speak. If I go over to the courthouse to pass some time, even old Lucian that sweeps ignores me. Of an evening I tip my hat to the people on their porches, or those I meet on the road, but they act like they don't see me. I'm near fifty years old, I've always lived here — I know it was partly wrong what I did, but I don't deserve this. It makes me not know what to do with myself. It makes me not see how I'm going to manage the rest of my days. It's worse now than it was in the fall, because there's nothing to do but look after the cow and chickens. After dark I stoke me up a good fire and listen to Paducah on the radio awhile before I go to bed. I've figured out one thing: people would have forgiven me it all if only I hadn't come to their doors the way I did.

My Blanche and our boy Howard stay at the hotel — Blanche's brother Bailey Carlisle runs it, and he gives them room and board. I haven't run into them for two or three weeks. The last time, they crossed to the other side of the street when they saw me coming. Frisky? — she looked friskier than ever, stepping right along with her nose in the air. She had on the black floppy hat she used to wear when we were courting. Howard was so embarrassed I thought he was going to fall on his face. I stood and watched them till they turned the corner and in spite of everything I couldn't help laughing. The house does seem empty without them, but it's not being able to talk to people that bothers me more. Blanche and Howard always seemed sort of like children to me.

Last February was Howard's twenty-first birthday and Blanche's fortieth. That gave me an excuse to do something I'd been studying about for a good while — have a kind of vacation for a whole year. I had forty-three hundred-dollar bills in a coffee can down next the southeast cornerstone doing me no good, and besides we had more than a year's provisions for ourselves and the animals, so I guessed we could afford a slack year. Most people go see relatives or take a trip through the Blue Ridge mountains on their vacations, but I wasn't interested in any such thing. I'd had a lot of ideas floating around in my head for a long time, and I wanted to stay right here and get them straight and worked out. And anyway there were odds and ends I wanted to see about at my leisure. On Howard's birthday I told them I'd have a surprise for them, and on Blanche's I told them what it was.

She started in talking about where we could go but I said no, I was staying put but they could go anywhere they wanted, and for them to think it over, take their time, because they had a year anyway, so there was no cause to fly off the handle yet. I said we'd each have seven hundred dollars to spend however we wanted during the year, no strings attached, and they'd have my love and my blessing to do what they wanted, so long as they didn't interfere with me doing what I wanted, and I wanted to start off by thinking and not running off somewhere.

Howard thought it was a joke at first — he just laughed and and shook his head, and he said, "That's a good one." But Blanche knew better; she looked hard at me and then she said, "Listen here, Louis, what is it you mean to think about, I'd like to know?" I said I myself wasn't sure yet, but I'd let her know as I got it worked out. Then I gave them the money. Howard began to realize I was serious about it, and he said, "I'll have to hand it to you, Daddy, you've really done it this time!" Blanche started to perk up too — "Well," she said, "I guess I could use a new dress or two, at that." "Sure you could," Howard said. "Why you know you could, Mother. Boy oh boy, this is really something!" Blanche said, "I can't help it, though, the whole thing does make me a little nervous. Just give me a few days to get over it — it's such a surprise, and I've never heard of anything like it." "I never have either," I said. "It's real nice of you," she said, and Howard said, "Lord, 'nice' ain't even the word for it!" I felt good, awful good that night when we blew out the lamps.

The vacation started the next day at breakfast. Blanche said, "Now, Louis, let's talk this over a little more. I can't really figure out what we're meant to do. I'd like to get a better idea of what you have in your mind."

"Well," I said, "I'm not exactly sure myself — I thought we could all figure it out ourselves, you know. What you're *meant* to do is whatever you *want* to do."

"Well now listen," she said. "Supposing I wanted to go off somewhere and you didn't: I don't see how I could, because who'd get your food for you and Howard, and so forth?"

Howard said, "Lord, I hadn't thought of that."

"Let's think about it, then," I said. I was curious to see what they would do. I felt like smiling at their timidity. I was timid too, or nervous at least, but it wasn't about who was to get my food for me!

I think Howard was afraid I might change my mind if any difficulties came up, because he said, "Wait a minute, now. If you took a trip somewhere, Mother, why we could fix our own meals, after all. We could buy our own butter and cheese, you know, there's no reason we couldn't. And if I went somewhere too, Daddy could do the same. Land, we could even hire Judy Dowdy for instance to come and take care of him, and I could hire Pete Corum to give him what help he needed with the work, and he wouldn't be needing much. He did say we could do what we wanted with the money." He looked at me out of the corner of his eye to see whether I approved or not, and Blanche was looking like she hoped I wouldn't.

I said, "I see I need to say a little more about this. This idea of mine: I want it to be the best thing in the world for all of us. But the point of it is, it has to depend on us, on each one, how it turns out. And even though when you first thought about it you might not have noticed it — you, Howard, especially — I expect problems. I mean it may not be as easy as it seems. For my part, anyway, I don't expect to know what it was until it's all over. We're having a vacation so we can *do* something, and if it's worth doing it's bound to be some trouble. Myself, I'll doubtless be up to things you couldn't imagine right now.

"Anyway," I said, "let's not for heaven's sake bog ourselves down with worrying about how we're to get food in our mouths. Each can see to his own. And you're not to pay for mine out of the money I gave you to pay for yours! And, Blanche, sweetheart, unless you have a particular yen to be at the stove, why you needn't even think about meals. Now you all do what you want today — you might start making some serious plans — I've put out paper and pencils in the parlor in case you want to write anything down."

Blanche said, "Well, I guess so . . . but what are you going to do now?"

"Well," I said, "what I'm going to do right now is, I'm going to walk over into the woods."

"Why, the hunting season hasn't even started!"

"I know," I said. "I'm just going. I don't even know what I'm going to do when I get there."

Blanche said, "I never heard of such a thing!"

"I know," I said.

They looked almost scared, so I held both their hands for a minute, and then I left them staring at me as I walked out.

I went to a place I'd stumbled onto once before. It was the kind of place I'd have liked when I was a boy — and I just wanted to spend some time there. The time I found it, the dog chased a rabbit back through some underbrush and then couldn't get back out, so I had to fight my way through to get to him. The opening had grown over, so I knew nobody had been there. When you get through the thicket you come to a sort of little clearing with big old shady maples and wild crabapple and blackberry and a little creek. It made me feel peaceful. I stretched myself out on a shelf of rock, and I thought awhile. The birds were singing and the stream was rippling, and the sandstone was warm from the sun. Fifty yards or so downstream there was a little hidden lake — I could hear a fish jump now and then. I decided that before the year was out I'd have to have a swim there. I talked to myself for a while. I said, "Now what shall I do with this year, after all?" because I myself didn't know yet. "Well," I said, "no need to rush, is there? No, no need to rush." Then I said, "You know, maybe I'll *make* something." I thought I might want to build me a cabin all my own out there in the woods, like Henry David Thoreau did at Walden Pond. I thought about that, and then I had a nap.

I spent the rest of the day walking around in the woods. When I got home, only Blanche was there — she'd been in to town and bought herself some dresses and a pair of shoes. Howard had gone over to Dawson with his buddies. Blanche was kind of quiet, but she perked up when I got her to try on her new clothes for me. We turned on the radio and did a waltz in the parlor. She said, "Have you decided what you want to do?" I said, "No, have you?" and she said no she hadn't yet, but she thought she might visit her folks in Louisville. I told her I thought the best thing would be for her to go on ahead, if she really wanted to, and then maybe I'd come later.

For about a week she dilly-dallied, making up her mind, and then she decided to go. I helped her as best I could. I knew I'd miss old Blanche — we hadn't been apart for more than a day or two since we'd been married — but I have to say I was glad to see her finally go, because I felt like I needed to do some thinking on my own. Howard meantime was spending most of his time carousing over in Dawson like I expected he would. The day after Blanche left he showed up with a used car he'd bought, and said he and Jimmie Thorne were going to drive down to Nashville. I told him to watch out for gambling and women, and I gave him my blessing.

II

The day after Howard left I went into town for the first time since Blanche's birthday. I thought I'd best take care of having my food sent to me and so forth right away, so I wouldn't have to bother about it. I met Otho Keezer in the grocery, and he said, "Well, now, Louis, it's good to see you up and about again," and he clapped me on the back. I had no idea what he meant — I thought he was joking, so I just laughed and went on about my business. But when the others kept asking me if I was better, I started asking them what they meant, and that way I finally got to the bottom of it: before she left, Blanche had told people I'd been feeling poorly, and hadn't been able to come to town. She'd told them I'd decided to lay off farming for a while because of my health — she hadn't told anybody about her birthday present except her brother Bailey Carlisle as it turned out. She must have been embarrassed or something I guess. I'd thought she would have bragged to the whole town about it, but no. Well, after that I didn't feel much like hanging around, so after I'd arranged for Otho's boy to leave groceries on my stoop once a week I just came on home and let them all think what they wanted.

I still didn't feel right, though, and when Moose Zacham came

over along about noon to borrow some tackle for plowing, I
blurted the whole thing out to him, about the vacation and how I
hadn't been sick at all. Moose is a good man, but he's none too
bright, so I didn't go into my reasons. Anyway, he said, "I wouldn't
want to take sides, Louis — seems to me you're both partly in the
wrong." I started to explain that there hadn't been any quarrel,
but then I thought there'd be no point in it, so I just said, "I wasn't
asking you to take sides, Moose." Of course, the time was coming
when I'd be hoping he would take sides.

That evening I had another visitor, Bailey Carlisle. He's a queer
sort. Since his Hilda died some years back he practically never sets
foot outside his hotel. He always was retiring — a little dried-up
fish of a man. Well, he keeps to that hotel — where Blanche and
Howard are staying now — but at the same time he has his nose
in everybody's business. We used to have Sunday dinner at the hotel
with him. He'd sit at the head of the table smiling and looking down
like some proper old lady. And he'd finagle every bit of gossip he
could out of us. He'd cluck and shake his head at the wild doings
of the youngsters nowadays, but he always wanted to hear more.

Like I say, he came to visit me — I don't think he'd set foot in our
house twice since we'd been married. He was polite and dainty,
but he was nervous too. It seems Blanche had told him the truth
she hadn't dared to tell anybody else. And he was worried. "I felt
I ought to offer you some advice," he said. "And whether you take
it is your concern" (of course, he damn well thought it was *his*
concern). He said, "I really think a month ought to be enough,
Louis, I really do. A month would be wonderful, and I know
Blanche and Howard would just love it. But much more — well,
I have to say it's bound to look peculiar to people, they're bound
to think things." He had the nerve to say, "Now I have a pretty
good idea of your financial situation, and I know something about
managing money, and even if you had twice as much as you do, I'd
call what you aim to do extravagant, I really would — extravagant
or even worse, Louis."

He didn't make me mad, though. I told him I'd think over what
he had to say (though I really didn't think it was worth a second
thought), and I even thanked him for his interest. And I knew
that he did want to help, the poor thing, at least part of him did,
because he was so lonesome.

We talked a while more, and then he said he ought to get back.

He'd come in his car — he never walks anywhere if he can help it. I stood outside· in the dark and watched his lights go down the hill through the trees, and then turn back up toward town. The wind was toward me — I could hear him a long time, till he went down behind the hill that's just this side of city limits. Then I looked around me, and I realized that I was finally on my own. There was a full moon — it felt like clean water on me. "Well, sir . . ." I said, but then I didn't say anything else. It was the last day of March. I went to the barn and put out some fodder for the cow — she woke up and looked at me, and then went back to sleep — and I threw out some grain in the chicken yard. Then I rolled me up an old army blanket and went to the woods.

It was a warm night, so I had myself a swim in that lake I'd been thinking about. Then I went back up to the flat rocks, where I could hear the stream. Made myself a bed of leaves, and lay down and wrapped my blanket around me. Somehow I didn't feel sleepy, so I just lay there quiet as could be. I watched the night birds, and toward morning I saw a pair of weasels come for a drink of water. I thought about a lot of things that night, an awful lot of things. I thought about Blanche and me, how we'd lived together and depended on each other for so long, and how we'd just about stopped even having to think about each other — and how, now that Howard was almost grown, people expected us just to stand back and keep quiet and not do anything more — and I guess that's really what Blanche wanted, too. I thought about how all my life I'd always done what people expected. I knew they liked me for it, but I also knew that, when I thought about the way I'd lived, I had to smile sometimes, the way I smiled over Blanche and Howard — because I seemed like no more than a good little frisky pup.

I thought I'd be getting a letter from Blanche the next day, and I knew what she'd say. Before too long I'd get a picture postcard of Nashville from Howard; he'd tell me all about what he'd seen that I'd never seen, thinking I wanted to hear it or that it made any difference, thinking he'd done something important just because he'd been able to send that card. And too, I knew the things he wouldn't tell me because he didn't know they didn't make any difference either — the scrapes and fixes he'd have got into because he was just a country rube. I felt pretty sure that neither of them, Blanche or Howard, would do much more with my gift than what they'd already done — buy some things and then run off somewhere — there was nothing I could do to help them except to go about my business, and maybe they'd understand a little more, watching me. Maybe they'd see that I was getting ready to . . . that I had my eye on the time when I was going to die. Maybe too they'd see that after all I didn't take much stock in heaven or what have you — and maybe then they'd realize that deep down they didn't either. If I'd had them there with me then, I could have told them some of what I had in my mind, maybe I could. I'd have liked to have hugged them to me in the woods there and talked to them about the way my mind was going. Well, there was nothing I could do about that, so I set myself to thinking about other things.

In the darkest part of the night, along about three or so, just before it started to get light, it seemed like I had a sort of vision or an inspiration that told me what it was I wanted to do with my time. It might have been a dream, but I really think I was awake, because I remember I saw the weasels afterward. I'd been thinking I ought to build something, but I really didn't want to build a house like Henry David Thoreau's, because I didn't want to copy anything. I was lying on my back, then, looking up at the sky. It was a clear night, but there were tree branches criss-crossing over my head and hiding some of the stars. All of a sudden I realized I couldn't find the big dipper, or anything else I knew — I must have been drowsy, and maybe I'd got turned around so I didn't know which direction I was lying in. Well, while I was trying to find the big dipper I had my vision — I don't exactly know how to say it, but it was something like this: every star had a line going from it to every other star, so that the whole sky was full of millions of letters. And then it came to me that what I'd make would be a statue of a word, a special word. I remember it was when I saw the weasels that I knew how to find this word. It was a complicated idea, and I wonder how I thought of it like that — but I did. It seemed kind of a miracle. I remember I said to myself, "Louis, you've found yourself something worthy!" Of course the real miracle was still to come.

III

When I'd gone swimming in the lake I'd noticed that near the middle there was a spur of granite and limestone some ten yards long and five feet wide, just below the water, I decided I'd build the statue there.

I guess the way to find the word came to me because I'd been listening to the creek and the animals and so forth. I figured out that every place in the world has its own special sounds that you'll hear if you're there. Now, of course, there are lots of sounds you can hear in more than one place. But it seemed to me that the whole combination of sounds you hear somewhere must be peculiar to that one place. And I thought I'd have done something if I could make a statue of that kind of a combination. Maybe I was mistaken, I'm not sure. What you'd hear would depend on when you were listening, too — you'd have to choose your time.

I built up the spur of rock with gravel and cement till it was well above water level, for the base of my statue. I had this done by the end of April, so I decided to spend May and June discovering the word, and then when I built it I could write on it "May and June," and the year. During May I stayed at the lake during the day and slept home at night, and in June, when it was warmer, I did the reverse — because I wanted to get the night sounds as well as the day ones. I wrote down every sound I heard on a tablet I'd got for this purpose. I wrote not only the sounds animals and birds and insects made, but also those of the wind and the water, and the trees, and the rain (I sat out in it, with my tablet protected by Blanche's breadbox) and everything else. I write a fine hand, but by the end of June the tablet was full and I had written some on the inside cover.

I didn't write down any sound more than three times in a day, no matter how often I heard it, so I had a good deal of spare time. I answered the letters I got from Blanche and Howard, and thought, and just rested. The two months passed faster than you'd think.

I spent the first two days of July figuring out what the word was. I decided it would have two syllables, since that was the average number; so then I made all the words into two-syllable ones. I just stretched out the shorter ones — for instance there was a sound a little water beetle made when it took off flying, that was *tiss*, and I made that into *ti-iss*. In the same way I squeezed down the ones longer than two syllables when I could, and if I couldn't I just cut off part of them and kept the part I thought was most important. From *whip-poor-will*, for instance, I kept *poor-will*, because it made more sense than *whip-poor* would. So then I had everything changed into two-syllable words, written out in a new tablet. Then I started counting. I didn't want to find it out all together, so I did the first syllable by itself first. I'd figured out ahead of time how it should be done.

The middle sound or vowel was easy. I just had to count which sound came up most often. It turned out to be *oo* like in *moo*. The outside parts or consonants were harder to do, because some of the syllables, like *spree*, might have as many as three consonants on one side, and none on the other. So I had to write them in a special way. If there weren't any, I wrote *000*. If there was one I wrote it two more times, and if there were two I stuck in a zero somewhere. So then I counted up the consonants the same way as the vowels, and I ended up with *0lloo000*. When I struck out the zeros I had *lloo*, and since I didn't see how you could say two l's together, I made it *Loo*. Well, then I figured out the second syllable of my word the same way as the first. It turned out to be *Iss*. I'd worked past midnight, and I must have gotten a little sleepy, because I didn't realize what had happened until I said it out loud: *Loo-iss*. It was my very own name, Louis! I almost fell off my chair. I shook my head, and said it again to make sure. And then I just sat back and smiled. It was a miracle. The combination of everything I'd heard from the middle of the pond for the two months was my name. I had to shake my head. I decided right then that, since it didn't matter how it was spelled, as long as it was the same word, the statue would be "Louis." I went outside and stood on the porch for a while, and then I went to sleep.

Well, maybe I shouldn't have done it, but first thing next morning I wrote a letter to Blanche and told her what had happened. She'd been saying she was about ready to come on back since she couldn't talk me into coming away, and I thought I ought to prepare her a little, so she wouldn't be too surprised. I thought about telling Howard too, but I thought he wouldn't understand anyway. When I went into town that morning to buy some nails, two or three people said I looked like the cat that had got the canary, and I guess I must have seemed pretty sly and perky — but I kept my secret. Jim Nisbett at the hardware store asked me if I was aiming to build a new barn with all those nails, and I just grinned. When I passed the hotel, I waved to Bailey Carlisle in his office. He was sitting at his desk, and he acted like he didn't see me, so I shrugged

my shoulders and went on about my business. I wasn't about to let
that little dried-up thing get on my nerves.

It took me most of July to get all the wood I figured to need
chopped down, and the platform for the statue built and cemented
to the rock. It was the hardest work I'd done in years. As soon as'I
fed the cow and chickens and made myself a lunch, I'd be down to
the lake, and I wouldn't be home till sundown. I cut trees as close
to the shoreline as possible so they'd fall straight into the water or
roll down to it. Then I'd have to tackle them and swim them out
to the rock. At first some of the animals were frightened away by all
the activity, but I left food for them and after a while they got used
to me and came back. And I was always careful not to cut any trees
that had nests in them. It was hot as could be there in the middle
of the lake with no shade, but then I could have me a swim whenever I wanted. When I got the base done it stood a little more than
three feet above the water; it was a yard deep and twelve yards long
— I'd expanded it out about a yard beyond each end of the rock.
I figured then that the letters could be ten feet tall and a yard wide,
with eighteen-inch spaces between them. I had drawn a picture
of the statue to scale, and it looked fine, so I started building.

The L was easy — it only took me three days to get it up. I nailed
the bottom part of it to the platform, and then I strengthened it
from behind with a couple of struts running from the back of the
platform to the middle of the upright part of the letter. The next
letter, O, was a good deal harder to build. Almost all the logs I had
were straight, so I had to make it out of a number of short pieces
with mitered ends. It took ten pieces altogether. I cut and shaped
them onshore, where I could handle the wood better, but I decided
to nail it together out on the platform, since I didn't think it would
stand much rough handling. I built it section by section from the
bottom up, attaching struts as I went along. I brought the stepladder down from the house because I knew I'd need it for the top
part. It was the second week in August and I'd done the bottom
half of the O already. It was near sundown, and I was getting ready
to stop for the day, when the birds over on the shore started screaming and flying away. Then I saw the bushes thrashing, and then
Howard came through. He looked like a city slicker in the picture
show. He had on a cream-colored suit and a straw hat, and he was
smoking a big cigar, grinning and waving to beat the band. It took
me a minute to even figure out who he was.

IV

He claimed he'd just gotten tired of the city life and was a little homesick. But it turned out later that he'd had two other reasons for coming back: he'd let some gal talk him into running through three quarters of his money already, and then Blanche had been writing him saying she was worried about me, and that she wanted him home when she got here. She'd even got Bailey Carlisle to write him, I later found out. But he didn't tell me any of that. The first time I suspected something was when I told him Blanche would be home in a couple of days, and he acted real surprised but he was blushing at the same time. I let it go.

All through supper he told me about what he'd seen and done — I thought he'd never stop. He kept that straw hat on till I told him he didn't need it in the house. In a while he said, "How's Uncle Bailey been doing?" and I said I couldn't say, since I hadn't seen him. I guess that sort of set Howard off. "Now, Daddy," he said, "now what the hell is it you're building down there in the woods?" I studied awhile before I said anything. Maybe it was wrong for me not to tell him the truth, I don't know. For one thing I wanted to make it as easy on him as I could — I figured he'd have a hard enough time understanding what I did tell him. "Well, sir," I said, "I'm building a statue of my name." And then I said, "Son, while you were a boy I made it my business to explain my doings to you, because you depended on me — because you couldn't under- stand any other way. Now you're grown up I'll give you whatever advice you want. But I won't justify myself anymore. Why should I? Especially not during our vacation." I'm not sure he understood that — he sort of shrugged and nodded and went off to bed.

Well, for the next two or three days it was raining and what with one thing and another I didn't get to the woods. I'd let the house get into a mess, so I spent most of the time straightening it up so it wouldn't be so bad for Blanche when she got here. She was so happy to see me that we hardly talked about anything until the day after she arrived. But then she started in. I remember she said, "Now heavens above, what do you want to go doing that to your name for, Louis? Your name was just fine without you putting up any statue of it!" I did explain to her again that it wasn't just a statue of my name, but she wouldn't listen to reason. I even showed her my tablets, but she said, "I don't care about all that, it's still your name, and every time I talk to you I'll have to think about that blasted lake! I think you're going to *ruin* your name, Louis, is what I think you're going to do. Why, what if the neighbors saw it while they were out hunting or something?" I tried to argue with her but she would just say, "I don't know how I can hold up my head if you keep on." I told her she was working her own self up but it didn't do any good so finally I said I'd hold off for a week. Of course I was disappointed in her, but I tried not to let her see it.

She brightened up. Almost every day she would flounce Howard and me into town to show everybody that we were back to normal. She wouldn't even let Howard wear his new hat and suit. He and I would sit and talk to some of the other men while she did her shopping or went to the beauty parlor. It was funny: I really did enjoy seeing my friends again, even though I hadn't missed them at all in the woods — particularly my neighbor Moose Zacham, because he so clearly was relieved to see that everything was all right. The one thing I could hardly stand was dinner at the hotel. I'd never seen Bailey Carlisle simper and smirk so. He nearly patted me on the head. And he served us the best meal we'd ever had there.

I admit it was partly because I was put out so by Bailey Carlisle that I went straight back to work on the statue first thing the next morning before Blanche and Howard were awake. About noon Blanche came running down to the lake white as a sheet. It was the first time she'd been there. I was up on the stepladder working on the top part of the O. I think the letters must have been even larger than she'd expected, because she stopped short, and just looked for a minute. Then she ran down to the shore and started saying something and beckoning for me to come in. When I yelled out, "What do you want?" she put her finger to her lips and said, "Shh," and stamped her foot for me to be quiet. So I swam on in.

She had seen Moose and some of the others walking down to the woods to go hunting, and she was afraid they'd catch me at work on the statue. I told her then that I aimed to go on with it, and she might as well reconcile herself to it. I told her she was letting it get all out of proportion. Besides, I said, if people thought it was peculiar, it looked to me like it was her place to side with me and not with them. I told her she might not understand it, but the important thing was, it was something I'd made up my mind to do. "Blanche," I said, "I've never done anything like this before, and

I'll never again, if it's any consolation to you. Besides," I said, "they probably won't be hunting in this part of the woods anyway."

She said, "It's just crazy, Louis, crazy," and I told her no it wasn't. She said, "Louis, Louis, think about me!"

I said, "I do think about you, don't you know that? I'm thinking about you this very second," but I didn't tell her what I was thinking. I was thinking how silly and pretty she seemed — younger than she had in years. She saw how I was looking at her, and she sort of blushed. I said, "Now you go on back to the house, Blanche, and don't you worry, little thing." I thought she was about to cry, so I kissed her and sent her off. I could tell by the way she stomped away that she was still angry.

I'd hoped to get the O done that day, so I kept working till it was too dark to see. I didn't quite finish it, but there was nothing to do but go on home. I thought it was odd that, when I got near the house, I didn't see any light. I found a note from Blanche on the table — she said she and Howard had gone in to town to spend the night at the hotel because Bailey Carlisle had taken sick, and they wanted me to come as soon as I could. Well, I took the lantern and set out, but I hadn't gone very far when two ideas came to me: first, that there was a good chance that Bailey wasn't really sick at all, but that they just wanted to distract me from my project, and, second, that with the very lantern I had in my hand I could finish up the O that night, like I'd wanted to do. I thought about it for a minute, and then I made up my mind. I cut back across the northeast corner of Moose Zacham's land into the woods. Since I knew my way I put out the lantern to save kerosene — I realized it was low. It occurs to me that if I only hadn't put it out they would have seen me coming back, and nothing would have happened. Because they weren't at the hotel at all. They were hiding some place where they could watch the house — maybe they were in the barn, they might even have been at the Zachams'.

I got the O finished pretty quickly. I was tired, though — I'd worked hard — and something seemed to tell me to stick close to my statue that night. It was warm but being so cloudy it looked like we might have a shower, so I put out the lantern again and crawled under the platform where I could keep pretty dry. I fell right to sleep — this must have been about 11:30 or so.

The next thing I remember is feeling something dripping on my hand — I guess at first I thought it had started raining. I was confused, and still half asleep. I smelled kerosene, but I thought it was just the lantern, and I remember I reached over to make sure I hadn't knocked it over. But my hand was stinging, and I realized I'd got kerosene on it somehow. Then, clear as could be, I heard Blanche's voice saying, "Be careful." I must have thought I was dreaming. But then I heard it again — it came from the shore, and she was yelling, "Now, be careful!" I turned over, and then I hear Howard's voice coming from directly over me saying, "God damn it! There's some kind of animal crawled up under here!" Then I hear a splash (it was Howard jumping into the water) and then the whole place lit up.

V

What can I say? I don't want it to sound like they were worse than they really were. After all, they didn't know what they were doing — they didn't know I was under there, and then for all my explaining they still didn't know what the statue was. In a way, they hadn't grown up. I've forgiven them in my heart, but no one's forgiven me.

I remember the first thing I did was to look out across the water. The light was so bright I could see everything. There was Howard splashing away — he always did swim like he was about to drown — and there on the shore were Blanche and Bailey Carlisle. Finally I saw what had happened. I peeped up between the logs of the platform, and I saw the L and the O that were standing over me all on fire. Howard had poured kerosene over them and set them on fire. There was nothing I could do to save them. A breeze had come up that whipped out long streamers of fire out behind the letters. Somehow it looked real fine, even though I did almost feel like crying. I remember I thought I wished I could have got the whole thing done before they burnt it, because it would have been a real fine sight.

Just as I started to crawl out, the fire jumped down and blocked my way. Howard had put most of the kerosene on the letters, but he had poured some over the platform itself, and some had dripped down through, so that there was fire every place I could have moved. Even though we'd had some rain during the summer, the wood had pretty much dried out sitting there in the sun day after day, so that it was burning fast. I know I'd have suffocated if it hadn't been for the breeze to carry the smoke away. When I could I looked across the lake again. I saw that the three of them were leaving. Even if I had felt like calling to them, they couldn't have heard me over the roar of the fire.

There was nothing I could do, so I got into a position where I could watch the letters burn, and waited. My clothes kept catching on fire but I managed to put them out. My hand that the kerosene had dripped over got burned — I've just lately been able to use it again. I lay there thinking I was probably going to burn to death before it was over. Like they say it does, my life went through my head, and I remember it was then that I began to get angry. I started trying to kick loose the platform from over me. The letters were about to fall anyway, and my kicking brought them down. Parts of them fell in the water, and other parts onto the platform over me, and the burning ash came sifting down through the logs. Then I started screaming, "Help! Help!" and then finally I guess I passed out. When I came to again it was pouring rain, and the fire was out. It was the rain that saved me.

I think I must have fallen asleep or lost consciousness several more times before I got myself free, just before dawn. I rested awhile, and then I swam to the shore and started walking. I had to go slow because I was burned and so tired. It must have been about six o'clock when I got to town. I walked through and started at the other end and worked my way back. I went to every house. I went to the door, and when they opened it, I said, "Look at me, look at what my family's done to me. My Blanche and my Howard did it, and that Bailey Carlisle." I was streaked black from the soot, my clothes were half burned off, my face was blistered, my hair was frizzled up. I held out my burned hand so they could see it.

Some of them said, "Louis, come on in here and let us fix you up," but I kept on. Lucy Patterson's little girl screamed and hid when she saw me, and Lucy said, "What are you saying, Louis? Why Blanche was out half the night, worried sick." All I said to her was, "They did this to me. What can a man do when his own family treats him so." I remember she said, "You should be ashamed of yourself, Louis," and slammed her door in my face. Maybe that should have warned me I was making a mistake, but it only made me madder. Before I was half through town there was a group of

people following me — some of them laughing, some telling me to
stop. A lot of them were youngsters. I didn't pay them any attention. But they were making a good deal of noise.

I was walking up to the hotel when the door opened and Blanche
stepped out to see what was happening. She took one look at me
and fainted right there. The people following me stopped talking.
Howard and Bailey Carlisle were close behind Blanche. I didn't
move till Howard had seen that she was all right, and then I started
saying my piece, pointing at the three of them. Howard was red as
a beet — he was bending over and pretending to pat Blanche's
cheek, so he'd have something to do, and so he could hide his face.
But Blanche had waked up, and she was looking me straight in the
eye. I've never seen her so angry. I shook my finger at them, and
I said, "Look at them. They did this to me." That Bailey Carlisle,
he listened for a minute, and then he just walked back into the
hotel and closed the door, leaving Blanche and Howard out on the
porch by themselves. You might know he'd do something of the
kind.

I imagine somebody had run ahead to tell Claude Witherspoon,
our sheriff, because he was waiting for me. He told me he didn't
want to, but he'd have to arrest me for disturbing the peace if I
didn't calm down. I said I had two more houses to go, and then I'd
be done, so if he aimed to arrest me he'd better do it (I'd gotten
a little carried away by then). He said, "It's not right, Louis, for a
man to treat his family this way. It's shameful, Louis, and you'll be
sorry for it." I said, "I may be — but what's shameful, Claude, is
the way they burned my statue," but he didn't answer me. He
just stood aside and let me go on. The last house was widow Thomas's — she's old and simple-minded. She was on her porch, and I
remember after I'd said my piece she burst out laughing, and then
she stopped and clapped her hands and said, "Go on, get out of
here! Get! Shoo! Get away from here." I guess I remember that
because those were the last words anybody said to me.

I had intended to stop and do my speech at the Zachams' but by
the time I got there I was so worn out I just went on home. "Well,"
I said to myself, "I guess they got more than they bargained for,
didn't they? If they hadn't been so concerned about people talking, everything would have been fine. Okay then: I've given people something to talk about for sure." Then I dressed my hand and
went to sleep. It seemed to me that I'd got everything worked out.

Things didn't happen the way I expected though. I thought people would be coming to commiserate with me and bring me food and so forth, so I waited mostly in bed for two or three days, but nobody came. Finally I walked over to the Zachams'. It was Sunday, and they'd just come back from church. They were sitting on the porch. When they saw me coming Alice said something to Moose and then she went inside. Moose sat there, but he looked real solemn and sad. I could practically read his mind. I didn't have to go through with it — I already knew what he'd say to me. I knew he'd say he couldn't ask me in. It came to me that people had set their hearts against me, and not against Blanche and Howard and Bailey Carlisle. Of course it made me feel bad, but when I saw poor old Moose in such a predicament, scratching his head and trying to figure out what he ought to do, I couldn't help chuckling to myself. So I just tipped my hat to him and kept going, like I was out for a walk and not coming to see them at all. I've kept away from them since then. I don't want to put old Moose on the spot. I can't resist crossing his land though now and again when he's out in the fields, just to see what he'll do. He always manages not to notice me.

For a while I did have some fun with the people in the stores and so on when I'd go into town. I'd speak to them and when they'd look down and not answer I'd say something like, "Cat got your tongue?" I got sick of it, though, after a while. Then I started explaining and apologizing to them, and taking all the blame on myself. I told them I'd been crazy and perverse even to think of building the statue. I said I'd been selfish and thoughtless — I told them anything I could think of, but still they looked away and pretended not to hear me. Part of the trouble was that they always looked so serious and angry I couldn't help laughing, even when I was apologizing. Now I've left off talking to them. I tried staying home all the time, but it got to be too lonesome, so now almost every day I go in and sit outside the courthouse so I can listen to people talking.

Like I say, I haven't talked to my family at all. They stay at the hotel, and it looks to me like they don't come out much more than Bailey Carlisle. There are a number of things I'd like to find out about them. I wonder, for instance, how they get along with the townspeople. I wonder whether Blanche feels disgraced — whether she feels she can "hold up her head." And then I'd like to know exactly what they had planned the night of the fire. It's pretty clear that Bailey Carlisle was only shamming sick. But I wonder what would have happened if I'd gone on to the hotel. Did they have somebody there to keep me occupied till they burned the statue? And then I wonder too whether or not they would have admitted doing it. Maybe they would have claimed to have been at the doctor's, and not to know anything about it. Or maybe they would have said they did it for my own benefit. Either way it would have been a good show.

The way I see it now is this. Most of the people never will forgive me, no matter what happens. But supposing Blanche and I get back together, things might ease up a little anyway. So the main question is Blanche — Howard will do anything the both of us tell him. Bailey Carlisle has probably advised Blanche never to have anything to do with me again, but I give her credit for having more sense than to take too much stock in what he says. So it depends on Blanche and me.

Now I've thought about writing her and telling her to come on back, and I expect she'd do it. On the other hand, it seems to me that it's her place to make the first move, so I've been waiting to see if she will. In fact I've decided I won't do anything till the end of the vacation. If she decides to come back before then, she can. If not, maybe I'll write her after the vacation, and then again I might not, I can't say. It might be that she's waiting for the year to be over too, I don't know. I'd thought about building the statue again, and sometimes I walk down to look at the lake; but I couldn't see much point in making a second try at it. I wonder if Blanche thinks I'm building it again. Anyway, what I have to do now is to get through the winter somehow, and get to the end of the vacation. And, like I told Blanche at the beginning, we won't know what it was till it's over. Whatever happens, I think that in the deepest part of my heart I'll be more proud than sorry, even if I'm lonely the rest of my days. I wouldn't tell anybody else, but I have to tell it to myself.

But sometimes I do miss my friends so much I wish we'd never taken the vacation — and so maybe before it's over I'll be able to apologize and not even smile at them.

PENELOPE STREET

The Magic Apple

(FROM OCCIDENT)

I

FIRST THING THAT MORNING, and it was a warm morning, being June and being in Michigan and sunny, I had gone to the delicatessen which was right around the corner from my dormitory, and bought a few salami sandwiches and some cheese for the trip. I wasn't particularly imaginative then. If I were to do it over again, I'd probably buy something more exotic: halvah, bagels and cream cheese, apples. It's not that exactly. I was just as imaginative then, only I didn't know you could be imaginative about food. I'd never cooked.

I was sixteen. It was the end of my freshman year at college because I'd skipped a few grades back in grammar school. When I started out, my mother was so proud. She had me skip the first grade; I went right from kindergarten to second grade and did fine. Then I went from second to third like normal and then from third to fifth. That was the bad one because I missed the multiplication tables, and as a result I was unpopular all the way through high school.

But that was all right, because I went away to college when I was fifteen and in college when you are an English literature major, they don't care about multiplication tables anymore.

My first day in Ann Arbor my first menstrual period began with a flourish. Some people call it a curse, but I called it a blessing. I was still a virgin, but I swore that wouldn't last for very long. My breasts were starting to grow!

A week later I went to my first class, freshman English composition and there it was that I met John.

John's the one that I was going to marry. We were sort of informally engaged. He'd called my father up to ask for the daughter's hand in marriage and my Dad had said, "Sure, why not?" without ever meeting the guy. That's my father for you. He never gave a shit. One way or the other.

So I was going to marry John, but not until the end of the summer because I had a job for the summer at home working in an employment agency, and we'd be able to use the money. So he got me a ride home from Ann Arbor to my front door with a friend of his.

There were four of us in the car and we didn't know each other. I had my sack of sandwiches and cheese and my luggage which was packed in the trunk. It was an old white Corvair — I watched the guy who was going to drive, Ed, load up the trunk — the trunk was in the front.

When I got engaged, I decided that my paranoid days were over. I was simply going to learn how to relax, so for a few months before the summer, I'd grown my quick-bitten nails to a superior length. I pruned them and polished them and buffed them. They were lovely. But there was simply no kidding that head of mine. It was the car and the worry of going home and the waiting for passengers and the long freeway ugly drive to and through Chicago (where we left one guy and picked up another) that meant doom for the nails. I chewed them off.

It was June of 1965 when we started out. Four of us rolled along all during the day and into the night on the Illinois, Indiana and Ohio turnpikes. Near the end of Ohio, Ed tired out and asked the other guy to drive. There were two girls and two guys.

The other guy started driving. There was a slight mist in the air, making the turnpike lighting only bulbous globs in the sky. We came to the end of the Ohio turnpike and paid the man the right amount of money. There is another tollgate at the entrance of the Pennsylvania turnpike where you pick up a ticket. It's a no man's land in between for about five miles. I guess the guy who was driving didn't know about the second gate. It approached at 80 miles per hour and never slowed down. Everyone in the car was taking a nap.

Ed, the guy who loaded the trunk, and the other girl were dead on arrival. Harry, the guy who was driving, wasn't hurt. But it was all an accident. Two years later the jury said it was Harry's fault, since he was sleeping.

I would think that a person would be able to tell when he was going to sleep. At least well enough to pull off the road. Maybe he was too proud to admit it.

We had, I heard later, been approaching the far right, eastbound gate, but when we hit, the side of our car hit the far left, westbound gate, ten gates over.

I awoke from the accident three distinct times before I came to into regular recognition of time and place.

At first the sirens shattered me into awareness where I was lying inside the moving ambulance. "Who am I?" I shouted. My brain network struggled to fit this situation into a logical context that it could understand. "What's going on?"

II

John is painting in the grotto on a short three-legged blue-enameled stool in front of his easel. The sun in his sky has an angry face — his hunks of trees are green blotches on a mean Y. Nugget is asleep on the floor in the room I'm in, under her blanket that I made her the winter I was in New York. The winter that I got raped by that big black man when I took that stroll through Harlem at night. That was the winter I decided to leave John and did.

John's a lot of fun I mean. He's a nice guy and we sit and cuddle in bed a lot and we read books and magazines together and cut out pictures in the Sears, Roebuck catalogue with manicure scissors and we tickle Pickle until she has tears streaming down her face. But John's very withdrawn and I'm outgoing I mean except for the usual regular fears I have like a fear of going outside. I'm afraid of even going to the store. It doesn't bother me, you know, if I'm going *with* somebody, or even when there's somebody at the house who'll be thinking of me and saying good-bye when I leave and who'll be there when I get home.

I was married when I was sixteen and it took me until I was nineteen to just leave the house alone to go to the store.

I've learned now how to go to the store alone. I'll go one of two places if necessary, either the bakery or the variety store. I've never driven a car. I guess it's because of the accident that I can't drive myself anywhere or even want to. Perhaps someday I'll get over it. But now if I have to go out in the car when John drives or particularly when someone else does, I get all nauseated and sullen and insist on open windows, and sometimes even vomit.

I want you to get to know me soon so that I'll have someone to talk to and someone who is close to me all the time. Someone who could be my sister if she could've or would've done it, and be my friend who knows me. Like if I happen to be mad, you'll be able to take me in and not make me go into the insane asylum.

Have you ever thought much about insane asylums? When I think of them I visualize the beds mostly which look like jail bars: that metal tubing that they've painted cream colored — and just the mattress ticking and no sheets. The window is the killer. The window is where you always have huge oak trees outside and just acres of the softest green grass all looking like it goes on forever — and a gravel driveway where you can hear the cars bringing patients and taking the old ones away, when they go. And maple trees that have those fliers that cover the seeds. You can peel them apart and make them stick to your nose.

Your fingers were always sticky after playing with those.

John. John's really a very wimpy guy I suppose. But he's got a fine expression on his face and eyes — transparent hazy blue eyes — you can see his nose through them when you look at a side view, through the clear part in the front of his eye. He had the deepest clear part I'd ever seen. It horrified me so I let him go all the way when I was only fifteen. He was a freshman in college. I was so proud to be going around with a college guy. And I wanted those eyes to belong to me. Well, it's so easy to lie. I think I just wanted to screw. My best friend in high school got me a blind date during summer vacation when I was fourteen. I gave him a hand job as naturally as I'd have kissed him. He enjoyed it while it happened, but he told his buddy. While it was happening we were lying at the foot of my parents' driveway on a hot summer night making a little triangle: our bodies, the driveway and the sidewalk. It was the first one I'd ever done, and I think I made a few mistakes. I think I rubbed too hard and hurt him or something. I wanted him to like me a lot. But fourteen-year-olds and fifteen- or sixteen-year-olds don't like you a lot when you give them a hand job, I discovered. They just think you are cheap. I could have acted prissy perfectly easily. I mean, I wasn't dying to give him a hand job. I just thought it would feel good to him. Isn't that silly? and then he goes and *complains* to his buddy as though it disgusted him. I'm surprised he wasn't proud. But maybe it was pride, of a sort. He was proud it was done to him, but he couldn't be proud of himself if the fellows knew he *knowingly* went out with a girl like that. So it was a one shot deal. He lived in a big mansion in Orange, New Jersey, and we went there on the blind date and sat around a swimming pool at night, and on the way home, about a couple of hours' drive, we made out in the back seat because I was drunk and the seat was gone and we had to ride along lying down. So when we got to my house and got out, the hand job thing seemed like the most logical conclusion, though I'd never done one and didn't know how exactly. I mean it just happened. I hadn't planned it. And then he never called me again.

But my friend, Lyn, the one who fixed me up with him, she called me the next day. She called me the next day to give me a lecture on being whory. She said that you definitely shouldn't give hand jobs to guys, particularly on first dates. Maybe even more particularly on blind first dates.

Since he can't see what you are doing.

You know why you shouldn't drink lake water? Because the fish fuck in it. It's full of fish sperm. And fish sweat. John never sweats. Even when we make love (though I've stopped calling it that), even when we screw he doesn't shed a drop of perspiration anywhere. Not even on his balls or his back. There should be some perfume called "Essence of B.O." for people like him. It turns me on. It turns me on or else I think it does because my man never has it. And my man usually turns me off. He's small, there's no doubt about that and he's weak and has very little energy, and that's not surprising I guess since he's real small. And since he doesn't turn me on very often or very much, we don't sleep together anymore. John has his own room, and I've walled off a room for myself and Jen under the eaves at one end of the living room. It was a patchwork I was working on for a long time. I made it into a sort of review of all the high points in our life. Little appliquéd pictures of the houses we'd stayed in and of Jenny as a baby and of our dog when he was a pup. I hung it from the ceiling to fence off the end part of the room. Jen's toys are in the room next to that.

So anyway, John is in the grotto working on his abstract painting

of an ugly hot day that is about four feet long and will probably
hang somewhere in the house, probably in here, in the living room,
when it's done.

The grotto is like the inside of a cave. It's concrete and damp and
we use it for a kitchen, I guess, though all it has is a refrigerator.
We cook in a Roto-broil and a toaster and an electric frying pan,
and wash the dishes in the bathroom sink. It's bad when you have
company over for a late dinner and everybody gets stoned and in
the morning the bathroom is mobbed and stacked with dirty dishes,
and nobody wants to wash them. So John does.

I just did a Tarot reading. I asked the cards if you would be able
to understand me. You know it would be a waste of time if I spent
all this energy on telling you about myself if you wouldn't be able
to decipher it at the end. It said no. It said yes and no. First of all
the cards show me lying on my belly with ten swords stabbing a row
down my back in a pool of blood. Which means I'll be laying it all
on the line and that's a pretty masochistic thing to do, but I think
it's necessary. In case you don't know how the Tarot is done, you
have a card according to your astrological sign. My card is Justice.
I think that this is the first reading I've done in a year that I didn't
build the reading on my own card. I decided that I wanted to ask
about this message I'm beginning. So as not to ever involve myself
in the answer I left my own personal card out of the reading. The
results were incredible. The results were outstanding. My own card,
the Justice card, came out as the best of possible outcomes. What
could be a more appropriate outcome for an epistle where I'm trying to get myself to come across? I've really enjoyed the Tarot.
There's something I've wanted to do for a very long time. I wanted
to write a book with a chapter on every card. Just what I think about
the card, what the picture means and what-not, more or less stream
of consciousness, and described in such a way that you would have
to have the card in front of you at all times to understand what I was
talking about.

He has shaggy hair and thick, almost white eyelashes, John. You
think you are looking at something you shouldn't.

III

I would walk the stroller with Jenny to the bakery where the nice
lady always gave her a free cookie and then we would go to the vari-

ety store and Jenny would get a small surprise. Oak Variety Store has a lot of 10¢ surprises like bubble soap and whistles and tiny rubber dolls in bassinettes covered with pinking-sheared blankets the size of a matchbook.

Every day I would see her. She was taller than I am and she always wore brown leather pants and a brown leather jacket that fitted her tightly across the back. And she wore red lipstick painted right along her lip lines and a hat. Always some outlandish hat with her high-heeled boots and a kind of satchel. I would see the Leather Lady walking and follow. Jenny would never notice: I would speed up the stroller until I was nearly running so I wouldn't lose sight.

The first day I saw her I was afraid to look. But I followed her. I followed her home and found out where she lived.

The second day I bought her a chocolate cake at the bakery and left it on her front porch. "For the Leather Lady from a Secret Admirer." And I began knitting the afghan. It was covered with gothic spires and castles and cathedrals which were all tree houses in the hugest, most ornate live oak trees ever beheld. A magnificent city in the trees, where no one could get to without a rope ladder made of the Leather Lady's hair, which was black and hung down gracefully beneath her hundred hats, black and wavy, and I was in love with her. She was so mysterious. For a long time I would just watch for her and follow her and look at her. I would never have said hello or have gotten close enough to really see her. I would work on the afghan day and night. I'd sit up in bed at night, Jenny asleep next to me in the light, John breathing and turning, out there in the dark. I'd knit some parts, crochet others. It was going to be magnificent. I worked so hard on it — knowing I couldn't just leave it, like the cake, on the porch. I'd have to take it to her in person. I'd have to ring that bell on that white Victorian doorframe and give her the blanket I'd made for her. I would get to talk to her in person.

Jenny liked the long walks we took that led us past the Leather Lady's house. She would make up songs about fire engines and bananas and would sing them on the way and would make me stop the stroller now and then so she could pick stolen flowers from old ladies' near-the-sidewalk plants.

John had finished his hot-day painting and it hung muggy in the living room like an oppressive summer rain cloud about to burst. If there had been trees inside the house, the leaves would be turned over in anticipation.

I remember when Jenny was born plain as day, watching her slimy perfect ten fingers ten toes red body slither out. I did that breathing method of natural childbirth called Lamaze, so I wasn't dopey, and it didn't hurt. Or it did hurt, but I didn't feel it. It was as though my eyes and my brain were stationed somewhere else than in my body, where that pain was registering, so I felt it, but I didn't feel it. I was too busy thinking about the pant-blow-pant-blow, and thinking about watching. It's not something you see every day.

They have a slanted mirror mounted at the feet end of the delivery table so you can watch, and it's such an unfamiliar angle that you feel as though you are watching someone else having a baby. And it's so fascinating that you almost forget it's you.

I saw her, Jenny, for a moment. Those sterile hands held her out for my eyes, but that sterility required my hands to stay under the white sheets and I couldn't touch or hold or suckle her. I didn't see her again until the next day. That wasn't natural. They shouldn't do it that way. The baby should be yours to hold, not theirs to test and prod, poke and scare. Next time, if there is a next time, it's going to be different.

I don't know what made me do it, but I ordered a huge Plexiglas aquarium the day I got home from the hospital.

Over and over again John griped, "Does your mother have to come out right after the baby's born?" When we got home from the hospital, there she was. Mother cooked her same-old-traditional meals with Campbell's soup and ground beef, pork chops, rice and tomatoes, frozen spinach. She repaired broken doorknobs, replaced the washer in the kitchen sink that had been dripping for years, and had John take the flash photos of Grandma holding Jenny in the rocking chair, Grandma holding Jenny on the front porch, Grandma holding Jenny dangling by the earlobe in the bathtub.

John was incidental to the grandchild miracle, and I nearly was. Mother took one picture of me, breast-feeding Jenny. It was a rear view: 80% chair, 20% hair.

I began to hate the baby's squall but she let me escape from John. I'd leap out of our bed, for it was *our* bed then, and bring her back in. The udder quieted the gaping mouth and we all would sleep, John angry at the intruder in his marriage bed. But he never said it. I often wonder if it would have made any difference if he had.

When the slurping kept him awake, the two of us, Jenny and I, would move out to the living room and I'd rock in a chair until we'd both fall asleep again, one drinking, one drugged with sleep. The morning light would wake us up and I would become used to waking up there in the swivel stuffed rocker with my feet on the ottoman and the baby asleep there two-pillow propped on my lap, with no resentful back angry against us.

I breast-fed for a long time. It was a fine excuse.

It took me two months to finish the afghan for the Leather Lady. It was time to take it to her. I arranged for a babysitter for Jenny for the whole afternoon and I folded the afghan carefully and put it in tissue paper in a toy-store shopping bag from Christmas. It wasn't a long walk. In a way it wasn't long enough. There I was ringing the bell. There she was answering the door. "Hello," I said. "Do you remember the chocolate cake?"

"Certainly I do," she said, and her voice: it was much lower than I'd expected, two octaves lower and foreign-sounding.

"Certainly I do. Come in." She was nice but her voice was so gruff. I followed her into the dark enormous entryway and we stood there feeling awkward and I said, "My name is Phebe. I've come to bring you a present I've made you."

"Another present? But you don't even know me! Come on into my apartment, and you can meet my boyfriend. By the way, my name is André."

André's boyfriend lounged across the day-bed in leotard bottoms. He had long thin child-hair that was yellowy-brown.

It was hard to believe that the Leather Lady was not the Leather Lady at all. I would have to change his name.

I gave him the afghan anyway. They spread it on their double bed and we all three sat on it and watched the color TV they had mounted on the wall. They laughed at my misunderstanding. They understood my misunderstanding. I liked them. They invited me back to watch color TV any time I liked and even suggested I bring Jenny along. She would like to watch color TV.

IV

My father liked me well enough, you know, but I always wanted my mother to like me. I inadvertently spoiled my chances for that when I was four, and five, and so on. I don't think she knew it exactly then, though, because she was at bridge club or PTA or somewhere.

I quit breast-feeding the day that John left, so I guess that Jenny felt more that she was losing her milk supply than that she was losing her father.

In the den with the leaded glass windows, I used to sit on those rose-colored furry chairs with the Red Monkey — that's what I called my boyfriend but his real name was Chip. Sometimes we'd even move to the floor. The door to the den was leaded glass too, and without curtains, and my parents sat out there in the living room and listened and half watched while they watched TV from opposite ends of the couch. There was Mom's end with the straight pins in the arm for when she felt inclined to pick her teeth and the manicure scissors and the orange Melmac cup and saucer emptied of coffee. And there was Dad's end with the *Salt Fishing* magazines and the *Mad* magazines and the black corduroy pillow he always leaned on and the edge of the Danish modern coffee table worn, there where he propped his feet. He propped his feet from exactly 7:45 until exactly 10 every night except for garbage night when it was only 9:45. Fifteen minutes to take out the garbage and to sing his song. He had a song for garbage night that went:

> *Stick out your can: Here comes the garbage man*
> *Stick out your can: Here comes the garbage man*
> *He's collecting all your garbage*
> *Just as fast as he can.*

It had become such a ritual that he usually just sang the first line and did the rest with "Da da's" real loud so that you could hear it all over the house as he went from room to room emptying all the wastepaper baskets into a grocery bag.

Actually, I imagine he still does it.

If I'd be necking in the den back then and it was garbage night, as it frequently was, he'd sing his song especially loudly, and as he passed the den door with the grocery bag in his hand, he'd leer in and say something like "Aha!" or "Caught in the act!"

I think it was just to show his pleasure, and relief that he hadn't destroyed my sex life. I was making out just fine.

I was telling you about the Red Monkey. Well, actually, his real

name was Charles Cameron O'Reilly John Anderson III, but he had
red hair and I guess that's why I once started calling him the Red
Monkey and it stuck. But I called him Chip a lot too.

He was the funniest person I'd ever met. He went to prep school,
boarding school, somewhere in the dim wilds of Maine where the
whole staff was homosexual and where it seemed to snow year-
round. Before he'd graduated from high school he had two illegiti-
mate children residing in the Maine wilderness.

When he'd try to finger fuck me on the den floor I frequently used
the excuse, "My mother wouldn't like it!" I don't know where I got
that one.

Chip would say, "Your mother isn't going to get it," which wasn't
at all what I meant. What I meant was that my mother wouldn't
have liked it if I did things like that, but that wasn't true either, because my mother would have liked it just fine.

I think she wished she'd been able to do things like that when she
was a girl. She wished she could have done it right there behind the
leaded glass doors when she was a girl.

I guess I just figured that I needed an excuse of some kind, but I
couldn't think of an appropriate one for the life of me. Why not?
After all, it feels good and a finger can't get you pregnant. Some
sort of defloweration was happening then in the den with its leaded
glass bookshelves covered with Signet paperbacks.

Chip had a kind of mystical effect on me. He always made it
quite clear that hundreds of *women* (and mind you, he was only sixteen) were doing it for him where he came from — women he cared
not one iota for — and here he is with you. Wonderful you the one
he loves most of all and you have the gall to deny him. He begged.
His cheeks turned frustration-red and it was more than obvious that
I had ample encouragement from the folks. There they were out
there on their couch loving every minute of it. It was the only love-
making they'd ever done, real or vicarious, that I knew of, aside
from the fact that my sister Lois and I were conceived once, a long
time ago.

"I go way up there to that rotten Godforsaken place," Chip would
say. "And all I do up there is think about you and write you letters
and walk out in the snow every day to see if there's a letter from
you and I come home and you won't *prove* that you love me."

"I think about you a lot when you're not here," I said thinking
of myself wondering all day in school if there would be a letter from

Maine on the end-table when I got home. And sometimes there was and it would be handwritten and gross and pleading for that one thing he wanted from me when he got home. His goal was always the next thing on the list that we hadn't done yet. First it was French kissing. It took him a year to get his tongue into my mouth. He finally pinned me against a wall at the beach house and stuck his tongue down my throat. I thought that I was going to hate it, find it disgusting. But I didn't.

Lyn and I talked about everything. She was my best friend. Around her I felt like a sex expert.

When I was fourteen Chip finger fucked me. I was wearing a bathing suit at the time. When you're fourteen it's not proper to take off your clothes to do stuff. From then on Lyn and I called it sixteening. It had a name. It wasn't because I'd been sixteen when it happened, but because a friend of ours named aula had already done it with sixteen guys.

Lyn and I had a private joke for everything. Every number was funny. But 16 was the funniest of all. We'd be watching TV with my parents and some commercial would come on that would have the number 16 in it somewhere and we'd roll around on the floor guffawing for about ten minutes.

Lyn thought sixteening was absolutely the worst, most impure, unvirtuous thing in the world.

My sixteening with Chip knocked me down a few notches on Lyn's purity list.

She said, "Some people really get a charge out of Cadillacs and opal tiaras, but this is no excuse for stealing. The fact remains that some things have a value which makes them worth waiting for.

"Phebe," she said, "I certainly don't know all the answers, but my mother keeps saying 'anything above the waist.' I just hope that you will think of things as a whole for their meaning and value and not for their appeal of the moment. You really deserve a better life than my Aunt Adelade in her crumby apartment across from the Paramount Theatre with my uncle bitching and throwing nail polish at the walls and stomping out to the nearest whorehouse."

I wasn't sure what I had to do with her Aunt Adelade, but I guess she figured that if I'd do what I did, it was downhill from then on unless I changed my ways drastically. And of course I didn't.

But I had to do that cavorting around in the den because of my father. You see we both needed for me to do that.

When I was four, which is what I've been trying to get at for this whole series of decoys and digressions, my father started to molest me when Lois was asleep and when Mom was off somewhere to one of her meetings or clubs. It happened every week or so for years, with me fearfully obliging his massive tongue in my mouth which was disgusting to me then, or whatever else he wanted to do. He made me afraid to tell and so of course I didn't. Suddenly one day, the same father, through some avalanche of guilt or self-control probably, quit touching me, and never mentioned it again. I began to wonder if it had really happened or if it was all in my mind. I was thirteen when it was all over and it never happened again.

I just wanted Mom to like me really. I guess I wanted her to forgive me for something that she didn't know I'd done and I couldn't tell her about.

Mom was always much more faithful to me in her own way. When I had that accident it was Mom who came to rescue me. She drove by herself three hundred miles to see how I was and Dad stayed home.

But messed up as Dad was, he was a nice guy. I wanted to prove to him that I could make it fine without him. Hence the den. And the Red Monkey and the mother who wouldn't like it. She would have loved it.

Poor Dad never got any sex, you see. Mom must have been frigid and that's why he ended up molesting his kid. It's perfectly logical and even though we haven't mentioned it since, it makes sense to me.

Chip was a high school romance. And when college came it *had* to happen that I marry my college romance, which I did. I had to get away from home, you know.

I've seen a psychiatrist pretty many times. A couple of them, in fact. They really think I'm mad. I've decided that it's not a very good idea to be around people who are pretty sure you're mad. It tends to make you start to believe it. And if you believe you're mad then you can start worrying about the asylums and being put away and having no one who's sane out there in the real world who can bail you out, who can say, "Don't worry folks. She's okay. I knew her when she was a little girl and she wasn't crazy then." Because everyone I knew when I was a little girl was nutty as a Mr. Goodbar. That's the kind of candy bar I always get when I go to the movies. But can you see my sex pervert father or my frigid mother or my nutty sister whom I haven't told you much about yet but I'll get to that, can you see them trying to get me out of the nut house once I'm in?

I'm not seeing any more shrinks, no siree. As long as nobody thinks you're crazy, nobody can put you in. I just try real hard every day to act sane.

I wash my dishes right after dinner and keep my papers in manila envelopes alphabetically in a drawer.

So Chip was my high school sweetheart who ended up marrying a girl he met when he was stationed in the air force in Ireland. And now he has a job writing news for a small-town East Coast newspaper somewhere and, since he's a Catholic, he's probably got about ten kids by now.

And then John was my college sweetheart. If you sixteen when you're fourteen, you are bound, as Lyn predicted, to wind up in the gutter.

When John got me pregnant, through no fault of his own, I told my parents. John was about the most virtuous, asexual person I'd ever met. He'd gone with a girl in high school for six years — for six years he went steady — and all he ever did was feel her up: under her sweater, but over her bra.

Maybe if I'd had big worthwhile breasts I'd have been a more virtuous girl. But I came to the unconscious conclusion that since there wasn't much at the top, I'd have to be one of the girls that prematurely gave the bottom up.

John's girlfriend didn't have much on the top either, as it turned out, but I practically raped poor John. I moved his hands around for him and forced him to open his mouth when he kissed me.

He was really a very naive guy. It was like me and Chip with me being the Chip and John being the me. I'd be panting and squirming and John would be groaning, "We can't. We can't." And I'd be saying, "Why not," just like Chip did and John should have said, "My mother wouldn't like it," but he didn't. I forget just what his excuse was, but he ran back to his old high school sweetheart everytime I got too fast for him. That was very frustrating.

When I got pregnant I told my parents. Nobody said anything. I guess it's because I told them on the phone. Dead silence. I guess they were shocked, you know, because generally Dad would say something funny and Mom would be concerned. Nobody said anything.

The next day Dad arrived, flown in directly from a thousand miles away.

Without saying a thing except for small talk, we left for Japan. Dad didn't even ask if I wanted an abortion. I guess I did, but we talked about the weather and Mom's sculpture class and the movie we saw on the plane.

I can't explain why, but Dad's just not the kind of guy who'll take you to Japan for an abortion. Maybe he felt responsible or something.

We crossed the street in Tokyo. The traffic was amazing. Tiny cars zipping around, soot hanging oppressively over the city like it had been permanently installed. On our way across the street I almost got hit by a sports car.

"You can get knocked *down* too," my father said. It was his first even offhand comment about the fact that I was pregnant. Until then I'd almost forgotten why we were there.

I didn't have to anymore, but when Dad and I got back, I married John. I think it was the stop in Hawaii that made me decide. I just had to get married to somebody, and John, baby or no baby, felt responsible. He was a nice guy, nearly as funny as Chip.

I got pregnant again immediately. Poor Dad. He must've felt the trip was a waste of money, you know.

ROBERT PENN WARREN

Meet Me in the Green Glen

(FROM PARTISAN REVIEW)

IT WAS DARK NOW. The big electric bulb that hung from the middle of the ceiling — there had to be a big bulb, the kitchen the size it was — blazed. You could see the freckles of flyspeck on the glass of the bulb, and the streaks where the grease-laden air had made deposits to settle and run down. Sometimes in the kitchen at night, she might suddenly stop whatever she was doing and stare at the blazing bulb. Sometimes it came closer and closer, so close she could see the flyspecks big and clear, but no matter how close it got, it never got to her and only kept coming. But sometimes it seemed to be going away from her, spinning away forever but never getting out of sight, never even getting smaller.

Tonight, she was staring at it, standing motionless with an empty saucepan — the one she meant to boil the potatoes in — hanging from her hand as though the wrist were too weak to support even that small burden. This was one of the times when the blazing bulb seemed to be going away from her, and though the going-away was awful, something else was growing in her head too, the notion that if you got to know that the way things happen to you, no matter how awful, couldn't happen any differently and that the way they happened was, really, just part of the way you were you, then you could keep forever this new feeling of strange joy.

She stood there, the saucepan dangling, bathed in that bleak whiteness of light that kept pouring from the bulb, even though the bulb was spinning away forever, and knew what joy meant. It meant that things would never again tease her and scare her by coming closer and closer and yet not coming. From now on everything, like the bulb there, like the walls of the kitchen, like the trees outside in the dark, and the hills, would keep on spinning away.

The going-awayness would never change — now at last she knew that, and suddenly, she felt the joy so strong she was dizzy and her eyes blurred.

Then she heard the noise. The door, the door to the back porch, swung slowly inward, open. There he was.

In her sight, he seemed to sway and swim there, as though the darkness from which he had come were a medium like water sustaining him. It was as though the pressure of all that darkness flooding down from the hills and woods had just pushed the door open, and in one second more, would come pouring in, filling up the room, washing him at her. She was sure that she saw the darkness swirling about his knees, ready to lift him off his feet, and flood in, bearing him to her, with his eyes fixed on her.

But that was not what happened. While he stood there, and the eyes kept looking at her out of his face, his hand went behind him and, though his body never moved, shoved the door shut. It made a little slam. The latch had caught. The dark would not come in.

But something else happened. She looked, one split second, at the electric bulb, and it was not going away now, it was coming back and she could see the flyspecks on it clear as could be.

She had been wrong. The going-awayness was over. The coming-closerness had begun again.

Then she was looking back at him, and his face was coming closer.

The eyes in his face were looking at her, and the mouth said: " 'Allo."

She felt her own mouth trying to move, but it wouldn't. His face was coming at her. She could see how the bristles that hadn't been shaved off today stuck out stiff and black around the pinkness of his mouth. His legs were moving, but it seemed that he was coming faster than the legs, faster than the walls were coming, or the stove, or the electric bulb, or anything. He was right at her when she closed her eyes.

She stood there in the darkness her eyelids made. Then she knew that the sound of him — no, it was the feel of him — had gone on by. She opened her eyes.

He was past her, over by the old zinc sink, by the window, running a glass of water, like he was nothing in the world but a man who had come in late and was thirsty.

Everything now had stopped coming at her, and had gone back where it belonged. Everything was like a dog you had told to go lie down.

He was looking at her face so hard it was as though the flesh would begin to hurt if he didn't stop.

"Did you go to Parkerton?" she said, and heard her voice way off asking that fool question.

"Yeah," he said, "Parkerton."

His gaze shifted from her face. She followed his eyes as they turned to look at the table she had set. There it was, as always, the red-check oilcloth on the table, the knife and fork and spoon, the coffee cup, the same pink-and-white plate, the last of the set of what they called Haviland china left from the old days, from her Aunt Josephine's time, from the set that had come as a wedding present and her aunt had been so proud of. It was the plate she had got in the habit of setting out for him to eat on.

He was staring at the plate, then strangely at her. "I go wash me," he said finally, and went out the door that led into the hall.

As she stood by the stove she did not feel anything. If she did not feel anything, then nothing would have happened, ever. And if nothing had ever happened, then she would not have to feel anything.

He was a long time coming back. She was glad of that, for now everything was ready, the mashed potatoes, the two porkchops, canned peas. In his chair, he looked down at the food, making not the slightest preparatory move to touch it, then up at her as she stood above him to pour the coffee. He looked down at the coffee, while the vapor rose thinly into the blank whiteness of the light of the bulb that hung almost directly above him. She had gone back to stand near the range, watching him.

All at once, having touched nothing, he shoved back the chair, with a scraping noise on the boards, and rose. Ignoring her, he went to the old electric icebox in the corner beyond the sink, got a tray of ice, put three cubes into the glass, poured it two-thirds full of water, and carried it back to the table. He set it carefully beside his plate, sat down, and, never having looked at her, having, in fact, mysteriously denied her presence, her very existence, by every motion made, drew a bottle of whiskey from his right hip pocket. He poured the glass nearly full.

Then he looked at her. He thrust the glass toward her, staring at her with bloodshot eyes.

She shook her head.

"You no wan', eh!" he said, and gave a sharp, bitten-off laugh. He took a long drink, then began to eat, not with appetite but in a slow fastidiousness, looking critically at each mouthful after he had lifted the fork, then chewing the food with a mincing motion of the jaws, the lids of his eyes lowered to shroud them from her sight. Each time, after he had swallowed, he took a delicate sip from the glass. The coffee went unnoticed.

He was more than half through the food on the plate, when he lifted his head. She stood frozen in the sudden unveiling of his gaze.

"You stand away there, why you stand there?" he demanded.

She tried to think why she was there. Every night after she had dished up the food, she had stood here by the range to watch him eat it. She had seen the light on his wet slicked-down hair like black enamel. But that was not an answer, she knew it wasn't, and she felt as she used to feel in school when she was a little girl in that schoolhouse up the road that wasn't there anymore, and the teacher asked her the question and the answer wouldn't come out of her mouth.

He was staring at her. "You no eat?" he said.

She shook her head.

"Why you no eat?" he said.

"I can't," she said.

"Why you can't?"

It was like school, and the answer wouldn't come. Always after he had finished eating and had left the kitchen and she was alone, she would warm up something to take to Sunder. After she had fed him, she would sit there by his bed and eat something.

But was that the answer?

"Why you no sit?" he was saying, with the bloodshot eyes on her.

She didn't answer.

"That chair, see?" he said, pointing to one by the wall beyond the sink. "You bring here now, eh?"

She brought the chair and placed it opposite him.

"*Bene,* sit."

She sat down, under the white glare of light.

He began to eat again, not noticing her. He finished, gazed directly across at her. Under that light her face was chalky white, but, as he stared at her, the flush began, first just a touch on each side, under the high cheekbones, the spot hectic and sudden like fever. As the check mantled, as she seemed about to lower her head, her eyes, from the dusky shadow of the sockets, suddenly met his with a look both bright and distant, like pleading.

Her eyes were there only an instant. Then her head dropped to press the chin on the breastbone. It was enough, however, to make the anger flash up in him.

"And now you sit but no talk. Why you no talk?"

He leaned at her.

"You talk."

She did not stir, and suddenly, his right hand leaped across the table and seized the wrist of the arm that lay opposite, humble, weak, and indifferent. His grip closed tight, lifting the arm from the table, holding it a foot or so above the surface, in the empty air.

"Talk! You talk!" he commanded.

But nothing happened, and he flung the wrist from him, in despair and outrage.

He rose from the table, seized the bottle, and stood there.

"Who you?" he cried out. *"Porca Madonna!* Who are you?"

By the time she had raised her head to look at him, to try to find something to say to that question that was filling her head, he was gone. Rather, his back was going through the door into the hall. Then the door closed.

He stood in the dark of the hall, breathing hard. If she had just said something. Then you would have known she was real.

Slowly, not bothering to turn on the light, he groped his way down the hall, turned the corner into the ell, and found his door. In the dark, he lay down on the bed, all his clothes on, even the shoes. He took a drink from the bottle, set it on the floor by the bed, lit a cigarette, and lay on his back, staring up into the dark.

When he took a drag of the cigarette, he held it between thumb and forefinger, cupped so that the brightness of the tip was concealed from his eyes, except for the faint bleeding away of pink glow upward into the darkness above the edge of his palm and little fin-

ger. When he took a drag, he kept his eyes on the upper darkness,
aware of the glow but not looking at it.

After a while he took another drink and lit another cigarette and
kept on staring at the darkness where the ceiling was.

It was raining again.

When he first jerked awake, he did not know where he was. But
his thumb and forefinger hurt, and he knew. He had gone to sleep,
and the cigarette had burned down to the fingers. The butt was
there on the blanket, smoldering. He crushed it out, and spat on
the spot on the blanket, and rubbed in the wetness. Then he put his
hurt fingers to his mouth, and with the other hand fumbled on the
floor for the bottle.

He found it. When he shook it in the dark there was a slosh, but
not a big one. He drank what there was.

He lay there and thought: *Santa Madonna, sono tornato. Back.*

He was lying there in the dark, the empty bottle loosely between
his fingers, on his chest, as though forgotten. He was remembering
all that had happened — or rather, he was seeing things happen in
the dark above his wide-open eyes — when he heard the sound.

It was the sound that came from that room down the hall. It was
like the sound he remembered from his uncle's farm in Ohio, when
you butchered a sheep. You hoisted the sheep up by the hind legs
and slit the throat and suddenly the last bleat with the blood in it
was like the sound from that room. But when the sound came from
the sheep, it did not keep on, the way the sound from that room
did sometimes. With the sheep dead the sound stopped.

The sound was loud now in the dark, louder than he had ever
heard it come to this room. He made a move to rise, but the sound
stopped, so he dropped back down. Then he decided he'd get up
anyway, to go outside to relieve himself, rain or not. He tiptoed
down the hall, to the back porch, to stand on the edge under the
eaves.

He had got back to the door of his room, when he realized that
just a minute back, when he came out, the door had been open.
That was why the sound had come so loud. Now he stood there in
the dark and tried to remember whether he had shut the door upon
entering the room after supper. Every other night, always when he
went in, he had shut it. He stood there thinking about shutting the
door.

Why was he worried about having left the door open?

There was nothing here, nothing but the woman and the noise in that room, and the rain falling outside, and upstairs the weight of darkness. He stood there, his hand on the doorjamb and looked upward toward the darkness of the ceiling, thinking of the rooms up there that he had never seen, of those spaces filled with darkness.

He could have gone up, any day or night, and nobody would have ever known or cared. There were the wide stairs in the front hall. He had wandered into the hall, just as he had wandered idly into the room where the piano was. But he had never even thought of going up those stairs. He hadn't had the curiosity even to open the two other doors in the ell on this floor, assuming that nothing, not here or upstairs, would be different from the room he was in.

But that was yesterday. It was not tonight, with him standing here now and saying in his head: *Ecco mi, Angelo. Back.*

The need was growing in him to touch every door, to go into every room, to stand in every room and breathe the dark there, to know — To know what?

He had come back. He did not say it, nor even think it, but he suddenly felt like a man on whom the door has been locked. If the door is open the man does not investigate the room he is in. The room has no walls to be investigated. The room is not, in fact, real. It is only part of the world. But once the key has turned, it is not part of the world. There are the walls. The room is real. You must run your hands over the walls.

He groped into his room, found the old syrup bottle he had stuck a candle in to go out back at night by, lit it, lit a cigarette, which he let hang from the left corner of his mouth, came back into the hall, and shut the door carefully behind him, as was his custom, and tried the door opposite his own.

He had been right in his assumption. It was like his own room, only more ruinous. The other door in the hall was to a bathroom, a big zinc tub set in a varnished wooden boxing, a marble surface on top about the tub. There was a zinc basin, set in a marble slab, with heavy brass fixtures, like those of the tub. There was the toilet in the corner near the window, with a pipe going up to the old-fashioned flush box, up near the ceiling.

Christ-a Jesus, the thought, *and Angelo evva morning — he go out to stink-house.*

But when he tried a faucet in the basin, no water came. He

leaned and held the candle over the bowl of the toilet. It was dry and dusty.

He came back into the hall and went toward the corner where the ell joined the main hall. He paused for a moment at the door of the room where the sound would come from, standing very still while the candle flame grew steady on the wick and the shadows froze to the walls as flat as black paper pasted on.

Then he turned right and moved the three paces that led to the door cutting off the front hall. He was still wearing his own clothes, the town clothes, and he set the toes of the patent-leather shoes down without sound. He looked down at the shoes and saw that they had no sheen in the candlelight. They were getting dry and cracked. Despair flooded his bosom.

But he laid hand to the hall door, entered, and ascended the stairs. The carpeting on the stairs was frayed through to the wood. Halfway up the stairs, he looked back. His own shadow, cast by the candle held breast-high before him, made the darkness darker behind him. There his shadow filled the air, enormous, hovering over him. When he had turned again up the stairs, he felt the weight on his shoulders.

He wandered the rooms. Out of the darkness, the furniture swayed slowly at him, swaying into the light of the candle like clumps of waterweed in the backwash of a sluggish current. In one room, a mattress, still on the bed, had been cut open by rats or squirrels, and the gray, clotted viscera spilled out over the floor. Standing there, he was aware, through the thin soles of the patent-leather shoes, of the gritty feel of dry rodent droppings under his feet. A moldy odor, streakily mixed of dust and damp, filled his nostrils. Here the sound of the rain was louder.

The last room he entered was toward the front, over the parlor, he calculated. It was much larger than the others, with a fireplace and, as he noticed, a marble mantle, this on the inner wall to the left, and a big tester bed jutting out toward him from the wall he faced. He moved toward the bed, veered to his left, the side the fireplace was on, and stood beside the bed. He looked up at the canopy. Some of the fabric had given way, slowly giving down of its own weight, hanging in motionless, raveling strips. He held the candle closer to a strip, studying it. It had once been rose color, as even in candlelight, he could tell from a few streaks not yet faded to a pinky-gray. He lifted his hand to touch the fabric, but in the

air the hanging cobwebs which he had not seen caught his hand
in their dry, sticky tangle, with a contact more loathsome for its
feebleness. He withdrew his hand, not having touched the hanging
strip, and wiped it against his trouser leg.

He looked down. There were two thick mattresses of gray-
striped ticking. He saw the bolster of ticking, and the two pillows,
in their places. He had never seen a bed like this. He wondered
what it would be like to sleep in such a bed.

He thought how people had really lain in that bed, on that mattress, sleeping while the rain came down outside as it was doing this
very minute, or had waked to turn and clasp each other in the dark.

That thought filled his head. It was the kind of thought he had
never had before. It was, literally, filling his head with a pressure
that hurt.

Here me, he thought.

All at once he jerked his hand back, and still looking at the bed,
the very spot on the mattress where his hand had been in contact,
withdrew a couple of slow backward steps. Then he lifted his right
hand, the hand that had been in contact with the mattress, and
studied it by the light of the candle.

He moved from the bed, and moving, caught the glint of the
candle flame in a· mirror, the tall mirror of the armoire across the
room — the candle flame and then, in the same instant, the shadowy image of a man with the flame glimmering pale on his face.
His blood froze, for in that instant he did not know there was a mirror, did not know that the shocked, forward-thrust, wide-eyed face,
glimmering so pale in light, with the cigarette hanging from the
corner of the mouth, was his own.

Then he knew, and stared into it, studying the image.

Me, he thought, in a wondering that grew more powerful and
benumbing with the confrontation, detail by detail, of the knowledge that this image was, really, himself.

The light on the face in the mirror flickered. The candle in the
mirror was, he suddenly saw, guttering. He was staring at the face
in the mirror when the flame flared up and then, all at once, had
died. In the mirror there was only the tiny illumination of the cigarette that hung from the left corner of the mouth. It showed
faintly the little area of the cheek and the left corner of the lips,
where it was burning down to the very flesh. That was all you could
see in the mirror.

With his tongue tip he pushed the butt free to fall, then delicately set the toe of a patent-leather shoe on the glowing spot.

He stood before the mirror, which he could not see now, and breathed, slowly and harshly, the dark air.

Whatever broke it, what was broken was the dream, with a sense, on waking, that something had been literally broken, like a plate dropped, or like a windowpane shattered because an old rotten window cord snapped when you touched the sash, and the sash fell. In that instant of waking, even before any consciousness of what the dream had been, she was flooded by that sense of the broken, the irremediable: not the numbness now, but the wild sadness that life had once, long ago, for a moment, been.

Then, in that awareness she knew what the dream had been. It had been a dream of Cy Grinder, not the thickening man in the torn red mackinaw standing on top of the bridge over the roaring creek, waving a bow against a darkening sky and calling to her some insult she could not make out, but of Cy Grinder young, towering above her as she lay, smiling down at her with the smile that had always made her want to cry with joy, now towering above her while his nakedness, which she had never seen and had dreamed only now, glimmered white against the darkness of the world.

He had been about to reach out to her, to say her name, but then the dream broke, and there was the wild sadness, followed by the flash of rage that she had had to have the dream at all. For she hadn't dreamed of Cy Grinder all these years. Oh, why did everything have to begin again!

Then, in that moment of waking in the dark, she thought, with a grim satisfaction, that the noise that woke her had been Sunder. But she could hear his breathing, and though it was ragged, it was not the kind of ragged it was after he had made his noise. So she lay listening.

Then she heard the noise again, knowing suddenly that it was the same kind of noise that had waked her. Somebody had bumped something, somebody upstairs, toward the front of the house. Even before that thought was framed, however, the cold prickles ran down from the back of her neck down the spine.

For she knew who it was. Her mind saw what it was: *him.*

Him, for he didn't have a name, at least not in her mind. Even if he had told her his name, as she knew he had, she never called

him by it; she rejected the name. He was no name, he was the shape
with no name: *him.*

She lay under the weight of the blankets, staring up where the
ceiling was, listening for something to move far off up there in the
dark hollowness of the house.

After he had fumbled his way down the dark stairs, he stopped
in the hall outside the door to that room, and listened.

There was no sound. He shrugged his shoulders. What was behind the door? Just that woman. And whatever — whoever — made
that noise like a sheep being slaughtered.

All at once, in the darkness of his head, as in the darkness of a
closed room, he saw the woman, this very instant, standing behind
the door just the other side, listening. He knew she was there.

He moved down the hall to his own door, and then, with his hand
yet on the knob, was, on the instant, totally convinced that when
he had entered the room tonight after supper, he had closed the
door. Somebody had opened the door while he slept. He could
see it happening.

The face, faintly white in the dark hall, had leaned close to the
panel of his shut door, listening for his breath. The white hand
had been laid to the knob, it had begun to turn the knob without
any sound.

He shivered.

For he was seeing, suddenly, the place laid for him tonight on the
table, the pink-and-white plate, the knife and fork and spoon, the
cup, all there on the red-check oilcloth that was beginning to show
gray where it was cracked, the table and everything there under the
blankness of light.

So she had known he would come back.

And as the knowledge of her knowledge filled his head, he felt
totally without defense.

When, at first light, his throat dry and head throbbing, he woke
up, the thought was already in his head, as though it had been waiting for him to wake up. She must have known everything. If not,
why, when she knew that the car was gone, hadn't she telephoned
the police? There was a telephone. How could she know he wasn't
running away with her car?

Suppose she had called the police.

He lay there sweating, thinking how near he had actually come to running away. He had got a hundred miles, up into Kentucky, running blind. Running blind, not from anything, not to anything, just blind, to be away. He had got up there in Kentucky before he remembered what day it was. It was the day to go to Parkerton.

So he had turned around and gone to Parkerton.

Suppose he had forgot Parkerton, and everything, running blind. He started sweating again.

"Well, Puss-Face," the man had said, cocking back in the swivel chair and removing the cigar from his mouth, "so you made it?"

"Yes, sir," he had said.

"Well, five minutes more and I'd a been long gone, Puss-Face. You expect me to wait round all night for you, Puss-Face?"

"No, sir," he had said, and later, down in the street, he had felt faint. He had leaned for a full minute against a building. He hadn't eaten all day, but he knew that was not the reason. It was the idea of coming here, and finding the door locked.

But on the way back from Parkerton to the valley, he had to keep fighting the impulse to turn off the road, to run blind, anywhere, let anything happen, no matter what. Then he kept thinking a drink would help. He hadn't had a drink in three years. He had got so he never missed it. But now the need was growing in him. The spit grew at the base of his tongue. There was a package store on the highway.

Back in the car he unscrewed the tin cap of the bottle and was about to put it to his mouth, when he decided he'd better get off the highway before he had the drink. So he waited until he had reached the Corners, and had turned off the highway up the valley. Then he took two deep drags, with no chaser, burning, raw.

He drove on up the valley, the feeble lights of the car muffled in the ground mist. It was going to rain, and he kept thinking how it had been raining the first time he came up this road, walking beside the roar of the creek. The creek was roaring now, and he was coming back.

He drove slower and slower, so slow the old car began to jerk and heave in high gear. He was approaching the spot where that *Sandy Claws cornuto, quello dannato,* had come flying in the air, and the arrow had whanged.

There was the house looming ahead, on the left. No light showed there. For an instant, he wondered what had happened, then realized that there was never any light in the front. Slowly, the tires slipping and sliding in the muddy ruts, the car moved on. He felt like a man who lets the reins go slack, lets the horse follow its head, in the dark.

The car had gone on past the house. It went up the valley. Until he saw the light of the shack he refused the knowledge of where he was. Now he pulled on past the shack, found a place to turn, turned, and came back past it, his lights off. Then he stopped. He fixed his eyes on the light in the shack yonder. Between him and the light he saw the faint glint of reflection on the slick, wet ground of the yard. He felt for the bottle on the seat, found it, and with his eyes still on the light, drank.

He sat there a long time, watching the light. Now and then he took a drink. He thought of himself, alone in his car, watching the light over there, through the rain, in the place where the girl was.

At last he started the car and drove on back to the big house. Through the window of the kitchen he saw the woman standing by the range, with a saucepan hanging off her limp hand.

He watched her from the deeper dark of the cedar under which he stood for protection from the last rain, and suddenly he knew he was trying to know what was going on in her head.

Christ-a Jesus, he thought, peering in at her from the darkness of the cedar, *Christ-a Jesus.*

If that morning, she had only said something. If she had moved. If she had fought him. If she had scratched him. If she had cried out. If — if anything —

Then, standing there under the cedar, peering in at the woman by the range, who was wrapped in that old baggy brown sweater, he saw the image of the body glimmering on the floor, motionless, as it had been that morning, when, after it was over, he had risen and was looking down at her, where she had been dropped to lie in limp and awkward beauty. Her eyes had been closed. She had never even opened her eyes.

It was like she was not real.

No — and at the instant of that realization his breath froze in his throat — it was like you, you yourself, were not real.

Then, through the window, he saw the table, under the electric bulb, the plate laid on it.

He stood there and waited, but he knew that he would, in the end, go in.

And she had known it all the time.

He lay there in bed while the dawn light hardened into day, and again, in his head, saw everything that had happened. It was all happening again — right up to this very minute, this very second. And he thought: *If I stay in this bed right now, nothing can never 'appen no more.*

He lay on his back and pulled the sheet up to his upper lip, just under his nose, drew it tight, and closed his eyes. This way, nothing could happen.

But, in the end, he got up.

He put on the old cut-down red bathrobe and went out into the hall, stopped before opening the back door, lit a cigarette, and knew that that door behind him had come open, and the eye at the crack was watching him. He went on out, to the privy.

On his way back to the house, he stopped, lit another cigarette, and stood there. The morning was clear and bright. The puddles from the rain of the night before, standing among the brown, sparse stems of grass, now glittered with skim ice. He stood there in the brightness of the world, with the smoke oozing slow from his nostrils, to pale to nothing in the sunlight. He stared at the window of his room. This side of the house was in shade, and the window was, in the gray paintlessness of the wall, a rectangle of darkly glimmering opacity.

He had to stand out here in the cold, not even dressed, waiting — waiting for what? — because that *cretina,* she might be in there, in his room. With anger there grew, too, a bitter stubbornness. He would go to the kitchen, he'd make the fire, he'd sit there and wait, he'd eat something, anything, to hell with coffee even, and wait till she came. He'd outwait her. That would show her.

He would not even go to look in the window to see if she was there.

But he did.

And there she was as before, crouching on the floor, wearing that faded flannel nightgown, mended now, he could see that much, her head leaning against the side of the bed, the eyes closed.

Idiota, he thought. He'd show her. He'd go to the kitchen and wait.

That was what he would have done. If she had not risen on her
knees and, with eyes still closed, groped for the pillow where his
head had lain.

The hands found the pillow, and drew it toward her. Then, still
on her knees, the eyes closed, she buried her face in it, in the very
spot where his head had lain.

With his vision of this act, another kind of anger rose in him,
more murderous but mixed with desolation, powerlessness, and
yearning.

Then he was racing toward the back door, then down the hall.
He did not hear what noise his feet made on the boards.

All happened as it had happened before.

With one difference:

Afterwards, the clothes he seized were not his own, the town
clothes, but what she had cut down for him to wear here.

He went to the kitchen, dressed, made the fire, and went out and
busied himself splitting stove lengths until he calculated that breakfast would be ready and his place laid.

If, earlier, work had been a flight, a refuge, now it became a fury.
That was what all the days were — a blind occupation. He had
long since replaced the broken pane of the window in his room.
Now he set about doing windows wherever needed, and many were
needed. He prowled the attic on rainy days to spot leaks, and on his
next trip to Parkerton bought five bales of shingles and patched the
roof. He bought paint and began painting the outside of the house
— the part, at least, under the protection of the high porch. When
he got beyond that, he found too much clapboarding in need of replacement, and all the wood too soggy with damp to take paint. He
would have to wait for warm weather to dry things out. But nevertheless he gave a second coat to the wall under the protection of the
porch, put a few boards in the porch floor, and laid on blue deck
paint. Then he began, bit by bit, to replace the worst pieces of
clapboarding.

But he interrupted that to work on the bathroom. One morning,
high on the ladder, ready to set a length of clapboard, he remembered the bathroom he had found the night he came back and
wandered in the dark house. Immediately, on impulse, he came
down the ladder, got the car, and drove to the Corners, where the

store was, and bought a flashlight. He came back, found a board-covered opening in the rough stone foundation, and crawled under.

It took all day to trace the pipes that led to that bathroom. For one thing he began by wasting time on those that led upstairs; for another, there was painfully little space for crawling. In some places the heavy timbers came down so low he had to inch along, belly down, thrusting himself forward with elbows and toes, driving his head forward through the veils of ancient cobweb that hung down into the jerky beam of the flashlight.

Now and then, he would roll over and stretch out to relieve the cramp of his muscles. Once, lying on his back with the light out, breathing the dry, cool dustiness of that secret earth, not drowsing, wide awake in that darkness, he felt a lassitude creep over him, rising from the earth beneath him, like water rising, and then, as the deliberate flood seemed to close over him in the dark, he knew that it was peace, a nothingness that was, strangely, a kind of sweetness. It would be sweet to lie here forever.

Flickeringly, he remembered what life had been long ago, the burning of whiskey in the throat, the smell of a girl, the roar of the exhaust as a car plunged at night into the tunnel of its own flung beams, the excitement of a fight, the sight of his own face in the mirror as the comb moved glossily through the blackness of his hair, the sway of colored lights in a dance hall while the music kept on and on. Like those flickering lights in the dance hall — that was what his whole life, what everything, had been.

Was that what it had been? A bright whirling and swaying, a hunting for something, a running after something, a going and coming and not knowing why? And now was everything this easy, after all? To lie in the dark, and not want anything?

He must have dozed off. For suddenly, he jerked into wakefulness, in the dark, not knowing where he was, then knowing, and knowing that the flashlight was gone, and knowing that the mass and weight of the house was over him, was coming slowly down on him.

He was groping wildly for the flashlight. He found it, and the beam struck forth to show, in their actuality and not in his nightmare vision, the timbers, the earth itself which, because the flashlight lay so close to the surface, was marked by unpredictable pools of shadow reaching from him, and the gray draperies of cobweb receding, timber after timber, into darkness.

He knew it had all been crazy, that panic.

I fix pipe, he said to himself. *Me, I fix 'im.*

If he just kept his mind on that, everything would be all right.

He found where the line from the kitchen had been disconnected and capped. Then he found the old leak. You could spot it by the delicate concentric circles where, long back, water had dripped on the undisturbed earth.

The work on the line meant two trips to Parkerton, to get pipe and rent tools to cut and thread it, and then carry the tools back. The work meant cutting off the water for the house. He had traced the supply line, a gravity feed from a big spring with a stone storage basin, up in the woods on the rise beyond the house. There was a valve there, beat up and corroded, but still workable. When he told the woman to stock up on water, he was going to cut it off to do some work, he made no further explanation.

He never explained more than he had to. If he did not explain, he protected something. He protected the fact that he was himself.

The first morning after he had fixed the line, he woke up with the immediate thought that he could go to the bathroom, he would not have to go down the hall, would not have to stand to light a cigarette at the porch door, would not have to know that that other door was opening a crack, would not have to suffer the eye at the crack spying on him. Then, back from the bathroom, standing in the hall, he wondered if, when he opened the door, she would be there.

His hand on the doorknob, he thought back on his confusion of feeling the first time he had not found her in his room when he opened the door. He hadn't known what he felt. He had dressed and gone to the kitchen, and there she was, silent, the eyes on him, the place laid for him. For five days it had been like that, and he had adapted himself to it, had found some relief, a sense of hope that life would offer something new, unexpected, and even joyful, though what he could not know.

Then one morning, the sixth morning, she had been there again, and he knew it had been her period. So everything was as it had been, and he did not know what he felt about that, either.

Now, with his hand on the knob, he remembered the first morning when she had not come, and opened the door.

But there she was. On the bed, on her back, the sheet to her chin, her eyes closed, lying like dead, waiting for the violation, waiting to be used, dropped, flung aside, all in silence except for the labor of breath, her own breath tight and hissing with the effort of control.

The bed — for long back now, that had begun. One morning he had opened the door, had seen the form crouching beside the bed, and had felt the burst of anger, had heard his own voice saying: "You crazy? — you make all time on floor? In bed if you wan' Angelo do you big-a — "

He used the dirty word, saw her eyes snap open, staring up at him, dark eyes sudden in the white face, and, in that instant wide, wild, and glittering as though surprised at seeing him and his obvious intention.

"Up!" he commanded; and with that glance still on him, she rose, and touched a hand to the bed.

"Bed," he said, "you get on bed."

With a cranky, tentative motion, like an old woman, her face now averted from him, she obeyed.

But otherwise, the ritual remained unchanged.

The ritual of work remained unchanged, too. After breakfast, with the last gulp of coffee still hot in his throat, he would shove the chair back and go out the back door, not even pausing to light his cigarette until he was free. If it was raining, he stood on the back porch, sucking on the cigarette, waiting for a break that would let him go to his task. If the break did not come, he would put on the old black slicker he had found in a closet and tear out for the barn to skulk there in that shadowy dampness, pretending to sort the debris that, over the years, had accumulated there.

Pretending, for he had already done all that was really needed. Not that the pretense was designed to deceive the woman in the house. No, he was not concerned to deceive her, but he had to deceive his own hands, make them think that the movements they made had a purpose. For if he deceived the hands into making those movements, then they, by those movements, could deceive him and he would not be left, occupationless, to sit in the chill shadows of the barn, with a cigarette in his mouth, with the cigarette butts accumulating on the packed earth about his feet, staring out the half-open door, up the slope where the woods were, at the gray, sopping sky. If he did not play that trick on the hands, then they would not play that trick on him, and if they did not, he would have to sit and think how things had once been and how they could never again be anything but what they now were.

Sometimes at noon, whether it was raining or not, whether he was in the barn or doing some job outside, he did not go to the house to eat. Not that he would have had to see her, for from the first, even if she had been visible outdoors, hanging wash, she would always be put out of sight by noon. In the kitchen would be the cold food laid out, a pot of coffee keeping hot on the back of the range, the kitchen empty and silent. Even so, he might keep at his job, or if it was raining and he was in the barn, he might keep watching his hands make those careful motions which pretended to be a job.

But the time always came when he would have to go to the house. He would avoid the kitchen, now that he did not have to get water for washing, and enter by the door to the back hall, and go to the bathroom which he had brought back to service. He would strip to the waist and wash himself, then lay out his razor, hoping that some water was still warm in the coil built into the kitchen range. When the shaving was over, he would comb his hair and then lean forward to inspect his face in the mirror — oval, olive-swarthy, dark-eyed, even-featured except for a fullness of the lips. Looking at it, he would think: *Puss-Face.*

That was what that man always called him. Someday he would kill that man.

After shaving he would take a drink from the bottle he now kept in his room, just one good one, put on a town shirt, and go to the kitchen. His place would be laid, one place on the red-check oil-cloth. The woman would be over there by the range, waiting.

But one night he took three pulls of the bottle before going to the kitchen, and when he entered and saw her staring at him, he went straight toward her, seized her and pressed his mouth hard and probingly against hers.

Releasing her, he stared into her face.

"*Santa Madonna,*" he cried out, "why you no talk?"

Nothing changed.

"*Santa Madonna,*" he cried, and heard his own voice thinning as into a wail in distance, "who you, please? Who you are?"

Just then the sound came. If he had not left the door open to the hall, they could not have heard it.

"Who that is?" he demanded, seizing her by the shoulders and shaking her. "You think Angelo stay here and no know!"

Then he shoved her from him. "I go see," he said, and strode toward the hall door. At the door he paused, and looked back. "I go see," he affirmed.

If she had said for him to stay, or even to go, he would have gone. But she said nothing. So in his rage and humiliation, he closed the door and went to sit down at the table.

After supper, he always went immediately to his room. There he lay down, and by the bare bulb of an old table lamp he had found in the barn and now kept on a chair by the bed, read one of his magazines. He had found them, stacks of them, in the armoire in the room upstairs with the tester bed — *True Detective, Argosy, Black Mask, True Confessions, Gangland, Ellery Queen,* dozens of titles, hundreds of copies, some dating back thirty-five years, none more recent than 1945, the pages gone yellow, the paper ready to flake under a touch, the colors of cover illustrations fading out, the dresses of girls and the shapes of cars in the pictures all looking funny now. He had brought the magazines down to his room, load after load, to stack along the wall, to the right of his bed. Now dozens of them were on the left side, where, at random, they had been flung. For when he had finished one, had really finished it, reading it steadily, even the advertisements, he flung it over to the left side.

It was not that he would have been able to identify a single story read a week, or perhaps even a night, earlier. He sensed this fact, but sensed, too, that the very blur of similarity was something he craved. The excitement evoked in the blur of violence and lust was allayed only to be reevoked by a new story which, in turn, would be nothing more than the old cycle repeated, the tale always empty of meaning but charged always with the heavy atmosphere of gunsmoke and sweetly sweating flesh.

For it was all a dream, like the dream his own past now seemed to be, and the two dreams could merge into one dream, not to be differentiated, and in that dream he was strong, he was real, men fell beneath the impact of his fist or the bullet he fired, and white arms stretched toward him, and red lips gone slack and distorted with yearning piteously called out his name — Angelo, Angelo.

Sometimes he would lie on the bed and think how there had

once been somebody named Angelo. People had called that name. But now only in a dream.

At a certain point, it might be in the middle of a story or while his eyes were fixed on an advertisement, he would let the magazine fall to his chest, and would fumble to locate the little radio he had got secondhand in Parkerton. Lying there, propped on a pillow, with the cigarette hanging from his lips, he would hunt for a station, and when he found the music he wanted, with the radio turned down till the music was little more than a whisper in a dream, a murmur coming from beyond the further edge of silence, he would lie back and watch the smoke unspooling upward in the naked light. He would be thinking what it would be like to be in a world where that music was.

He would lie there with closed eyes, while the music murmured from beyond the further edge of silence, and try to remember something — anything — that had once happened to him. Shapes, gestures, sounds would come into the darkened theater of his head, but colors, they never came. He knew that there had been colors, but the colors had been bleached away, and behind the shut eyes he watched the gray flickering of a world that had once been real.

Or as he watched the flickering, he would try to remember what feelings he had had in that world when it was real. But it seemed that all feeling, like the colors, had been drained away from these stances and movements of memory. Then, one night, listening to the rustle of music from the radio, he became aware that he did not even know what feelings he had now.

He was suddenly aware of this, but was not aware that he had been trying, in fact, not to have any. Day by day, he watched his hands in the fury of occupation, and tried not to have any feeling. He ate food and tried not to taste it. He looked at the woman standing by the range. He rose in the morning and evacuated, he came back to the room to find her there, he did what he would do, and everything was like everything else.

Was this the way things always were in the end? If all you had out of living was the memories you couldn't remember the feelings of, did that mean that your living itself, even now while you lived it, was like that too, and everything you did, even in the instant of doing, was nothing more than the blank motions the shadow of your body made in those memories which now, without meaning, were all you had out of the living and working you had done before?

He thought how his mother's hands had always been moving, all the years, and how he had watched them move. He thought of his father's hands. He had watched their hands moving, and their eyes as they looked down at their own hands, and he had sworn that he would never be like that. And he had not been, not for a while, but now he himself was like that.

He remembered how, in the last years, his father had sat in a chair in the kitchen, far off in Savoca, in Sicily, a dying hulk, and the hands had not been moving then, lying swollen on the knees. But a foot, always the right foot, had always been twitching, just a little, inside the torn felt slipper, with the big toe sticking through, twitching with a rhythmic regularity. The old man sat with eyes fixed on the floor, and everything, everything in the world, was just that twitch that you waited for, and then it came, always in that feeble and merciless regularity that made you want to get up and yell and run out into the street, anywhere.

Now night after night, remembering his father and the motion of the foot, he would rise from the bed, and go from the room. He would go upstairs and wander about, and in the end, shut off the flashlight and stand breathing the dark air that was harsh with dustiness and cold. It was always the big front room with the tester bed where he cut off the light. In the dark he would move toward a window and look off in what he knew was the direction of the ruined dairy house.

The first night when he wandered upstairs, he came back to his room, to find the radio still emitting its whispery music. He seized it, lifted his arm high as though to hurl it from him. But he lowered it, turned it off, and in the silence stared down at it, there in his hand.

On subsequent nights, if he had forgotten to turn it off, he merely picked it up, turned the switch, and then undressed as quickly as possible, and lay down to sleep.

At least, in this world of changelessness, where nothing had ever happened and nothing would ever happen, he could, if he waited long enough, sleep. For he knew that the dream that used to wake him in the sweat of fear and guilt did not come now. The dream might be there, waiting in the dark to be dreamed. But now, night by night, he closed his eyes and knew that, at least not yet, he would not have to dream it.

He knew that he was living another dream, and the living of that dream was the price he paid not to dream the other.

Back in the fall, sorting out the plunder in the barn, he had found a 12-gauge shotgun. It was old and rusty, but he dismantled it, soaked it in kerosene, worked it over with steel wool and oiled it. Now in the protracted spell of hard clear weather that came in January, he would slip away in the afternoon and go hunting for rabbits. He felt some uneasiness in breaking from the rigid ritual of his occupations, but now, in this new brightness of sky, he could not stand the proximity of the house. When he came into the kitchen at dusk and flung down a couple of rabbits, gutted and peeled, he was doing something that seemed to expiate whatever had, in the afternoon, needed expiation.

The first day he wandered over the ridge east of the house, and into the woods and old fields beyond, but each day as he made the loop homeward, he moved closer and closer to the other woods to the south and west, toward the road. On the fifth day, it was still daylight when he crouched behind deadfall at the edge of the open ground where the dairy house was.

There was no movement in that space. A squirrel chittered somewhere, far off. After a time, a single crow, very high above the spot where he crouched, labored, in a stubborn, methodical motion, across the visible sky. The glitter of sun, at that height, on the blackness of those moving wings, made him realize the thickening shadow of the woods.

He rose and took the track toward the house.

When he came around the corner of the barn, he saw the cream-colored Buick convertible. He had seen that car three times before. It had come every month. Peering out from the protection of the barn, he waited until the man in the gray suit and gray overcoat came out and got in the Buick.

Suddenly, with the powerful glide of its take-off, the car disappeared beyond the house, so suddenly he was not sure it had been there at all. Staring at the place where it had been and was not now, he thought that if he had not gone away, or if going away, he had not gone into those other woods, then the car would not have been there.

But he knew that thinking that was crazy.

The car came every month.

THEODORE WEESNER

Stealing Cars

(FROM AUDIENCE)

ALEX HOUSMAN WAS DRIVING a Buick Riviera. The Buick, copper-tone, white sidewalls, was the model of the year, a '59, although
the 1960 models were already out. The upholstery in the car was
black, the windshield was tinted a thin color of motor oil. The
Buick's heater was issuing a stale and odorous warmth, but Alex
remained chilled. He had walked several blocks through snow and
slush to the car, wearing neither hat nor gloves nor rubbers. The
steering wheel was icy in his hands, and he felt icy within, throughout his veins and bones. Alex was sixteen; the Buick was his fourteenth car.

The storm was early to Michigan's Thumb. It was not yet November. The previous day had been predictably autumn, drizzling
all day, leaves still hanging apple-colored overhead among the city's
black wires, and lying soggy underfoot. But by evening a chilling
breeze had begun moving through the city, blowing over the wide
bypasses and outerdrives. In the morning the snow covering was
overall. It was five or six inches deep, as wet as a blanket soaked in
water, as gray and full in the sky as smoke from the city's automobile factories.

A cigarette Alex had not wanted so early in the morning was
wedged in the teeth of the ashtray drawer. He could not remember
having lighted it, and he thought to snuff it out, but made no move
to do so. The dry smoke reached over the dashboard like a girl's
hair in water. Taking the cigarette up, discovering either weakness or nervousness in his fingers, he drew his lungs full and replaced it in the teeth of the drawer. The smoke seemed to burn his

eyes from within. He squinted as they watered, and shivered. Before him the windshield wipers slapped back and forth quietly, slapping the melting snow to streams trailing to the sides. The view was on again, off again.

He saw that he was heading out of town. He had crossed a line somewhere and now he was no longer going in the direction of Central High School, he was going away. There was little traffic on his side of the street but on the other side crept a double line of cars and buses. Their headlights sparkled by, in the gray and white of the storm. Glimpsing himself going in the wrong direction once again, on an edge of consciousness, he turned to the radio to search for music. Before long, still turning the dial, he was not listening to the stations. Soon he removed his hand. Driving. On the thought alone, the tediousness of driving raised its head.

He drove on. He pressed the accelerator and the heavy Buick moved out faster. He had switched license plates the first night he took the Buick, but he had been driving it ten or twelve days now, too long, he knew, to keep a car so easily identified. He knew he should trade the Buick for a Chevrolet, if only to save on gas money. He knew it every day, but he did not trade it. His father left him a dollar bill on their kitchen table each morning for his lunch and bus fare, and he suffered through giving up the dollar (for gas, never oil; regular, never ethyl) as he suffered through other things he had given up, other things he was leaving undone.

Alex had been driving to the country schools since September. He had discovered the first one by accident, merely driving one day when he should have been in his own; thereafter he searched them out intentionally. In easy fantasies, imagining he was the owner of the car, he drove around the corners and fronts of the strange schools in the movements of their lunch hours, to let himself be seen. Riding a copper-tone stallion. He returned to one school or another for several days running, picking out a girl and looking at her, and looking for her, and partially following her, returning to the same place the next day to watch for her to appear, almost never speaking or approaching. Then, frightened by the 4-H football types in threes and fours who always began to stare at him and say things to each other, he went on to another school, to Flushing and Linden and Grand Blanc and Atlas and Montrose. They were schools only an eighth or a tenth the size of his city high school — two or three hundred students versus three thousand

— but there had been a wonder and excitement those fall days of discovering that the students were, incredibly, always fifteen and sixteen and seventeen, with the same recognizable bodies and backs and leg lengths and postures, except, when they turned, for their faces. Their faces were different: unknown and unknowing. He drove among them, and walked among them. He intentionally parked his Chevrolet Bel Air or his Buick Riviera under their eyes, left the car and reentered the car under their eyes, able to see himself in these moments as he imagined he was seen by them, as a figure from a movie, a stranger, some newcomer come to town, some new cock of the walk with a new car, with a plume of city hair.

Fifteen miles from the city he took the familiar ramp off the highway and continued right on the road to Shiawassee. Within a half-mile he passed the side road down which Eugenia Rodgers lived, down which she had walked several times to meet him, for she was not allowed to have boys pick her up at her house.

His brother, Howard, also lived in this direction. Howard, who was three years younger, lived with their mother and her second husband some twenty-five miles from the city, where they operated a lakeside tavern. Alex did not know where they lived, but he knew where the tavern was. He was thinking of Howard, now, trying to call up images of him, trying to make the images stand still as he drove. What would Howard think if he saw him in the Buick? The thought of seeing Howard, of actually seeing him, made Alex shudder.

He leaned closer over the steering wheel, to concentrate on the on-again, off-again view presented by the wipers. In the weeks that he had been driving to Shiawassee he had thought of Howard a few times, but he had never considered going there, to Lake Nepessing. Nor did he plan on going there now. What he saw of himself he did not wish his brother to see. He had not seen Howard since a day late in the summer, three years before, when their mother, a stranger — they had not seen her in five or six years — came and took Howard away in her car, carrying his possessions, his clothes. in cardboard boxes. It was a miserable thing to remember, and shuddering again, Alex admitted to himself only that it had been a bad time, a bad week, and looked away from thinking about it. But the idea of seeing Howard became more pleasant, and he let it have its pleasant way, let it occupy him, and drove on, with no intention of going there.

Eugenia Rodgers was his age, sixteen, although he had told her he was nineteen. Nineteen seemed a proud age to his mind; sixteen possessed no such quality. He had met Eugenia, or picked her up, several weeks before, and now, even if it was no more than nine-thirty or ten and she would be in school, her town and her country school were a place to drive to, a place to believe he was headed for, rather than the lake beyond, rather than nowhere.

If he saw Eugenia he might apologize, after a fashion. He had picked her up at school two days before, during her lunch hour, and when they had driven into the country, to a lake, and the lunch hour was ending, he had refused to take her back. It had been autumn then, two days ago. They had gone, as they had several times before, to a lakeside park which was deserted in October. She wanted to go back, because if she missed again, the teacher was going to call her mother again, and her mother, who had remarried not long ago, was going to confine her. But he had refused to take her back, not when she begged, not when she let him feel her breasts, not when she became angry and started walking. He followed her with the car, and stopped before her on the shoulder of the road, watching her through the rearview mirror as she bent forward to begin running, pressing the accelerator as she came close. He convinced her twice more that he was stopping to pick her up, and left both times. The next time he stopped, she walked past the car and did not look at him, and he let her walk perhaps a quarter of a mile before he went after her again. When she finally got into the car, it was nearly two o'clock. She sat still and said nothing, and he looked at her now and then as he drove. In town, when he stopped at a corner, she left the car, slammed the door, and he had not seen her since. He felt like a fool, remembering, but he knew if he told her some story, that he had killed someone, had hit them with the car, or that he had killed his father, that she would listen, and would not believe him, but would, in her way, forgive.

He decided to go ahead and drive to Lake Nepessing. He did not care now; he felt he could talk to Howard somehow. What did it matter what he said, what they said, what they did not say? The idea of actually seeing Howard swept through him and from the tinted interior of the car, in the surrounding whiteness, he began to fantasize that there had been a catastrophe, that a war had come home, that he and Howard were two who were lost and all they needed in the world was to find each other, that with their ratlike cunning they would survive, they would effect a new life. Automobiles, schools, families, all would vanish. They would effect life itself.

Lake Nepessing was both a lake and a village, east on a winding road off the highway, north of Shiawassee. By the time he was on the road and undeniably headed for the village, his resolve had faded some, but not enough to make him turn back. The tavern was several miles past the village. He passed houses here and there along the winding road, then there were houses along both sides, and then a sign:

LAKÉ NEPESSING

SPEED LIMIT

25 MPH.

He drove slowly, beginning to feel nervous again.

Driving through the town he noticed a woman leaving a car, keeping her head down as she stepped over to the sidewalk, and he wondered if she might be his mother. He wondered, given all the times he had walked on sidewalks in the city, if she had ever passed him? Had she known she was passing him? It did not matter if she did; he felt neither love nor hate for her. If he felt anything it was a distant curiosity. He did not want to talk to her; but he'd like to see her to look her over without being seen.

The tavern had not opened yet. The front windows were dark and there were no cars or tire marks in the parking lot in front. The neon sign LAKEVIEW TAVERN was unlighted and hardly visible inside one of the windows, although some small neon beer signs along the windowsill were lighted, Blatz and Falstaff, red and yellow. He had all but stopped on the highway, and now he pulled over, into the parking lot. He sat in the car with the motor running and looked around. He felt as nervous as he had the first time he took a car. Then, as if climbing further into the thin branches of a tree, he opened the door, and left the motor running, stepped out into the snow and damp air. He heard a car coming on the highway behind him, and stood still, without looking, as it passed.

At the dark glass of the tavern he held his hands like blinders. He had never seen the inside of the tavern. Empty of people it looked disappointingly worn and threadbare. The lights over a shuffleboard were out, but behind the bar, among mirrors and bottles and glasses, a Miller's Highlife clock was lighted. It was twenty-three minutes after ten, the second hand revolving. For no reason, he tapped the window lightly with his fingers. However loud the tapping seemed, no one appeared, nothing happened. There was his reflection in the dark glass, in the gray air, and it occurred to him that the figure he saw was lost in some way he could not understand.

Against the rising of nervousness he walked around the end of the tavern, stepping through the unmarked slush, along a driveway which led down behind the building to a boat launching ramp. A T-shaped dock was in the water, and an old red gas pump stood on the bank. A rowboat was in the water, moving slightly, lifting a little toward shore and out again on a slack rope. On the dock he looked down into the water; it was more green here than black. Crouching to see better, he felt the snow fall on the back of his neck. The sky reflected its gray colors on the surface, and as he leaned forward his face and shoulders reflected darkly. The shreds of snow parachuted onto the water, shriveled gray and disappeared; his mind was ranging off as if in judgment of things the size of the universe, and of himself, but of nothing he could see in particular.

Turning his neck down, looking directly into his reflection, he found he could see through his face into the water. He worked his reflection like a flashlight to reveal the bottom. It was still autumn down there, brown and green, the sand blond, the moss hair wavering black from green stones, from the dock piles. Two nearly translucent fish, no deeper or longer than a finger, hovered unconcerned. A slight seizure came turning into his stomach and he leaned over all the more, bent his head between his knees to tighten his stomach against it. He glimpsed the sweep of his trouble and it was so wide and unknown, his face began trembling while his mind told him nothing.

An hour later he had driven back to Shiawassee. It was a town of five or six blocks of stores, with a movie theater and new parking meters, and with the streetlights lighted under the dark sky. The high school was on Main Street, set back from the street, with two dairy bars directly opposite. The two floors of school windows in the brick building were lighted, the same diamond color through the storm as car headlights. He saw a woman teacher's back close to a window on the second floor. He parked where he always parked to wait for Eugenia, where he could see the door of her school. He did not know what he was going to do and did not think much about it; it was not a new problem.

He sat in the car a long time, smoking and looking around. Then he yawned, yawned within the yawn, and deflated into himself. His eyes watered from exhaustion; they itched and he rubbed them. He had not known he was so tired. He considered lying over on his side in the front seat, to sleep, but did not. It was dangerous, inviting to strolling policemen. Still he slumped in the seat, and his head bobbed; he was waiting for Eugenia Rodgers to come out, and not waiting for her either, but merely waiting.

He heard no bells ring, but at last, as he was watching, the main door opened and two boys came out. Then a girl came out, alone, and he was not sure at first that it was her. He looked at the door again, which did not close all the way as one student after another kept it swinging open. Then he looked at the girl again and realized it was her. She walked with her face down against the snow, without a hat, her coat collar turned up and her shoulders high against her neck.

The coat: she was wearing the coat he had given her. It had been in the back seat of one car or another, a lady's camel's-hair coat with a small chain sewn inside the collar. He had forgotten the coat. It was too large for her, too long, and she walked with her hands drawn into the sleeves. He imagined her fuzzed and ratted sweater, her thickness of lipstick, the odors of her neck and hair, her large and firm breasts, and he felt aroused to see her. If he touched the horn for the slightest beep he knew she would look over at him, and she would turn away from her bearing across the street and walk to the car as she had before, without looking at him on the way. In the car she might pause before looking at him; she might ask for a cigarette and conceal herself with a search for matches, or she might ask for a light and conceal herself in a search for a cigarette, or she might close her eyes and lean over to kiss his ear, to use her tongue, or in their game of profanity she might say *you son of a bitch* and smile her shy and uncertain smile.

He did not touch the horn. He watched her walk along. She, like himself, had not worn boots. He knew she was on her way to one of the dairy bars, and he thought of taking her off somewhere to buy her some warm hamburgers. She usually bought cigarettes with the few coins she scraped or stole from her mother, and she loved hamburgers and French fries. But he watched her pass from view, like a thin song, and was relieved when it was over.

He drove through the students who were too concerned with the snow, or too sure of their world to look for cars, although they seemed to see the Buick's brushing fenders and headlights as he inched among them. Passing the dim windows of the dairy bar he glanced to see if she might see him, and he saw bodies and faces inside the glass, and the gold-flecked backside of one of the pinball machines. He imagined she had seen him; he had never driven away like this from anyone and it gave him a little strength, as if something were finally passing, finally ending.

For a moment, driving through Shiawassee, he saw a clarity in his life, or a determination. His troubles seemed for the moment to focus away. If they did not actually catch him driving a car, how could they prove it? With the cars recovered, would they care? It was a soothing idea; it seemed an easy road to follow. If he could begin, if he drove back to the city, and parked the car, and walked to school — It seemed that if he could begin, if he could stay calm, he could follow the road to its end, and there, where it stood waiting, he could secretly step into a new idea of himself.

He parked the Buick three blocks from the school, where he had parked the day before, and walked back. The snow was turning to rain by now and the leather of his shoes was quickly soaked black. He had thought to clear the car of evidence, to wipe away fingerprints and to empty the ashtray, but for no clear reason he simply parked it and let it stand. About ten minutes remained in the lunch hour, and as he walked back, the feeling of drawing nearer to the school moved through him with the air of a wind rising and falling, rising again.

Within the warmth of the heavy double door, he foolishly stomped his feet on the link-metal mat, splashing the water the mat lay in on his pants legs. He walked on into the first floor corridor. In spite of all else there was a faint feeling of coming home after having been away. Here was the tile floor, the familiar hallways lined with dark green lockers, the whiskey-colored varnished molding, the globes hanging from the ceiling. Except for two girls walking away on the right, the corridor was empty. Far off, also to the right, music was playing, record music from the noon-hour dance in the girls' gym, which because he had never learned how to dance, he had avoided.

His locker was to the left, in the basement near his homeroom. He walked along. Going down the stairs to the basement, he met his homeroom teacher, Mr. Hewitt, coming up. Mr. Hewitt, besides teaching history, was the varsity baseball coach, and a quiet man, neither popular nor unpopular. He nodded lightly at Alex as they passed, then, behind him, Alex heard Mr. Hewitt say, "Alex, were you here this morning?"

Pausing, Alex said, "No."

"Where were you?"

Rather than condemnation there was some kindness in the man's voice, and Alex, stopped on the steps, was affected and weakened by it. He found it hard to look up at Mr. Hewitt, who stood waiting. At last, glancing up, Alex said, "I'm back to school now."

Mr. Hewitt was amused. "You're back. Good, I'm glad to hear that. Where have you been?"

"Nowhere," Alex said. "Just messing around." He stood where he was, looking down again, knowing that Mr. Hewitt was standing there looking at him.

"You have a minute?" Mr. Hewitt said. "I'd like to talk with you."

Alex hunched his shoulders, to say yes, and walked along slightly to the rear of the teacher. They went past Alex's locker, and into the homeroom, and Alex still found it hard to look up. It seemed if he did, something like whimpering would spread from his chest to his throat. He glanced up enough to see that a girl was sitting at a desk in the homeroom, reading, and looked away as Mr. Hewitt said to her, "Would you excuse us a minute, please?"

She did not quite understand, and Mr. Hewitt added after a pause, "We'd like to have a talk in private for a minute."

"Oh," she said. Alex heard her gather her things and heard Mr. Hewitt step over to close the door behind her.

Mr. Hewitt said, "Sit down."

Alex sat down, looking ahead to look away. He saw the bottom half of Mr. Hewitt move to a seat on a desktop. Mr. Hewitt said, "You've gotten yourself into some kind of dilemma, haven't you? Can you tell me what's happened?"

"Oh, I don't know," Alex said quickly.

"Why are you so upset?" Mr. Hewitt said.

Alex hunched his shoulders and lips again, as if not knowing, or not wanting to say.

"Something at home?"

"Nah," Alex said.

"I know you've missed a lot of school lately. What have you been doing? I'm not going to punish you or anything. Perhaps I can help."

"Ah, just a lot of bad things," Alex said. But his voice failed to work clearly — it rose at the end — and he continued to look ahead at nothing, angry with his voice, with himself.

"What kind of bad things? You mean skipping school?"

"No."

"What, exactly? Can you tell me? You feel free to tell me?"

Unable to speak and unable to look, Alex hunched his shoulders again — he didn't know. He felt his lower lip reaching out.

Someone opened the door and came walking in. Alex's view to the door was blocked and he did not look anyway, but Mr. Hewitt said, impatiently, "Please wait outside and close the door."

After a pause, almost in a whisper, Mr. Hewitt said, "Serious bad things?"

Alex nodded once. He did not look up. He knew Mr. Hewitt was studying him and, in his pause, that Mr. Hewitt believed him. For a moment neither of them spoke or moved. Then Mr. Hewitt said, "I'm afraid the class is about to start. But I want you to do me a favor — I want you to come back this afternoon after school — immediately after — will you do that?"

Alex moved his shoulders again and more or less nodded that he would.

He stood up as Mr. Hewitt stood up, but he still could not look at the man. He walked over toward the door without looking back, and heard Mr. Hewitt say behind him, "Don't get too worried now. It'll work itself out."

Alex said nothing; before him through the glass half of the door he saw faces on top of and beside each other, beginning to separate and back off before he touched the doorknob.

He stepped through them without looking at a face, saw bodies before him in the thickening corridor, and heard someone whisper, *"What's going on?"* The bell, ringing suddenly, startled him.

At his locker, facing the wall and holding his lock in his hand, he

tried to tell himself the numbers. They floated close but he could
not quite catch them. He fingered the lock's black face, and beside
him, someone said, "Hey, what was that all about?"

Alex turned and looked at the boy beside his shoulder but could
not think of his name, however familiar his face. *"What?"* he said
to the boy.

The boy spoke again, but Alex's mind was hearing Mr. Hewitt
again and he did not hear the boy. Alex turned his back on him,
as if to conceal the working of his combination, and the boy's
hand fell on his shoulder. "Hey," the boy said, and Alex, not looking back, suddenly, violently, whipped his shoulder to shake off the
hand. The hand did not return. Nor did Alex look back. He continued staring down, hardly seeing the lock cupped in his hand.

In a moment he knew, decided in the knowing, that he was not
going to the afternoon classes. What was he doing here? How could
he have thought of coming to school? Sitting at a desk, sitting there,
sitting there, sitting there. He closed his eyes for a moment, still
facing the wall. But he could not see what he seemed to have been
trying to see. At last he let the lock drop and turned to leave, making his way as calmly as he could through the confusion of corridor
movement, aiming for the side door on the landing, fifty feet
away, aiming for the gray and cold air outside.

Moving down the steps, walking away, he felt the school itself
was watching his back, and he felt diminished being watched. He
hurried along. Some relief came when he made it around a corner
and out of sight of the buildings. His feet were so wet by now they
were squishing water inside his shoes. He thought of going home,
to undress and put on dry clothes, but he would have to wait until
his father had left for work. He walked on. Water was dripping
from his hair, down his neck and down his forehead, and from his
sideburns. Clear water was gathering in the slush over the sidewalk,
small pools in the nickel-colored foot marks. He walked along at
a good pace, thinking he had never been so wet, but it was not until
he was among the stores and buildings of downtown that it occurred
to him that he had left the Buick behind. He had forgotten it
completely. Not sure if it was funny or crazy, he tried again, without
success, to laugh at himself.

In the men's room of the Fox Theater he used paper towels to
wipe his hair and neck and face. Downstairs at the curtained aisle
entrance he removed his coat and walked in. An orange-tinted ad-

vertisement for a dry cleaner was on the screen, but the lights were not yet completely dark. Perhaps fifteen people were scattered about the cavern, and he took a seat as removed from any of them as possible, on the right, the second seat in, opening his coat over the back of the third seat to dry. He never felt at ease until a theater was completely dark — the worst moment was when a movie ended and the lights came on, a moment he usually avoided by turning to watch the end as he walked up the hill of the aisle, slipping out and away before the lights came on. Now, his timing was lucky. Just as he slouched down into the cushioned seat, to conceal himself, the remaining overhead lights dimmed to darkness and *Previews of Coming Attractions* was fanning over the screen.

When the telephone rang, Alex was asleep on the couch in the living room. He was in his underwear, wrapped in an old Indian blanket he and his father kept on the couch, his clothes on the floor beside him where he had pulled them off. The only light in the room came from the opened door to the bathroom, off the living room at the end of a short hallway.

In the blur of his sleep — it had been short, but long enough to thicken his response — he made his way into the kitchen to the phone, and took up the receiver. As he answered, holding his forehead with his other hand, someone began half whispering in a hurry, and it was a moment before he realized it was Eugenia Rodgers. She was in a state of some kind, but he hardly had voice enough yet for talking and asked no questions. And even when he began to understand what had happened and why she had called, he did not want to appear frightened, and said little. More or less whispering, because she was whispering, he said, "Oh," and "They found the coat?" She carried on like a child herself, no longer bluffing, saying something about hating her stepfather for his promise not to tell if she told and about his telling just the same.

He stood, cold in his underwear, and closed his eyes for a moment. Then he opened them. The call seemed to have taken place in a dream from which he was now awakening. Off in the dream Eugenia Rodgers said she had told them "everything" and they had "called the police."

Stepping over to feel the wall for the light switch, he discovered that his hand was weak. The fluorescent lights came faltering on. He squinted. By the wall clock it was nine or ten minutes after ten. The day was refusing to die. He stood still a moment, not knowing

what to do. He remembered the call again as if he had already forgotten. They found the coat. He was thinking she should have said
they found her wearing the coat, and he was thinking he should have
thanked her for calling — he had not — and he should have apologized for the other day. A yawn took him then, journeyed him a
second or two to the tip of his head, made his eyes water with exhaustion. He exhaled to nearly collapsing, envisioned the blue-
uniformed police, and felt far too tired to fight, or to run, or to think,
felt no more than a thought away from anything.

In the bathroom he looked at himself in the mirror. Except that
he had no need of shaving, there was a resemblance to his father
when his father got up from sleeping after he'd been drinking. His
hair, extra thick like his father's hair, was pressed high on the right,
as were the veins on the side of his face. He felt another, stranger
resemblance on the inside — felt gummed and swollen — and he
was beginning to tremble. He tried to decide what to do. Should he
run or should he stay? The idea of running, out in the rain, hitch-
hiking, taking another car, was like something from a movie. He
had no energy to think about it. It only meant more trouble, more
fear. He would stay. His decision was easy. Whatever might happen, he would stay.

He sat on the toilet stool as a place to sit. With his elbows on his
knees he rested his eye sockets and head on the heels of his hands.
He had not forgotten the call, but still he kept remembering. His
father. The thought of his father was different now. It made his
heart wince somewhat. He knew at last what his father would feel.
He would not feel anger, he would have no strong words. His father
would feel as he felt now.

He drew bath water. He did not like baths and usually did his
bathing at school in the showers. But he had not showered for
several days, and besides, a bath was a way to get warm, to wake up.
He drew the tub half-full, wadded his underclothes and laid them
on the floor, and stepped into the water. He did not wash at first,
but lay soaking. The telephone call kept returning to his thoughts,
like something he could still not quite remember, or believe, or
forget. Of all the places of disclosure — his teachers, the basketball
team, Mr. Hewitt, students — only one made him shudder now, his
father.

The police? Would they actually come here, rap on the door, take
him away? Were they coming here now? He moved along more

quickly on the idea, not to be caught in the tub, to be dressed. He wondered if the police would be impressed with his ingenuity of switching license plates, siphoning gas, impressed with his cooperative answers, impressed with him? How could such an intelligent young man, a fine young man, a basketball player, get into such a mess? No, he thought, they would not see it that way.

In his bedroom he put on clean underwear and socks, and a pair of clean khaki pants, and for its little flair of style, his only white shirt. He had grown some since his father gave him money to buy the shirt, together with a tie and a jacket. They were for his ninth grade graduation dance, which he walked to, dateless, to spend the evening in the corner with some other boys who did not know how to dance, telling jokes, less angered or nervous in their presence, leaving the corner only once, when everyone circled around Miss Long, the music teacher, dancing with Mr. Fulton, the metal-shop teacher.

Before the mirror, he combed his hair. He looked better now; he was shiny-faced, combed, in a clean shirt. Something was over; he felt lean. And he began to feel hungry. He had drunk water and pop, but he could not remember having eaten all day. The feeling of hunger was pleasant, but tenuous, and he tried to sustain it. He tried to believe that something was in fact over.

He fixed an elaborate meal: bacon and eggs, chopped onion and green pepper in the eggs, scrambled, rye bread toasted, cold milk. It was the only meal Alex knew how to cook for himself, and his dinner was usually a choice between this and a slab of rubbery cheese on dry bread, or peanut butter, stuffing the sandwich home on his way back down the stairs and down the driveway, clearing his throat somewhere along the way with a bottle of pop.

He ate until he remembered again. He had eaten a little more than half. As he remembered, his stomach filled and his appetite immediately disappeared. He sat at the table, holding his fork aloft, and a moment later he was hurrying to the bathroom. He stood several minutes over the toilet, bending as if to work a snake from his throat, resting his hand against the wall, and bending again. He placed his hand against the wall again finally, trying to even his breath. He believed it now. Sitting on the stool, his stomach cramping but with nothing there to be released, he shivered with goose bumps. He felt as able as a six-year-old; he was afraid.

*

By the clock in the kitchen it was ten minutes to twelve. His father was out of work by now. But his father seldom came home before twelve-thirty, or one, or sometime in the night after the bars closed at two-thirty. He had no thought of telling his father, but like a child alone in a house, he longed for his father to be there.

There were the dirty dishes. They had a pact of always washing their dishes and wiping the table and counter. It was only when things went bad for his father that the dishes began to stack — a mess which started at the start of heavy weekend drinking, so Alex failed as well and the sink soon filled with dishes and cloudy water and bits of egg and bread and cigarette butts floating. When the drinking ended, the kitchen was cleaned. It might be shining some afternoon when Alex came home from school, peace floating comfortably throughout the apartment. Or they might do the job together on a weekend morning, washing the dishes and scalding them with water from the tea kettle, cleaning the refrigerator, mopping the floor, beginning another string of fixing separate meals, washing a separate set of dishes, one leaving it clean for the other.

He left the mess. In the living room he looked down at Chevrolet Avenue from the window, thinking of the police, thinking it might be better if they came first, or at the same time, to counter his having to face his father.

He was in the kitchen again when he heard someone outside. It was still no more than twenty to one, and if it was his father, he was probably sober. He heard the several sounds, the car, the car door slamming, and in a moment, footsteps on the stairway, coming up. He stepped from the kitchen, and reentered as his father was coming through the door. His father looked pleased to see him, and spoke quietly, saying, "You're still up," as he was closing the door.

The sweep of cold air he had admitted passed over the room. Alex felt chilled anyway. His father placed his lunch bucket on the table and removed his coat, a blue denim fingertip-length workcoat. He was clearly sober, and in a calm mood. He rubbed his hands together. "Whatcha doing up so late? Schoolwork?"

Alex nodded.

"Why so glum, chum? Everything okay?"

"Sure."

His father was turning back his cuffs. The odor he carried of the factory was following now over the kitchen, an odor of oil, of machines. He turned to the sink to wash his hands. He wore a khaki shirt, from the army, and blue denim work pants. Alex thought to tell him now, to say, when he turned back, that something was wrong, that he had done something awful, that he was in trouble. But he did not. Always before when he wanted something, some dollars, or permission, or a baseball glove or a white shirt and tie, he approached his father when he was drinking, when he was flushed with love or generosity or something. It was different when he was sober.

Drying his hands, his father said, "You hungry? How about some bacon and eggs?"

"I already ate."

His father was at the refrigerator, removing the carton of eggs and the bacon. Alex began picking up his dirty dishes, but his father said, "Don't worry about those, I'll do them with mine."

"I guess I'll go to bed," Alex said.

"You tired?"

"Oh, a little."

For a moment then, as his father was working at the counter, neither of them spoke. Then Alex said, "I guess I'll go to bed then."

"Sure you won't have a bite to eat?" His father was looking at him now.

"No, I'm pretty tired," Alex said, looking away from looking at his father. He paused a moment, aware that his father was watching him, and then he walked from the kitchen, saying no more.

In his bedroom, not turning on his light, he sat on the edge of his bed to remove his socks, and when they were off, he still sat on the bed. At last, standing, he removed his shirt and pants. He knew his father knew something was wrong, and he knew this was the time to talk to him, but he still could not do it.

Then his father came to the door. Alex was turning his covers down, straightening the pillow of his unmade bed. His father half-whispered from the doorway, "You going to bed now?"

"Yes."

"Well — okay. You have yourself a good sleep now, son."

"I will."

"Good night now."

"Good night."

Still his father paused. Then he said, "You want your door closed?"

"Okay."

"Good night now, son. Have a good sleep." His father closed the door softly, as if not to disturb something.

Pushing in between his old sheets, pulling up his covers, Alex lay on his side and kept his eyes open. In a moment he recognized the sound of the rain on his window, and then he could see more clearly the light which came around his shade from the lights in the street outside. His place in bed grew a little warmer and it was almost comfortable lying there, more comfortable than otherwise, he knew, with his father there, and sober, and a little worried about him. Nor could he help seeing the reversal of things. The misery was usually in those outer rooms, the old records playing, perhaps a sudden smashing of something, a dish, a cup, a fist against a wall or door, or a sudden laugh, or perhaps the throwing open of his bedroom door and the black silhouette of his father in the harsh light of the doorway — *son, hey son, old pal, wake up a minute* — perhaps nothing but the music and his father's silent presence through the night.

He was arrested the next day, but not until school had nearly ended. With no more than five minutes remaining in his last class, geometry, a girl from the principal's office entered the room with a white slip of paper.

It had been a day of questions and answers, of failures to answer. In homeroom that morning, Mr. Hewitt had leaned over his desk and whispered, "What happened to you yesterday? I looked for you."

"I guess I forgot," Alex had whispered back. "Everything's okay now."

Mr. Hewitt had looked at him as he straightened up, as if asking with his eyebrows if Alex was sure, and Alex had signaled with a small nod that he was.

During lunch hour he had walked past the parked Buick. It stood as he had left it, but looking somehow larger. He did not turn his eyes to it as he passed, but looked ahead, as if both he and the car were being watched. He circled the block so as not to pass it again, and this time he crossed the street and entered the lunchroom on the corner. It was filled with bodies and noise, cigarette smoke layering toward the ceiling, the juke box playing. Entering, not knowing just where to go or stand, he overheard someone say something about the noon-hour dance being about to start, and something grated within him, as always.

He recognized the girl entering the room as one who worked in the principal's office. When the teacher, Mrs. Scholls, read the note and looked in his direction, he was not surprised. But he may have been stunned in a way, for he could not quite recall afterward how the next minute or two passed. Mrs. Scholls came to his desk and said softly, "You're to report to the principal's office," and as if transferred by magic, a moment later he was in front of the wooden counter in the office where four or five girls and women were working at desks. He knew Mr. Spencer's office was to the left, but as a girl looked at him for his question, he said, his voice quite clear, "I'm supposed to see the principal." The girl directed him, but he hardly heard her words. In an outer office, a lady at a desk said from a distance, "Alex Housman?" and he nodded that he was.

He stopped at the doorway to the principal's office. He had never been here before. Mr. Spencer, from his desk, and two men, standing, in suits and unbuttoned topcoats, had their faces turned to the door. Alex had never met Mr. Spencer, but the man said, "Come in, Alex."

He took two or three steps into the office, and Mr. Spencer rose and came around his desk as if to shake hands, but stepped past him to close the door.

One of the men was walking over to him, reaching inside his topcoat to remove his wallet, which he flopped open. Alex glimpsed an intricate gold badge, some blue on it, then it was gone. Mr. Spencer was behind his desk again, standing, although Alex had not seen him return. The man introduced himself, Lieutenant Somebody, and the other man, Detective Somebody, but Alex did not listen carefully enough to register their names. He saw their faces looking at him. The lieutenant said, "I guess you know why we're here?"

"Yes," Alex said.

A moment later they were in the corridor, and the first students, the fast-walkers, were already in motion, although Alex had not heard the first bell ring. But classroom doors were open, or opening, classes were on their feet, and the day was ending.

They had to go to the basement for Alex to get his coat from his locker. Both detectives walked with him. He laid his books on the shelf and slipped his coat on, and locked up again. When they returned the way they had come, the corridor had thickened to a slow herding. Alex was not between the two men — both were on his right — but he noticed passing students glancing from him to them and back again, and he tried then to walk without looking into faces. Just before they reached the outside door, the men both slipped on porkpie rain hats. The man who had done the talking, the lieutenant, held the door for them, and when he came up he was on the other side so Alex was in the middle. He thought for the first time to run; it was one thing he could somehow do well.

Their car was parked in the no-parking space where the sidewalk met the street, half blocking the way over to the bus stops and lunchrooms. It was a black car, unmarked except for a small antenna coming from the roof. The mass of students was passing around the car as water passes around a dock pile. The lieutenant opened the rear door for Alex, and when he had stepped in and sat down, the door was slammed behind him. The lieutenant took the seat in front of him, and the other detective, a younger man, went around to the driver's side. The car was dirty, cigarette ashes all around, the floor ribbed metal without carpet; the motor was as noisy and loose as a truck's motor. They nosed through the flow of students in a J-turn, and headed downtown.

He spent several hours in the police station, from about three-thirty until eight or eight-thirty, getting stranded somehow in a shift change and in the dinner hour. A man finally came from the first office, folded handcuffs hanging from his belt, catching Alex smoking, and said, "That's all right — don't put it out. Come on in."

The man was conversational. He asked Alex how he was doing, how was school, and who was going to win the Pontiac game, and he asked many questions about full name and date of birth and address, and then if Alex had a girl friend, and what he wanted to be when he grew up. Alex cooperated. He said he sort of had a girl friend, but that he did not know what he wanted to be when he grew up. They talked about drafting and apprenticeships in the factories and the General Motors Institute of Technology, and at last the man said, "What about the cars? Let's talk about them. When did you take the first one?"

"You mean the exact date?"

"Sure. Do you remember it?"

"Well, it was Friday. The first Friday in September. After school started."

"What was the car?"

"It was a Chevrolet, a Bel Air. Green, two-door."

"You got a good memory. Where did you find it? How long did you keep it? Where did you leave it?"

"I just kept it one night. I found it out at Lakeside Park, and I left it down on East Kearsley Street, about two in the morning."

"Who was with you?"

"Nobody."

"Come on. Was was with you?"

"Nobody."

"You took these cars alone?"

"Yes."

The man eyed him. Then he said, "Okay — keep your memory going. What was the next car. All the details."

Alex's memory remained clear. He could remember all but the numbers of the license plates he had switched. He talked for about an hour, told of smashing one car into a parked truck, and of trading the spare tire of another for three dollars in gas, up to and including the copper-tone Buick Riviera, telling where they could pick it up. When he finished, the man said, "Go on."

"That's it," Alex said.

"You sure?"

"Yes."

The man took up a sheet of paper. "What about the Olds Eighty-eight you took on September twenty-seventh? Why'd you leave that off the list?"

"I didn't take it," Alex said.

"Let's see your wallet."

Alex laid his wallet on the desk. The man picked it up and looked through it.

"This your phone number?" he said.

"Must be."

"Who's home?"

"Nobody."

"Your mother's not home? She work?"

"I just live with my father."

"Aah so. Where's he?"

"At work."

"Where?"

"Chevie."

"What shift does he work?"

"Second."

"You and your old man get along okay?"

"Sure."

The man was shaking his head, looking at him. "Why?" he said. "It makes no sense."

Alex said nothing; he knew no answer.

The man, rising, said, "What you doing in a mess like this? You nuts? Don't you know this is for real?"

Alex said nothing.

"Well, let's go," the man said. "I'm gonna have to put you in the detention home."

Alex was taken to another part of the police station. He was left sitting on a bench, not far from the main door and opposite the complaint desk, a moon-shaped counter with openings like those at a bank. He was waiting for the ID Clerk to come on duty. The blue-shirted policemen behind the counter paid little attention to him, much less than he paid to them. He listened to their radio and telephone conversations and orders and questions. He smoked. He stood up several times to relieve the numb pain growing on his tail-bone from sitting, and he stepped over several times to press a swig of water from a cooler. The fact that he was waiting to be taken to the detention home floated over his thoughts as coolly as an impending basketball game, or an impending fight between others. He did not quite believe it.

At last a young man came hurrying in, wearing civilian clothes, popular, for it seemed all the policemen behind the counter called out something — *Hey, DJ, where the hell you been? DJ, how's duck hunting? Hey, old Murphy's hot after your ass.* And, among them: *You got a customer there.*

The young man was already past Alex but he looked back and said, "Be with you in a minute." He went on through a door and lights came on all along the upper half of a milk-colored glass wall. Alex saw the young man's shadow move across the room, then disappear. Ten minutes later he opened the door and said, "Okay, let's go."

Alex was photographed in an alcove marked with heights — look to the right, flash, chin up, flash — and his fingers were separated, rolled over an ink pad and then over a white card. The young man moved very fast. He wore a white shirt and tie, but with his sleeves rolled above his elbows, a cigarette behind one ear. He asked questions and clicked at a typewriter as Alex answered, spun the card out, and Alex was soon left sitting at another bench, within the ID room this time, to wait.

Two men passed through while he sat there, each accompanied by a uniformed policeman — one a tough, mean-looking man of about thirty who had been in a fight, little more than his eyebrow showing from one eye, and blood on his face, neck, and shirt, the other an egg-shaped old man dressed in a mismatched coat and tie and pants. Later Alex heard DJ on the phone — "Where the hell is Watt? I got a prisoner over here. No, no, juvenile."

Alex sat smoking, reaching out to throw matches and flick ashes into a metal wastebasket beside a desk. In time a uniformed policeman walked in, with a card in his hand. "Housman?" he said to Alex. Alex nodded. "Let's take a ride," he said. Alex rose. He put out his cigarette against the inside of the wastebasket.

Outside it was dark. They went down to the garage in one of the elevators, and out into the cold air. It was shivering cold to Alex, for all this time he had not removed his coat. Nor had he eaten, had barely eaten all day, but he was not hungry. He did not know the time. He felt it must have been past eight, perhaps close to nine. He and the policeman walked across a low-ceilinged garage, and, coming to a marked police cruiser, the policeman told him to get in front. They pulled out from under the building and across the lighted parking lot. Alex sat with his hands in his coat pockets, still shivering. The policeman said almost nothing. It had been raining, but the rain had stopped and there were only wet spots left, with traces of snow in the gutters.

They drove through the city, for a time in the direction of Alex's house, then turning east. They passed close to the factories along the river where his father worked, and must have been working at the time.

Some ten minutes later, in the country, going along a dark, paved road, the policeman suddenly put on his blinker — it flashed green on the dashboard — then braked and turned to enter a long drive-way. The buildings were there, but they were poorly lighted and just visible in the sweep of headlights. Alex saw the brick to the right, with blacker spaces in the receding darkness where the windows must have been. He could not see how high the brick went, for there were small outdoor lights on the corners of the building, and blackness above. To the left, in a glimpse, the headlights flashed over part of a

wire fence about eight feet high. The policeman said, "Let's go,"
and Alex realized the man had automatically disliked him.

The policeman came around from the driver's side, leaving the motor running, tall with his hat and his leather gear squeaking, and
walking beside Alex to a door. Alex could see now that the building
went on perhaps another hundred feet, that the other end was not
lighted and disappeared in darkness. He glanced up and saw that the
building was even higher than he had imagined, not two stories but
three, perhaps four. From the darkness overhead, not very loud in
the stillness, a Negro voice said, *"Hey, you new man — poleece catch
yo ass?"* Laughter, barely audible, came from within.

The policeman said nothing. At the doorway he pressed a button
and they stood waiting. A faint clicking came from inside the door,
then it opened and a man was standing there. The policeman
handed the card he had carried to the man. He said, "Here's a new
one for you."

The man, who was short, said, "Give you any trouble?"

"No," said the policeman.

The policeman did not go in. The man nodded for Alex to enter,
and Alex stepped inside. The man said something to the policeman
and then closed the door. It caught cleanly and locked, a heavy door.

In the corridor the man told Alex to walk ahead. Alex walked
ahead of him to where the corridor ended, where the door on the
left was made of metal. With a key extracted from a ring on his
belt, the man unlocked the door, reached in to switch on another
light, and said, "Up you go."

Alex went up a circular metal stairway ahead of the man. Overhead somewhere he thought he heard something, voices, or the creaking of beds, within the sound of their footsteps on the metal. At the
top, at a landing, there was another metal door, one with a hole
about four inches wide in the center. The light switch here was on
the outside. The man flipped the switch and looked in before he
unlocked the door. Alex entered first. It was another corridor, not
much wider than the door itself, lined with doors on one side some
six or seven feet apart. Both walls were marked the full length with
initials and messages and drawings dug and scratched into the white
plaster. Two or three caged lights along the runway were lighted.
The man closed the door behind him before he continued. Alex
felt the sense now of confinement, of being cornered.

"Go on," the man said.

Each door along the way had a hole like that in the main door, with numbers stenciled over the holes, several of the numbers rubbed and scratched as if from within, all marked from without, but still readable.

"Right here," the man said.

It was number 11. Alex stood waiting while the man found another key to unlock the door. He pushed it open but did not go in himself. "In you go," he said.

Alex stepped into the room. For just a moment, from the light around his shadow, he saw more marked walls, a cot, a commode against the wall. The door was pulled shut at once behind him and there was only the circle of light from the hole in the door. Then the door was being locked, the key was working, and he turned to look back. There was nothing to see but the hole. A moment later he heard the door at the other end of the runway being opened. Immediately he was in full darkness, although he had not heard the click of the light switch. The sound of footsteps on the metal stairway followed, then, fainter, the opening, closing, and locking of the door at the bottom of the stairs.

He realized the room had a window.

Someone spoke then, calmly and soft. "Hey man, what you in for?"

Alex looked toward the door again, but did not answer.

Someone else said, "Hey, how you like the service in this hotel?" A high-pitched *hee-hee-hee* followed, and other laughter, but it settled quickly.

Alex stood waiting, listening. He thought he also heard the sound of steady breathing, someone asleep. There was also a light hissing sound of steam.

The lighter shape of the window was visible now, and he stepped over to it. The window was not barred, but it was covered on the outside with heavy mesh wire. The wire crossed at right angles in squares of about an inch, and was not quite as thick as a pencil.

There was little to see, except that it must have been the back of the building, away from the road. There were no lights. Nor did he see any stars visible in the dark sky. But then, far off, perhaps a mile away, he saw lights which seemed to come from a house.

He stood by the window. He was not very tired; it could not be much later than nine-thirty. He could see the shape of the cot now but he had no feeling to lie down. He stood quite a long time this way, thinking but barely following his thoughts. The excitement of being in jail, the notoriety, had already faded away. He thought he had been here about an hour, but was not sure. It may have been no more than fifteen minutes. He stood thinking, thinking naturally of himself, scanning his life as if to see what it was that had brought him here, and unable at the same time to see anything very clearly.

He wondered if there was any talk of him at the football game over in the city, any talk of his being here, of the detectives taking him from school. Probably not, for not many would know where he had been taken, and if they did, it did not much matter. He remembered the years he had sold popcorn at the stadium, for both football and baseball games. He had made one cent of each ten he collected, and on a good night, besides his admission, he made about two dollars. He worked at the stadium until he went to high school; he quit because he wanted to join the spectators sitting in the stands.

Right now his father was probably working at Plant 4, across the river from the lighted stadium. From there as well as from their apartment, the big plays and the touchdowns could be heard. He wondered if his father, hearing the crowd tonight, would think of him and think he was there. Or would his father know by now? He doubted it. He doubted the police would have notified him at the factory. His father would probably go home and find the apartment empty and think he was out late. Would he think he was at a party, a dance? It was something they never talked about.

Football games; he had always felt depressed during and after football games. He never liked to simply go back home, and he was afraid to go to the dances. He usually left in the general crowded movement and walked along into town, along with the lines of cars moving bumper to bumper, the policeman waving red flashlights. But in town the procession soon passed. The people who stopped there were always older people who parked and disappeared into the cocktail bars, and he continued walking along, looking in store windows, never in a mood at those times to go to a late movie, sometimes trying to pick up stray girls at bus stops, inviting them to milk shakes, or to walk, but with little luck. Usually, before long, he shot a few games of pool somewhere and walked home again. It was only that first night, and the nights after, when he had a car, that he did not go home early.

He shivered. The air around the window made it seem colder.

The fear, and then the excitement, and then the calm he had felt since being locked up, were gone now, replaced by a small sickness of self-pity. The warmth of work and life in a factory seemed now all the richness one wanted to ask for under the sun. Life in school, with books and dreams and romance — it seemed the private, far-off world of the privileged, lying safe over there, sleeping well now after a night out.

He remembered the night at Lakeside Park, when he had stood looking as he stood now, and shivering, without being cold. He stood at the edge of the dark gymnasium floor that night, and all the time he was there he hardly moved a foot. The backboards had been raised, unseen in the overhead darkness, to make room for the dance, and colored lights, reds and greens, blues and violets, revolved overhead, over all, over his face where he stood, over the shadowed bodies of those dancing on the floor. Music was furnished by musicians from his school he had not known were musicians. He had taken two buses, the second to the end of the line, and walked another three quarters of a mile to get there; it was the first time he had ever gone to a school dance. And he thought he had been the last to have the back of his hand stamped at the door — where two girls had to check his name in a book to be sure he was from Central High School — but after a time the victorious football team came in and a brief uproar passed through the half-dark room. He still did not move. The uproar settled quickly, was absorbed quickly, as if by the darkness, and the music, and the dancers continued to dance, and he stood watching. Occasionally, passing, the brighter red or yellow light caught someone's upturned face, and when it caught his own, he stiffened and did not change his expression. He did not stay long. When he left, on his way to the door, sidestepping politely through the dancers, he had to pause once to let a couple not looking avoid bumping into him. He smiled lightly over this, as if over something cute, something youthful, but if they had bumped into him, and if he had had a knife, he would have ripped their throats with it. Out in the parking lot, he took his first car, a Chevrolet Bel Air with keys hanging in the ignition.

JOSE YGLESIAS

The Guns in the Closet

(FROM THE NEW YORKER)

UNTIL NOW, Tony believed he had been liberated by his Venezuelan grandfather's name — freed to be the special person that for years he unthinkingly felt himself to be. Ybarra. "Basque, you know," he would say when the subject came up. He was an editor in a New York publishing house, and author of an occasional essay, and it was understood, especially by European editors visiting his office, that his name set him apart from — well, whatever American foolishness or provinciality or philistinism infected the scene at the moment. He was aware that there was more than a trace of snobbery in this; aware, too, of the defensive residue, for he never forgot the discrimination that his name had subjected him to — mild, he admitted — during his adolescence in New York public schools and even at Harvard, though never in publishing, he liked to believe. Motel desk clerks in New England and the Midwest still took a second look at him when they noticed the name on the charge card, and allowed his appearance and his speech to convince them that he was all right. Those tiny encounters when he stood for inspection kept him, he thought, open to the world of the ghettos — the blacks, Puerto Ricans, and Chicanos — and it pleased him that his son Bill, who he had made sure learned Spanish fluently, should have lately come alive to the name. It amused him when Bill referred to himself in company — so as not, perhaps, to be challeneged by his parents — as a Third World person. Today, Tony was uneasy.

Bill had come down from the apartment near Columbia University that he shared with other students — like him, activists who had been suspended after the campus strike — to have Sunday brunch at home. A surprise, for these were not family brunches, and Tony knew that Bill could no longer bear the two or three writers and editors, all West Side liberal neighbors, who would be there. "It's the Third World that's important, not the American moral conscience!" he had yelled one Sunday three months earlier. "Up the NLF!" And he had not been back since. Today, Bill sat out the two pitchers of Bloody Marys, the quiche, the fruit salad, the French loaves and cheeses from Zabar's, and tension grew between him and Tony as suppressed as Bill's opinions were today.

Tony thought about his old friend Clifford, who would have been here if he were not in Algiers on a writing assignment. "Dear chaps, you're luckier with Bill than others are with their children," he'd said the last time Tony and his wife, Gale, had discussed Bill with him. "*They* deal with their kids as if they were a declining power negotiating with a newly emerged nation. The new diplomacy, right?"

Right. Tony saw that Gale had caught him studying Bill, and he smiled thinly, as if to say *Don't ask me.* And Bill of course intercepted all this and, unseen by the guests, winked at his parents, as if he in turn were replying *I'm here, that's all.* But later, when the others had left, he offered to go down with his father to walk the dog, and Gale exclaimed triumphantly, "Aha!" Bill laughed helplessly as in the days when he was a boy and they had uncovered one of his ruses.

"Shall I take money with me?" Tony asked as if asking an audience.

"No money," Gale said.

Bill shook his head and threw up his arms. A routine family charade, and Tony decided that his anxiety was baseless. But when Bill was saying good-bye, Gale took the boy's head between her hands, as she had begun to do during the strike at Columbia, and kissed him. Trouble, Tony thought; she always knows.

Going down in the elevator, both quiet in the presence of other tenants, Tony noticed that Bill wore a J. Press jacket he had not seen in a long time. No army fatigue jacket. His hair was almost short, his pants were not jeans, his shoes were not work boots, and there were no Panther buttons on his chest. He seemed to have abandoned the new life-style, and it surprised Tony that his son's appearance did not please him; he looked ordinary.

Ordinary? Then he must not be a Weatherman. Thinking about Bill afflicted Tony with non sequiturs. "Bill, you don't have money to keep your apartment, do you?" he said. "You're not there anymore. We haven't been able to reach you for two weeks."

Bill shook his head. "No," he said, "but I don't want to be up there anymore."

So he was downtown. "Are you in a commune?"

Bill pulled the dog toward Riverside Drive. "Too many people on Broadway," he explained, and crossed the Drive to the park. When Tony caught up with him, he was bending down to unleash the dog and let him run.

"Well, are you in a commune?" Tony asked, and smiled to appear casual.

From his bent position, Bill looked up and smiled a mocking smile; he shook his head. Tony was not reassured — not even when Bill straightened, threw out his arms, and took a deep breath, as if that was what he had come out for. Bill began to jog down the path to the esplanade and motioned his father on. "Good for you!" he called, and again he went through the motions of inhaling and exhaling with vigor.

When Tony got to him, he said, "Listen, Dad, I'd like to bring some stuff down tonight from my place. For you to keep for me. Just for a couple of days."

There were people brushing by. "Sure," Tony said, thinking it was books or clothes. "We're not going out. Anyway, you have a key." Bill looked at him so seriously that Tony stopped, suspicious again. "What stuff?"

Bill turned his head away. They were alone on the path now. "Guns," he said quietly.

Later, Tony wished he could have seen his son's face when he said that, but only the back of his neck was in view. There were wet leaves on the ground, and everything was still. Then a burst of laughter from a group of young people who appeared in the path on their way out of the park. They crowded Tony to one side and gave him time to think. I must not show my fear, he thought, especially my fear for him. But the questions burst out of him like exclamations. "They're not yours, are they? Whose are they?"

"No questions like that," Bill said. In a moment, he added, "Of course they don't belong to *me*."

"I see," Tony said, subdued. They had come onto the esplanade and there were people everywhere, walking their dogs, sitting on the benches, or simply strolling. Tony did not know whether it was their presence that forced him to speak casually, that created a new equality between him and Bill, or the boundaries that Bill had set up. I do not own this part of him, he thought; I can say yes or no, but that is all. He had liked being a father and it shamed him now that he was elated, as he walked alongside him, to find that Bill had his own mysterious corners, his own densities.

Finally, he said, "I shall have to talk to Gale first. It's her decision, too." He had never, with Bill, called Gale anything but "your mother," and he knew he was being mean in his new equality. Both to Bill and to his wife. Bill could walk away from their lives — perhaps even should — but parentage cannot be removed. He reached out and touched Bill's shoulder.

"O.K.," Bill said. "You tell me when I phone you later."

But he has come to me — *me* — and in the wind that blew from the river Tony's eyes teared. "You said they were at your place," he said. "Is that uptown?"

Bill nodded.

"And your friends living there — do they know?"

Bill exhaled and began his explanations. "They were away last weekend and the FBI broke in. The kids next door told them about it. The agents went through their apartment to get to the fire escape — it's kind of hard to get into ours with the locks I have on the door — and the kids came home while the agents were there. The super had let the two of them in, but the kids told them to get out. So the pieces have to be removed right away. They were just lying under the bed in duffel bags — they must have seen them. My friends have been trying to get to me all week."

"And the apartment is in your name!"

Bill did not answer.

"You can bring them," Tony said. "It will be all right with your mother, I'm sure."

"O.K.," Bill said. "I have to go now." He handed his father the leash. "I'll call you tonight." The dog followed him, and he turned back after a few paces. "Listen, when I call I'll ask if I can sleep over and tell you how soon I'll be there. You be down on the street when I arrive."

"All right," Tony said, and the sound of his voice was so strange to him that he leaned down to hold the dog to hide his sensation.

Bill's legs did not move away, so Tony looked up and saw him bring a hand up to his waist and make it into a fist quickly, casually.

"All power to the people," Bill said in a conversational voice. Then he smiled, in order, as they said in their family, to take the curse off it. "See you."

Alone, Tony felt cool and light-headed. He wanted to run and did, and the dog ran after him. Nothing unusual — the kind of sprint that men walking dogs in the park will often break into. During the war, he had reacted this way when, as pilot on a scout observation plane, he climbed to the catwalk and into his plane to be catapulted from the ship: his hands checked the canopy, the stick between his legs — all concentration while his emotions unreeled without control and unrelated images flitted in and out of his mind. He knew only that he was being observed and that he must be true to some unconfessed vision of himself.

He walked back to the apartment slowly. How to tell Gale. Dinner guests would have to be put off. Last summer, the caretaker of the Maine estate they rented had asked him what kind of name his was, and when he replied that it was Spanish — no use saying Basque — the old man had said, "Spanish! Now, there's nothing wrong with that, is there?" The guns must go in the closet in his study — that was one place their thirteen-year-old daughter, who now should be back from her friend's apartment, never looked.

In the elevator, he thought, But if *they* didn't come back to the apartment with warrants, then they must have a reason to wait. Do they hope to catch Bill? Do they have a watch on the place and if Bill walks out in a few hours with . . . He would not say this to Gale. She was lying on the living room couch with the Sunday *Times,* and he got a pad and pen and sat next to her and wrote out the conversation — the gist of it — he had had with Bill.

Gale smiled when he handed it to her but when she had read it she sat up. "But —" she began. Behind her came the wail of a Beatles record from their daughter's room.

Tony put a finger to his lips. "Not here," he said.

The color went out of her face. "I've got to go out for a cup of coffee," she said. "Right now!"

They walked up and down Broadway and sat in a coffee shop and talked. She wanted to be angry at someone. "Couldn't you have brought him back to the apartment?" she said.

Tony felt like putting his head in his hands. "I didn't think . . ."

She waved a hand defeatedly, in understanding. "And there's no way of getting in touch with him?"

By the time they returned to the apartment, the exhilaration he had first felt was gone. They were no sooner inside than Gale had to take up the pad and write on it a warning about their daughter. *She must not know unless it is absolutely neccesary.* He nodded, noticing the misspelling. And the cleaning woman who came three times a week, she wrote. She must be kept out of his study. He nodded again and took the sheet from the pad and went into the small bath off the study and tore it into small pieces and flushed them down the toilet. Thank God, Gale had not thought of the danger to Bill when he removed the guns from the apartment uptown.

Tony sat in the study and knew that Gale was restlessly tidying the apartment. Later, he heard her on the phone calling off the evening's appointment, arguing with their daughter to keep her from having friends in. Then silence. He could not read or write. He kept visualizing the walkup near Columbia, which he had visited only three or four times. So many of the tenants were young people moving in and out that surely duffel bags would attract no attention. He thought of the solution: a decoy. Someone must first leave with the duffel bags that had been under the bed but with something else in them. Of course. He got up from his chair to tell Gale. No. It was Bill he should get to. Run up to the apartment? Ten minutes by taxi. Gale wouldn't notice.

He had taken his jacket out of the hall closet when he realized that he dare not be seen up there today. Which of Bill's friends could he call? Which of them had gone this far with him in his politics? He did not know. He told Gale, who was lying on the couch again, that he was going down for cigarettes. She looked blank, then questioning, and Tony smiled and shook his head. From a street booth, he called a friend of Bill's who had been with him in the Columbia strike. The operator came on and asked what number he was calling. He told her — safe enough in a public booth, he thought. In a moment, she came back on to say the number had been disconnected. When he got back to the apartment, Gale did not look up from the couch. As he put his jacket back in the closet he saw that she would not look up. She had thought of the danger.

He went to his study and tried not to think. There was a manuscript in his briefcase that one of the young editors liked. Another book on Vietnam. They already had one for the winter list. It was foolish not to talk aloud to Gale in the apartment. He could not believe the FBI had time to listen to his phone, to the hours of his daughter's, his wife's, and his own conversations, just because of Bill. He remembered a manuscript on surveillance that his house had turned down. To cover the whole apartment, the sound would have to be transmitted to a nearby station no more than two or three blocks away, to be either recorded or monitored. Thank God, he was not a paranoid left-winger.

Yet when the phone rang at eleven forty-five and he heard Bill say, "Dad?" he gave way to the fear that had made him write on the pad. He had to clear his throat before he could answer.

"Listen, Dad, I'm in the neighborhood." His voice was easy — he was a good actor. "I'm at a party and I don't want to go all the way downtown when I leave, so I'm going to do you and Mom the honor of staying with you overnight. O.K.?"

"O.K.," he said and knew he was not playing his part well. He tried to ask the question. "Bill . . ."

"I'll be there in an hour," Bill said with that touch of highhanded misuse of parents that had once been genuinely his. "Thanks," he added, out of character.

"Bill . . ." Tony began again and then did not risk it.

After a pause Bill said, "See you then," and hung up.

The next hour would tell. Tony went to the bedroom where Gale was watching a talk show and said with the casualness he had not managed on the phone that Bill was coming by in an hour to spend the night. She looked at him with the kind of reproach that women transmit with a glance when they think their men are acting like boys. He shrugged, went to the kitchen, heated some coffee, and drank it in his study. Once *this* was over, he told himself, he would make Bill have a long talk with him. There had been no battles during his adolescence — none of the rows that are usual with fathers and sons — and he did not want Bill's activities now, whatever they were, to be surrogates for them. He had been proud when Bill so suddenly, at Columbia, had become political; he had alerted everyone at the office when Bill was scheduled to appear on a program last year of the show Gale was now watching. He had not used parental concern as an excuse for trying to keep him at school or to deflect him — not even when, after Dean Rusk had spoken at the new Hilton, Bill came home battered from a fight with the cops on Sixth Avenue.

Ten minutes before the hour was up, Tony went downstairs. Between midnight and one, the doorman was always in the basement helping the janitor wheel the garbage cans onto the street by the side entrance. A police car was parked at the corner, its lights on; one cop stood at the back entrance of the bakery two doors down, waiting for the pastry they cadged each night, and the other was at the all-night diner for coffee. Tony lit a cigarette and stood at the door of the building as if he had come out for a breath of air. There were still many people on Broadway, but fewer, and the prostitutes were more visible. The cops went back to their car to drink the coffee and eat the Danish. He raised a hand in greeting when one looked his way, and both of them grinned. Nothing suspicious about me, he thought; I'm a respectable, middle-aged West Sider.

The cops pulled out as soon as they were finished, having lit cigarettes and set their faces into the withdrawn, contemptuous expressions that signified they were back on the job. A Volks station wagon turned into the street, paused, and then parked where the patrol car had been. Bill sat next to the driver; the friend Tony had tried to call earlier was behind the wheel. Tony walked over as Bill got out; his friend stayed inside and did not turn off the engine.

"Everything all right?" Tony asked.

"Great!" Bill said. He walked to the back of the car, opened the window, and beckoned with his head. There were two long leather cases lying in the car; they looked handsome and rich. "Golf clubs," Bill said, and picked up one and handed it to Tony. He took the other, fitted an arm through its strap, and carried it over one shoulder. With his free hand he waved to his friend, and the car drove off.

"Thank God, you didn't bring them in the duffel bags," Tony said, almost gaily. "I wanted to call and tell you that you should first have left the house with the duffel bags and then . . ."

"That's what we did," he said. "Sent a decoy out first."

Tony put his arm through the strap of the second case and walked alongside Bill to the entrance of the apartment building. We are the perfect picture of the middle-class father and son, he thought. I would say, seeing the two of us, that we belong to a country club in Westchester, play tennis from spring to late fall, swim, golf, of course, and keep a boat at the Seventy-ninth Street Basin. During the winter, we get together at the Athletic Club for handball, followed by a short swim in the heated pool. The son dashes out immediately after, but the father gets a rubdown and later joins two or three others his age for lunch upstairs by the wide, tall windows looking down on Central Park. Ah, yes. His Venezuelan grandfather's name and his childhood in the Spanish section of Chelsea would keep him always on a circular stage slowly revolving to the view: you never cease to act the role that the eyes of others create.

Tony said, "You're going to find your mother very upset."

"About this?" Bill said. "I'll talk to her."

"Well, not inside," Tony advised. "We've been careful to say nothing that we wouldn't want overheard."

Bill looked down, but Tony saw he was amused. "Well, Dad, it's not very likely," he said in the lobby. "Their tapping equipment must be overtaxed these days. Too many groups into heavy stuff, you know." And in the elevator he explained, in such detail that it alarmed Tony that he should know the subject so well, how you can detect with the use of an FM radio whether there is a bug in the apartment.

"We have to talk about you," Tony said. "I don't know what *you* are into, and it worries me."

"Sure, O.K.," Bill said. They were on their floor, about to turn to the door of their apartment. "Look, you know I'm grateful to you that I learned Spanish and something about the culture. I got you to thank for that." He stopped, and Tony thought there must be many things Bill did not thank him for. "But I'm a Third World person, you know, and that's how I'm going to live."

Gale was not at the front of the apartment. Tony led Bill through the dining room and kitchen to the study. They leaned the cases against the back wall of the closet, and when they closed the door on them Bill said, "It'll only be for a couple of days. We'll let you know when."

"Remember I stay home Tuesdays to read manuscripts," Tony said.

"O.K.," Bill said, nodding, and on the way to the living room turned and added, "It won't be me."

Gale was standing in the living room in her robe. She held one

hand up in a fist and shook it at Bill in pretended anger. He
laughed. Well, for Christ's sake, Tony thought.

She asked, "Can I make you something to eat?"

"No time, Mom," Bill said. "I've got to go."

"But you said — " Tony began.

Gale completed it: "You were staying overnight!"

Bill's expression reminded them of his old joke that his parents
talked like an orchestra. "I can't. My friend is waiting for me."

"But he drove away," Tony said.

"I saw him from my window," Gale added.

"He's two blocks farther down, waiting." Bill walked over to his
mother to say good-bye. "I'll be in touch."

Tony watched her hug him but could not hear what she whispered
in his ear. When she let him go, she was pale and ready to cry. Tony
said, "I'm coming down with you."

In the hall, he tried to tell Bill some of the things he had thought
that day. They came out badly. "I have to tell you that I don't
agree with what you're doing. They're the wrong tactics. They
won't work here. You don't know what real Americans are. You'll
bring down the most —"

"Christ, Dad, you're not on the Susskind program." That special
hardness was in his voice; Tony did not know where he got it. "You
know all the arguments as well as I do. Remember the time you
came off his talk show and said there's just no way to make radical
change palatable to liberals like that?"

"You're not going to compare me to him!"

"Not unless you force me," Bill said, and stopped because people
had got on the elevator.

In the lobby, Tony let them go ahead. He said quietly, as if making a new start, "I'm worried about what's going to happen to you."

"Don't worry, I'm learning karate," Bill said seriously. "No pig
is going to run me down and twist my arm behind my back. From
now on we're doing the bogarting. Twice a week I go to Connecticut
to the rifle ranges and practice shooting." He laughed. "I need a lot
of practice."

"What's that for!"

"I've got a very simple test for radicals," Bill said. "When I read
about some radical movement, I ask, did they arm themselves, did
they pick up the gun? If they didn't, they aren't serious."

On Broadway, Tony flinched when he saw a middle-aged writer

coming toward them with his young wife — his third. They had the giggly look of people who have been turning on. And an after-the-party boredom with one another. Tony introduced them to Bill, and the writer made an effort to focus on him. "Pretty quiet at Columbia this year," he said. "Anything happening?"

"I wouldn't know," Bill said.

Quickly, Tony asked the writer how his new novel was doing. He began to talk about the reviews. Tony saw Bill edge away, and the writer tried to hold him by saying, "Say, you ought to take a look at it. It's a revolutionary book."

"We have to go," Tony said. "I'll call you tomorrow."

Bill was down the block and the writer called, "Read the book, kid. It'll blow your mind!"

Tony was breathless with the need to say something to his son that would somehow get to — what? He didn't know; he simply exhaled when he reached his side.

Bill shook his head. "Don't worry," he said, as if he understood. The Volks station wagon was at the corner waiting, and Bill paused. "You know, I've been down to Fourteenth Street several times, eating at the Spanish restaurants and sitting at the bars. A couple of old Republicans like Fidel, but none speak well about the Puerto Ricans." He shook his head again.

"Well . . ."

"You say your grandfather was an anarchist — right?" Bill asked. "Did you talk to him much? I got to talk to you about him. Sometime. O.K.?"

"Yes, yes," Tony said. He wondered what that old man — wearing a beret while he fixed the windows and doors in the worn-out apartment and built cages for the pigeons on the roof—had thought of him and his books.

When he got back home, he found Gale lying in bed reading. He felt sure she had been to the closet in his study. She looked up when he took out his robe and began to undress. "I don't want to talk about it until they're gone," she said, "and that had better be soon or I shall go out of my mind." He didn't answer, and after a moment she asked, "When is that going to be?"

"Two days," he said, but he did not really know. He lay next to her, his arms folded over his chest, and went over everything Bill had said. He could not quite remember what was to happen. Someone would get in touch with him. There were the facts of Bill's day-to-day life to piece together. And all that rhetoric. He was going to live like a Third World person. What the hell did that mean? This is the real generation gap, he thought — you can't grab hold of these kids; they sum up your life and their own in a phrase and leave you gasping. They wrench you out of the dense element that is your daily life and there you are — on the shore, on the shore, on the shore.

At breakfast next morning, Gale announced that she was going to do volunteer work at the public school all week. Penance for sending their own to private schools, but also this week, he suspected, to be out of the way.

Tony went to the office late. There had been no call at the apartment, and there was no call here, either. He returned early with three manuscripts to read the next day. Again, no call. Gale was not home and he took the dog and headed for the Drive, as if that would help him recall his talk with Bill. He let the dog loose and stood at the parapet at the esplanade and smoked and stared at the river.

A short dark man who looked to Tony like a typical Puerto Rican came over with an unlit cigarette, asking for a light. Tony handed him his cigarette and he held it delicately and took a light from it. He looked Tony directly in the eye when he thanked him. He did not walk away but turned to study the river, too, and it was then Tony realized that the man had spoken to him in Spanish. "If you are home tomorrow morning," he said now, still in Spanish, "someone will come to pick up the packages you have been so kind to hold for us."

Tony smiled in a kind of reflex and found that he could not turn on his fake smile. He thought, This is a trap; I must get away. Instead, he replied in Spanish, "For us?"

"Your son did not tell you whose they are?" He had the sweet accent of Puerto Ricans.

Tony shook his head.

The man said, "MIRA. Have you heard of us?"

Tony nodded. The bombings in the Bronx. An underground terrorist group operating in New York. A bad manuscript called "Colonies in the Mother Country" had mentioned them. Crazily, he wondered if he had been right to reject it.

The man seemed to watch all this going on in his head, and as if to help him added, "We are madmen."

"Talk to me," Tony said and pointed to a bench. "What about my son?"

"Your son?" The man waited for him to sit first, bowing a little and standing to one side. "But you must know better than we do — if he trusted you with packages. What can I tell you?"

"We are very worried about his activities," Tony replied. "I do not want you to divulge anything that is confidential but if you can tell me something . . ."

"Oh, there do not have to be any mysteries between us," the man said, and looked around at a man going by with a dog. He waited until he had passed. "Your son is very much of an Hispano. He is closer in feeling to us, he says, than to any of the others."

"Others?"

"The other revolutionary groups," he explained. "American ones. We are all in touch. He is a liaison man with us. There are certain things that a Puerto Rican cannot do. It looks funny for us to be in certain places or buy certain things. Too conspicuous. You understand?"

Tony nodded and looked at the river, trying to place Bill in all this. His dog came back to the bench and the man leaned down and patted him. "What a friendly little dog he is," he said. "My younger brother was killed in the independence uprising after the war. Just one of the many killed in Puerto Rican towns all over the island . . . One of our problems is getting guns to comrades on the island," he said inconsequentially, talking as if this might help Tony. "What better proof that we are an oppressed colony than the fact that guns, which are so easy to come by in these states, are almost impossible for Puerto Ricans to obtain."

"The laws are not the same?" Tony said.

"Jesus Christ himself could not qualify to own a gun there."

Tony took out a pack of cigarettes and offered it. The Puerto Rican accepted with the grace that only a Latin seems able to put into such a gesture. "I admired your article on the Latin-American revolutionaries very much," he said, and Tony was startled — could this man have read the quarterly where he had published two essays in the last five years? "The one on their situation after the death of Che. I had not known that wonderful saying of Martí's: 'El árbol *que más crece es el que tiene un muerto por debajo.'* " ("The tree that grows tallest has a dead man buried beneath it.")

"That is what I fear," Tony said.

The man squinted and then struck himself on the forehead. "What a fool I am! You ask me about your son, you are worried like a good father, and all I talk about is dying and killing. Forgive me, *compañero*." They were quiet a moment. The Puerto Rican looked at his cigarette and flicked the ash off it carefully. "It is true that for us it is specially necessary to think about the possibility of death, to get used to it even. But that is not what interests us — that does not interest us one bit."

"Forgive me if I tell you that I do not think you have a chance," Tony said.

"That, too, does not interest us," the Puerto Rican replied very gently, in a tone that seemed solely concerned with Tony's feelings.

Tony got up, and because he was suddenly ashamed at the abruptness with which he was ending their talk extended his hand.

The man took it in both of his. "I know what it is you are too polite to say," he said. "That your son is not a Puerto Rican. But do you not find that wonderful? Is not that the best guarantee that we will win this time? Look, those Young Lords in the barrio want to free Puerto Rico, too, but almost none of them can really speak Spanish. Some of the older nationalists cannot believe in them, but I say it is what is here" — he stopped to place a hand on his own heart — "that matters."

"I wish you success," Tony said.

The man nodded slowly, solemnly. Then he smiled. "Perhaps we shall see one another again. If you go to the island to write one of your studies, there are people we would like you to meet. See what Yankees we have become — we know the value of publicity now, even if only among the professors who read the magazines where you publish." He laughed and added, "At ten tomorrow morning then, a girl will ring your bell. A beautiful American girl. And she will ask you one more favor — to help her take the packages to her car."

It was Gale's custom to look at him carefully when she greeted him — her way of asking for news — but today she began a story about a Taiwanese child at school, so pointedly, Tony felt, that it was a rebuff. When she stopped, he said, "Tomorrow."

She stepped over to him and pecked him on the cheek. "How do you know?" she whispered.

He lied. "Bill called."

The phone rang, and Gale picked it up. "Cliff!" she exclaimed.

"Tell him to come over," Tony called. Back from Algiers, thank God — the one person he could talk to about all this.

"He heard you," Gale said, "but he hasn't unpacked."

Tony insisted, as eager as when they had been undergraduates, "Tell him to come over and we'll open cans for dinner — I want to discuss business."

Clifford had spent a month in Algiers talking to Eldridge Cleaver. The last time they had spent an old-fashioned evening together, Tony had come up with the idea of the trip, and he did want to know if Clifford was going to get a book out of it. He wanted to talk about simultaneous hardcover and paperback publication, but it was really the chance to spend the evening with something in mind other than the guns in the closet that attracted him. And the possibility that Clifford could help with Bill.

Clifford had got a bottle of Cuban *añejo* through customs and he held it out in greeting. "Limes and Seven-Up!" he called. "I feel like my comic-strip name — Clifford Moon!"

Gale said, "You don't look it!"

He was wearing a Pierre Cardin vest suit and a flowered silk shirt with wide sleeves. In the month he had been away his sideburns had grown long and bushy; his mustache curved over the corners of his lips. He stretched out on a chair and showed his Moroccan slippers — sheepskin with embroidery.

"In Algiers everyone is stoned all the time," Clifford said, beginning on his first Mojito — a Cuban drink he had brought back from trips made to cover the Cuban revolution. "You really should have fresh mint for this, but it'll do. They just don't know what the joys of drinking are in Algiers. I think I shall have to take a stand against hash, pot, grass — what inelegant names! It turns everyone into lobotomized types."

"Never mind all that," Tony said. "Have you got a book?"

"Dear chaps, I've scarcely been allowed to turn the experience over in my mind," he replied, and he let his arms droop down the sides of his chair. "I haven't even called my agent."

Tony waved a hand. "Oh, your agent — we've already discussed it."

"Did he say there won't be any minimum royalty on the paperback?" Clifford asked, sitting forward.

"Well . . ."

"I want more than the five per cent for my share," Clifford said. He laughed. "I'm getting myself a fur coat this winter."

"Well!" Tony said, and he didn't know if it was envy that made him decide then that he could not discuss Bill.

Gale said, "Let's drive down to Washington together for the Kent State demonstration. Or do you have to work?"

"Yes, no — yes!" Clifford said. "Dear me, I mean yes. There'll be beautiful young people there from all over the country. They're bound to get stoned and disrobe — like Woodstock. And I can work that into the book." He picked up his drink from the floor and looked slyly at Tony over the rim of his glass. "How the revolution sells nowadays. Though I don't know to whom. The young don't read. I daresay it's the anxious middle-aged who want to know what their children are doing. In the fifties they would've gone to their analysts. This is better for us." He looked sly again. "Right, chaps?"

Promptly at ten the next morning, the downstairs buzzer sounded. Alone in the apartment, Tony opened the door, and a few minutes later watched the girl walk from the elevator toward him. She wore a maxi raincoat unbuttoned over a mini skirt. Her legs were stunning. "Is everything all right?" he asked.

"Oh, hi!" she said, delighted. "I'm parked just across from you."

He had thought that if she was alone he would have to make two trips with the cases, but she touched her right biceps and said, "Muscles," and took one of them. Tony watched the doorman study her legs when he held the door open for them. Damn. The writer whose new novel was just out was on the sidewalk — alone this time.

"Hey!" the writer said. "You didn't call."

"Stay right there," Tony said, following the girl. "I'll be right back." She opened the trunk of a Mercedes Benz at the opposite curb, and while he placed his case in it Tony was aware that the writer watched them.

She brushed her long hair back when she straightened, and said, "Thanks."

"O.K.?" Tony said, wondering if he should shake hands.

"A message from Bill — he won't be in touch for a while," she said with a smile.

"What!" he said.

"Your friend is waiting," she said, and turned away.

He hovered as she got in behind the wheel. "Tell him we want to see him, please," he said, and watched her smile in that nonwavering, idiotic way.

When he got back to the writer, they watched her drive off. Without looking at him, the writer said, "You play golf?"

"Me?" Tony asked. "Oh no, just helping a neighbor."

"Wow!" he replied. "You got that in your building!"

When Tony walked into the apartment, it felt eerie, like the time they returned from the theater to find that someone had broken in. He went straight to the study and closed the door to the closet. He could not concentrate on the manuscripts he had brought home. He made a cup of coffee and tried to think of what Bill's message meant. He would not tell Gale. On the radio in the study, the news commentators said that the national revulsion against the Kent State killings was escalating. The third time he heard the same news on the hour break, he turned the radio off and remembered Bill's instructions about how to find a tapping bug. He flicked the radio on again and dialed to the low end of the band and slowly moved up. On the third try, he caught a faint beep. He held the dial there; it built in volume. With both hands he picked up the radio and moved it in the direction of the wall phone. The beep became steadier and louder: the tap was there. With shaking hands Tony put the radio back on its shelf and turned it off. Something else to keep to himself.

Later in the week, he and Gale went to Washington with Clifford and walked among the young people on the green. He looked for Bill, letting Gale and Clifford sit through the speeches while he roamed. He came back exhausted, and when Gale said, "Aren't they beautiful?" he could only nod, because his eyes were full of tears and his throat was tight. He felt better for being there, but on the way home anxiety returned; and each time a bomb exploded that winter he fought back the desire to call the police and find out, before the *Times* got to the stands, who was involved. He went to all the demonstrations. They were dear to him. He looked at the young people, no longer searching for his son, who had never called, and said inwardly, over and over, without irony, accepting his country at last while he repeated Bill's name in Spanish — Guillermo Ybarra — *I commend my son, fellow Americans, to your care.*

BIOGRAPHICAL NOTES

Biographical Notes

M. F. BEAL was born in New York City in 1937. She spent part of her youth in Germany and France, attended Cornell, and graduated from Barnard in 1960. Her stories have appeared in magazines and anthologies, including *The Atlantic Monthly* and *New American Review*. With her husband, the novelist David Shetzline, and three daughters, she has shared in building houses on their Oregon Coast ranch and in the Sierra foothills. Recently she completed a novel, *Amazon One*, about a radical women's collective.

RICHARD BRAUTIGAN was born in the Pacific Northwest in 1935. He is the author of *Trout Fishing in America, The Pill Versus the Springhill Mine Disaster*, and *In Watermelon Sugar* published in one volume by Delacorte Press/Seymour Lawrence. The books were first published by the Four Seasons Foundation in San Francisco. His verse includes *The Galilee Hitch-Hiker, Lay the Marble Tea, The Octopus Frontier, All Watched Over by Machines of Loving Grace*, and *Please Plant This Book*. He lives in San Francisco.

KELLY CHERRY was born in Baton Rouge, Louisiana, and grew up in Richmond, Virginia. After an unsuccessful attempt to major in paleontology, she took her degree in philosophy, and was a DuPont Fellow in graduate philosophy at the University of Virginia before going to the University of North Carolina at Greensboro for her Masters. She has published stories and poetry in little magazines, including *The Red Clay Reader, The Southern*

Poetry Review, and *The Carolina Quarterly.* She is completing a novel in New York City.

HERBERT GOLD was born in Cleveland, attended Columbia College and the Sorbonne, and has taught at the University of California, Stanford, Cornell, and Harvard. His essays and stories have appeared in magazines ranging from *Playboy, Esquire, Harper's* and *The Atlantic Monthly* to *Hudson Review* and *Tri-Quarterly Review.* His books have been widely translated abroad. Among his published works are a volume of stories, *Love and Like,* and one of essays, *The Age of Happy Problems.* His most recent collection is *The Magic Will: Stories and Essays of a Decade.* He is also the author of six novels, and has recently completed an autobiographical study of a writer in America entitled *My Last Two Thousand Years.* Mr. Gold and his family live in San Francisco.

JOANNE GREENBERG was born in Brooklyn, New York, in 1932. She is a graduate of American University, Washington, D.C., and the University of London and has studied at Colorado University. Using the pseudonym Hannah Green, she is the author of the highly acclaimed work *I Never Promised You a Rose Garden,* which won the Fromm-Reichmann Award for 1965. Under her own name she has published two collections of short stories and three novels. Her novel *The King's Persons* received the Daroff Memorial Award for fiction in 1962. Mrs. Greenberg is a qualified teacher of sign language and in her latest novel, *In This Sign,* she concerns herself with the silent world of the deaf. Mrs. Greenberg lives with her husband, Albert, and two teen-age sons in a mountaintop home in Colorado.

MARY HEATH was born and raised in Pennsylvania. She is a graduate of Mount Holyoke College (1952), associate editor of the *Massachusetts Review,* and a student in the Master of Fine Arts Program at the University of Massachusetts. Her husband teaches at Amherst College and they have two daughters. "The Breadman," her first published story, won second prize in the Emily Clark Balch Prize Contest for fiction in 1971.

EDWARD M. HOLMES was born in Montclair, New Jersey, in 1910. He holds degrees from Dartmouth, the University of Maine, and

Brown. Now a professor at the University of Maine, he has been a clerk on Wall Street, newspaper reporter, business manager, stage and shipyard carpenter, buyer and trucker of lobsters, organizer of fishermen's cooperatives and credit unions, high school teacher and principal. Several of his short stories have been reprinted in collections and "Drums Again," included in this volume, received an Emily Clark Balch Prize in 1971. He and his wife live in Westport, Maine.

MARY GRAY HUGHES, who was born and raised in Texas, attended the University of Texas for one year, and received a B.A. from Barnard College and a B.Litt. from Oxford University. She has published stories in *Redbook*, the Swiss magazine *Ann Belle*, *Esquire*, and *The Atlantic Monthly*. One of her stories was selected for inclusion in *The Best American Short Stories 1969* and a collection of her stories, *The Thousand Springs*, appeared in 1971 as the first publication of the recently founded Puckerbruch Press in Orono, Maine.

ANN JONES was born in 1926 and raised in Rodeo, California. Her stories have been published in *The University of Windsor Review*, *Four Quarters*, *The Virginia Quarterly Review*, and *The Iowa Review*. She received the Phelan Award in 1966 and an Emily Clark Balch Award in 1971. She and her husband live in Three Rivers, California, and have one son.

WARD JUST was born in 1935 and raised in the suburbs of Chicago. For twelve years he worked in the United States and abroad for *Newsweek*, *The Reporter*, and the Washington *Post*. He is the author of three books, *To What End*, a memoir of the Vietnam War; *Military Men*, a study of the U.S. Army; and a novel, *A Soldier of the Revolution*. In 1970 he left the Washington *Post* to devote full time to fiction. "Three Washington Stories" is his first short fiction to be published anywhere. He lives in the District of Columbia with his wife and children.

ROBERTA KALECHOFSKY was born in Brooklyn, New York, in 1931. She attended Brooklyn College, the University of Connecticut, and New York University, where she received an M.A. and a Ph.D. She taught for a year as a part-time instructor at the University of Connecticut and for four years in the School of General Studies at Brooklyn College. Her stories have been published in various magazines, and she has written two novels. Several chapters from her most recent novel, *Orestes in Progress,* have been published in *Works.* She is now completing a volume of short stories, entitled *Solomon's Wisdom,* and a book on George Orwell. She is married, has two sons and a three-legged dog who has a part in her last novel. They live in Marblehead, Massachusetts.

REBECCA KAVALER was born in Georgia in 1920 and was raised in the South. After graduating from the University of Georgia, she went on to study at the Sorbonne in Paris and the New School for Social Research in New York City. Her short stories have previously appeared in two anthologies, *American Vanguard* and *New Voices,* and in *Nimrod,* a journal that included one of her stories in an issue devoted to the best stories of the past decade. She lives in New York City with her husband and two children.

JOHN L'HEUREUX, born in 1934, is a Contributing Editor of *The Atlantic Monthly.* He is the author of four books of poetry, an autobiography, and two novels. His short stories have appeared in *The Atlantic Monthly, Work in Progress, Four Quarters,* and *Transatlantic Review.* A collection of his stories, *Nine Lives and Mrs. Bludd,* will appear in 1973. For sixteen years a Jesuit, he was laicized in 1971 and married with Vatican approval. He and his wife make their home in Boston.

RALPH MALONEY, a graduate of Harvard, is a full-time writer now living in the Boston area. He is a regular contributor to *The Atlantic Monthly,* where most of his short stories were first published. In the fall of 1972 W. W. Norton & Company is publishing a collection of his short stories entitled *Fish in a Stream in a Cave.* He is also the author of the best-selling novel *The Nixon Recession Caper,* soon to be released as a motion picture. Mr. Maloney is married and has three children.

MARVIN MANDELL was born in Rochester, New York, in 1927. He served with the U.S. Army in Italy during World War II. An honors graduate of the University of Rochester, he was elected to Phi Beta Kappa and later received his Masters from Columbia and Ph.D. from the University of Iowa. He has worked as a machinist and as a teacher. He is now teaching English and comparative literature at Curry College in Milton, Massachusetts, and working on a collection of short stories. He lives with his wife and two daughters in Boston during the winter and on Cuttyhunk Island, Massachusetts, in the summer.

CYNTHIA OZICK, author of the novel *Trust* and *The Pagan Rabbi and Other Stories,* has been a teacher of literature at Ohio State University and New York University. She has also taught at the Chautauqua Fiction Workshop. In 1970 she delivered the America-Israel Address on Cultural Affairs at the Weizman Institute, Rehovot, Israel. Among her honors are the Edward Lewis Wallant Award, B'nai B'rith Jewish Heritage Award, Jewish Book Council of America Award, and the National Endowment of the Arts. Her fiction, poetry, essays, criticism, reviews, and translations appear in numerous periodicals and her work is included in eight anthologies, including *The Best American Short Stories 1970.* She is currently a Stolmitz Memorial Lecturer at Indiana University.

JOE ASHBY PORTER was born in Kentucky in 1942. He has studied at Harvard, Oxford, and Berkeley. Since completing a group of ten linked stories, of which "The Vacation" is one, he has begun a novel. At present he lives in Charlottesville, Virginia, where he teaches at the university.

PENELOPE STREET was born in Long Beach, New Jersey, in 1944 and went to school in eight different places in the East and Midwest. She graduated from the University of California in 1971 with honors in English literature and is presently working toward a Master of Arts degree in creative writing at the University of British Columbia in Vancouver. She is completing a novel, of which "The Magic Apple" is a part, and has a book-length manuscript of poetry ready for publication. In 1971 the University of California at Berkeley awarded her the Eisner Prize for fiction and she received the Joseph Henry Jackson Prize in 1970 for some of her poetry. All her writing in the recent past has been published under her married name, Lowenthal. She now uses her maiden name, Street, and lives with her four-year-old son A.J. and their two cats, Lillian Hellman and Waring Blendor.

ROBERT PENN WARREN was born in Guthrie, Kentucky, in 1905. After graduating *summa cum laude* from Vanderbilt University at the age of sixteen, he earned his Masters at the University of California at Berkeley, attended Yale, and went on to England as a Rhodes Scholar at Oxford, which granted him the B.Litt. degree in 1930. He has taught at Southwestern College, Vanderbilt, Louisiana State, the University of Minnesota, and Yale, where he has been Professor of English since 1961. Among his honors are his appointment to the Chair of Poetry of the Library of Congress for 1944–45 and his election to the American Academy of Arts and Letters in 1959. He is the author of several volumes of poetry and prose. His various works have been awarded the Pulitzer Prize in poetry and fiction, the National Book Award and the Edna St. Vincent Millay Memorial Award. His latest novel, *Meet Me in the Green Glen,* was published by Random House in the fall of 1971. Mr. Warren lives in Connecticut with his wife and two children.

THEODORE WEESNER is the author of the novel *The Car Thief,* of which "Stealing Cars" is a part. He grew up in Flint, Michigan, served three years in the Army, and later attended Michigan State University and the University of Iowa. His stories have appeared in *The New Yorker, The Atlantic Monthly, Esquire, Audience,* and in other magazines. He makes his home in Durham, New Hampshire, but with his wife and three children will spend most of 1973 in Europe at work on a new novel.

JOSE YGLESIAS was born in 1919 in the Latin section of Tampa, Florida. Although he left it one day after graduating from high school, he has written about it in the six books he has published: three novels, a personal narrative, and two works of social reportage. He now lives in North Brooklin, Maine, with his wife, the novelist Helen Yglesias.

THE
YEARBOOK
OF THE
AMERICAN SHORT STORY

January 1 to December 31, 1971

Roll of Honor, 1971

I. American Authors

ADAMS, ALICE
Ripped Off. The New Yorker, May 22.
ARKLEY, GAIL
The Staff of Life. New American Review, #13.

BERGSTEIN, ELEANOR
Stuart. Miscellany, Spring–Summer.
BINGHAM, SALLY
Rachel's Island. Audience, July–August.
BONTEMPS, ARNA
Talk to the Music. Cimarron Review, July.
BUMPUS, JERRY
The Sorrow of Dreams. The South Dakota Review, Autumn.

CALDWELL, PRICE
A Sense of Place. Georgia Review, Summer.
CANZONERI, ROBERT
Reflections. McCall's, March.
CLARKE, AUSTIN C.
Griff! Tamarack Review, #58.
CLEARMAN, MARY
I Beat the Midget. North American Review, Summer.

DEEMER, CHARLES
Presenting the Annual Interracial Roast Pig. Prism International, Spring.

FETLER, ANDREW
To Byzantium. New American Review, #12.
FOX, GEORGE
The Twenty-Sixth Second. Paris Review, #51.
FRANCIS, H. E.
Sully. The Kansas Quarterly, Winter.

GERALD, JOHN BART
Conventional Wisdoms. Harper's, July.
GOLDSTEIN, SANFORD
Outside Person. Arizona Quarterly, Spring.
GRANAT, ROBERT
Herr Bruderman. Event, Spring.

HARTER, EVELYN
Odor of Sandalwood. South Dakota Review, Autumn.
HAYDEN, JULIE
A Touch of Nature. The New Yorker, August 21.
HENDERSON, ROBERT
The Wanderers. The New Yorker, November 27.
HOFFMAN, WILLIAM
Breaking Cover. Cosmopolitan, July.

KIMBALL, GEORGE ROBERT
The Enchantment of Mrs. Hedgepeth. Audience, September–October.

KRAUSE, ERVIN D.
The Crossing. Literary Review, Summer.

LARSON, CHARLES R.
Confounding Sophocles. Colorado Quarterly, Summer.
LAVIN, MARY
Trastevere. The New Yorker, December 11.
LEVIN, BEATRICE
Ghosts from an Enchanter Fleeing. Forum, Summer.

McCULLERS, CARSON
Breath from the Sky. Redbook, October.
Instant of the Hour After. Redbook, October.
MALONEY, RALPH
Happy Ending. Atlantic Monthly, September.
MASSA, RONALD XAVIER
The Man Who Tried to Marry My Sister. Massachusetts Review, Winter.
MIDWOOD, BARTON
The Riddle. Esquire, March.

NEMEC, DAVID
Gladya When Last Seen. Works, Vol. III, #1.
NEWMAN, CHARLES
There Must Be More to Love Than Death. Antioch Review, Summer.

OATES, JOYCE CAROL
Other Dreams. New American Review, #13.
Scenes of Passion and Despair, Shenandoah, Summer.
The Obsession. Ladies' Home Journal, October.

POWER, VICTOR
The Threshold. North American Review, Summer.
PUTMAN, CLAY
Some Grass Roots of Peace in Pacific Heights South. Atlantic Monthly, October.

REEVE, F. D.
Upbringing. Audience, March–April.
RICHLER, MORDECAI
The Passing of Issy Hersh. Tamarack Review, Second Quarter.

SALTER, JAMES
The Destruction of the Goetheanum. Paris Review, #51.
SCHAFER, WILLIAM J.
When the War Breaks Out in Mexico, I'll Head for Montreal. Miscellany, Spring–Summer.
SCHULTZ, PHILIP
A Sorting Place. Iowa Review, Summer.
SINGER, ISAAC BASHEVIS
Two Children's Stories. Audience, January.
SPANIER, MURIEL
The Reception. Colorado Quarterly, Summer.
SPENCER, SCOTT
The News. Redbook, May.

TOBIAS, TOBI
Peas in a Pod. Southern Humanities Review, Summer.
TUROW, SCOTT
A Classic Case. Transatlantic Review, #40.

ZELNER, PATRICIA
The Flood. Virginia Quarterly Review, Autumn.

II. *Foreign Authors*

ALVAREZ, A.
Night Out. The New Yorker, September 4.

BARTHOLD, JAMES
What's Happenin'. Transatlantic Review, #40.

COOGAN, TIM PAT
The Compromise. Transatlantic Review, #40.

GILLIAT, PENELOPE
As We Have Learned from Freud, There Are No Jokes. The New Yorker, October 2.
The Position of the Planets. The New Yorker, August 14.

GORDIMER, NADINE
No Place Like. Southern Review, Summer.

HAZZARD, SHIRLEY
The Statue and the Bust. McCall's, August.

KIELY, BENEDICT
The Green Lanes. Audience, May–June.

LELAND, JEREMY
The Last Sandcastle. Mademoiselle, October.

LESSING, DORIS
Spies I Have Known. Partisan Review, #1.

MEACOCK, NORMA
Thinking Girl. Partisan Review, #3.

MEYRINK, GUSTOW
The Toad's Curse, trans. by Michael Bullock. Prism International, Spring.

NAIPAUL, SLIWA
The Father, Son and Holy Ghost. Denver Quarterly, Autumn.

NOVIS, LESLIE
The Highland Boy. Atlantic Monthly, June.

OZ, AMOS
Crusade. Commentary, August.

WALKER, TED
Stephen, Steve, Stevie. The New Yorker, July 24.

YESHOSHUA, A. B.
Another Hot Day. Audience, January.

Distinctive Short Stories, 1971

I. American Authors

ADLER, RENATA
Quiet. The New Yorker, April 24.
AMES, BERNICE
This Frequent Rearrangement. Kansas Quarterly, Winter.
ANGOFF, CHARLES
The Life of Letters. Literary Review, Summer.
ATWOOD, MARGARET
Polarities. Tamarack Review, #58.
AUKEMA, CHARLES
Running the Whole Board. Panache, 1971.

BAMBARA, TONI CADE
I Ain't Playin', I'm Hurtin'. Redbook, November.
BARTHELME, DONALD
The Catechist. The New Yorker, November 13.
BARTHELME, STEVE
Oily Rag. Transatlantic Review, Spring.
BERKMAN, SYLVIA
The Saffron Boat. Aphra, Vol. II, #4.
BLAKE, GEORGE
Night Watch. Kansas Quarterly, Summer.
BOLES, PAUL DARCY
Jayess. Seventeen, July.
BORAZZI, ROBERT
Summer Reading. Cimarron Review, April.

BRIAN, LEE
Commitments. Kansas Quarterly, Winter.
BRIGHAM, BESMILR
The Death of Manuel Garcia. North American Review, Fall.
BRONER, E. M.
The Saga of Great Men. Commentary, December.
BROWN, BRUCE BENNETT
Guest and Host. Wind, Spring.
BUMPUS, JERRY
Away in Night. Iowa Review, Fall.

CANSON, JACK
Friday Night Smith. Southwest Review, Autumn.
CARVER, RAYMOND
Nightschool. North American Review, Fall.
CATES, JAY
Hunt. North American Review, Fall.
CHACKO, DAVID
Up from Djibouti and Covered in Braid. Panache, 1971.
CHOSEK, JUDITH
Saturday Walk. Jewish Frontier, February.
CLIFTON, LUCILLE
The End of Love Is Death and the End of Death Is Love. Atlantic Monthly, March.
CONROY, FRANK
The Movie Star. Cosmopolitan, November.

CONSTANT, NICHOLAS
Bound Away. Iowa Review, Winter.
CUPO, HORTENSE
The Last Circle. Kansas Quarterly, Summer.
CURLEY, DANIEL
Litany for the Loving. Kansas Quarterly, Winter.

DEASY, MARY
Like Fireflies in August. Redbook, August.
DILLARD, LEONA M.
Indians in Tall Grass. South Dakota Review, Autumn.
DONLEY, MICHAEL
Laboratory Experiment. Transatlantic Review, Spring.
DUNN, STEPHEN
Initiation. Shenandoah, Summer.

EATON, CHARLES EDWARD
Daughter of a Poet. Kansas Quarterly, Winter.
EDKINS, ANTHONY
Scapegoat in Sheep's Clothing. Black Swamp Review, #2.
ELLIOTT, GEORGE P.
Muriel. Esquire, February.
ELLIOTT, WILLIAM D.
The Road to Monterrey, Kansas Quarterly, Winter.
EMSHWILLER, CAROL
Yes, Virginia. Transatlantic Review, Spring.
ERNST, PAUL
Our Little Girl Is Lost. Good Housekeeping, March.
EVANIER, DAVID
Guidance. Transatlantic Review, Spring.

FITZGERALD, F. SCOTT
Lo, The Poor Peacock. Esquire, September.
FLYTHE, STARKEY, JR.
Point of Conversion. Antioch Review, Spring.
FOX, HUGH
Countdown. Kansas Quarterly, Summer.
FRIEDMAN, BRUCE JAY
High, Wide and Handsome. Esquire, October.

GALLO, PHILIP
The Confidante. Prism International, Autumn.
GARDNER, JOHN
The Song of Grendel. Esquire, October.
GERBER, YANCY
The Lovers and Another Level. Epoch, Spring.
GOLDSCHMIDT, JEAN
Pursuits. Atlantic Monthly, June.
GOTTLIEB, ELAINE
The Lizard. Southern Review, Spring.
GRANT, C. L.
Afternoon of the Banjo. Little Magazine, Spring.
GRIMM, CHERRY
A Chronic Condition. Prism International, Autumn.

HALL, JAMES BAKER
Any More Alive. Cimarron Review, April.
HARGRAVE, HARRY A.
A Man: a Story. Southern Humanities Review, Fall.
HARRISON, WILLIAM
A Nice Enough Funeral. Playboy, February.
HARTER, EVELYN
The Black Razor. Kansas Quarterly, Summer.
HARVEY, ANN CAMERON
A Short Dance. Iowa Review, Spring.
HARVOR, BETH
Our Lady of All the Distances. Colorado Quarterly, Winter.
HYDE, ELEANOR
Wesley's Wife. Aphra, Vol. II, #2.

ISRAEL, PETER
Nuestra Señora, Reina de Los Angeles. Iowa Review, Summer.

JACKEL, KAREN
The Engagement. Epoch, Spring.
JACOBSEN, JOSEPHINE
Vermont Fall. Epoch, Fall.
JERRARD, MARGOT
A Very Small Shipwreck. Redbook, November.
JOHNSON, DIANE
An Apple, An Orange. Epoch, Fall.

NABOKOV, VLADIMIR
The Dashing Fellow. Playboy, December.
NOWLAN, ALDEN
Life and Times. Fiddlehead, Spring.

OATES, JOYCE CAROL
Bloodstains. Harper's, August.
Loving, Losing, Loving. Southern Review, Autumn.
O'CONNOR, PHILIP F.
Constants. Kansas Quarterly, Winter.
OLIVER, CHARLES
The Changeling. Southwest Review, Spring.
OWENS, PETER
Georgie. North American Review, Fall.

PAIGE, HARRY W.
The Vision Quest. South Dakota Review, Autumn.
PESTA, JOHN
The Possibility of Freedom. Kansas Quarterly, Summer.
PETRIE, GRAHAM
The Test. Playboy, October.
POSNER, GRACE
Stone and Shell. Twigs, VII.
POLLEY, GEORGE
Jonah's Birth. South Dakota Review, Autumn.
POUND, E. F.
The Trophy. North American Review, Fall.

REIFLER, SAMUEL
Salt Point Seance. Transatlantic Review, Spring.
REINHOLD, JAMES
Family Portrait. Esquire, March.
REYNOLDS, LAWRENCE JUDSON
My Friend and Colleague. Greensboro Review, Summer.
ROBERTSON, STROWAN
Vida. Malahat Review, October.
ROGERS, MICHAEL
A Great Feeling. Esquire, April.

SALMON, ELON
The Moroccan Duck. Midstream, May.

SCHONNING, GUNNAR
The Vampire. Epoch, Fall.
SIKES, SHIRLEY
The Birds of Sadness. Denver Quarterly, Spring.
Burial. Kansas Quarterly, Winter.
Pioneers. Transatlantic Review, Winter.
SILVERMAN, PAUL
The Rat Was There. Denver Quarterly, Winter.
SINCLAIR, BENNIE LEE
At the Heart of the Prodigal. South Carolina Review, December.
SINCLAIR, THOMAS
Dee Scahboro Road. Cimarron Review, April.
SINGER, ISAAC BASHEVIS
Grandfather and Grandson. Southern Review, Autumn.
The Magazine. The New Yorker, May 22.
The Third One. The New Yorker, July 17.
SINTETOS, LORRE
Big John Blows the Haps. Transpacific, Vol. II, #2.
SORRENTINO, GILBERT
The Moon in Its Flight. New American Review, #13.
SPIEGEL, JOY G.
They're Deep in California. Cimarron Review, April.
STEPHENS, MARK
The Lady Who Stole Trees. Redbook, September.
STEPHENS, ROSEMARY
Pink Roses. Seventeen, September.
STEWART, DONALD C.
The Bear and the Mountain. Kansas Quarterly, Summer.
STUART, JESSE
Tree Frog. Southwest Review, Winter.
A Spider in the Dumplings. Kansas Quarterly, Winter.
STUART, SHIRLEY
The Lizard's Treadmill. Antioch Review, Spring.
STURBAHN, LAURENCE
All the King's Horses and All the King's Men Couldn't Put Mr. Wil-

berforce Together Again. Kansas Quarterly, Winter.
The First Spectator and the Last. North American Review, Summer.

SWENSON, ALAN
The Train. Kansas Quarterly, Winter.

SYKES, DOUGLAS M.
Tell Me, Bethabara. Greensboro Review, Summer.

TARGAN, BARRY
Leaving. Denver Quarterly, Autumn.

TAYLOR, HARRY H.
Carolyn. Epoch, Spring.
Teasing. Forum, Winter.

THOMPSON, KENT
Hero, O Heroine. Tamarack Review, Second Quarter.

TROTT, SUSAN
Bones of Contention. Redbook, May.

TURNER, KENNETH
Masks. Phylon, Summer.

TYLER, ANNE
Outside. Southern Review, Autumn.

ULLIAN, ROBERT
A Snag in the Harp. Esquire, February.

URBAN, JOHN
Savings. Transatlantic Review, Spring.

UPDIKE, JOHN
Love: First Lessons. The New Yorker, November 6.
Sublimating. Harper's, September.

VALGARDSON, W. D.
Dominion Day. Fiddlehead, Spring.

VEDER, BOB
The Eighteen Karat Gold Pin. Forum, Winter.

WASSER, MARGARET
The Balloon. Miscellany, Spring–Summer.

WEIR, ALLEN
Cop and Robbers. Southern Review, Summer.

WHITE, DORI
The Clay Feet of Miss Merivale. Woman's Day, April.

WHITE, JAMES P.
Summer. Kansas Quarterly, Summer.

WISER, WILLIAM
Keepers. Miscellany, Spring–Summer.

WOIWODE, L.
Marie. The New Yorker, December 25.

WUB, HUBBNER
Tale of the Lithuanian Sheets. Epoch, Fall.

YU-HWA, LEE
The Fresh Start. Arizona Quarterly, Winter.

II. Foreign Authors

AGNON, S. Y.
Friendship. Transatlantic Review, Winter.

BANVILLE, JOHN
Mr. Mallin's Quest. Transatlantic Review, Autumn–Winter.
Nativity. Transatlantic Review, Autumn–Winter.

BORGES, JORGE LUIS
The Congress. The New Yorker, November 6.
Six Pieces. Antioch Review, Winter.
Tom Castro, The Implausible Impostor. Harper's, October.

ESSA, AHMED
The Prisoner. Literary Review, Fall.

FRANCIS, H. E.
The Moment of Fish. Southern Review, Autumn.

FERNANDES
Loss. Southwest Review, Autumn.

GARLAND, PATRICK
A Dublin Winter. Transatlantic Review, #39.

GILLIATT, PENELOPE
Nobody's Business. The New Yorker, July 3.

GORDIMER, NADINE
Why Haven't You Written? The New Yorker, February 27.

HAMELINK, JACQUES
Delayed Thunder, trans. by Martha Veerman. Prism International, Summer.

HUNT, HUGH ALLYN
A Kind of Recovery. Transatlantic Review, Winter.

JENS, WALTER
Brecht in the Underworld. Transatlantic Review, Spring.

JHABVALA, R. PRAWER
Two More Under the Indian Sun. The New Yorker, May 29.
Rose Petals. The New Yorker, July 10.

LAWRENCE, VINCENT
Cantata. Transatlantic Review, #40.

LESSING, DORIS
Report on the Threatened City. Playboy, November.

LURIE, MORRIS
The Cardplayers. The New Yorker, December 18.
Last Strings. Transatlantic Review, #40.

MARQUEZ, GABRIEL GARCIA
A Very Old Man with Enormous Wings, trans. by Gregory Rabassa. New American Review, #13.
The Handsomest Drowned Man in the World. Playboy, November.
"Isabel's Monologue" While Watching It Rain in Macondo. Prism International, Autumn.

MOYANO, DANIEL
Et Cetera, trans. by H. E. Francis. Kansas Quarterly, Summer.
The Rescue, trans. by H. E. Francis. Southern Review, Summer.
The Thousand Days, trans. by H. E. Francis. Transatlantic Review, Winter.

NAKAMURA, SHINICHIRO
The Genie and Her Magic. Prism International, Autumn.

NOVIS, LESLIE
The Waxwings. Atlantic Monthly, February.

NXELE, LANGA
In Our Time. Literary Review, Fall.

SERCAMBI
Novella of Love and Lust, trans. by Joseph Ranallo. Malahat Review, April.

TALBOT, KATHRINE
The Lion of Heyst. Paris Review, #51.

VAID, KRISHNA BALDEV
Portrait of Old Maya. Literary Review, Summer.

VOGEL, BRUNO
Protea. Literary Review, Fall.

WAIN, JOHN
A Man in a Million. Malahat Review, October.

WALKER, TED
The Skein. The New Yorker, March 6.

WARNER, SYLVIA TOWNSEND
The Music at Long Verney. The New Yorker, August 28.

Addresses of American and Canadian Magazines Publishing Short Stories

Amistad, Vintage Books, 33 West 60th Street, New York, New York 10023
Antioch Review, 212 Xenia Avenue, Yellow Springs, Ohio 45387
Aphra, R.F.D. Box 355, Springtown, Pennsylvania 18081
Ararat, 109 East 40th Street, New York, New York 10016
Argosy, 205 East 42nd Street, New York, New York 10017
Arlington Quarterly, P.O. Box 366, University Station, Arlington, Texas 76010
Atlantic Monthly, 8 Arlington Street, Boston, Massachusetts 02116
Audience, 207 East 32nd Street, New York, New York 10016
Canadian Forum, 30 Front Street West, Toronto, Ontario, Canada
Carleton Miscellany, Carleton College, Northfield, Minnesota 55057
Carolina Quarterly, P.O. Box 1117, Chapel Hill, North Carolina 27514
Cimarron Review, 203B Morrill Hall, Oklahoma State University, Stillwater, Oklahoma 74074
Colorado Quarterly, University of Colorado, Boulder, Colorado 80303
Commentary, 165 East 56th Street, New York, New York 10022
Cosmopolitan, 1775 Broadway, New York, New York 10019
Ellery Queen's Mystery Magazine, 229 Park Avenue South, New York, New York 10003
Epoch, 252 Goldwin Smith Hall, Cornell University, Ithaca, New York 14850
Esquire, 488 Madison Avenue, New York, New York 10022
Event, 422 South Fifth Street, Minneapolis, Minnesota 55415
Evidence, Box 245, Station F, Toronto, Ontario, Canada
Falcon, Mansfield State College, Mansfield, Pennsylvania 16933
Fantasy and Science Fiction, P.O. Box 271, Rockville Centre, New York 11571
Fiddlehead, Department of English, University of New Brunswick, Fredericton, New Brunswick, Canada
Florida Quarterly, University of Florida, 330 Reitz Union, Gainesville, Florida 32601
Forum, Ball State University, Muncie, Indiana 47302
Four Quarters, LaSalle College, Philadelphia, Pennsylvania 19143
Georgia Review, University of Georgia, Athens, Georgia 30601

Good Housekeeping, 959 Eighth Avenue, New York, New York 10019
Green River Review, Box 594, Owensboro, Kentucky 42301
Greensboro Review, University of North Carolina at Greensboro, Box 96, McIver Building, Greensboro, North Carolina 27401
Harper's Bazaar, 717 Fifth Avenue, New York, New York 10022
Harper's Magazine, 2 Park Avenue, New York, New York 10016
Hudson Review, 65 East 55th Street, New York, New York 10022
Husk, Cornell College, Mount Vernon, Iowa 52314
Intro, Associated Writing Programs, Brown University, Providence, Rhode Island 02912
Iowa Review, University of Iowa, Iowa City, Iowa 52240
Kansas Quarterly, Kansas State University, Manhattan, Kansas 66502
Ladies' Home Journal, 641 Lexington Avenue, New York, New York 10022
Laurel Review, West Virginia Wesleyan College, Buckhannon, West Virginia 26201
Literary Review, Fairleigh Dickinson University, Rutherford, New Jersey 07070
McCall's, 230 Park Avenue, New York, New York 10017
Mademoiselle, 420 Lexington Avenue, New York, New York 10017
Malahat Review, University of Victoria, Victoria, British Columbia, Canada
Manhattan Review, 229 East 12th Street, New York, New York 10003
Massachusetts Review, Memorial Hall, University of Massachusetts, Amherst, Massachusetts 01002
Michigan Quarterly Review, University of Michigan, 3032 Rackham Building, Ann Arbor, Michigan 48104
Modern Occasions, 5A Bigelow Street, Cambridge, Massachusetts 02139
Motive, P.O. Box 871, Nashville, Tennessee 37202
New American Review, 630 Fifth Avenue, New York, New York 10020
New Letters, University of Missouri, Kansas City, Missouri 64110
New Orleans Review, Loyola University, New Orleans, Louisiana 70118
New Renaissance, 9 Heath Road, Arlington, Massachusetts 02174
New Yorker, 25 West 43rd Street, New York, New York 10036
North American Review, University of Northern Iowa, Cedar Falls, Iowa 50613
Northern Minnesota Review, Bemidji State College, Bemidji, Minnesota 56601
Northwest Review, Erb Memorial Union, University of Oregon, Eugene, Oregon 97403
Occident, Eshelman Hall, University of California, Berkeley, California 94720
Panache, P.O. Box 89, Princeton, New Jersey 08540
Paris Review, 45–39 171st Place, Flushing, New York 11358
Partisan Review, Rutgers University, 191 College Avenue, New Brunswick, New Jersey 08903
Pathway Magazine, P.O. Box 1483, Charleston, West Virginia 25325
Penthouse, 1560 Broadway, New York, New York 10036

Perspective, Washington University Post Office, St. Louis, Missouri 63130

Phylon, Atlanta University, Atlanta, Georgia 30314

Playboy, 919 North Michigan Avenue, Chicago, Illinois 60611

Ploughshares, P.O. Box 529, Cambridge, Massachusetts 02139

Prairie Schooner, Room 201, Andrews Hall, University of Nebraska, Lincoln, Nebraska 68508

Prism International, University of British Columbia, Vancouver, British Columbia, Canada

Quarterly Review of Literature, 26 Haslet Avenue, Princeton, New Jersey 08540

Quartet, 1701 Puryear Drive (Apartment 232), College Station, Texas 77840

Queens Quarterly, Queens University, Kingston, Ontario, Canada

Redbook, 230 Park Avenue, New York, New York 10017

Salmagundi Magazine, Skidmore College, Saratoga Springs, New York 12866

San Francisco Review, P.O. Box 671, San Francisco, California 94100

Seneca Review, Box 115, Hobart and William Smith Colleges, Geneva, New York 14456

Seventeen, 320 Park Avenue, New York, New York 10022

Sewanee Review, University of the South, Sewanee, Tennessee 37375

Shenandoah, P.O. Box 722, Lexington, Virginia 24450

South Carolina Review, P.O. Box 28661, Furman University, Greenville, South Carolina 29613

South Dakota Review, P.O. Box 111, University Exchange, University of South Dakota, Vermillion, South Dakota 57069

Southern Humanities Review, Auburn University, Auburn, Alabama 36830

Southwest Review, Southern Methodist University Press, Dallas, Texas 75222

Tamarack Review, P.O. Box 157, Postal Station K, Toronto, Ontario, Canada

Texas Quarterly, P.O. Box 7527, University Station, Austin, Texas 78712

Transatlantic Review, P.O. Box 3348, Grand Central Station, New York, New York 10017

Transpacific, P.O. Box 486, Laporte, Colorado 80535

Tri-Quarterly, University Hall 101, Northwestern University, Evanston, Illinois 60201

Twigs, Hilltop Editions, Pikeville College Press, Pikeville, Kentucky 41501

University Review, University of Missouri, 5100 Rockhill Road, Kansas City, Missouri 64110

Virginia Quarterly Review, 1 West Range, Charlottesville, Virginia 22903

Wascana Review, Wascana Parkway, Regina, Saskatchewan, Canada

Western Humanities Review, Building 41, University of Utah, Salt Lake City, Utah 84112

Western Review, Western New Mexico University, Silver City, New Mexico 88061

Yale Review, 28 Hillhouse Avenue, New Haven, Connecticut 06520